Also available from Silhouette Books
and Harlequin Books by

NORA ROBERTS

FINDING FOREVER
Never let go of love...

O'HURLEY'S RETURN
Family together at last...

O'HURLEY BORN
A dynasty of love...

KEEP YOU CLOSE
A dangerous attraction...

FIRST SNOW
Walking in a winter wonderland...

CHRISTMAS WITH YOU
True love feels like coming home...

* * *

Be sure to look for more Nora Roberts titles
at your local stores, or contact our
Harlequin Reader Service Center:
USA: 3010 Walden Avenue
PO Box 1325, Buffalo, NY 14269
Canada: PO Box 609, Fort Erie, Ontario L2A 5X3

Visit Silhouette Books at www.Harlequin.com

NORA ROBERTS

A TOUCH OF SUN

Silhouette Books

Published by Silhouette Books
America's Publisher of Contemporary Romance

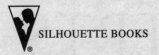

SILHOUETTE BOOKS
®

Recycling programs for this product may not exist in your area.

A Touch of Sun

ISBN-13: 978-1-335-89796-1

Copyright © 2019 by Harlequin Books S.A.

The publisher acknowledges the copyright holder of the individual works as follows:

Mind Over Matter
Copyright © 1987 by Nora Roberts

Dual Image
Copyright © 1985 by Nora Roberts

Printed in U.S.A.

CONTENTS

MIND OVER MATTER

Chapter 1

He'd expected a crystal ball, pentagrams and a few tea leaves. Burning candles and incense wouldn't have surprised him. Though he wouldn't admit it to anyone, he'd actually looked forward to it. As a producer of documentaries for public television, David Brady dealt in hard facts and meticulous research. Anything and everything that went into one of his productions was checked and rechecked, most often personally. The truth was, he'd thought an afternoon with a fortune teller would bring him a refreshing, even comic, relief from the daily pressure of scripts, storyboards and budgets. She didn't even wear a turban.

The woman who opened the door of the comfortable suburban home in Newport Beach looked as though she would more likely be found at a bridge table than a séance. She smelled of lilacs and dusting powder, not musk and mystery. David's impression that she was housekeeper or companion to the renowned psychic was immediately disabused.

"Hello." She offered a small, attractive hand and a smile. "I'm Clarissa DeBasse. Please come in, Mr. Brady. You're right on time."

"Miss DeBasse." David adjusted his thinking and accepted her hand. He'd done enough research so far to be prepared for the normalcy of people involved in the paranormal. "I appreciate your seeing me. Should I wonder how you know who I am?"

As their hands linked, she let impressions of him come and go, to be sorted out later. Intuitively she felt he was a man she could trust and rely on. It was enough for the moment. "I could claim precognition, but I'm afraid it's simple logic. You were expected at one-thirty." Her agent had called to remind her, or Clarissa would still be knee-deep in her vegetable garden. "I suppose it's possible you're carrying brushes and samples in that briefcase, but I have the feeling it's papers and contracts. Now I'm sure you'd like some coffee after your drive down from L.A."

"Right again." He stepped into a cozy living room with pretty blue curtains and a wide couch that sagged noticeably in the middle.

"Sit down, Mr. Brady. I just brought the tray out, so the coffee's hot."

Deciding the couch was unreliable, David chose a chair and waited while Clarissa sat across from him and poured coffee into two mismatched cups and saucers. It took him only a moment to study and analyze. He was a man who leaned heavily on first impressions. She looked, as she offered cream and sugar, like anyone's favorite aunt—rounded without being really plump, neat without being stiff. Her face was soft and pretty and had lined little in fifty-odd years. Her pale blond hair was cut stylishly and showed no gray, which David attributed to her hairdresser. She was entitled to her vanity, he thought. When she offered the cup, he noted the symphony of rings on her hands. That, at least, was in keeping with the image he had projected.

"Thank you. Miss DeBasse, I have to tell you, you're not at all what I expected."

Comfortable with herself, she settled back. "You were expecting me to greet you at the door with a crystal ball in my hands and a raven on my shoulder."

The amusement in her eyes would have had some men shifting in their chairs. David only lifted a brow. "Something like that." He sipped his coffee. The fact that it was hot was the only thing going for it. "I've read quite a bit about you in the past few weeks. I also saw a tape of your appearance on *The Barrow Show*." He probed gently for the right phrasing. "You have a different image on camera."

"That's showbiz," she said so casually he wondered if she was being sarcastic. Her eyes remained clear and friendly. "I don't generally discuss business, particularly at home, but since it seemed important that you see me, I thought we'd be more comfortable this way." She smiled again, showing the faintest of dimples in her cheeks. "I've disappointed you."

"No." And he meant it. "No, you haven't." Because his manners went only so far, he put the coffee down. "Miss DeBasse—"

"Clarissa." She beamed such a bright smile at him he had no trouble returning it.

"Clarissa, I want to be honest with you."

"Oh, that's always best." Her voice was soft and sincere as she folded her hands on her lap.

"Yeah." The childlike trust in her eyes threw him for a moment. If she was a hard-edged, money-oriented con, she was doing a good job disguising it. "I'm a very practical man. Psychic phenomena, clairvoyance, telepathy and that sort of thing, don't fit into my day-to-day life."

She only smiled at him, understanding. Whatever thoughts came into her head remained there. This time David did shift in his chair.

"I decided to do this series on parapsychology mainly for its entertainment value."

"You don't have to apologize." She lifted her hand just as a large black cat leaped into her lap. Without looking at it, Clarissa stroked it from head to tail. "You see, David, someone in my position understands perfectly the doubts and the fascination people have for… such things. I'm not a radical." As the cat curled up in her lap, she continued to pet it, looking calm and content. "I'm simply a person who's been given a gift, and a certain responsibility."

"A responsibility?" He started to reach in his pocket for his cigarettes, then noticed there were no ashtrays.

"Oh, yes." As she spoke, Clarissa opened the drawer of the coffee table and took out a small blue dish. "You can use this," she said in passing, then settled back again. "A young boy might receive a toolbox for his birthday. It's a gift. He has choices to make. He can use his new tools to learn, to build, to repair. He can also use them to saw the legs off tables. He could also put the toolbox in his closet and forget about it. A great many of us do the last, because the tools are too complicated or simply too overwhelming. Have you ever had a psychic experience, David?"

He lit a cigarette. "No."

"No?" There weren't many people who would give such a definitive no. "Never a sense of déjà vu, perhaps?"

He paused a moment, interested. "I suppose everyone's had a sense of doing something before, being somewhere before. A feeling of mixed signals."

"Perhaps. Intuition, then."

"You consider intuition a psychic gift?"

"Oh, yes." Enthusiasm lit her face and made her eyes young. "Of course it depends entirely on how it's developed, how it's channeled, how it's used. Most of us use only a fraction of what we have because our minds are so crowded with other things."

"Was it impulse that led you to Matthew Van Camp?"

A shutter seemed to come down over her eyes. "No."

Again he found her puzzling. The Van Camp case was the one that had brought her prominently into the public eye. He would have thought she would have been anxious to speak of it, elaborate, yet she seemed to close down at the mention of the name. David blew out smoke and noticed that the cat was watching him with bored but steady eyes. "Clarissa, the Van Camp case is ten years old, but it's still one of the most celebrated and controversial of your successes."

"That's true. Matthew is twenty now. A very handsome young man."

"There are some who believe he'd be dead if Mrs. Van Camp hadn't fought both her husband and the police to have you brought in on the kidnapping."

"And there are some who believe the entire thing was staged for publicity," she said so calmly as she sipped from her cup. "Alice Van Camp's next movie was quite a box-office success. Did you see the film? It was wonderful."

He wasn't a man to be eased off-track when he'd already decided on a destination. "Clarissa, if you agree to be part of this documentary, I'd like you to talk about the Van Camp case."

She frowned a bit, pouted almost, as she petted her cat. "I don't know if I can help you there, David. It was a very traumatic experience for the Van Camps, very traumatic. Bringing it all up again could be painful for them."

He hadn't reached his level of success without knowing how and when to negotiate. "If the Van Camps agreed?"

"Oh, then that's entirely different." While she considered, the cat stirred in her lap, then began to purr loudly. "Yes, entirely different. You know, David, I admire your work. I saw your documentary on child abuse. It was gripping and very upsetting."

"It was meant to be."

"Yes, exactly." She could have told him a great deal of the world was upsetting, but didn't think he was ready to understand how she knew, and how she dealt with it. "What is it you're looking for with this?"

"A good show." When she smiled he was sure he'd been right not to try to con her. "One that'll make people think and question."

"Will you?"

He tapped out his cigarette. "I produce. How much I question I suppose depends on you."

It seemed like not only the proper answer, but the truest one. "I like you, David. I think I'd like to help you."

"I'm glad to hear that. You'll want to look over the contract and—"

"No." She cut him off as he reached for his briefcase.

"Details." She explained them away with a gesture of her hand. "I let my agent bother with those things."

"Fine." He'd feel more comfortable discussing terms with an agent. "I'll send them over if you give me a name."

"The Fields Agency in Los Angeles."

She'd surprised him again. The comfortable aunt-like lady had one of the most influential and prestigious agencies on the Coast. "I'll have them sent over this afternoon. I'd enjoy working with you, Clarissa."

"May I see your palm?"

Every time he thought he had her cataloged, she shifted on him. Still, humoring her was easy. David offered his hand. "Am I going to take an ocean voyage?"

She was neither amused nor offended. Though she took his hand, palm up, she barely glanced at it. Instead she studied him with eyes that seemed abruptly cool. She saw a man in his early thirties, attractive in a dark, almost brooding way despite the well-styled black hair and casually elegant clothes. The bones in his face were strong, angular enough to warrant a second glance. His brows were thick, as black as his hair, and dominated surprisingly quiet eyes. Or their cool, pale green appeared quiet at first glance. She saw a mouth that was firm, full enough to gain a woman's attention. The hand in hers was wide, long fingered, artistic. It vied with a rangy, athletic build. But she saw beyond that.

"You're a very strong man, physically, emotionally, intellectually."

"Thank you."

"Oh, I don't flatter, David." It was a gentle, almost maternal reproof. "You haven't yet learned how to temper this strength with tenderness in your relationships. I suppose that's why you've never married."

She had his attention now, reluctantly. But he wasn't wearing a ring, he reminded himself. And anyone who cared to find out about his marital status had only to make a few inquiries. "The standard response is I've never met the right woman."

"In this case it's perfectly true. You need to find someone every bit as strong as you are. You will, sooner than you think. It won't be easy, of course, and it will only work between you if you both remember the tenderness I just spoke of."

"So I'm going to meet the right woman, marry and live happily ever after?"

"I don't tell the future, ever." Her expression changed again, becoming placid. "And I only read palms of people who interest me. Shall I tell you what my intuition tells me, David?"

"Please."

"That you and I are going to have an interesting and long-term relationship." She patted his hand before she released it. "I'm going to enjoy that."

"So am I." He rose. "I'll see you again, Clarissa."

"Yes. Yes, of course." She rose and nudged the cat onto the floor. "Run along now, Mordred."

"Mordred?" David repeated as the cat jumped up to settle himself on the sagging sofa cushion.

"Such a sad figure in folklore," Clarissa explained. "I always felt he got a bad deal. After all, we can't escape our destiny, can we?"

For the second time David felt her cool, oddly intimate gaze on him. "I suppose not," he murmured, and let her lead him to the door.

"I've so enjoyed our chat, David. Please come back again."

David stepped out into the warm spring air and wondered why he felt certain he would.

"Of course he's an excellent producer, Abe. I'm just not sure he's right for Clarissa."

A. J. Fields paced around her office in the long, fluid gait that always masked an overflow of nervous energy. She stopped to straighten a picture that was slightly tilted before she turned back to her associate. Abe Ebbitt was sitting with his hands folded on his round belly, as was his habit. He didn't bother to push back the glasses that had fallen down his nose. He watched A.J. patiently before he reached up to scratch one of the two clumps of hair on either side of his head.

"A.J., the offer is very generous."

"She doesn't need the money."

His agent's blood shivered at the phrase, but he continued to speak calmly. "The exposure."

"Is it the right kind of exposure?"

"You're too protective of Clarissa, A.J."

"That's what I'm here for," she countered. Abruptly she stopped, and sat on the corner of her desk. When Abe saw her brows draw together, he fell silent. He might speak to her when she was in this mood, but she wouldn't answer. He respected and admired her. Those were the reasons he, a veteran Hollywood agent, was working for the Fields Agency, instead of carving up the town on his own. He was old enough to be her father, and realized that a decade before their roles would have been reversed. The fact that he worked for her didn't bother him in the least. The best, he was fond of saying, never minded answering to the best. A minute passed, then two.

"She's made up her mind to do it," A.J. muttered, but

again Abe remained silent. "I just—" Have a feeling, she thought. She hated to use that phrase. "I just hope it isn't a mistake. The wrong director, the wrong format, and she could be made to look like a fool. I won't have that, Abe."

"You're not giving Clarissa enough credit. You know better than to let your emotions color a business deal, A.J."

"Yeah, I know better." That's why she was the best. A.J. folded her arms and reminded herself of it. She'd learned at a very young age how to channel emotion. It had been more than necessary; it had been vital. When you grew up in a house where your widowed mother often forgot little details like the mortgage payment, you learned how to deal with business in a business-like way or you went under. She was an agent because she enjoyed the wheeling and dealing. And because she was damn good at it. Her Century City office with its lofty view of Los Angeles was proof of just how good. Still, she hadn't gotten there by making deals blindly.

"I'll decide after I meet with Brady this afternoon."

Abe grinned at her, recognizing the look. "How much more are you going to ask for?"

"I think another ten percent." She picked up a pencil and tapped it against her palm. "But first I intend to find out exactly what's going into this documentary and what angles he's going for."

"Word is Brady's tough."

She sent him a deceptively sweet smile that had fire around the edges. "Word is so am I."

"He hasn't got a prayer." He rose, tugging at his belt. "I've got a meeting. Let me know how it goes."

"Sure." She was already frowning at the wall when he closed the door.

David Brady. The fact that she personally admired his work would naturally influence her decision. Still, at the right time and for the right fee, she would sign a client to play a tea bag in a thirty-second local commercial. Clarissa was a different matter. Clarissa DeBasse had been her first client. Her only client, A.J. remembered, during those first lean years. If she was protective of her, as Abe had said, A.J. felt she had a right to be. David Brady might be a successful producer of quality documentaries for public television, but he had to prove himself to A. J. Fields before Clarissa signed on the dotted line.

There'd been a time when A.J. had had to prove herself. She hadn't started out with a staff of fifteen in an exclusive suite of offices. Ten years before, she'd been scrambling for clients and hustling deals from an office that had consisted of a phone booth outside a corner deli. She'd lied about her age. Not too many people had been willing to trust their careers to an eighteen-year-old. Clarissa had.

A.J. gave a little sigh as she worked out a kink in her shoulder. Clarissa didn't really consider what she did, or what she had, a career as much as a calling. It was up to A.J. to haggle over the details.

She was used to it. Her mother had always been such a warm, generous woman. But details had never been her strong point. As a child, it had been up to A.J. to remember when the bills were due. She'd balanced the checkbook, discouraged door-to-door salesmen and juggled her schoolwork with the household budget. Not that her mother was a fool, or neglectful of her daughter. There had always been love, conversation and interest. But their roles had so often been reversed. It was the mother who would claim the stray puppy had followed her home and the daughter who had worried how to feed it.

Still, if her mother had been different, wouldn't A.J. herself be different? That was a question that surfaced often. Destiny was something that couldn't be outmaneuvered. With a laugh, A.J. rose. Clarissa would love that one, she mused.

Walking around her desk, she let herself sink into the deep, wide-armed chair her mother had given her. The chair, unlike the heavy, clean-lined desk, was extravagant and impractical. Who else would have had a chair made in cornflower-blue leather because it matched her daughter's eyes?

A.J. realigned her thoughts and picked up the De-Basse contract. It was in the center of a desk that was meticulously in order. There were no photographs, no flowers, no cute paperweights. Everything on or in her desk had a purpose, and the purpose was business.

She had time to give the contract one more thorough going-over before her appointment with David Brady. Before she met with him, she would understand every phrase, every clause and every alternative. She was just making a note on the final clause, when her buzzer rang. Still writing, A.J. cradled the phone at her ear.

"Yes, Diane."

"Mr. Brady's here, A.J."

"Okay. Any fresh coffee?"

"We have sludge at the moment. I can make some."

"Only if I buzz you. Bring him back, Diane."

She turned her notepad back to the first page, then rose as the door opened. "Mr. Brady." A.J. extended her hand, but stayed behind her desk. It was, she'd learned, important to establish certain positions of power right from the start. Besides, the time it took him to cross the office gave her an opportunity to study and judge. He looked more like someone she might have for a client than a producer. Yes, she was certain she could have sold that hard, masculine look and rangy walk. The laconic, hard-boiled detective on a weekly series; the solitary, nomadic cowboy in a feature film. Pity.

David had his own chance for study. He hadn't expected her to be so young. She was attractive in that streamlined, no-nonsense sort of way he could respect professionally and ignore personally. Her body seemed almost too slim in the sharply tailored suit that was rescued from dullness by a fire-engine-red blouse. Her pale blond hair was cut in a deceptively casual style that shagged around the ears, then angled back to sweep her collar. It suited the honey-toned skin that had been kissed by the sun—or a sunlamp. Her face was oval, her mouth just short of being too wide. Her eyes were a rich blue, accentuated by clever smudges of shadow and framed now with oversize glasses. Their hands met, held and released as hands in business do dozens of times every day.

"Please sit down, Mr. Brady. Would you like some coffee?"

"No, thank you." He took a chair and waited until she settled behind the desk. He noticed that she folded her hands over the contract. No rings, no bracelets, he mused. Just a slender, black-banded watch. "It seems we have a number of mutual acquaintances, Ms. Fields. Odd that we haven't met before."

"Yes, isn't it?" She gave him a small, noncommittal smile. "But, then, as an agent, I prefer staying in the background. You met Clarissa DeBasse."

"Yes, I did." So they'd play stroll around the bush for a while, he decided, and settled back. "She's charming. I have to admit, I'd expected someone, let's say, more eccentric."

This time A.J.'s smile was both spontaneous and generous. If David had been thinking about her on a personal level, his opinion would have changed. "Clarissa is never quite what one expects. Your project sounds interesting, Mr. Brady, but the details I have are sketchy. I'd like you to tell me just what it is you plan to produce."

"A documentary on psychic phenomena, or psi, as I'm told it's called in studies, touching on clairvoyance, parapsychology, ESP, palmistry, telepathy and spiritualism."

"Séances and haunted houses, Mr. Brady?"

He caught the faint disapproval in her tone and wondered about it. "For someone with a psychic for a client, you sound remarkably cynical."

"My client doesn't talk to departed souls or read tea leaves." A.J. sat back in the chair in a way she knew registered confidence and position. "Miss DeBasse has proved herself many times over to be an extraordinarily sensitive woman. She's never claimed to have supernatural powers."

"Supernormal."

She drew in a quiet breath. "You've done your homework. Yes, 'supernormal' is the correct term. Clarissa doesn't believe in overstatements."

"Which is one of the reasons I want Clarissa DeBasse for my program."

A.J. noted the easy use of the possessive pronoun. Not the program, but *my* program. David Brady obviously took his work personally. So much the better, she decided. Then he wouldn't care to look like a fool. "Go on."

"I've talked to mediums, palmists, entertainers, scientists, parapsychologists and carnival gypsies. You'd be amazed at the range of personalities."

A.J. stuck her tongue in her cheek. "I'm sure I would."

Though he noticed her amusement, he let it pass. "They run from the obviously fake to the absolutely sincere. I've spoken with heads of parapsychology departments in several well-known institutions. Every one of them mentioned Clarissa's name."

"Clarissa's been generous with herself." Again he thought he detected slight disapproval. "Particularly in the areas of research and testing."

And there would be no ten percent there. He decided that explained her attitude. "I intend to show possibilities, ask questions. The audience will come up with its own answers. In the five one-hour segments I have, I'll have room to touch on everything from cold spots to tarot cards."

In a gesture she'd thought she'd conquered long ago, she drummed her fingers on the desk. "And where does Miss DeBasse fit in?"

She was his ace in the hole. But he wasn't ready to play her yet. "Clarissa is a recognizable name. A woman who's 'proved herself,' to use your phrase, to be extraordinarily sensitive. Then there's the Van Camp case."

Frowning, A.J. picked up a pencil and began to run it through her fingers. "That was ten years ago."

"The child of a Hollywood star is kidnapped, snatched from his devoted nanny as he plays in the park. The ransom call demands a half a million. The mother's frantic—the police are baffled. Thirty-six hours pass without a clue as the boy's parents desperately try to get the cash together. Over the father's objection, the mother calls a friend, a woman who did her astrological chart and occasionally reads palms. The woman comes, of course, and sits for an hour holding some of the boy's things—his baseball glove, a stuffed toy, the pajama top he'd worn to bed the night before. At the end of that hour, the woman gives the police a description of the boy's kidnappers and the exact location of the house where he's being held. She even describes the room where he's being held, down to the chipped paint on the ceiling. The boy sleeps in his own bed that night."

David pulled out a cigarette, lit it and blew out smoke, while A.J. remained silent. "Ten years doesn't take away that kind of impact, Ms. Fields. The audience will be just as fascinated today as they were then."

It shouldn't have made her angry. It was sheer foolishness to respond that way. A.J. continued to sit silently as she worked back the surge of temper. "A great many people call the Van Camp case a fraud. Dredging that up after ten years will only dredge up more criticism."

"A woman in Clarissa's position must have to deal with criticism continually." He saw the flare come into her eyes—fierce and fast.

"That may be, but I have no intention of allowing her to sign a contract that guarantees it. I have no intention of seeing my client on a televised trial."

"Hold it." He had a temper of his own and could respect hers—if he understood it. "Clarissa goes on trial every time she's in the public eye. If her abilities can't stand up to cameras and questions, she shouldn't be doing what she does. As her agent, I'd think you'd have a stronger belief in her competence."

"My beliefs aren't your concern." Intending to toss him and his contract out, A.J. started to rise, when the phone interrupted her. With an indistinguishable oath, she lifted the receiver. "No calls, Diane. No—oh." A.J. set her teeth and composed herself. "Yes, put her on."

"Oh, I'm so sorry to bother you at work, dear."

"That's all right. I'm in a meeting, so—"

"Oh, yes, I know." Clarissa's calm, apologetic voice came quietly in her ear. "With that nice David Brady."

"That's a matter of opinion."

"I had a feeling you wouldn't hit it off the first time." Clarissa sighed and stroked her cat. "I've been giving that contract business a great deal of thought." She didn't mention the dream, knowing her agent wouldn't want to hear it. "I've decided I want to sign it right away. Now, now, I know what you're going to say," she continued before A.J. could say a word. "You're the agent— you handle the business. You do whatever you think best about clauses and such, but I want to do this program."

A.J. recognized the tone. Clarissa had a feeling. There was never any arguing with Clarissa's feelings. "We need to talk about this."

"Of course, dear, all you like. You and David iron out the details. You're so good at that. I'll leave all the terms up to you, but I will sign the contract."

With David sitting across from her, A.J. couldn't take the satisfaction of accepting defeat by kicking her desk. "All right. But I think you should know I have feelings of my own."

"Of course you do. Come to dinner tonight."

She nearly smiled. Clarissa loved to feed you to smooth things over. Pity she was such a dreadful cook. "I can't. I have a dinner appointment."

"Tomorrow."

"All right. I'll see you then."

After hanging up, A.J. took a deep breath and faced David again. "I'm sorry for the interruption."

"No problem."

"As there's nothing specific in the contract regarding the Van Camp case, including that in the program would be strictly up to Miss DeBasse."

"Of course. I've already spoken to her about it."

A.J. very calmly, very deliberately bit her tongue. "I see. There's also nothing specific about Miss De-Basse's position in the documentary. That will have to be altered."

"I'm sure we can work that out." So she was going to sign, David mused, and listened to a few other minor changes A.J. requested. Before the phone rang, she'd been ready to pitch him out. He'd seen it in her eyes. He held back a smile as they negotiated another minor point. He was no clairvoyant, but he would bet his grant that Clarissa DeBasse had been on the other end of that phone. A.J. Fields had been caught right in the middle. Best place for agents, he thought, and settled back.

"We'll redraft the contract and have it to you tomorrow."

Everybody's in a hurry, she thought, and settled back herself. "Then I'm sure we can do business, Mr. Brady, if we can settle one more point."

"Which is?"

"Miss DeBasse's fee." A.J. flipped back the contract and adjusted the oversize glasses she wore for reading. "I'm afraid this is much less than Miss De-Basse is accustomed to accepting. We'll need another twenty percent."

David lifted a brow. He'd been expecting something along these lines, but he'd expected it sooner. Obviously A.J. Fields hadn't become one of the top in her profession by doing the expected. "You understand we're working in public television. Our budget can't compete with network. As producer, I can offer another five percent, but twenty is out of reach."

"And five is inadequate." A.J. slipped off her glasses and dangled them by an earpiece. Her eyes seemed larger, richer, without them. "I understand public television, Mr. Brady, and I understand your grant." She gave him a charming smile. "Fifteen percent."

Typical agent, he thought, not so much annoyed as fatalistic. She wanted ten, and ten was precisely what his budget would allow. Still, there was a game to be played. "Miss DeBasse is already being paid more than anyone else on contract."

"You're willing to do that because she'll be your biggest draw. I also understand ratings."

"Seven."

"Twelve."

"Ten."

"Done." A.J. rose. Normally the deal would have left her fully satisfied. Because her temper wasn't completely under control it was difficult to appreciate the fact that she'd gotten exactly what she'd intended to get. "I'll look for the revised contracts."

"I'll send them by messenger tomorrow afternoon. That phone call..." He paused as he rose. "You wouldn't be dealing with me without it, would you?"

She studied him a moment and cursed him for being sharp, intelligent and intuitive. All the things she needed for her client. "No, I wouldn't."

"Be sure to thank Clarissa for me." With a smile smug enough to bring her temper back to boil he offered his hand.

"Goodbye, Mr....." When their hands met this time, her voice died. Feelings ran into her with the impact of a slap, leaving her weak and breathless. Apprehension, desire, fury and delight rolled through her at the touch of flesh to flesh. She had only a moment to berate herself for allowing temper to open the door.

"Ms. Fields?" She was staring at him, through him, as though he were an apparition just risen from the floorboards. In his, her hand was limp and icy. Automatically David took her arm. If he'd ever seen a woman about to faint, he was seeing one now. "You'd better sit down."

"What?" Though shaken, A.J. willed herself back. "No, no, I'm fine. I'm sorry, I must have been thinking of something else." But as she spoke, she broke all contact with him and stepped back. "Too much coffee, too little sleep." And stay away from me, she said desperately to herself as she leaned back on the desk. Just stay away. "I'm glad we could do business, Mr. Brady. I'll pass everything along to my client."

Her color was back, her eyes were clear. Still David hesitated. A moment before she'd looked fragile enough to crumble in his hands. "Sit down."

"I beg your—"

"Damn it, sit." He took her by the elbow and nudged her into a chair. "Your hands are shaking." Before she could do anything about it, he was kneeling in front of her. "I'd advise canceling that dinner appointment and getting a good night's sleep."

She curled her hands together on her lap to keep him from touching her again. "There's no reason for you to be concerned."

"I generally take a personal interest when a woman all but faints at my feet."

The sarcastic tone settled the flutters in her stomach. "Oh, I'm sure you do." But then he took her face in his hand and had her jerking. "Stop that."

Her skin was as soft as it looked, but he would keep that thought for later. "Purely a clinical touch, Ms. Fields. You're not my type."

Her eyes chilled. "Where do I give thanks?"

He wondered why the cool outrage in her eyes made him want to laugh. To laugh, and to taste her. "Very good," he murmured, and straightened. "Lay off the coffee," he advised, and left her alone before he did something ridiculous.

And alone, A.J. brought her knees up to her chest and pressed her face to them. What was she going to do now? she demanded as she tried to squeeze herself into a ball. What in God's name was she going to do?

Chapter 2

A.J. seriously considered stopping for a hamburger before going on to dinner at Clarissa's. She didn't have the heart for it. Besides, if she was hungry enough she would be able to make a decent showing out of actually eating whatever Clarissa prepared.

With the sunroof open, she sat back and tried to enjoy the forty-minute drive from her office to the suburbs. Beside her was a slim leather portfolio that held the contracts David Brady's office had delivered, as promised. Since the changes she'd requested had been made, she couldn't grumble. There was absolutely no substantial reason for her to object to the deal, or to her client working with Brady. All she had was a feeling. She'd been working on that since the previous afternoon.

It had been overwork, she told herself. She hadn't felt anything but a quick, momentary dizziness because she'd stood so fast. She hadn't felt anything for or about David Brady.

But she had.

A.J. cursed herself for the next ten miles before she brought herself under control.

She couldn't afford to be the least bit upset when she arrived in Newport Beach. There was no hiding such things from a woman like Clarissa DeBasse. She would have to be able to discuss not only the contract terms, but David Brady himself with complete objectivity or Clarissa would home in like radar.

For the next ten miles she considered stopping at a phone booth and begging off. She didn't have the heart for that, either.

Relax, A.J. ordered herself, and tried to imagine she was home in her apartment, doing long, soothing yoga exercises. It helped, and as the tension in her muscles eased, she turned up the radio. She kept it high until she turned the engine off in front of the tidy suburban home she'd helped pick out.

A.J. always felt a sense of self-satisfaction as she strolled up the walk. The house suited Clarissa, with its neat green lawn and pretty white shutters. It was true that with the success of her books and public appearances Clarissa could afford a house twice as big in Beverly Hills. But nothing would fit her as comfortably as this tidy brick ranch.

Shifting the brown bag that held wine under her arm, A.J. pushed open the door she knew was rarely locked. "Hello! I'm a six-foot-two, three-hundred-and-twenty-pound burglar come to steal all your jewelry. Care to give me a hand?"

"Oh, did I forget to lock it again?" Clarissa came bustling out of the kitchen, wiping her hands on an already smeared and splattered apron. Her cheeks were flushed from the heat of the stove, her lips already curved in greeting.

"Yes, you forgot to lock it again." Even with an armload of wine, A.J. managed to hug her. Then she kissed both cheeks as she tried to unobtrusively sniff out what was going on in the kitchen.

"It's meat loaf," Clarissa told her. "I got a new recipe."

"Oh." A.J. might have managed the smile if she hadn't remembered the last meat loaf so clearly. Instead she concentrated on the woman. "You look wonderful. I'd swear you were running into L.A. and sneaking into Elizabeth Arden's once a week."

"Oh, I can't be bothered with all that. It's too much worrying that causes lines and sags, anyway. You should remember that."

"So I look like a hag, do I?" A.J. dropped her portfolio on the table and stepped out of her shoes.

"You know I didn't mean that, but I can tell you're worried about something."

"Dinner," A.J. told her, evading. "I only had time for a half a sandwich at lunch."

"There, I've told you a dozen times you don't eat properly. Come into the kitchen. I'm sure everything's about ready."

Satisfied that she'd distracted Clarissa, A.J. started to follow.

"Then you can tell me what's really bothering you."

"Doesn't miss a trick," A.J. muttered as the doorbell rang.

"Get that for me, will you?" Clarissa cast an anxious glance at the kitchen. "I really should check the brussels sprouts."

"Brussels sprouts?" A.J. could only grimace as Clarissa disappeared into the kitchen. "Bad enough I have to eat the meat loaf, but brussels sprouts. I should have had the hamburger." When she opened the door her brows were already lowered.

"You look thrilled to see me."

One hand still on the knob, she stared at David. "What are you doing here?"

"Having dinner." Without waiting for an invitation, David stepped forward and stood with her in the open doorway. "You're tall. Even without your shoes."

A.J. closed the door with a quiet snap. "Clarissa didn't explain this was a business dinner."

"I think she considers it purely social." He hadn't yet figured out why he hadn't gotten the very professional Ms. Fields out of his mind. Maybe he'd get some answers before the evening was up. "Why don't we think of it that way—A.J.?"

Manners had been ingrained in her by a quietly determined mother. Trapped, A.J. nodded. "All right, David. I hope you enjoy living dangerously."

"I beg your pardon?"

She couldn't resist the smile. "We're having meat loaf." She took the bottle of champagne he held and examined the label. "This should help. Did you happen to have a big lunch?"

There was a light in her eyes he'd never noticed before. It was a laugh, a joke, and very appealing. "What are you getting at?"

She patted his shoulder. "Sometimes it's best to go into these things unprepared. Sit down and I'll fix you a drink."

"Aurora."

"Yes?" A.J. answered automatically before she bit her tongue.

"Aurora?" David repeated, experimenting with the way it sounded in his voice. "That's what the *A* stands for?"

When A.J. turned to him her eyes were narrowed. "If just one person in the business calls me that, I'll know exactly where they got it from. You'll pay."

He ran a finger down the side of his nose, but didn't quite hide the smile. "I never heard a thing."

"Aurora, was that—" Clarissa stopped in the kitchen doorway and beamed. "Yes, it was David. How lovely." She studied both of them, standing shoulder to shoulder just inside her front door. For the instant she concentrated, the aura around them was very clear and very bright. "Yes, how lovely," she repeated. "I'm so glad you came."

"I appreciate your asking me." Finding Clarissa as charming as he had the first time, David crossed to her. He took her hand, but this time brought it to his lips. Pleasure flushed her cheeks.

"Champagne, how nice. We'll open it after I sign the contracts." She glanced over his shoulder to see A.J. frowning. "Why don't you fix yourself and David a drink, dear? I won't be much longer."

A.J. thought of the contracts in her portfolio, and of her own doubts. Then she gave in. Clarissa would do precisely what Clarissa wanted to do. In order to protect her, she had to stop fighting it and accept. "I can guarantee the vodka—I bought it myself."

"Fine—on the rocks." David waited while she went to a cabinet and took out a decanter and glasses.

"She remembered the ice," A.J. said, surprised when she opened the brass bucket and found it full.

"You seem to know Clarissa very well."

"I do." A.J. poured two glasses, then turned. "She's much more than simply a client to me, David. That's why I'm concerned about this program."

He walked to her to take the glass. Strange, he thought, you only noticed her scent when you stood close, very close. He wondered if she used such a light touch to draw men to her or to block their way. "Why the concern?"

If they were going to deal with each other, honesty might help. A.J. glanced toward the kitchen and kept her voice low. "Clarissa has a tendency to be very open with certain people. Too open. She can expose too much of herself, and leave herself vulnerable to all manner of complications."

"Are you protecting her from me?"

A.J. sipped from her drink. "I'm trying to decide if I should."

"I like her." He reached out to twine a lock of A.J.'s hair around his finger, before either of them realized his intention. He dropped his hand again so quickly she didn't have the chance to demand it. "She's a very likable woman," David continued as he turned to wander around the room. He wasn't a man to touch a business associate, especially one he barely knew, in so casual a manner. To give himself distance, he walked to the window to watch birds flutter around a feeder in the side yard. The cat was out there, he noticed, sublimely disinterested as it sunned itself in a last patch of sunlight.

A.J. waited until she was certain her voice would be properly calm and professional. "I appreciate that, but your project comes first, I imagine. You want a good show, and you'll do whatever it takes to produce one."

"That's right." The problem was, he decided, that she

wasn't as tailored and streamlined as she'd been the day before. Her blouse was soft and silky, the color of poppies. If she'd had a jacket to match the snug white skirt, she'd left it in her car. She was shoeless and her hair had been tossed by the wind. He took another drink. She still wasn't his type. "But I don't believe I have a reputation for exploiting people in order to get it. I do my job, A.J., and expect the same from anyone who works with me."

"Fair enough." She finished the unwanted drink. "My job is to protect Clarissa in every way."

"I don't see that we have a problem."

"There now, everything's ready." Clarissa came out to see her guests not shoulder to shoulder, but with the entire room between them. Sensitive to mood, she felt the tension, confusion and distrust. Quite normal, she decided, for two stubborn, self-willed people on opposing ends. She wondered how long it would take them to admit attraction, let alone accept it. "I hope you're both hungry."

A.J. set down her empty glass with an easy smile. "David tells me he's starved. You'll have to give him an extra portion."

"Wonderful." Delighted, she led the way into the dining area. "I love to eat by candlelight, don't you?" She had a pair of candles burning on the table, and another half-dozen tapers on the sideboard. A.J. decided the romantic light definitely helped the looks of the meat loaf. "Aurora brought the wine, so I'm sure it's lovely. You pour, David, and I'll serve."

"It looks wonderful," he told her, and wondered why A.J. muffled a chuckle.

"Thank you. Are you from California originally, David?" Clarissa asked as she handed A.J. a platter.

"No, Washington State." He tipped Beaujolais into Clarissa's glass.

"Beautiful country." She handed Aurora a heaping bowl of mashed potatoes. "But so cold."

He could remember the long, windy winters with some nostalgia. "I didn't have any trouble acclimating to L.A."

"I grew up in the East and came out here with my husband nearly thirty years ago. In the fall I'm still the tiniest bit homesick for Vermont. You haven't taken any vegetables, Aurora. You know how I worry that you don't eat properly."

A.J. added brussels sprouts to her plate and hoped she'd be able to ignore them. "You should take a trip back this year," A.J. told Clarissa. One bite of the meat loaf was enough. She reached for the wine.

"I think about it. Do you have any family, David?"

He'd just had his first experience with Clarissa's cooking and hadn't recovered. He wondered what recipe she'd come across that called for leather. "Excuse me?"

"Any family?"

"Yes." He glanced at A.J. and saw the knowing smirk. "Two brothers and a sister scattered around Washington and Oregon."

"I came from a big family myself. I thoroughly enjoyed my childhood." Reaching out, she patted A.J.'s hand. "Aurora was an only child."

With a laugh A.J. gave Clarissa's hand a quick squeeze. "And I thoroughly enjoyed my childhood." Because she saw David politely making his way through a hill of lumpy potatoes, she felt a little tug on her conscience. A.J. waited until it passed. "What made you choose documentaries, David?"

"I'd always been fascinated by little films." Picking

up the salt, he used it liberally. "With a documentary, the plot's already there, but it's up to you to come up with the angles, to find a way to present it to an audience and make them care while they're being entertained."

"Isn't it more of a learning experience?"

"I'm not a teacher." Bravely he dipped back into the meat loaf. "You can entertain with truth and speculation just as satisfyingly as you can entertain with fiction."

Somehow watching him struggle with the meal made it more palatable for her. "No urge to produce the big film?"

"I like television," he said easily, and reached for the wine. They were all going to need it. "I happen to think there's too much pap and not enough substance."

A.J.'s brow lifted, to disappear under a thin fringe of bangs. "Pap?"

"Unfortunately network television's rife with it. Shows like *Empire,* for instance, or *It Takes Two.*"

"Really." A.J. leaned forward. "*Empire* has been a top-rated show for four years." She didn't add that it was a personal favorite.

"My point exactly. If a show like that retains consistently high ratings—a show that relies on steam, glitter and contrivance—it proves that the audience is being fed a steady stream of garbage."

"Not everyone feels a show has to be educational or 'good' for it to be quality. The problem with public television is that it has its nose up in the air so often the average American ignores it. After working eight hours, fighting traffic, coping with children and dealing with car repair bills, a person's entitled to relax."

"Absolutely." Amazing, he thought, how lovely she became when you lit a little fire under her. Maybe she was a woman who needed conflict in her life. "But that same person doesn't have to shut off his or her intelligence to be entertained. That's called escapism."

"I'm afraid I don't watch enough television to see the difference," Clarissa commented, pleased to see her guests clearing their plates. "But don't you represent that lovely woman who plays on *Empire?*"

"Audrey Cummings." A.J. slipped her fingers under the cup of her wineglass and swirled it lightly. "A very accomplished actress, who's also played Shakespeare. We've just made a deal to have her take the role of Maggie in a remake of *Cat on a Hot Tin Roof.*" The success of that deal was still sweet. Sipping her wine, she tilted her head at David. "For a play that deals in a lot of steam and sweat, it's amazing what longevity it's had. We can't claim it's a Verdi opera, can we?"

"There's more to public television than Verdi." He'd touched a nerve, he realized. But, then, so had she. "I don't suppose you caught the profile on Taylor Brooks? I thought it was one of the most detailed and informative on a rock star I'd ever seen." He picked up his wine in a half toast. "You don't represent him, too, do you?"

"No." She decided to play it to the hilt. "We dated casually a couple of years ago. I have a rule about keeping business and personal relationships separated."

"Wise." He lifted his wine and sipped. "Very wise."

"Unlike you, I have no prejudices when it comes to television. If I did, you'd hardly be signing one of my top clients."

"More meat loaf?" Clarissa asked.

"I couldn't eat another bite." A.J. smiled at David. "Perhaps David would like more."

"As much as I appreciate the home cooking, I can't."

He tried not to register too much relief as he stood. "Let me help you clear up."

"Oh, no." Rising, Clarissa brushed his offer aside. "It relaxes me. Aurora, I think David was just a bit disappointed with me the first time we met. Why don't you show him my collection?"

"All right." Picking up her wineglass, A.J. gestured to him to follow. "You've scored points," she commented. "Clarissa doesn't show her collection to everyone."

"I'm flattered." But he took her by the elbow to stop her as they started down a narrow hallway. "You'd prefer it if I kept things strictly business with Clarissa."

A.J. lifted the glass to her lips and watched him over the rim. She'd prefer, for reasons she couldn't name, that he stayed fifty miles from Clarissa. And double that from her. "Clarissa chooses her own friends."

"And you make damn sure they don't take advantage of her."

"Exactly. This way." Turning, she walked to a door on the left and pushed it open. "It'd be more effective by candlelight, even more with a full moon, but we'll have to make do." A.J. flicked on the light and stepped out of his view.

It was an average-size room, suitable to a modern ranch house. Here, the windows were heavily draped to block the view of the yard—or to block the view inside. It wasn't difficult to see why Clarissa would use the veil to discourage the curious. The room belonged in a tower—or a dungeon.

Here was the crystal ball he'd expected. Unable to resist, David crossed to a tall, round-topped stand to examine it. The glass was smooth and perfect, reflecting only the faintest hint of the deep blue cloth beneath it. Tarot cards, obviously old and well used, were displayed in a locked case. At a closer look he saw they'd been hand painted. A bookshelf held everything from voodoo to telekinesis. On the shelf with them was a candle in the shape of a tall, slender woman with arms lifted to the sky.

A Ouija board was set out on a table carved with pentagrams. One wall was lined with masks of pottery, ceramic, wood, even papier-mâché. There were dowsing rods and pendulums. A glass cabinet held pyramids of varying sizes. There was more—an Indian rattle, worn and fragile with age, Oriental worry beads in jet, others in amethyst.

"More what you expected?" A.J. asked after a moment.

"No." He picked up another crystal, this one small enough to rest in the palm of his hand. "I stopped expecting this after the first five minutes."

It was the right thing for him to say. A.J. sipped her wine again and tried not to be too pleased. "It's just a hobby with Clarissa, collecting the obvious trappings of the trade."

"She doesn't use them?"

"A hobby only. Actually, it started a long time ago. A friend found those tarot cards in a little shop in England and gave them to her. After that, things snowballed."

The crystal was cool and smooth in his hand as he studied her. "You don't approve?"

A.J. merely shrugged her shoulders. "I wouldn't if she took it seriously."

"Have you ever tried this?" He indicated the Ouija board.

"No."

It was a lie. He wasn't sure why she told it, or why he was certain of it. "So you don't believe in any of this."

"I believe in Clarissa. The rest of this is just showmanship."

Still, he was intrigued with it, intrigued with the fascination it held for people through the ages. "You've never been tempted to ask her to look in the crystal for you?"

"Clarissa doesn't need the crystal, and she doesn't tell the future."

He glanced into the clear glass in his hand. "Odd, you'd think if she can do the other things she's reported to be able to do, she could do that."

"I didn't say she couldn't—I said she doesn't."

David looked up from the crystal again. "Explain."

"Clarissa feels very strongly about destiny, and the tampering with it. She's refused, even for outrageous fees, to predict."

"But you're saying she could."

"I'm saying she chooses not to. Clarissa considers her gift a responsibility. Rather than misuse it in any way, she'd push it out of her life."

"Push it out." He set the crystal down. "Do you mean she—a psychic—could just refuse to be one. Just block out the...let's say power, for lack of a better term. Just turn it off?"

Her fingers had dampened on the glass. A.J. casually switched it to her other hand. "To a large extent, yes. You have to be open to it. You're a receptacle, a transmitter—the extent to which you receive or transmit depends on you."

"You seem to know a great deal about it."

He was sharp, she remembered abruptly. Very sharp. A.J. smiled deliberately and moved her shoulders again.

"I know a great deal about Clarissa. If you spend any amount of time with her over the next couple of months, you'll know quite a bit yourself."

David walked to her. He watched her carefully as he took the wineglass from her and sipped himself. It was warm now and seemed more potent. "Why do I get the impression that you're uncomfortable in this room. Or is it that you're uncomfortable with me?"

"Your intuition's missing the mark. If you'd like, Clarissa can give you a few exercises to sharpen it."

"Your palms are damp." He took her hand, then ran his fingers down to the wrist. "Your pulse is fast. I don't need intuition to know that."

It was important—vital—that she keep calm. She met his eyes levelly and hoped she managed to look amused. "That probably has more to do with the meat loaf."

"The first time we met you had a very strong, very strange reaction to me."

She hadn't forgotten. It had given her a very restless night. "I explained—"

"I didn't buy it," he interrupted. "I still don't. That might be because I found myself doing a lot of thinking about you."

She'd taught herself to hold her ground. She'd had to. A.J. made one last attempt to do so now, though his eyes seemed much too quiet and intrusive, his voice too firm. She took her wineglass back from him and drained it. She learned it was a mistake, because she could taste him as well as the wine. "David, try to remember I'm not your type." Her voice was cool and faintly cutting. If she'd thought about it a few seconds longer, she would have realized it was the wrong tactic.

"No, you're not." His hand cupped her nape, then slid up into her hair. "But what the hell."

When he leaned closer, A.J. saw two clear-cut choices. She could struggle away and run for cover, or she could meet him with absolute indifference. Because the second choice seemed the stronger, she went with it. It was her next mistake.

He knew how to tempt a woman. How to coax. When his lips lowered to hers they barely touched, while his hand continued to stroke her neck and hair. A.J.'s grip on the wineglass tightened, but she didn't move, not forward, not away. His lips skimmed hers again, with just the hint of his tongue. The breath she'd been holding shuddered out.

As her eyes began to close, as her bones began to soften, he moved away from her mouth to trace his lips over her jaw. Neither of them noticed when the wineglass slipped out of her hand to land on the carpet.

He'd been right about how close you had to get to be tempted by her scent. It was strong and dark and private, as though it came through her pores to hover on her skin. As he brought his lips back to hers, he realized it wasn't something he'd forget. Nor was she.

This time her lips were parted, ready, willing. Still he moved slowly, more for his own sake now. This wasn't the cool man-crusher he'd expected, but a warm, soft woman who could draw you in with vulnerability alone. He needed time to adjust, time to think. When he backed away he still hadn't touched her, and had given her only the merest hint of a kiss. They were both shaken.

"Maybe the reaction wasn't so strange after all, Aurora," he murmured. "Not for either of us."

Her body was on fire; it was icy; it was weak. She

couldn't allow her mind to follow suit. Drawing all her reserves of strength, A.J. straightened. "If we're going to be doing business—"

"And we are."

She let out a long, patient breath at the interruption. "Then you'd better understand the ground rules. I don't sleep around, not with clients, not with associates."

It pleased him. He wasn't willing to ask himself why. "Narrows the field, doesn't it?"

"That's my business," she shot back. "My personal life is entirely separate from my profession."

"Hard to do in this town, but admirable. However…" He couldn't resist reaching up to play with a stray strand of hair at her ear. "I didn't ask you to sleep with me."

She caught his hand by the wrist to push it away. It both surprised and pleased her to discover his pulse wasn't any steadier than hers. "Forewarned, you won't embarrass yourself by doing so and being rejected."

"Do you think I would?" He brought his hand back up to stroke a finger down her cheek. "Embarrass myself."

"Stop it."

He shook his head and studied her face again. Attractive, yes. Not beautiful, hardly glamorous. Too cool, too stubborn. So why was he already imagining her naked and wrapped around him? "What is it between us?"

"Animosity."

He grinned, abruptly and completely charming her. She could have murdered him for it. "Maybe part, but even that's too strong for such a short association. A minute ago I was wondering what it would be like to make love with you. Believe it or not, I don't do that with every woman I meet."

Her palms were damp again. "Am I supposed to be flattered?"

"No. I just figure we'll deal better together if we understand each other."

The need to turn and run was desperate. Too desperate. A.J. held her ground. "Understand this. I represent Clarissa DeBasse. I'll look out for her interests, her welfare. If you try to do anything detrimental to her professionally or personally, I'll cut you off at the knees. Other than that, we really don't have anything to worry about."

"Time will tell."

For the first time she took a step away from him. A.J. didn't consider it a retreat as she walked over and put her hand on the light switch. "I have a breakfast meeting in the morning. Let's get the contracts signed, Brady, so we can both do our jobs."

Chapter 3

Preproduction meetings generally left his staff frazzled and out of sorts. David thrived on them. Lists of figures that insisted on being balanced appealed to the practical side of him. Translating those figures into lights, sets and props challenged his creativity. If he hadn't enjoyed finding ways to merge the two, he never would have chosen to be a producer.

He was a man who had a reputation for knowing his own mind and altering circumstances to suit it. The reputation permeated his professional life and filtered through to the personal. As a producer he was tough and, according to many directors, not always fair. As a man he was generous and, according to many women, not always warm.

David would give a director creative freedom, but only to a point. When the creative freedom tempted the director to veer from David's overall view of a project, he stopped him dead. He would discuss, listen and at times compromise. An astute director would realize that the compromise hadn't affected the producer's wishes in the least.

In a relationship he would give a woman an easy, attentive companion. If a woman preferred roses, there would be roses. If she enjoyed rides in the country, there would be rides in the country. But if she attempted to get beneath the skin, he stopped her dead. He would discuss, listen and at times compromise. An astute woman would realize the compromise hadn't affected the man in the least.

Directors would call him tough, but would grudgingly admit they would work with him again. Women would call him cool, but would smile when they heard his voice over the phone.

Neither of these things came to him through carefully thought-out strategy, but simply because he was a man who was careful with his private thoughts—and private needs.

By the time the preproduction meetings were over, the location set and the format jelled, David was anxious for results. He'd picked his team individually, down to the last technician. Because he'd developed a personal interest in Clarissa DeBasse, he decided to begin with her. His choice, he was certain, had nothing to do with her agent.

His initial desire to have her interviewed in her own home was cut off quickly by a brief memo from A. J. Fields. Miss DeBasse was entitled to her privacy. Period. Unwilling to be hampered by a technicality, David arranged for the studio to be decorated in precisely the same homey, suburban atmosphere. He'd have her interviewed there by veteran journalist Alex Marshall.

David wanted to thread credibility through speculation. A man of Marshall's reputation could do it for him.

David kept in the background and let his crew take over. He'd had problems with this director before, but both projects they'd collaborated on had won awards. The end product, to David, was the bottom line.

"Put a filter on that light," the director ordered. "We may have to look like we're sitting in the furniture department in the mall, but I want atmosphere. Alex, if you'd run through your intro, I'd like to get a fix on the angle."

"Fine." Reluctantly Alex tapped out his two-dollar cigar and went to work. David checked his watch. Clarissa was late, but not late enough to cause alarm yet. In another ten minutes he'd have an assistant give her a call. He watched Alex run through the intro flawlessly, then wait while the director fussed with the lights. Deciding he wasn't needed at the moment, David opted to make the call himself. Only he'd make it to A.J.'s office. No harm in giving her a hard time, he thought as he pushed through the studio doors. She seemed to be the better for it.

"Oh, David, I do apologize."

He stopped as Clarissa hurried down the hallway. She wasn't anyone's aunt today, he thought, as she reached out to take his hands. Her hair was swept dramatically back, making her look both flamboyant and years younger. There was a necklace of silver links around her neck that held an amethyst the size of his thumb. Her makeup was artfully applied to accent clear blue eyes, just as her dress, deep and rich, accented them. This wasn't the woman who'd fed him meat loaf.

"Clarissa, you look wonderful."

"Thank you. I'm afraid I didn't have much time to

prepare. I got the days mixed, you see, and was right in the middle of weeding my petunias when Aurora came to pick me up."

He caught himself looking over her shoulder and down the hall. "She's here?"

"She's parking the car." Clarissa glanced back over her shoulder with a sigh. "I know I'm a trial to her, always have been."

"She doesn't seem to feel that way."

"No, she doesn't. Aurora's so generous."

He'd reserve judgment on that one. "Are you ready, or would you like some coffee or tea first?"

"No, no, I don't like any stimulants when I'm working. They tend to cloud things." Their hands were still linked when her gaze fastened on his. "You're a bit restless, David."

She said it the moment he'd looked back, and seen A.J. coming down the hall. "I'm always edgy on a shoot," he said absently. Why was it he hadn't noticed how she walked before? Fast and fluid.

"That's not it," Clarissa commented, and patted his hand. "But I won't invade your privacy. Ah, here's Aurora. Should we start?"

"We already have," he murmured, still watching A.J.

"Good morning, David. I hope we haven't thrown you off schedule."

She was as sleek and professional as she'd been the first time he'd seen her. Why was it now that he noticed small details? The collar of her blouse rose high on what he knew was a long, slender neck. Her mouth was unpainted. He wanted to take a step closer to see if she wore the same scent. Instead he took Clarissa's arm. "Not at all. I take it you want to watch."

"Of course."

"Just inside here, Clarissa." He pushed open the door. "I'd like to introduce you to your director, Sam Cauldwell. Sam." It didn't appear to bother David that he was interrupting his director. A.J. noticed that he stood where he was and waited for Cauldwell to come to him. She could hardly censure him for it when she'd have used the same technique herself. "This is Clarissa DeBasse."

Cauldwell stemmed obvious impatience to take her hand. "A pleasure, Miss DeBasse. I read both your books to give myself a feel for your segment of the program."

"That's very kind of you. I hope you enjoyed them."

"I don't know if 'enjoyed' is the right word." He gave a quick shake of his head. "They certainly gave me something to think about."

"Miss DeBasse is ready to start whenever you're set."

"Great. Would you mind taking a seat over here. We'll take a voice test and recheck the lighting."

As Cauldwell led her away, David saw A.J. watching him like a hawk. "You make a habit of hovering over your clients, A.J.?"

Satisfied that Clarissa was all right for the moment, A.J. turned to him. "Yes. Just the way I imagine you hover over your directors."

"All in a day's work, right? You can get a better view from over here."

"Thanks." She moved with him to the left of the studio, watching as Clarissa was introduced to Alex Marshall. The veteran newscaster was tall, lean and distinguished. Twenty-five years in the game had etched a few lines on his face, but the gray threading through his hair contrasted nicely with his deep tan. "A wise choice for your narrator," she commented.

"The face America trusts."

"There's that, of course. Also, I can't imagine him putting up with any nonsense. Bring in a palm reader from Sunset Boulevard and he'll make her look like a fool regardless of the script."

"That's right."

A.J. sent him an even look. "He won't make a fool out of Clarissa."

He gave her a slow, acknowledging nod. "That's what I'm counting on. I called your office last week."

"Yes, I know." A.J. saw Clarissa laugh at something Alex said. "Didn't my assistant get back to you?"

"I didn't want to talk to your assistant."

"I've been tied up. You've very nearly recreated Clarissa's living room, haven't you?"

"That's the idea. You're trying to avoid me, A.J." He shifted just enough to block her view, so that she was forced to look at him. Because he'd annoyed her, she made the look thorough, starting at his shoes, worn canvas high-tops, up the casual pleated slacks to the open collar of his shirt before she settled on his face.

"I'd hoped you'd catch on."

"And you might succeed at it." He ran his finger down her lapel, over a pin of a half-moon. "But she's going to get in the way." He glanced over his shoulder at Clarissa.

She schooled herself for this, lectured herself and rehearsed the right responses. Somehow it wasn't as easy as she'd imagined. "David, you don't seem to be one of those men who are attracted to rejection."

"No." His thumb continued to move over the pin as he looked back at her. "You don't seem to be one of those women who pretend disinterest to attract."

"I don't pretend anything." She looked directly into

his eyes, determined not a flicker of her own unease would show. "I am disinterested. And you're standing in my way."

"That's something that might get to be a habit." But he moved aside.

It took nearly another forty-five minutes of discussion, changes and technical fine-tuning before they were ready to shoot. Because she was relieved David was busy elsewhere, A.J. waited patiently. Which meant she only checked her watch half a dozen times. Clarissa sat easily on the sofa and sipped water. But whenever she glanced up and looked in her direction, A.J. was glad she'd decided to come.

The shoot began well enough. Clarissa sat with Alex on the sofa. He asked questions; she answered. They touched on clairvoyance, precognition, Clarissa's interest in astrology. Clarissa had a knack for taking long, confusing phrases and making them simple, understandable. One of the reasons she was often in demand on the lecture circuit was her ability to take the mysteries of psi and relate them to the average person. It was one area A.J. could be certain Clarissa DeBasse would handle herself. Relaxing, she took a piece of hard candy out of her briefcase in lieu of lunch.

They shot, reshot, altered angles and repeated themselves for the camera. Hours passed, but A.J. was content. Quality was the order of the day. She wanted nothing less for Clarissa.

Then they brought out the cards.

She'd nearly taken a step forward, when the slightest signal from Clarissa had her fuming and staying where she was. She hated this, and always had.

"Problem?"

She hadn't realized he'd come up beside her. A.J. sent

David a killing look before she riveted her attention on the set again. "We didn't discuss anything like this."

"The cards?" Surprised by her response, David, too, watched the set. "We cleared it with Clarissa."

A.J. set her teeth. "Next time, Brady, clear it with me."

David decided that whatever nasty retort he could make would wait when Alex's broadcaster's voice rose rich and clear in the studio. "Miss DeBasse, using cards to test ESP is a rather standard device, isn't it?"

"A rather limited test, yes. They're also an aid in testing telepathy."

"You've been involved in testing of this sort before, at Stanford, UCLA, Columbia, Duke, as well as institutions in England."

"Yes, I have."

"Would you mind explaining the process?"

"Of course. The cards used in laboratory tests are generally two colors, with perhaps five different shapes. Squares, circles, wavy lines, that sort of thing. Using these, it's possible to determine chance and what goes beyond chance. That is, with two colors, it's naturally a fifty-fifty proposition. If a subject hits the colors fifty percent of the time, it's accepted as chance. If a subject hits sixty percent, then it's ten percent over chance."

"It sounds relatively simple."

"With colors alone, yes. The shapes alter that. With, say, twenty-five cards in a run, the tester is able to determine by the number of hits, or correct answers, how much over chance the subject guessed. If the subject hits fifteen times out of twenty-five, it can be assumed the subject's ESP abilities are highly tuned."

"She's very good," David murmured.

"Damned right she is." A.J. folded her arms and tried

not to be annoyed. This was Clarissa's business, and no one knew it better.

"Could you explain how it works—for you, that is?" Alex idly shuffled the pack of cards as he spoke to her. "Do you get a feeling when a card is held up?"

"A picture," Clarissa corrected. "One gets a picture."

"Are you saying you get an actual picture of the card?"

"An actual picture can be held in your hand." She smiled at him patiently. "I'm sure you read a great deal, Mr. Marshall."

"Yes, I do."

"When you read, the words, the phrasings make pictures in your head. This is very similar to that."

"I see." His doubt was obvious, and to David, the perfect reaction. "That's imagination."

"ESP requires a control of the imagination and a sharpening of concentration."

"Can anyone do this?"

"That's something that's still being researched. There are some who feel ESP can be learned. Others believe psychics are born. My own opinion falls in between."

"Can you explain?"

"I think every one of us has certain talents or abilities, and the degree to which they're developed and used depends on the individual. It's possible to block these abilities. It's more usual, I think, to simply ignore them so that they never come into question."

"Your abilities have been documented. We'd like to give an impromptu demonstration here, with your co-operation."

"Of course."

"This is an ordinary deck of playing cards. One of the crew purchased them this morning, and you haven't handled them. Is that right?"

"No, I haven't. I'm not very clever with games." She smiled, half apologetic, half amused, and delighted the director.

"Now if I pick a card and hold it like this." Alex pulled one from the middle of the deck and held its back to her. "Can you tell me what it is?"

"No." Her smile never faded as the director started to signal to stop the tape. "You'll have to look at the card, Mr. Marshall, think of it, actually try to picture it in your mind." As the tape continued to roll, Alex nodded and obliged her. "I'm afraid you're not concentrating very hard, but it's a red card. That's better." She beamed at him. "Nine of diamonds."

The camera caught the surprise on his face before he turned the card over. Nine of diamonds. He pulled a second card and repeated the process. When they reached the third, Clarissa stopped, frowning.

"You're trying to confuse me by thinking of a card other than the one in your hand. It blurs things a bit, but the ten of clubs comes through stronger."

"Fascinating," Alex murmured as he turned over the ten of clubs. "Really fascinating."

"I'm afraid this sort of thing is often no more than a parlor game," Clarissa corrected. "A clever mentalist can do nearly the same thing—in a different way, of course."

"You're saying it's a trick."

"I'm saying it can be. I'm not good at tricks myself, so I don't try them, but I can appreciate a good show."

"You started your career by reading palms." Alex set down the cards, not entirely sure of himself.

"A long time ago. Technically anyone can read a palm, interpret the lines." She held hers out to him.

"Lines that represent finance, emotion, length of life. A good book out of the library will tell you exactly what to look for and how to find it. A sensitive doesn't actually read a palm so much as absorb feelings."

Charmed, but far from sold, Alex held out his. "I don't quite see how you could absorb feelings by looking at the palm of my hand."

"You transmit them," she told him. "Just as you transmit everything else, your hopes, your sorrows, your joys. I can take your palm and at a glance tell you that you communicate well and have a solid financial base, but that would hardly be earth-shattering news. But..." She held her own out to him. "If you don't mind," she began, and cupped his hand in hers. "I can look again and say that—" She stopped, blinked and stared at him. "Oh."

A.J. made a move forward, only to be blocked by David. "Let her be," he muttered. "This is a documentary, remember. We can't have it staged and tidy. If she's uncomfortable with this part of the tape we can cut it."

"If she's uncomfortable you will cut it."

Clarissa's hand was smooth and firm under Alex's, but her eyes were wide and stunned. "Should I be nervous?" he asked, only half joking.

"Oh, no." With a little laugh, she cleared her throat. "No, not at all. You have very strong vibrations, Mr. Marshall."

"Thank you. I think."

"You're a widower, fifteen, sixteen years now. You were a very good husband." She smiled at him, relaxed again. "You can be proud of that. And a good father."

"I appreciate that, Miss DeBasse, but again, it's hardly news."

She continued as if he hadn't spoken. "Both your children are settled now, which eases your mind, as it does any parent's. They never gave you a great deal of worry, though there was a period with your son, during his early twenties, when you had some rough spots. But some people take longer to find their niche, don't they?"

He wasn't smiling anymore, but staring at her as intensely as she stared at him. "I suppose."

"You're a perfectionist, in your work and in your private life. That made it a little difficult for your son. He couldn't quite live up to your expectations. You shouldn't have worried so much, but of course all parents do. Now that he's going to be a father himself, you're closer. The idea of grandchildren pleases you. At the same time it makes you think more about the future—your own mortality. But I wonder if you're wise to be thinking of retiring. You're in the prime of your life and too used to deadlines and rushing to be content with that fishing boat for very long. Now if you'd—" She stopped herself with a little shake of the head. "I'm sorry. I tend to ramble on when someone interests me. I'm always afraid of getting too personal."

"Not at all." He closed his hand into a loose fist. "Miss DeBasse, you're quite amazing."

"Cut!" Cauldwell could have gotten down on his knees and kissed Clarissa's feet. Alex Marshall considering retirement. There hadn't been so much as a murmur of it on the grapevine. "I want to see the playback in thirty minutes. Alex, thank you. It's a great start. Miss DeBasse—" He'd have taken her hand again if he hadn't been a little leery of giving off the wrong vibrations. "You were sensational. I can't wait to start the next segment with you."

Before he'd finished thanking her, A.J. was at her

side. She knew what would happen, what invariably happened. One of the crew would come up and tell Clarissa about a "funny thing that happened to him." Then there would be another asking for his palm to be read. Some would be smirking, others would be curious, but inside of ten minutes Clarissa would be surrounded.

"If you're ready, I'll drive you home," A.J. began.

"Now I thought we'd settled that." Clarissa looked idly around for her purse without any idea where she'd set it. "It's too far for you to drive all the way to Newport Beach and back again."

"Just part of the service." A.J. handed her the purse she'd been holding throughout the shoot.

"Oh, thank you, dear. I couldn't imagine what I'd done with it. I'll take a cab."

"We have a driver for you." David didn't have to look at A.J. to know she was steaming. He could all but feel the heat. "We wouldn't dream of having you take a cab all the way back."

"That's very kind."

"But it won't be necessary," A.J. put in.

"No, it won't." Smoothly Alex edged in and took Clarissa's hand. "I'm hoping Miss DeBasse will allow me to drive her home—after she has dinner with me."

"That would be lovely," Clarissa told him before A.J. could say a word. "I hope I didn't embarrass you, Mr. Marshall."

"Not at all. In fact, I was fascinated."

"How nice. Thank you for staying with me, dear." She kissed A.J.'s cheek. "It always puts me at ease. Good night, David."

"Good night, Clarissa. Alex." He stood beside A.J. as they linked arms and strolled out of the studio. "A nice-looking couple."

Before the words were out of his mouth, A.J. turned on him. If it had been possible to grow fangs, she'd have grown them. "You jerk." She was halfway to the studio doors before he stopped her.

"And what's eating you?"

If he hadn't said it with a smile on his face, she might have controlled herself. "I want to see that last fifteen minutes of tape, Brady, and if I don't like what I see, it's out."

"I don't recall anything in the contract about you having editing rights, A.J."

"There's nothing in the contract saying that Clarissa would read palms, either."

"Granted. Alex ad-libbed that, and it worked very well. What's the problem?"

"You were watching, damn it." Needing to turn her temper on something, she rammed through the studio doors.

"I was," David agreed as he took her arm to slow her down. "But obviously I didn't see what you did."

"She was covering." A.J. raked a hand through her hair. "She felt something as soon as she took his hand. When you look at the tape you'll see five, ten seconds where she just stares."

"So it adds to the mystique. It's effective."

"Damn your 'effective'!" She swung around so quickly she nearly knocked him into a wall. "I don't like to see her hit that way. I happen to care about her as a person, not just a commodity."

"All right, hold it. Hold it!" He caught up to her again as she shoved through the outside door. "There didn't seem to be a thing wrong with Clarissa when she left here."

"I don't like it." A.J. stormed down the steps toward

the parking lot. "First the lousy cards. I'm sick of see-ing her tested that way."

"A.J., the cards are a natural. She's done that same test, in much greater intensity, for institutes all over the country."

"I know. And it makes me furious that she has to prove herself over and over. Then that palm business. Something upset her." She began to pace on the patch of lawn bordering the sidewalk. "There was something there and I didn't even have the chance to talk to her about it before that six-foot reporter with the golden voice muscled in."

"Alex?" Though he tried, for at least five seconds, to control himself, David roared with laughter. "God, you're priceless."

Her eyes narrowed, her face paled with rage, she stopped pacing. "So you think it's funny, do you? A trusting, amazingly innocent woman goes off with a virtual stranger and you laugh. If anything happens to her—"

"Happens?" David rolled his eyes skyward. "Good God, A.J., Alex Marshall is hardly a maniac. He's a highly respected member of the news media. And Clarissa is certainly old enough to make up her own mind—and make her own dates."

"It's not a date."

"Looked that way to me."

She opened her mouth, shut it again, then whirled around toward the parking lot.

"Now wait a minute. I said wait." He took her by both arms and trapped her between himself and a parked car. "I'll be damned if I'm going to chase you all over L.A."

"Just go back inside and take a look at that take. I want to see it tomorrow."

"I don't take orders from paranoid agents or anyone else. We're going to settle this right here. I don't know what's working on you, A.J., but I can't believe you're this upset because a client's going out to dinner."

"She's not just a client," A.J. hurled back at him. "She's my mother."

Her furious announcement left them both momentarily speechless. He continued to hold her by the shoulders while she fought to even her breathing. Of course he should have seen it, David realized. The shape of the face, the eyes. Especially the eyes. "I'll be damned."

"I can only second that," she murmured, then let herself lean back against the car. "Look, that's not for publication. Understand?"

"Why?"

"Because we both prefer it that way. Our relationship is private."

"All right." He rarely argued with privacy. "Okay, that explains why you take such a personal interest, but I think you carry it a bit too far."

"I don't care what you think." Because her head was beginning to pound, she straightened. "Excuse me."

"No." Calmly David blocked her way. "Some people might say you interfere with your mother's life because you don't have enough to fill your own."

Her eyes became very dark, her skin very pale. "My life is none of your business, Brady."

"Not at the moment, but while this project's going on, Clarissa's is. Give her some room, A.J."

Because it sounded so reasonable, her hackles rose. "You don't understand."

"No, maybe you should explain it to me."

"What if Alex Marshall presses her for an interview

over dinner? What if he wants to get her alone so he can hammer at her?"

"What if he simply wanted to have dinner with an interesting, attractive woman? You might give Clarissa more credit."

She folded her arms. "I won't have her hurt."

He could argue with her. He could even try reason. Somehow he didn't think either would work quite yet. "Let's go for a drive."

"What?"

"A drive. You and me." He smiled at her. "It happens to be my car you're leaning on."

"Oh, sorry." She straightened again. "I have to get back to the office. There's some paperwork I let hang today."

"Then it can hang until tomorrow." Drawing out his keys, he unlocked the door. "I could use a ride along the beach."

So could she. She'd overreacted—there was no question of it. She needed some air, some speed, something to clear her head. Maybe it wasn't wise to take it with him, but... "Are you going to put the top down?"

"Absolutely."

It helped—the drive, the air, the smell of the sea, the blare of the radio. He didn't chat at her or try to ease her into conversation. A.J. did something she allowed herself to do rarely in the company of others. She relaxed.

How long had it been, she wondered, since she'd driven along the coast, no time frame, no destination? If she couldn't remember, then it had been too long. A.J. closed her eyes, emptied her mind and enjoyed.

Just who was she? David asked himself as he watched her relax, degree by degree, beside him. Was she the tough, no-nonsense agent with an eye out for ten percent of a smooth deal? Was she the fiercely protective, obviously devoted daughter—who was raking in that same ten percent of her mother's talent on one hand and raising the roof about exploitation the next? He couldn't figure her.

He was a good judge of people. In his business he'd be producing home movies if he weren't. Yet when he'd kissed her he hadn't found the hard-edged, self-confident woman he'd expected, but a nervous, vulnerable one. For some reason, she didn't entirely fit who she was, or what she'd chosen to be. It might be interesting to find out why.

"Hungry?"

Half dreaming, A.J. opened her eyes and looked at him. How was it he hadn't seen it before? David asked himself. The eyes, the eyes were so like Clarissa's, the shape, the color, the…depth, he decided for lack of a better word. It ran through his head that maybe she was like Clarissa in other ways. Then he dismissed it.

"I'm sorry," she murmured, "I wasn't paying attention." But she could have described his face in minute detail, from the hard cheekbones to the slight indentation in his chin. Letting out a long breath, she drew herself in. A wise woman controlled her thoughts as meticulously as her emotions.

"I asked if you were hungry."

"Yes." She stretched her shoulders. "How far have we gone?"

Not far enough. The thought ran unbidden through his mind. Not nearly far enough. "About twenty miles. Your choice." He eased over to the shoulder of the road and indicated a restaurant on one side and a hamburger stand on the other.

"I'll take the burger. If we can sit on the beach."

"Nothing I like better than a cheap date."

A.J. let herself out. "This isn't a date."

"I forgot. You can pay for your own." He'd never heard her laugh like that before. Easy, feminine, fresh. "Just for that I'll spring." But he didn't touch her as they walked up to the stand. "What'll it be?"

"The jumbo burger, large fries and the super shake. Chocolate."

"Big talk."

As they waited, they watched a few early-evening swimmers splash in the shallows. Gulls swooped around, chattering and loitering near the stand, waiting for handouts. David left them disappointed as he gathered up the paper bags. "Where to?"

"Down there. I like to watch." A.J. walked out on the beach and, ignoring her linen skirt, dropped down on the sand. "I don't get to the beach often enough." Kicking off her shoes, she slid stockinged feet in the sand so that her skirt hiked up to her thighs. David took a good long look before he settled beside her.

"Neither do I," he decided, wondering just how those legs—and the rest of her—might look in a bikini.

"I guess I made quite a scene."

"I guess you did." He pulled out her hamburger and handed it to her.

"I hate to," she said, and took a fierce bite. "I don't have a reputation as an abrasive or argumentative agent, just a tough one. I only lose objectivity with Clarissa."

He screwed the paper cups into the sand. "Objectivity is shot to hell when we love somebody."

"She's so good. I don't just mean at what she does, but inside." A.J. took the fries he offered and nibbled one. "Good people can get hurt so much easier than others, you know. And she's so willing to give of herself.

If she gave everything she wanted, she'd have nothing left."

"So you're there to protect her."

"That's right." She turned, challenging.

"I'm not arguing with you." He held up a hand. "For some reason I'd like to understand."

With a little laugh she looked back out to sea. "You had to be there."

"Why don't you tell me what it was like? Growing up."

She never discussed it with anyone. Then again, she never sat on a beach eating hamburgers with associates. Maybe it was a day for firsts. "She was a wonderful mother. Is. Clarissa's so loving, so generous."

"Your father?"

"He died when I was eight. He was a salesman, so he was away a lot. He was a good salesman," she added with the ghost of a smile. "We were lucky there. There were savings and a little bit of stock. Problem was the bills didn't get paid. Not that the money wasn't there. Clarissa just forgot. You'd pick up the phone and it would be dead because she'd misplaced the bill. I guess I just started taking care of her."

"You'd have been awfully young for that."

"I didn't mind." This time the smile bloomed fully. There were, as with her mother, the faintest of dimples in her cheeks. "I was so much better at managing than she. We had a little more coming in once she started reading palms and doing charts. She really just sort of blossomed then. She has a need to help people, to give them—I don't know—reassurance. Hope. Still, it was an odd time. We lived in a nice neighborhood and people would come and go through our living room. The neighbors were fascinated, and some of them came in regularly for readings, but outside the house there was a kind of distance. It was as if they weren't quite sure of Clarissa."

"It would have been uncomfortable for you."

"Now and then. She was doing what she had to do. Some people shied away from us, from the house, but she never seemed to notice. Anyway, the word spread and she became friends with the Van Camps. I guess I was around twelve or thirteen. The first time movie stars showed up at the house I was awestruck. Within a year it became a matter of course. I've known actors to call her before they'd accept a role. She'd always tell them the same thing. They had to rely on their own feelings. The one thing Clarissa will never do is make decisions for anyone else. But they still called. Then the little Van Camp boy was kidnapped. After that the press camped on the lawn, the phone never stopped. I ended up moving her out to Newport Beach. She can keep a low profile there, even when another case comes up."

"There was the Ridehour murders."

She stood up abruptly and walked closer to the sea. Rising, David walked with her. "You've no idea how she suffered through that." Emotions trembled in her voice as she wrapped her arms around herself. "You can't imagine what a toll something like that can take on a person like Clarissa. I wanted to stop her, but I knew I couldn't."

When she closed her eyes, David put a hand on her shoulder. "Why would you want to stop her if she could help?"

"She grieved. She hurt. God, she all but lived it, even before she was called in." She opened her eyes and turned to him then. "Do you understand, even before she was called in, she was involved?"

"I'm not sure I do."

"No, you can't." She gave an impatient shake of her head for expecting it. "I suppose you have to live it. In any case, they asked for help. It doesn't take any more than that with Clarissa. Five young girls dead." She closed her eyes again. "She never speaks of it, but I know she saw each one. I know." Then she pushed the thought aside, as she knew she had to. "Clarissa thinks of her abilities as a gift…but you've no idea what a curse that can be."

"You'd like her to stop. Shut down. Is that possible?"

A.J. laughed again and drew both hands through hair the wind had tossed. "Oh, yes, but not for Clarissa. I've accepted that she needs to give. I just make damn sure the wrong person doesn't take."

"And what about you?" He would have sworn something in her froze at the casual question. "Did you become an agent to protect your mother?"

She relaxed again. "Partly. But I enjoy what I do." Her eyes were clear again. "I'm good at it."

"And what about Aurora?" He brought his hands up her arms to her shoulders.

A yearning rose up in her, just from the touch. She blocked it off. "Aurora's only there for Clarissa."

"Why?"

"Because I know how to protect myself as well as my mother."

"From what?"

"It's getting late, David."

"Yeah." One hand skimmed over to her throat. Her skin was soft there, sun kissed and soft. "I'm beginning to think the same thing. I never did finish kissing you, Aurora."

His hands were strong. She'd noticed it before, but it seemed to matter more now. "It's better that way."

"I'm beginning to think that, too. Damn if I can figure out why I want to so much."

"Give it a little time. It'll pass."

"Why don't we test it out?" He lifted a brow as he looked down at her. "We're on a public beach. The sun hasn't set. If I kiss you here, it can't go any further than that, and maybe we'll figure out why we unnerve each other." When he drew her closer, she stiffened. "Afraid?" Why would the fact that she might be, just a little, arouse him?

"No." Because she'd prepared herself she almost believed it was true. He wouldn't have the upper hand this time, she told herself. She wouldn't allow it. Deliberately she lifted her arms and twined them around his neck. When he hesitated, she pressed her lips to his.

He'd have sworn the sand shifted under his feet. He was certain the crash of the waves grew in volume until it filled the air like thunder. He'd intended to control the situation like an experiment. But intentions changed as mouth met mouth. She tasted warm—cool, sweet— pungent. He had a desperate need to find out which of his senses could be trusted. Before either of them was prepared, he plunged himself into the kiss and dragged her with him.

Too fast. Her mind whirled with the thought. Too far. But her body ignored the warning and strained against him. She wanted, and the want was clearer and sharper than any want had ever been. She needed, and the need was deeper and more intense than any other need. As the feelings drummed into her, her fingers curled into his hair. Hunger for him rose so quickly she moaned with it. It wasn't right. It couldn't be right. Yet the feeling swirled through her that it was exactly right and had always been.

A gull swooped overhead and was gone, leaving only the flicker of a shadow, the echo of a sound.

When they drew apart, A.J. stepped back. With distance came a chill, but she welcomed it after the enervating heat. She would have turned then without a word, but his hands were on her again.

"Come home with me."

She had to look at him then. Passion, barely controlled, darkened his eyes. Desire, edged with temptation, roughened his voice. And she felt…too much. If she went, she would give too much.

"No." Her voice wasn't quite steady, but it was final. "I don't want this, David."

"Neither do I." He backed off then. He hadn't meant for things to go so far. He hadn't wanted to feel so much. "I'm not sure that's going to make any difference."

"We have control over our own lives." When she looked out to sea again, the wind rushed her hair back, leaving her face unframed. "I know what I want and don't want in mine."

"Wants change." Why was he arguing? She said nothing he hadn't thought himself.

"Only if we let them."

"And if I said I wanted you?"

The pulse in her throat beat quickly, so quickly she wasn't sure she could get the words around it. "I'd say you were making a mistake. You were right, David, when you said I wasn't your type. Go with your first impulse. It's usually the best."

"In this case I think I need more data."

"Suit yourself," she said as though it made no difference. "I have to get back. I want to call Clarissa and make sure she's all right."

He took her arm one last time. "You won't always be able to use her, Aurora."

She stopped and sent him the cool, intimate look so like her mother's. "I don't use her at all," she murmured. "That's the difference between us." She turned and made her way back across the sand.

Chapter 4

There was moonlight, shafts of it, glimmering. There was the scent of hyacinths—the faintest fragrance on the faintest of breezes. From somewhere came the sound of water, running, bubbling. On a wide-planked wood floor there were shadows, the shifting grace of an oak outside the window. A painting on the wall caught the eye and held it. It was no more than slashes of red and violet lines on a white, white canvas, but somehow it portrayed energy, movement, tensions with undercurrents of sex. There was a mirror, taller than most. A.J. saw herself reflected in it.

She looked indistinct, ethereal, lost. With shadows all around it seemed to her she could just step forward into the glass and be gone. The chill that went through her came not from without but from within. There was something to fear here, something as nebulous as her own reflection. Instinct told her to go, and to go quickly, before she learned what it was. But as she turned something blocked her way.

David stood between her and escape, his hands firm on her shoulders. When she looked at him she saw that his eyes were dark and impatient. Desire—his or hers—thickened the air until even breathing was an effort.

I don't want this. Did she say it? Did she simply think it? Though she couldn't be sure, she heard his response clearly enough, clipped and annoyed.

"You can't keep running, Aurora. Not from me, not from yourself."

Then she was sliding down into a dark, dark tunnel with soft edges just beginning to flame.

A.J. jerked up in bed, breathless and trembling. She didn't see moonlight, but the first early shafts of sun coming through her own bedroom windows. Her bedroom, she repeated to herself as she pushed sleep-tousled hair from her eyes. There were no hyacinths here, no shadows, no disturbing painting.

A dream, she repeated over and over. It had just been a dream. But why did it have to be so real? She could almost feel the slight pressure on her shoulders where his hands had pressed. The turbulent, churning sensation through her system hadn't faded. And why had she dreamed of David Brady?

There were several logical reasons she could comfort herself with. He'd been on her mind for the past couple of weeks. Clarissa and the documentary had been on her mind and they were all tangled together. She'd been working hard, maybe too hard, and the last true relaxation she'd had had been those few minutes with him on the beach.

Still, it was best not to think of that, of what had happened or nearly happened, of what had been said or left unsaid. It would be better, much better, to think of schedules, of work and of obligations.

There'd be no sleeping now. Though it was barely six, A.J. pushed the covers aside and rose. A couple of strong cups of black coffee and a cool shower would put her back in order. They had to. Her schedule was much too busy to allow her to waste time worrying over a dream.

Her kitchen was spacious and very organized. She allowed no clutter, even in a room she spent little time in. Counters and appliances gleamed in stark white, as much from the diligence of her housekeeper as from disuse. A.J. went down the two steps that separated the kitchen from the living area and headed for the appliance she knew best. The coffeemaker.

Turning off the automatic alarm, which would have begun the brewing at 7:05, A.J. switched it to Start. When she came out of the shower fifteen minutes later, the scent of coffee—of normalcy—was back. She drank the first cup black, for the caffeine rather than the taste. Though she was an hour ahead of schedule, A.J. stuck to routine. Nothing as foolish and insubstantial as a dream was going to throw her off. She downed a handful of vitamins, preferring them to hassling with breakfast, then took a second cup of coffee into the bedroom with her to dress. As she studied the contents of her closet, she reviewed her appointments for the day.

Brunch with a very successful, very nervous client who was being wooed for a prime-time series. It wouldn't hurt to look over the script for the pilot once more before they discussed it. A prelunch staff meeting in her own conference room was next. Then there was a late business lunch with Bob Hopewell, who'd begun casting his new feature. She had two clients she felt were tailor-made for the leads. After mentally reviewing her appointments, A.J. decided what she needed was a touch of elegance.

She went with a raw silk suit in pale peach. Sticking to routine, she was dressed and standing in front of the full-length mirrors of her closet in twenty minutes. As an afterthought, she picked up the little half-moon she sometimes wore on her lapel. As she was fastening it, the dream came back to her. She hadn't looked so confident, so—was it aloof?—in the dream. She'd been softer, hadn't she? More vulnerable.

A.J. lifted a hand to touch it to the glass. It was cool and smooth, a reflection only. Just as it had only been a dream, she reminded herself with a shake of the head. In reality she couldn't afford to be soft. Vulnerability was out of the question. An agent in this town would be eaten alive in five minutes if she allowed a soft spot to show. And a woman—a woman took terrifying chances if she let a man see that which was vulnerable. A. J. Fields wasn't taking any chances.

Tugging down the hem of her jacket, she took a last survey before grabbing her briefcase. In less than twenty minutes, she was unlocking the door to her suite of offices.

It wasn't an unusual occurrence for A.J. to open the offices herself. Ever since she'd rented her first one-room walk-up early in her career, she'd developed the habit of arriving ahead of her staff. In those days her staff had consisted of a part-time receptionist who'd dreamed of a modeling career. Now she had two receptionists, a secretary and an assistant, as well as a stable of agents. A.J. turned the switch so that light gleamed on brass pots and rose-colored walls. She'd never regretted calling in a decorator. There was class here, discreet, understated class with subtle hints of power.

Left to herself, she knew she'd have settled for a couple of sturdy desks and gooseneck lamps.

A glance at her watch showed her she could get in several calls to the East Coast. She left the one light burning in the reception area and closeted herself in her own office. Within a half-hour she'd verbally agreed to have her nervous brunch appointment fly east to do a pilot for a weekly series, set out prenegotiation feelers for a contract renewal for another client who worked on a daytime drama and lit a fire under a producer by refusing his offer on a projected mini-series.

A good morning's work, A.J. decided, reflecting back on the producer's assessment that she was a near-sighted, money-grubbing python. He would counteroffer. She leaned back in her chair and let her shoes drop to the floor. When he did, her client would get over-the-title billing and a cool quarter million. He'd work for it, A.J. thought with a long stretch. She'd read the script and understood that the part would be physically demanding and emotionally draining. She understood just how much blood and sweat a good actor put into a role. As far as she was concerned, they deserved every penny they could get, and it was up to her to squeeze it from the producer's tightfisted hand.

Satisfied, she decided to delve into paperwork before her own phone started to ring. Then she heard the footsteps.

At first she simply glanced at her watch, wondering who was in early. Then it occurred to her that though her staff was certainly dedicated enough, she couldn't think of anyone who'd come to work thirty minutes before they were due. A.J. rose, fully intending to see for herself, when the footsteps stopped. She should just call out, she thought, then found herself remembering every suspense movie she'd ever seen. The trusting heroine called out, then found herself trapped in a room with a maniac. Swallowing, she picked up a heavy metal paperweight.

The footsteps started again, coming closer. Still closer. Struggling to keep her breathing even and quiet, A.J. walked across the carpet and stood beside the door. The footsteps halted directly on the other side. With the paperweight held high, she put her hand on the knob, held her breath, then yanked it open. David managed to grab her wrist before she knocked him out cold.

"Always greet clients this way, A.J.?"

"Damn it!" She let the paperweight slip to the floor as relief flooded through her. "You scared me to death, Brady. What are you doing sneaking around here at this hour?"

"The same thing you're doing sneaking around here at this hour. I got up early."

Because her knees were shaking, she gave in to the urge to sit, heavily. "The difference is this is *my* office. I can sneak around anytime I like. What do you want?"

"I could claim I couldn't stay away from your sparkling personality."

"Cut it."

"The truth is I have to fly to New York for a location shoot. I'll be tied up for a couple of days and wanted you to pass a message on to Clarissa for me." It wasn't the truth at all, but he didn't mind lying. It was easier to swallow than the fact that he'd needed to see her again. He'd woken up that morning knowing he had to see her before he left. Admit that to a woman like A. J. Fields and she'd either run like hell or toss you out.

"Fine." She was already up and reaching for a pad. "I'll be glad to pass on a message. But next time try to remember some people shoot other people who wander into places before hours."

"The door was unlocked," he pointed out. "There was no one at reception, so I decided to see if anyone was around before I just left a note."

It sounded reasonable. Was reasonable. But it didn't suit A.J. to be scared out of her wits before 9:00 a.m. "What's the message, Brady?"

He didn't have the vaguest idea. Tucking his hands in his pockets, he glanced around her meticulously ordered, pastel-toned office. "Nice place," he commented. He noticed even the papers she'd obviously been working with on her desk were in neat piles. There wasn't so much as a paper clip out of place. "You're a tidy creature, aren't you?"

"Yes." She tapped the pencil impatiently on the pad. "The message for Clarissa?"

"How is she, by the way?"

"She's fine."

He took a moment to stroll over to study the single painting she had on the wall. A seascape, very tranquil and soothing. "I remember you were concerned about her—about her having dinner with Alex."

"She had a lovely time," A.J. mumbled. "She told me Alex Marshall was a complete gentleman with a fascinating mind."

"Does that bother you?"

"Clarissa doesn't see men. Not that way." Feeling foolish, she dropped the pad on her desk and walked to her window.

"Is something wrong with her seeing men? That way?"

"No, no, of course not. It's just…"

"Just what, Aurora?"

She shouldn't be discussing her mother, but so few people knew of their relationship, A.J. opened up before she could stop herself. "She gets sort of breathy and vague whenever she mentions him. They spent the day together on Sunday. On his boat. I don't remember Clarissa ever stepping foot on a boat."

"So she's trying something new."

"That's what I'm afraid of," she said under her breath. "Have you any idea what it's like to see your mother in the first stages of infatuation?"

"No." He thought of his own mother's comfortable relationship with his father. She cooked dinner and sewed his buttons. He took out the trash and fixed the toaster. "I can't say I have."

"Well, it's not the most comfortable feeling, I can tell you. What do I know about this man, anyway? Oh, he's smooth," she muttered. "For all I know he's been smooth with half the women in Southern California."

"Do you hear yourself?" Half-amused, David joined her at the window. "You sound like a mother fussing over her teenage daughter. If Clarissa were an ordinary middle-aged woman there'd be little enough to worry about. Don't you think the fact that she is what she is gives her an advantage? It seems she'd be an excellent judge of character."

"You don't understand. Emotions can block things, especially when it's important."

"If that's true, maybe you should look to your own emotions." He felt her freeze. He didn't have to touch her; he didn't have to move any closer. He simply felt it. "You're letting your affection and concern for your mother cause you to overreact to a very simple thing. Maybe you should give some thought to targeting some of that emotion elsewhere."

"Clarissa's all I can afford to be emotional about."

"An odd way of phrasing things. Do you ever give any thought to your own needs? Emotional," he murmured, then ran a hand down her hair. "Physical."

"That's none of your business." She would have turned away, but he kept his hand on her hair.

"You can cut a lot of people off." He felt the first edge of her anger as she stared up at him. Oddly he enjoyed it. "I think you'd be extremely good at picking up the spear and jabbing men out of your way. But it won't work with me."

"I don't know why I thought I could talk to you."

"But you did. That should give you something to consider."

"Why are you pushing me?" she demanded. Fire came into her eyes. She remembered the dream too clearly. The dream, the desire, the fears.

"Because I want you." He stood close, close enough for her scent to twine around him. Close enough so that the doubts and distrust in her eyes were very clear. "I want to make love with you for a long, long time in a very quiet place. When we're finished I might find out why I don't seem to be able to sleep for dreaming of it."

Her throat was dry enough to ache and her hands felt like ice. "I told you once I don't sleep around."

"That's good," he murmured. "That's very good, because I don't think either of us needs a lot of comparisons." He heard the sound of the front door of the offices opening. "Sounds like you're open for business, A.J. Just one more personal note. I'm willing to negotiate terms, times and places, but the bottom line is that I'm going to spend more than one night with you. Give it some thought."

A.J. conquered the urge to pick up the paperweight

and heave it at him as he walked to the door. Instead she reminded herself that she was a professional and it was business hours. "Brady."

He turned, and with a hand on the knob smiled at her. "Yeah, Fields?"

"You never gave me the message for Clarissa."

"Didn't I?" The hell with the gingerbread, he decided. "Give her my best. See you around, lady."

David didn't even know what time it was when he unlocked the door of his hotel suite. The two-day shoot had stretched into three. Now all he had to do was figure out which threads to cut and remain in budget. Per instructions, the maid hadn't touched the stacks and piles of paper on the table in the parlor. They were as he'd left them, a chaotic jumble of balance sheets, schedules and production notes.

After a twelve-hour day, he'd ordered his crew to hit the sheets. David buzzed room service and ordered a pot of coffee before he sat down and began to work. After two hours, he was satisfied enough with the figures to go back over the two and a half days of taping.

The Danjason Institute of Parapsychology itself had been impressive, and oddly stuffy, in the way of institutes. It was difficult to imagine that an organization devoted to the study of bending spoons by will and telepathy could be stuffy. The team of parapsychologists they'd worked with had been as dry and precise as any staff of scientists. So dry, in fact, David wondered whether they'd convince the audience or simply put them to sleep. He'd have to supervise the editing carefully.

The testing had been interesting enough, he decided. The fact that they used not only sensitives but people more or less off the street. The testing and conclusions were done in the strictest scientific manner. How had it been put? The application of math probability theory to massive accumulation of data. It sounded formal and supercilious. To David it was card guessing.

Still, put sophisticated equipment and intelligent, highly educated scientists together, and it was understood that psychic phenomena were being researched seriously and intensely. It was, as a science, just beginning to be recognized after decades of slow, exhaustive experimentation.

Then there had been the interview on Wall Street with the thirty-two-year-old stockbroker-psychic. David let out a stream of smoke and watched it float toward the ceiling as he let that particular segment play in his mind. The man had made no secret of the fact that he used his abilities to play the market and become many times a millionaire. It was a skill, he'd explained, much like reading, writing and calculating were skills. He'd also claimed that several top executives in some of the most powerful companies in the world had used psychic powers to get there and to stay there. He'd described ESP as a tool, as important in the business world as a computer system or a slide rule.

A science, a business and a performance.

It made David think of Clarissa. She hadn't tossed around confusing technology or littered her speech with mathematical probabilities. She hadn't discussed market trends or the Dow Jones Average. She'd simply talked, person to person. Whatever powers she had...

With a shake of his head, David cut himself off. Listen to this, he thought as he ran his hands over his face. He was beginning to buy the whole business himself, though he knew from his own research that for every lab-contained experiment there were dozens of card-wielding, bell-ringing charlatans bilking a gullible audience. He drew smoke down an already raw throat before he crushed out the cigarette. If he didn't continue to look at the documentary objectively, he'd have a biased mess on his hands.

But even looking objectively, he could see Clarissa as the center of the work. She could be the hinge on which everything else hung. With his eyes half-closed, David could picture it—the interview with the somber-eyed, white-coated parapsychologists, with their no-nonsense laboratory conditions. Then a cut to Clarissa talking with Alex, covering more or less the same ground in her simpler style. Then there'd be the clip of the stockbroker in his sky-high Wall Street office, then back to Clarissa again, seated on the homey sofa. He'd have the tuxedoed mentalist they'd lined up in Vegas doing his flashy, fast-paced demonstration. Then Clarissa again, calmly identifying cards without looking at them. Contrasts, angles, information, but everything would lead back to Clarissa DeBasse. She was the hook—instinct, intuition or paranormal powers, she was the hook. He could all but see the finished product unfolding.

Still, he wanted the big pull, something with punch and drama. This brought him right back to Clarissa. He needed that interview with Alice Van Camp, and another with someone who'd been directly involved in the Ridehour case. A.J. might try to block his way. He'd just have to roll over her.

How many times had he thought of her in the past three days? Too many. How often did he catch his mind drifting back to those few moments on the beach? Too often. And how much did he want to hold her like that again, close and hard? Too much.

Aurora. He knew it was dangerous to think of her as Aurora. Aurora was soft and accessible. Aurora was passionate and giving and just a little unsure of herself. He'd be smarter to remember A. J. Fields, tough, uncompromising and prickly around the edges. But it was late and his rooms were quiet. It was Aurora he thought of. It was Aurora he wanted.

On impulse, David picked up the phone. He punched buttons quickly, without giving himself a chance to think the action through. The phone rang four times before she answered.

"Fields."

"Good morning."

"David?" A.J. reached up to grab the towel before it slipped from her dripping hair.

"Yeah. How are you?"

"Wet." She switched the phone from hand to hand as she struggled into a robe. "I just stepped out of the shower. Is there a problem?"

The problem was, he mused, that he was three thousand miles away and was wondering what her skin would look like gleaming with water. He reached for another cigarette and found the pack empty. "No, should there be?"

"I don't usually get calls at this hour unless there is. When did you get back?"

"I didn't."

"You didn't? You mean you're still in New York?"

He stretched back in his chair and closed his eyes. Funny, he hadn't realized just how much he'd wanted to hear her voice. "Last time I looked."

"It's only ten your time. What are you doing up so early?"

"Haven't been to bed yet."

This time she wasn't quick enough to snatch the towel before it landed on her bare feet. A.J. ignored it as she dragged her fingers through the tangle of wet hair. "I see. The night life in Manhattan's very demanding, isn't it?"

He opened his eyes to glance at his piles of papers, overflowing ashtrays and empty coffee cups. "Yeah, it's all dancing till dawn."

"I'm sure." Scowling, she bent down to pick up her towel. "Well, you must have something important on your mind to break off the partying and call. What is it?"

"I wanted to talk to you."

"So I gathered." She began, more roughly than necessary, to rub the towel over her hair. "About what?"

"Nothing."

"Brady, have you been drinking?"

He gave a quick laugh as he settled back again. He couldn't even remember the last time he'd eaten. "No. Don't you believe in friendly conversations, A.J.?"

"Sure, but not between agents and producers long-distance at dawn."

"Try something new," he suggested. "How are you?"

Cautious, she sat on the bed. "I'm fine. How are you?"

"That's good. That's a very good start." With a yawn, he realized he could sleep in the chair without any trouble at all. "I'm a little tired, actually. We spent most of the day interviewing parapsychologists who use computers and mathematical equations. I talked to a woman who claims to have had a half a dozen out-of-body experiences. 'OOBs.'"

She couldn't prevent the smile. "Yes, I've heard the term."

"Claimed she traveled to Europe that way."

"Saves on airfare."

"I suppose."

She felt a little tug of sympathy, a small glimmer of amusement. "Having trouble separating the wheat from the chaff, Brady?"

"You could call it that. In any case, it looks like we're going to be running around on the East Coast awhile. A palmist in the mountains of western Maryland, a house in Virginia that's supposed to be haunted by a young girl and a cat. There's a hypnotist in Pennsylvania who specializes in regression."

"Fascinating. It sounds like you're having just barrels of fun."

"I don't suppose you have any business that would bring you out this way."

"No, why?"

"Let's just say I wouldn't mind seeing you."

She tried to ignore the fact that the idea pleased her. "David, when you put things like that I get weak in the knees."

"I'm not much on the poetic turn of phrase." He wasn't handling this exactly as planned, he thought with a scowl. Then again, he hadn't given himself time to plan. Always a mistake. "Look, if I said I'd been thinking about you, that I wanted to see you, you'd just say something nasty. I'd end up paying for an argument instead of a conversation."

"And you can't afford to go over budget."

"See?" Still, it amused him. "Let's try a little experiment here. I've been watching experiments for days and I think I've got it down."

A.J. lay back on the bed. The fact that she was already ten minutes behind schedule didn't occur to her. "What sort of experiment?"

"You say something nice to me. Now that'll be completely out of character, so we'll start with that premise.... Go ahead," he prompted after fifteen seconds of blank silence.

"I'm trying to think of something."

"Don't be cute, A.J."

"All right, here. Your documentary on women in government was very informative and completely unbiased. I felt it showed a surprising lack of male, or female, chauvinism."

"That's a start, but why don't you try something a little more personal?"

"More personal," she mused, and smiled at the ceiling. When had she last lain on her bed and flirted over the phone? Had she ever? She supposed it didn't hurt, with a distance of three thousand miles, to feel sixteen and giddy. "How about this? If you ever decide you want to try the other end of the camera, I can make you a star."

"Too clichéd," David decided, but found himself grinning.

"You're very picky. How about if I said I think you might, just might, make an interesting companion. You're not difficult to look at, and your mind isn't really dull."

"Very lukewarm, A.J."

"Take it or leave it."

"Why don't we take the experiment to the next stage? Spend an evening with me and find out if your hypothesis is correct."

"I'm afraid I can't dump everything here and fly out to Pennsylvania or wherever to test a theory."

"I'll be back the middle of next week."

She hesitated, lectured herself, then went with impulse. "*Double Bluff* is opening here next week. Friday. Hastings Reed is a client. He's certain he's going to cop the Oscar."

"Back to business, A.J.?"

"I happen to have two tickets for the premiere. You buy the popcorn."

She'd surprised him. Switching the phone to his other hand, David was careful to speak casually. "A date?"

"Don't push your luck, Brady."

"I'll pick you up on Friday."

"Eight," she told him, already wondering if she was making a mistake. "Now go to bed. I have to get to work."

"Aurora."

"Yes?"

"Give me a thought now and then."

"Good night, Brady."

A.J. hung up the phone, then sat with it cradled in her lap. What had possessed her to do that? She'd intended to give the tickets away and catch the film when the buzz had died down. She didn't care for glittery premieres in the first place. And more important, she knew spending an evening with David Brady was foolish. And dangerous.

When was the last time she'd allowed herself to be charmed by a man? A million years ago, she remembered with a sigh. And where had that gotten her? Weepy and disgusted with herself. But she wasn't a child anymore, she remembered. She was a successful, self-confident woman who could handle ten David

Bradys at a negotiating table. The problem was she just wasn't sure she could handle one of him anywhere else.

She let out a long lingering sigh before her gaze passed over her clock. With a muffled oath she was tumbling out of bed. Damn David Brady and her own foolishness. She was going to be late.

Chapter 5

She bought a new dress. A.J. told herself that as the agent representing the lead in a major motion picture premiering in Hollywood, she was obligated to buy one. But she knew she had bought it for Aurora, not A.J.

At five minutes to eight on Friday night, she stood in front of her mirror and studied the results. No chic, professional suit this time. But perhaps she shouldn't have gone so far in the other direction.

Still, it was black. Black was practical and always in vogue. She turned to the right profile, then the left. It certainly wasn't flashy. But all in all, it might have been wiser to have chosen something more conservative than the pipeline strapless, nearly backless black silk. Straight on, it was provocative. From the side it was downright suggestive. Why hadn't she noticed in the dressing room just how tightly the material clung? Maybe she had, A.J. admitted on a long breath. Maybe she'd been giddy enough, foolish enough, to buy it because it didn't make her feel like an agent or any other sort of professional. It just made her feel like a woman. That was asking for trouble.

In any case, she could solve part of the problem with the little beaded jacket. Satisfied, she reached for a heavy silver locket clipped to thick links. Even as she was fastening it, A.J. heard the door. Taking her time, she slipped into the shoes that lay neatly at the foot of her bed, checked the contents of her purse and picked up the beaded jacket. Reminding herself to think of the entire process as an experiment, she opened the door to David.

She hadn't expected him to bring her flowers. He didn't seem the type for such time-honored romantic gestures. Because he appeared to be as off-balance as she, they just stood there a moment, staring.

She was stunning. He'd never considered her beautiful before. Attractive, yes, and sexy in the coolest, most aloof sort of way. But tonight she was breathtaking. Her dress didn't glitter, it didn't gleam, but simply flowed with the long, subtle lines of her body. It was enough. More than enough.

He took a step forward. Clearing her throat, A.J. took a step back.

"Right on time," she commented, and worked on a smile.

"I'm already regretting I didn't come early."

A.J. accepted the roses and struggled to be casual, when she wanted to bury her face in them. "Thank you. They're lovely. Would you like a drink while I put them in water?"

"No." It was enough just to look at her.

"I'll just be a minute."

As she walked away, his gaze passed down her nape,

over her shoulder blades and the smooth, generously exposed back to her waist, where the material of her dress again intruded. It nearly made him change his mind about the drink.

To keep his mind off tall blondes with smooth skin, he took a look around her apartment. She didn't appear to have the same taste in decorating as Clarissa.

The room was cool, as cool as its tenant, and just as streamlined. He couldn't fault the icy colors or the un-cluttered lines, but he wondered just how much of her-self Aurora Fields had put into the place she lived in. In the manner of her office, nothing was out of place. No frivolous mementos were set out for public viewing. The room had class and style, but none of the passion he'd found in the woman. And it told no secrets, not even in a whisper. He found himself more determined than ever to discover how many she had.

When A.J. came back she was steady. She'd arranged the roses in one of her rare extravagances, a tall, slim vase of Baccarat crystal. "Since you're prompt, we can get there a bit early and ogle the celebrities. It's different than dealing with them over a business lunch or watching a shoot."

"You look like a witch," he murmured. "White skin, black dress. You can almost smell the brimstone."

Her hands were no longer steady as she reached for her jacket. "I had an ancestor who was burned as one."

He took the jacket from her, regretting the fact that once it was on too much of her would be covered. "I guess I shouldn't be surprised."

"In Salem, during the madness." A.J. tried to ig-nore the way his fingers lingered as he slid the jacket over her. "Of course she was no more witch than Clarissa, but she was…special. According to the journals and documents that Clarissa gathered, she was twenty-five and very lovely. She made the mistake of warning her neighbors about a barn fire that didn't happen for two days."

"So she was tried and executed?"

"People usually have violent reactions to what they don't understand."

"We talked to a man in New York who's making a killing in the stock market by 'seeing' things before they happen."

"Times change." A.J. picked up her bag, then paused at the door. "My ancestor died alone and penniless. Her name was Aurora." She lifted a brow when he said nothing. "Shall we go?"

David slipped his hand over hers as the door shut at their backs. "I have a feeling that having an ancestor executed as a witch is very significant for you."

After shrugging, A.J. drew her hand from his to push the button for the elevator. "Not everyone has one in his family tree."

"And?"

"And let's just say I have a good working knowledge of how different opinions can be. They range from everything from blind condemnation to blind faith. Both extremes are dangerous."

As they stepped into the elevator he said consideringly, "And you work very hard to shield Clarissa from both ends."

"Exactly."

"What about you? Are you defending yourself by keeping your relationship with Clarissa quiet?"

"I don't need defending from my mother." She'd

swung through the doors before she managed to bank the quick surge of temper. "It's easier for me to work for her if we keep the family relationship out of it."

"Logical. I find you consistently logical, A.J."

She wasn't entirely sure it was a compliment. "And there is the fact that I'm very accessible. I didn't want clients rushing in to ask me to have my mother tell them where they lost their diamond ring. Is your car in the lot?"

"No, we're right out front. And I wasn't criticizing, Aurora, just asking."

She felt the temper fade as quickly as it had risen. "It's all right. I tend to be a little sensitive where Clarissa's concerned. I don't see a car," she began, glancing idly past a gray limo before coming back to it with raised brows. "Well," she murmured. "I'm impressed."

"Good." The driver was already opening the door. "That was the idea."

A.J. snuggled in. She'd ridden in limos countless times, escorting clients, delivering or picking them up at airports. But she never took such cushy comfort for granted. As she let herself enjoy, she watched David take a bottle out of ice.

"Flowers, a limo and now champagne. I am impressed, Brady, but I'm also—"

"Going to spoil it," he finished as he eased the cork expertly out. "Remember, we're testing your theory that I'd make an interesting companion." He offered a glass. "How'm I doing?"

"Fine so far." She sipped and appreciated. If she'd had experience in anything, she reminded herself, it was in how to keep a relationship light and undemanding. "I'm afraid I'm more used to doing the pampering than being pampered."

"How's it feel to be on the other side?"

"A little too good." She slipped out of her shoes and let her feet sink into the carpet. "I could just sit and ride for hours."

"It's okay with me." He ran a finger down the side of her throat to the edge of her jacket. "Want to skip the movie?"

She felt the tremor start where his finger skimmed, then rush all the way to the pit of her stomach. It came home to her that she hadn't had experience with David Brady. "I think not." Draining her glass, she held it out for a refill. "I suppose you attend a lot of these."

"Premieres?" He tilted wine into her glass until it fizzed to the rim. "No. Too Hollywood."

"Oh." With a gleam in her eye, A.J. glanced slowly around the limo. "I see."

"Tonight seemed to be an exception." He toasted her, appreciating the way she sat with such careless elegance in the plush corner of the limo. She belonged there. Now. With him. "As a representative of some of the top names in the business, you must drop in on these things a few times a year."

"No." A.J.'s lips curved as she sipped from her glass. "I hate them."

"Are you serious?"

"Deadly."

"Then what the hell are we doing?"

"Experimenting," she reminded him, and set her glass down as the limo stopped at the curb. "Just experimenting."

There were throngs of people crowded into the roped

off sections by the theater's entrance. Cameras were clicking, flashes popping. It didn't seem to matter to the crowd that the couple alighting from the limo weren't recognizable faces. It was Hollywood. It was opening night. The glitz was peaking. A.J. and David were cheered and applauded. She blinked twice as three paparazzi held cameras in her face.

"Incredible, isn't it?" he muttered as he steered her toward the entrance.

"It reminds me why I agent instead of perform." In an instinctive defense she wasn't even aware of, she turned away from the cameras. "Let's find a dark corner."

"I'm for that."

She had to laugh. "You never give up."

"A.J. A.J., *darling!*"

Before she could react, she found herself crushed against a soft, generous bosom. "Merinda, how nice to see you."

"Oh, I can't tell you how thrilled I am you're here." Merinda MacBride, Hollywood's current darling, drew her dramatically away. "A friendly face, you know. These things are such zoos."

She glittered from head to foot, from the diamonds that hung at her ears to the sequined dress that appeared to have been painted on by a very appreciative artist. She sent A.J. a smile that would have melted chocolate at ten paces. "You look divine."

"Thank you. You aren't alone?"

"Oh, no. I'm with Brad…." After a moment's hesitation, she smiled again. "Brad," she repeated, as if she'd decided last names weren't important. "He's fetching me a drink." Her gaze shifted and fastened on David. "You're not alone, either."

"Merinda MacBride, David Brady."

"A pleasure." He took her hand and, though she turned her knuckles up expectantly, didn't bring it to his lips. "I've seen your work and admired it."

"Why, thank you." She studied, measured and rated him in a matter of seconds. "Are we mutual clients of A.J.'s?"

"David's a producer." A.J. watched Merinda's baby-blue eyes sharpen. "Of documentaries," she added, amused. "You might have seen some of his work on public television."

"Of course." She beamed at him, though she'd never watched public television in her life and had no intention of starting. "I desperately admire producers. Especially attractive ones."

"I have a couple of scripts I think you'd be interested in," A.J. put in to draw her off.

"Oh?" Instantly Merinda dropped the sex-bomb act. A. J. Fields didn't recommend a script unless it had meat on it. "Have them sent over."

"First thing Monday."

"Well, I must find Brad before he forgets about me. David." She gave him her patented smoldering look. Documentaries or not, he was a producer. And a very attractive one. "I hope we run into each other again. Ta, A.J." She brushed cheeks. "Let's do lunch."

"Soon."

David barely waited for her to walk out of earshot. "You deal with that all the time?"

"Shh!"

"I mean *all* the time," he continued, watching as Merinda's tightly covered hips swished through the crowd. "Day after day. Why aren't you crazy?"

"Merinda may be a bit overdramatic, but if you've seen any of her films, you'll know just how talented she is."

"The woman looked loaded with talent to me," he began, but stopped to grin when A.J. scowled. "As an *actress,*" he continued. "I thought she was exceptional in *Only One Day.*"

A.J. couldn't quite conquer the smile. She'd hustled for weeks to land Merinda that part. "So you have seen her films."

"I don't live in a cave. That film was the first one that didn't—let's say, focus on her anatomy."

"It was the first one I represented her on."

"She's fortunate in her choice of agents."

"Thank you, but it goes both ways. Merinda's a very hot property."

"If we're going to make it through this evening, I'd better not touch that one."

They were interrupted another half a dozen times before they could get into the theater. A.J. ran into clients, acquaintances and associates, greeted, kissed and complimented while turning down invitations to after-theater parties.

"You're very good at this." David took two seats on the aisle near the back of the theater.

"Part of the job." A.J. settled back. There was nothing she enjoyed quite so much as a night at the movies.

"A bit jaded, A.J.?"

"Jaded?"

"Untouched by the glamour of it all, unaffected by the star system. You don't get any particular thrill out of exchanging kisses and hugs with some of the biggest and most distinguished names in the business."

"Business," she repeated, as if that explained it all. "That's not being jaded—it's being sensible. And the only time I saw you awestruck was when you found yourself face-to-face with three inches of cleavage on a six-foot blonde. Shh," she muttered before he could comment. "It's started and I hate to miss the opening credits."

With the theater dark, the audience quiet, A.J. threw herself into the picture. Ever since childhood, she'd been able to transport herself with the big screen. She wouldn't have called it "escape." She didn't like the word. A.J. called it "involvement." The actor playing the lead was a client, a man she knew intimately and had comforted through two divorces. All three of his children's birthdays were noted in her book. She'd listened to him rant; she'd heard his complaints, his doubts. That was all part of the job. But the moment she saw him on film, he was, to her, the part he played and nothing else.

Within five minutes, she was no longer in a crowded theater in Los Angeles, but in a rambling house in Connecticut. And there was murder afoot. When the lights went out and thunder boomed, she grabbed David's arm and cringed in her seat. Not one to pass up an age-old opportunity, he slipped an arm around her.

When was the last time, he wondered, that he'd sat in a theater with his arm around his date? He decided it had been close to twenty years and he'd been missing a great deal. He turned his attention to the film, but was distracted by her scent. It was still light, barely discernible, but it filled his senses. He tried to concentrate on the action and drama racing across the screen. A.J. caught her breath and shifted an inch closer. The tension on the screen seemed very pedestrian compared to his own. When the lights came up he found himself regretting that there was no longer such a thing as the double feature.

"It was good, wasn't it?" Eyes brilliant with pleasure, she turned to him. "It was really very good."

"Very good," he agreed, and lifted his hand to toy with her ear. "And if the applause is any indication, your client's got himself a hit."

"Thank God." She breathed a sigh of relief before shifting away to break what was becoming a very unnerving contact. "I talked him into the part. If he'd flopped, it would have been my head."

"And now that he can expect raves?"

"It'll be because of his talent," she said easily. "And that's fair enough. Would you mind if we slipped out before it gets too crazy?"

"I'd prefer it." He rose and steered her through the pockets of people that were already forming in the aisles. They hadn't gone ten feet before A.J.'s name was called out three times.

"Where are you going? You running out?" Hastings Reed, six feet three inches of down-home sex and manhood, blocked the aisle. He was flushed with the victory of seeing himself triumph on the screen and nervous that he might have misjudged the audience reaction. "You didn't like it?"

"It was wonderful." Understanding his need for reassurance, A.J. stood on tiptoe to brush his cheek. "You were wonderful. Never better."

He returned the compliment with a bone-crushing hug. "We have to wait for the reviews."

"Prepare to accept praise humbly, and with good grace. Hastings, this is David Brady."

"Brady?" As Hastings took David's hand, his etched in bronze face creased into a frown. "Producer?"

"That's right."

"God, I love your work." Already flying, Hastings pumped David's hand six times before finally releasing it. "I'm an honorary chairman of Rights for Abused Children. Your documentary did an incredible job of bringing the issue home and making people aware. Actually, it's what got me involved in the first place."

"It's good to hear that. We wanted to make people think."

"Made me think. I've got kids of my own. Listen, keep me in mind if you ever do a follow-up. No fee." He grinned down at A.J. "She didn't hear that."

"Hear what?"

He laughed and yanked her against him again. "This lady's incredible. I don't know what I'd have done without her. I wasn't going to take this part, but she badgered me into it."

"I never badger," A.J. said mildly.

"Nags, badgers and browbeats. Thank God." Grinning, he finally took a good look at her. "Damn if you don't look like something a man could swallow right up. I've never seen you dressed like that."

To cover a quick flush of embarrassment, she reached up to straighten his tie. "And as I recall, the last time I saw you, you were in jeans and smelled of horses."

"Guess I did. You're coming to Chasen's?"

"Actually, I—"

"You're coming. Look, I've got a couple of quick interviews, but I'll see you there in a half hour." He took two strides away and was swallowed up in the crowd.

"He's got quite an...overwhelming personality," David commented.

"To say the least." A.J. glanced at her watch. It was still early. "I suppose I should at least put in an appearance, since he'll count on it now. I can take a cab if you'd rather skip it."

"Ever hear of the expression about leaving with the guy who brought you?"

"This isn't a country dance," A.J. pointed out as they wove through the lingering crowd.

"Same rules apply. I can handle Chasen's."

"Okay, but just for a little while."

The "little while" lasted until after three.

Cases of champagne, mountains of caviar and piles of fascinating little canapés. Even someone as practical as A.J. found it difficult to resist a full-scale celebration. The music was loud, but it didn't seem to matter. There were no quiet corners to escape to. Through her clientele and David's contacts, they knew nearly everyone in the room between them. A few minutes of conversation here, another moment there, ate up hours of time. Caught up in her client's success, A.J. didn't mind.

On the crowded dance floor, she allowed herself to relax in David's arms. "Incredible, isn't it?"

"Nothing tastes so sweet as success, especially when you mix it with champagne."

She glanced around. It was hard not to be fascinated with the faces, the names, the bodies. She was part of it, a very intricate part. But through her own choice, she wasn't an intimate part. "I usually avoid this sort of thing."

He let his fingers skim lightly up her back. "Why?"

"Oh, I don't know." Weariness, wine and pleasure combined. Her cheek rested against his. "I guess I'm more of a background sort of person. You fit in."

"And you don't?"

"Ummm." She shook her head. Why was it men smelled so wonderful—so wonderfully different? And felt so good when you held and were held by one. "You're part of the talent. I just work with clauses and figures."

"And that's the way you want it?"

"Absolutely. Still, this is nice." When his hand ran down her back again, she stretched into it. "Very nice."

"I'd rather be alone with you," he murmured. Every time he held her like this he thought he would go crazy. "In some dim little room where the music was low."

"This is safer." But she didn't object when his lips brushed her temple.

"Who needs safe?"

"I do. I need safe and ordered and sensible."

"Anyone who chooses to be involved in this business tosses safe, ordered and sensible out the window."

"Not me." She drew back to smile at him. It felt so good to relax, to flow with the evening, to let her steps match his without any conscious thought. "I just make the deals and leave the chances up to others."

"Take ten percent and run?"

"That's right."

"I might have believed that a few weeks ago. The problem is I've seen you with Clarissa."

"That's entirely different."

"True enough. I also saw you with Hastings tonight. You get wrapped up with your clients, A.J. You might be able to convince yourself they're just signatures, but I know better. You're a marshmallow."

Her brows drew together. "Ridiculous. Marshmallows get swallowed."

"They're also resilient. I admire that in you." He touched his lips to hers before she could move. "I'm beginning to realize I admire quite a bit in you."

She would have pulled away then, but he kept her close easily enough and continued to sway. "I don't mix business and personal feelings."

"You lie."

"I might play with the truth," she said, abruptly dignified, "but I don't lie."

"You were ready to turn handsprings tonight when that movie hit."

A.J. tossed her hair out of her face. He saw too much too easily. A man wasn't supposed to. "Have you any idea how I can use that as a lever? I'll get Hastings a million-five for his next movie."

"You'll 'get Hastings,'" David repeated. "Even your phrasing gives you away."

"You're picking up things that aren't there."

"No, I think I'm finding things you've squirreled away. Have you got a problem with the fact that I've decided I like you?"

Off-balance, she missed a step and found herself pressed even closer. "I think I'd handle it better if we still got on each other nerves."

"Believe me, you get on my nerves." Until his blood was on slow boil, his muscles knotting and stretching and the need racing. "There are a hundred people in this room and my mind keeps coming back to the fact that I could have you out of what there is of that dress in thirty seconds flat."

The chill arrowed down her back. "You know that's not what I meant. You'd be smarter to keep your mind on business."

"Smarter, safer. We're looking for different things, A.J."

"We can agree on that, anyway."

"We might agree on more if we gave ourselves the chance."

She didn't know exactly why she smiled. Perhaps it was because it sounded like a fantasy. She enjoyed watching them, listening to them, without really believing in them. "David." She rested her arms on his shoulders. "You're a very nice man, on some levels."

"I think I can return that compliment."

"Let me spell things out for you in the way I understand best. Number one, we're business associates at the moment. This precludes any possibility that we could be seriously involved. Number two, while this documentary is being made my first concern is, and will continue to be, Clarissa's welfare. Number three, I'm very busy and what free time I have I use to relax in my own way—which is alone. And number four, I'm not equipped for relationships. I'm selfish, critical and disinterested."

"Very well put." He kissed her forehead in a friendly fashion. "Are you ready to go?"

"Yes." A little nonplussed by his reaction, she walked off the dance floor to retrieve her jacket. They left the noise and crowd behind and stepped out into the cool early-morning air. "I forget sometimes that the glamour and glitz can be nice in small doses."

He helped her into the waiting limo. "Moderation in all things."

"Life's more stable that way." Cut off from the driver and the outside by thick smoked glass, A.J. settled back against the seat. Before she could let out the first contented sigh, David was close, his hand firm on her chin. "David—"

"Number one," he began, "I'm the producer of this project, and you're the agent for one, only one, of the talents. That means we're business associates in the broadest sense and that doesn't preclude an involvement. We're already involved."

There'd been no heat in his eyes on the dance floor, she thought quickly. Not like there was now. "David—"

"You had your say," he reminded her. "Number two, while this documentary is being made, you can fuss over Clarissa all you want. That has nothing to do with us. Number three, we're both busy, which means we don't want to waste time with excuses and evasions that don't hold water. And number four, whether you think you're equipped for relationships or not, you're in the middle of one right now. You'd better get used to it."

Temper darkened her eyes and chilled her voice. "I don't have to get used to anything."

"The hell you don't. Put a number on this."

Frustrated desire, unrelieved passion, simmering anger. She felt them all as his mouth crushed down on hers. Her first reaction was pure self-preservation. She struggled against him, knowing if she didn't free herself quickly, she'd be lost. But he seemed to know, somehow, that her struggle was against herself, not him.

He held her closer. His mouth demanded more, until, despite fears, despite doubts, despite everything, she gave.

With a muffled moan, her arms went around him. Her fingers slid up his back to lose themselves in his hair. Passion, still unrelieved, mounted until it threatened to consume. She could feel everything, the hard line of his body against hers, the soft give of the seat at her back. There was the heat of his lips as they pressed and rubbed on hers and the cool air blown in silently through the vents.

And she could taste—the lingering punch of champagne as their tongues tangled together. She could taste a darker flavor, a deeper flavor that was his flesh. Still wilder, less recognizable, was the taste of her own passion.

His mouth left hers only to search out other delights. Over the bare, vulnerable skin of her neck and shoulders he found them. His hands weren't gentle as they moved over her. His mouth wasn't tender. Her heart began to thud in a fast, chaotic rhythm at the thought of being taken with such hunger, such fury.

Driven by her own demons she let her hands move, explore and linger. When his breath was as uneven as hers their lips met again. The contact did nothing to soothe and everything to arouse. Desperate for more, she brought her teeth down to nip, to torment. With an oath, he swung her around until they were sprawled on the long, wide seat.

Her lips parted as she looked up at him. She could see the intermittent flash of streetlights as they passed overhead. Shadow and light. Shadow and light. Hypnotic. Erotic. A.J. reached up to touch his face.

She was all cream and silk as she lay beneath him. Her hair was tousled around a face flushed with arousal. The touch of her fingers on his cheek was light as a whisper and caused the need to thunder through him.

"This is crazy," she murmured.

"I know."

"It's not supposed to happen." But it was. She knew it. She had known it from the first meeting. "It can't happen," she corrected.

"Why?"

"Don't ask me." Her voice dropped to a whisper. She couldn't resist letting her fingers play along his face even as she prepared herself to deny both of them. "I can't explain. If I could you wouldn't understand."

"If there's someone else I don't give a damn."

"No, there's no one." She closed her eyes a moment, then opened them again to stare at him. "There's no one else."

Why was he hesitating? She was here, aroused, inches away from total surrender. He had only to ignore the confused plea in her eyes and take. But even with his blood hot, the need pressing, he couldn't ignore it. "It might not be now, it might not be here, but it will be, Aurora."

It would be. Had to be. The part of her that knew it fought a frantic tug-of-war with the part that had to deny it. "Let me go, David."

Trapped by his own feelings, churning with his own needs, he pulled her up. "What kind of game are you playing?"

She was cold. Freezing. She felt each separate chill run over her skin. "It's called survival."

"Damn it, Aurora." She was so beautiful. Why did she suddenly have to be so beautiful? Why did she suddenly have to look so fragile? "What does being with me, making love with me, have to do with your survival?"

"Nothing." She nearly laughed as she felt the limo cruise to a halt. "Nothing at all if it were just that simple."

"Why complicate it? We want each other. We're both adults. People become lovers every day without doing themselves any damage."

"Some people." She let out a shuddering breath. "I'm not some people. If it were so simple, I'd make love with you right here, in the back seat of this car. I won't tell you I don't want to." She turned to look at him and the vulnerability in her eyes was haunted by regrets. "But it's not simple. Making love with you would be easy. Falling in love with you wouldn't."

Before he could move, she'd pushed open the door and was on the street.

"Aurora." He was beside her, a hand on her arm, but she shook him off. "You can't expect to just walk off after a statement like that."

"That's just what I'm doing," she corrected, and shook him off a second time.

"I'll take you up." With what willpower he had left, he held on to patience.

"No. Just go."

"We have to talk."

"No." Neither of them was prepared for the desperation in her voice. "I want you to go. It's late. I'm tired. I'm not thinking straight."

"If we don't talk this out now, we'll just have to do it later."

"Later, then." She would have promised him anything for freedom at that moment. "I want you to go now, David." When he continued to hold her, her voice quivered. "Please, I need you to go. I can't handle this now."

He could fight her anger, but he couldn't fight her fragility. "All right."

He waited until she had disappeared inside her building. Then he leaned back on the car and pulled out a cigarette. Later then, he promised himself. They'd talk. He stood where he was, waiting for his system to level.

They'd talk, he assured himself again. But it was best to wait until they were both calmer and more reasonable.

Tossing away the cigarette, he climbed back into the limo. He hoped to God he could stop thinking of her long enough to sleep.

Chapter 6

She wanted to pace. She wanted to walk up and down, pull at her hair and walk some more. She forced herself to sit quietly on the sofa and wait as Clarissa poured tea.

"I'm so glad you came by, dear. It's so seldom you're able to spend an afternoon with me."

"Things are under control at the office. Abe's covering for me."

"Such a nice man. How's his little grandson?"

"Spoiled rotten. Abe wants to buy him Dodger Stadium."

"Grandparents are entitled to spoil the way parents are obliged to discipline." She kept her eyes lowered, anxious not to show her own longings and apply pressure. "How's your tea?"

"It's...different." Knowing the lukewarm compliment would satisfy Clarissa saved her from an outright lie. "What is it?"

"Rose hips. I find it very soothing in the afternoons. You seem to need a little soothing, Aurora."

A.J. set down her cup and, giving in to the need for movement, rose. She'd known when she'd deliberately cleared her calendar that she would come to Clarissa. And she'd known that she would come for help, though she'd repeatedly told herself she didn't need it.

"Momma." A.J. sat on the sofa again as Clarissa sipped tea and waited patiently. "I think I'm in trouble."

"You ask too much of yourself." Clarissa reached out to touch her hand. "You always have."

"What am I going to do?"

Clarissa sat back as she studied her daughter. She'd never heard that phrase from her before, and now that she had, she wanted to be certain to give the right answers. "You're frightened."

"Terrified." She was up again, unable to sit. "It's getting away from me. I'm losing the controls."

"Aurora, it isn't always necessary to hold on to them."

"It is for me." She looked back with a half smile. "You should understand."

"I do. Of course I do." But she'd wished so often that her daughter, her only child, would be at peace with herself. "You constantly defend yourself against being hurt because you were hurt once and decided it would never happen again. Aurora, are you in love with David?"

Clarissa would know he was at the core of it. Naturally she would know without a word being said. A.J. could accept that. "I might be if I don't pull myself back now."

"Would it be so bad to love someone?"

"David isn't just someone. He's too strong, too overwhelming. Besides…" She paused long enough to steady herself. "I thought I was in love once before."

"You were young." Clarissa came as close as she ever did to true anger. She set her cup in its saucer with a little snap. "Infatuation is a different matter. It demands more and gives less back than love."

A.J. stood in the middle of the room. There was really no place to go. "Maybe this is just infatuation. Or lust."

Clarissa lifted a brow and sipped tea calmly. "You're the only one who can answer that. Somehow I don't think you'd have cleared your calendar and come to see me in the middle of a workday if you were concerned about lust."

Laughing, A.J. walked over to drop on the sofa beside her. "Oh, Momma, there's no one like you. No one."

"Things were never normal for you, were they?"

"No." A.J. dropped her head on Clarissa's shoulder. "They were better. You were better."

"Aurora, your father loved me very much. He loved, and he accepted, without actually understanding. I can't even comprehend what my life might have been like if I hadn't given up the controls and loved him back."

"He was special," A.J. murmured. "Most men aren't."

Clarissa hesitated only a moment, then cleared her throat. "Alex accepts me, too."

"Alex?" Uneasy, A.J. sat up again. There was no mistaking the blush of color in Clarissa's cheeks. "Are you and Alex…" How did one put such a question to a mother? "Are you serious about Alex?"

"He asked me to marry him."

"What?" Too stunned for reason, A.J. jerked back and gaped. "Marriage? You barely know him. You met only weeks ago. Momma, certainly you're mature enough to realize something as important as marriage takes a great deal of thought."

Clarissa beamed at her. "What an excellent mother you'll make one day. I was never able to lecture quite like that."

"I don't mean to lecture." Mumbling, A.J. picked up her tea. "I just don't want you to jump into something like this without giving it the proper thought."

"You see, that's just what I mean. I'm sure you got that from your father's side. My family's always been just the tiniest bit flighty."

"Momma—"

"Do you remember when Alex and I were discussing palm reading for the documentary?"

"Of course." The uneasiness increased, along with a sense of inevitability. "You felt something."

"It was very strong and very clear. I admit it flustered me a bit to realize a man could be attracted to me after all these years. And I wasn't aware until that moment that I could feel like that about anyone."

"But you need time. I don't doubt anything you feel, anything you see. You know that. But—"

"Darling, I'm fifty-six." Clarissa shook her head, wondering how it had happened so quickly. "I've been content to live alone. I think perhaps I was meant to live alone for a certain amount of time. Now I want to share the rest of my life. You're twenty-eight and content and very capable of living alone. Still, you mustn't be afraid to share your life."

"It's different."

"No." She took A.J.'s hands again. "Love, affection, needs. They're really very much the same for everyone. If David is the right man for you, you'll know it. But after knowing, you have to accept."

"He may not accept me." Her fingers curled tightly around her mother's. "I have trouble accepting myself."

"And that's the only worry you've ever given me. Aurora, I can't tell you what to do. I can't look into tomorrow for you, as much as part of me wants to."

"I'm not asking that. I'd never ask you that."

"No, you wouldn't. Look into your heart, Aurora. Stop calculating risks and just look."

"I might see something I don't want to."

"Oh, you probably will." With a little laugh, Clarissa settled back on the sofa with an arm around A.J. "I can't tell you what to do, but I can tell you what I feel. David Brady is a very good man. He has his flaws, of course, but he is a good man. It's been a pleasure for me to be able to work with him. As a matter of fact, when he called this morning, I was delighted."

"Called?" Immediately alert, A.J. sat up straight. "David called you? Why?"

"Oh, a few ideas he'd had about the documentary." She fussed with the little lace napkin in her lap. "He's in Rolling Hills today. Well, not exactly in, but outside. Do you remember hearing about that old mansion no one ever seems able to live in for long? The one a few miles off the beach?"

"It's supposed to be haunted," A.J. muttered.

"Of course there are differing opinions on that. I think David made an excellent choice for his project, though, from what he told me about the background."

"What do you have to do with that?"

"That? Oh, nothing at all. We just chatted about the house. I suppose he thought I'd be interested."

"Oh." Mollified, A.J. began to relax. "That's all right then."

"We did set up a few other things. I'll be going into the studio—Wednesday," she decided. "Yes, I'm sure it's Wednesday of next week, to discuss spontaneous phenomena. And then, oh, sometime the following week, I'm to go to the Van Camps'. We'll tape in Alice's living room."

"The Van Camps'." She felt the heat rising. "He set all this up with you."

Clarissa folded her hands. "Yes, indeed. Did I do something wrong?"

"Not you." Fired up, she rose. "He knew better than to change things without clearing it with me first. You can't trust anyone. Especially a producer." Snatching up her purse, she strode to the door. "You don't go anywhere on Wednesday to discuss any kind of phenomena until I see just what he has up his sleeve." She caught herself and came back to give Clarissa a hug. "Don't worry, I'll straighten it out."

"I'm counting on it." Clarissa watched her daughter storm out of the house before she sat back, content. She'd done everything she could—set energy in motion. The rest was up to fate.

"Tell him we'll reschedule. Better yet, have Abe meet with him." A.J. shouted into her car phone as she came up behind a tractor-trailer.

"Abe has a three-thirty. I don't think he can squeeze Montgomery in at four."

"Damn." Impatient, A.J. zoomed around the tractor-trailer. "Who's free at four?"

"Just Barbara."

While keeping an eye peeled for her exit, A.J. turned that over in her mind. "No, they'd never jell. Reschedule, Diane. Tell Montgomery...tell him there was an emergency. A medical emergency."

"Check. There isn't, is there?"

Her smile was set and nothing to laugh about. "There might be."

"Sounds promising. How can I reach you?"

"You can't. Leave anything important on the machine. I'll call in and check."

"You got it. Hey, good luck."

"Thanks." Teeth gritted, A.J. replaced the receiver.

He wasn't going to get away with playing power games. A.J. knew all the rules to that one, and had made up plenty of her own. David Brady was in for it. A.J. reached for her map again. If she could ever find him.

When the first raindrop hit the windshield she started to swear. By the time she'd taken the wrong exit, made three wrong turns and found herself driving down a decrepit gravel road in a full-fledged spring storm, she was cursing fluently. Every one of them was aimed directly at David Brady's head.

One look at the house through driving rain and thunderclouds proved why he'd chosen so well. Braking viciously, A.J. decided he'd arranged the storm for effect. When she swung out of the car and stepped in a puddle of mud that slopped over her ankle, it was the last straw.

He saw her through the front window. Surprise turned to annoyance quickly at the thought of another interruption on a day that had seen everything go wrong. He hadn't had a decent night's sleep in a week, his work was going to hell and he itched just looking at her. When he pulled open the front door, he was as ready as A.J. for an altercation.

"What the hell are you doing here?"

Her hair was plastered to her face; her suit was soaked. She'd just ruined half a pair of Italian shoes. "I want to talk to you, Brady."

"Fine. Call my office and set up an appointment. I'm working."

"I want to talk to you now!" Lifting a hand to his chest, she gave him a hefty shove back against the door. "Just where do you come off making arrangements with one of my clients without clearing it with me? If you want Clarissa in the studio next week, then you deal with me. Understand?"

He took her damp hand by the wrist and removed it from his shirt. "I have Clarissa under contract for the duration of filming. I don't have to clear anything with you."

"You'd better read it again, Brady. Dates and times are set up through her representative."

"Fine. I'll send you a schedule. Now if you'll excuse me—"

He pushed open the door, but she stepped in ahead of him. Two electricians inside the foyer fell silent and listened. "I'm not finished."

"I am. Get lost, Fields, before I have you tossed off the set."

"Watch your step, or my client might develop a chronic case of laryngitis."

"Don't threaten me, A.J." He gripped her lapels with both hands. "I've had about all I'm taking from you. You want to talk, fine. Your office or mine, tomorrow."

"Mr. Brady, we need you upstairs."

For a moment longer he held her. Her gaze was locked on his and the fury was fierce and very equal. He wanted, God, he wanted to drag her just a bit closer, wipe that maddening look off her face. He wanted to crush his mouth to hers until she couldn't speak, couldn't breathe, couldn't fight. He wanted, more than anything, to make her suffer the way he suffered. He released her so abruptly she took two stumbling steps back.

"Get lost," he ordered, and turned to mount the stairs.

It took her a minute to catch her breath. She hadn't known she could get this angry, hadn't allowed herself to become this angry in too many years to count. Emotions flared up inside her, blinding her to everything else. She dashed up the stairs behind him.

"Ms. Fields, nice to see you again." Alex stood on the top landing in front of a wall where the paint had peeled and cracked. He gave her an easy smile as he smoked his cigar and waited to be called back in front of the camera.

"And I want to talk to you, too," she snapped at him. Leaving him staring, she strode down the hall after David.

It was narrow and dark. There were cobwebs clinging to corners, but she didn't notice. In places there were squares of lighter paint where pictures had once hung. A.J. worked her way through technicians and walked into the room only steps behind David.

It hit her like a wall. No sooner had she drawn in the breath to shout at him again than she couldn't speak at all. She was freezing. The chill whipped through her and to the bone in the matter of a heartbeat.

The room was lit for the shoot, but she didn't see the cameras, the stands or the coils of cable. She saw wallpaper, pink roses on cream, and a four-poster draped in the same rose hue. There was a little mahogany stool beside the bed that was worn smooth in the center. She could smell the roses that stood fresh and a little damp in an exquisite crystal vase on a mahogany vanity that gleamed with beeswax and lemon. And she saw—much more. And she heard.

You betrayed me. You betrayed me with him, Jessica.

No! No, I swear it. Don't. For God's sake don't do this. I love you. I—

Lies! All lies. You won't tell any more.

There were screams. There was silence, a hundred times worse. A.J.'s purse hit the floor with a thud as she lifted her hands to her ears.

"A.J." David was shaking her, hands firm on her shoulders, as everyone else in the room stopped to stare. "What's wrong with you?"

She reached out to clutch his shirt. He could feel the iciness of her flesh right through the cotton. She looked at him, but her eyes didn't focus. "That poor girl," she murmured. "Oh, God, that poor girl."

"A.J." With an effort, he kept his voice calm. She was shuddering and pale, but the worst of it was her eyes, dark and glazed as they looked beyond him. She stared at the center of the room as if held in a trance. He took both of her hands in his. "A.J., what girl?"

"He killed her right here. There on the bed. He used his hands. She couldn't scream anymore because his hands were on her throat, squeezing. And then…"

"A.J." He took her chin and forced her to look at him. "There's no bed in here. There's nothing."

"It—" She struggled for air, then lifted both hands to her face. The nausea came, a too-familiar sensation. "I have to get out of here." Breaking away, she pushed through the technicians crowded in the doorway and ran. She stumbled out into the rain and down the porch steps before David caught her.

"Where are you going?" he demanded. A flash of lightning highlighted them both as the rain poured down.

"I've got to…" She trailed off and looked around blindly. "I'm going back to town. I have to get back."

"I'll take you."

"No." Panicked, she struggled, only to find herself held firmly. "I have my car."

"You're not driving anywhere like this." Half leading, half dragging, he pulled her to his car. "Now stay here," he ordered, and slammed the door on her.

Unable to gather the strength to do otherwise, A.J. huddled on the seat and shivered. She needed only a minute. She promised herself she needed only a minute to pull herself together. But however many it took David to come back, the shivering hadn't stopped. He tossed her purse in the back, then tucked a blanket around her. "One of the crew's taking your car back to town." After starting the engine, he headed down the bumpy, potholed gravel road. For several moments there was silence as the rain drummed and she sat hunched under the blanket.

"Why didn't you tell me?" he said at length.

She was better now. She took a steady breath to prove she had control. "Tell you what?"

"That you were like your mother."

A.J. curled into a ball on the seat, cradled her head in her arms and wept.

What the hell was he supposed to say? David cursed her, then himself, as he drove through the rain with her sobbing beside him. She'd given him the scare of his life when he'd turned around and seen her standing there, gasping for air and white as a sheet. He'd never felt anything as cold as her hands had been. Never seen anything like what she must have seen.

Whatever doubts he had, whatever criticisms he could make about laboratory tests, five-dollar psychics and executive clairvoyants, he knew A.J. had seen something, felt something, none of the rest of them had.

So what did he do about it? What did he say?

She wept. She let herself empty. There was no use berating herself, no use being angry with what had happened. She'd long ago resigned herself to the fact that every now and again, no matter how careful she was, no matter how tightly controlled, she would slip and leave herself open.

The rain stopped. There was milky sunlight now. A.J. kept the blanket close around her as she straightened in her seat. "I'm sorry."

"I don't want an apology. I want an explanation."

"I don't have one." She wiped her cheeks dry with her hand. "I'd appreciate it if you'd take me home."

"We're going to talk, and we're going to do it where you can't kick me out."

She was too weak to argue, too weak to care. A.J. rested her head against the window and didn't protest when they passed the turn for her apartment. They drove up into the hills, high above the city. The rain had left things fresh here, though a curling mist still hugged the ground.

He turned into a drive next to a house with cedar shakes and tall windows. The lawn was wide and trimmed with spring flowers bursting around the borders.

"I thought you'd have a place in town."

"I used to, then I decided I had to breathe." He took her purse and a briefcase from the back seat. A.J. pushed the blanket aside and stepped from the car. Saying nothing, they walked to the front door together.

Inside wasn't rustic. He had paintings on the walls and thick Turkish carpets on the floors. She ran her hand along a polished rail and stepped down a short flight of steps into the living room. Still silent, David went to the fireplace and set kindling to blaze. "You'll want to get out of those wet clothes," he said matter-of-factly. "There's a bath upstairs at the end of the hall. I keep a robe on the back of the door."

"Thank you." Her confidence was gone—that edge that helped her keep one step ahead. A.J. moistened her lips. "David, you don't have to—"

"I'll make coffee." He walked through a doorway and left her alone.

She stood there while the flames from the kindling began to lick at split oak. The scent was woodsy, comfortable. She'd never felt more miserable in her life. The kind of rejection she felt now, from David, was the kind she'd expected. It was the kind she'd dealt with before.

She stood there while she battled back the need to weep again. She was strong, self-reliant. She wasn't about to break her heart over David Brady, or any man. Lifting her chin, A.J. walked to the stairs and up. She'd shower, let her clothes dry, then dress and go home. A. J. Fields knew how to take care of herself.

The water helped. It soothed her puffy eyes and warmed her clammy skin. From the small bag of emergency cosmetics in her purse, she managed to repair the worst of the damage. She tried not to notice that the robe carried David's scent as she slipped it on. It was better to remember that it was warm and covered her adequately.

When she went back downstairs, the living area was still empty. Clinging to the courage she'd managed to build back up, A.J. went to look for him.

The hallway twisted and turned at angles when least expected. If the situation had been different, A.J. would have appreciated the house for its uniqueness. She didn't take much notice of polished paneling offset by stark white walls, or planked floors scattered with intricately patterned carpets. She followed the hallway into the kitchen. The scent of coffee eased the beginning of flutters in her stomach. She took a moment to brace herself, then walked into the light.

He was standing by the window. There was a cup of coffee in his hand, but he wasn't drinking. Something was simmering on the stove. Perhaps he'd forgotten it. A.J. crossed her arms over her chest and rubbed her hands over the sleeves of the robe. She didn't feel warm any longer.

"David?"

He turned the moment she said his name, but slowly. He wasn't certain what he should say to her, what he could say. She looked so frail. He couldn't have described his own feelings at the moment and hadn't a clue to hers. "The coffee's hot," he told her. "Why don't you sit down?"

"Thanks." She willed herself to behave as normally as he and took a seat on a stool at the breakfast bar.

"I thought you could use some food." He walked to the stove to pour coffee. "I heated up some soup."

Tension began to beat behind her eyes. "You didn't have to bother."

Saying nothing, he ladled out the soup, then brought both it and the coffee to her. "It's an old family recipe. My mother always says a bowl of soup cures anything."

"It looks wonderful," she managed, and wondered why she had to fight back the urge to cry again. "David…"

"Eat first." Taking no food for himself, he drew up a stool across from her and cradled his coffee. He lit a cigarette and sat, sipping his coffee and smoking, while she toyed with her soup. "You're supposed to eat it," he pointed out. "Not just rearrange the noodles."

"Why don't you ask?" she blurted out. "I'd rather you just asked and got it over with."

So much hurt there, he realized. So much pain. He wondered where it had its roots. "I don't intend to start an interrogation, A.J."

"Why not?" When she lifted her head, her face was defiant, her eyes strong. "You want to know what happened to me in that room."

He blew out a stream of smoke before he crushed out his cigarette. "Of course I do. But I don't think you're ready to talk about what happened in that room. At least not in detail. A.J., why don't you just talk to me?"

"Not ready?" She might have laughed if her stomach wasn't tied up in knots. "You're never ready. I can tell you what she looked like—black hair, blue eyes. She was wearing a cotton gown that buttoned all the way up to her throat, and her name was Jessica. She was barely eighteen when her husband killed her in a jealous rage, strangled her with his own hands, then killed himself in grief with the pistol in the table beside the bed. That's what you want for your documentary, isn't it?"

The details, and the cool, steady way she delivered them, left him shaken. Just who was this woman who sat across from him, this woman he'd held and desired? "What happened to you has nothing to do with the project. I think it has a great deal to do with the way you're reacting now."

"I can usually control it." She shoved the soup aside so that it lapped over the edges of the bowl. "God knows I've had years of practice. If I hadn't been so angry, so out of control when I walked in there—it probably wouldn't have happened."

"You can block it."

"Usually, yes. To a large extent, anyway."

"Why do you?"

"Do you really think this is a gift?" she demanded as she pushed away from the counter. "Oh, maybe for someone like Clarissa it is. She's so unselfish, so basically good and content with herself."

"And you?"

"I hate it." Unable to remain still, she whirled away. "You've no idea what it can be like, having people stare at you, whisper. If you're different, you're a freak, and I—" She broke off, rubbing at her temple. When she spoke again, her voice was quiet. "I just wanted to be normal. When I was little, I'd have dreams." She folded her hands together and pressed them to her lips. "They were so incredibly real, but I was just a child and thought everyone dreamed like that. I'd tell one of my friends—oh, your cat's going to have kittens. Can I have the little white one? Then weeks later, the cat would have kittens and one of them would be white. Little things. Someone would lose a doll or a toy and I'd say, well, your mother put it on the top shelf in your closet. She forgot. When they looked it would be there. Kids didn't think much of it, but it made some of the parents nervous. They thought it would be best if their children stayed away from me."

"And that hurt," he murmured.

"Yes, that hurt a lot. Clarissa understood. She was comforting and really wonderful about it, but it hurt. I still had the dreams, but I stopped talking about them. Then my father died."

She stood, the heels of her hands pressed to her eyes as she struggled to rein in her emotions. "No, please." She shook her head as she heard David shift on the stool as if to rise. "Just give me a minute." On a long breath, she dropped her hands. "I knew he was dead. He was away on a selling trip, and I woke up in the middle of the night and knew. I got up and went to Clarissa. She was sitting up in bed, wide awake. I could see on her face that she was already grieving. We didn't even say anything to each other, but I got into bed with her, and we just lay there together until the phone rang."

"And you were eight," he murmured, trying to get some grip on it.

"I was eight. After that, I started to block it off. Whenever I began to feel something, I'd just pull in. It got to the point where I could go for months—at one point, two years—without something touching it off. If I get angry or upset to the point where I lose control, I open myself up for it."

He remembered the way she'd stormed into the house, strong and ready for a fight. And the way she'd run out again, pale and terrified. "And I make you angry."

She turned to look at him for the first time since she'd begun to speak. "It seems that way."

The guilt was there. David wasn't certain how to deal with it, or his own confusion. "Should I apologize?"

"You can't help being what you are any more than I can stop being what I am."

"Aurora, I think I understand your need to keep a handle on this thing, not to let it interfere with the day-to-day. I don't understand why you feel you have to lock it out of your life like a disease."

She'd gone this far, she thought as she walked back to the counter. She'd finish. "When I was twenty, scrambling around and trying to get my business rolling, I met this man. He had this little shop on the beach, rent-

ing surfboards, selling lotion, that sort of thing. It was
so, well, exciting, to see someone that free-spirited,
that easygoing, when I was working ten hours a day
just to scrape by. In any case, I'd never been involved
seriously with a man before. There hadn't been time.
I fell flat on my face for this one. He was fun, not too
demanding. Before I knew it we were on the point of
being engaged. He bought me this little ring with the
promise of diamonds and emeralds once we hit it big.
I think he meant it." She gave a little laugh as she slid
onto the stool again. "In any case, I felt that if we were
going to be married we shouldn't have any secrets."

"You hadn't told him?"

"No." She said it defiantly, as if waiting for disapproval. When none came, she lowered her gaze and
went on. "I introduced him to Clarissa, and then I told
him that I—I told him," she said flatly. "He thought it
was a joke, sort of dared me to prove it. Because I felt
so strongly about having everything up front between
us, well, I guess you could say I proved it. After—he
looked at me as though…" She swallowed and struggled
to keep the hurt buried.

"I'm sorry."

"I suppose I should have expected it." Though she
shrugged it off, she picked up the spoon and began to
run the handle through her fingers. "I didn't see him for
days after that. I went to him with some grand gesture in
mind, like giving him back his ring. It's almost funny,
looking back on it now, the way he wouldn't look at me,
the way he kept his distance. Too weird." She looked up
again with a brittle smile. "I was just plain too weird."

And she was still hurting. But he didn't reach out to
her. He wasn't quite sure how. "The wrong man at the
wrong time."

A.J. gave an impatient shake of her head. "I was the wrong woman. Since then, I've learned that honesty isn't always the most advantageous route. Do you have any idea what it would do to me professionally if my clients knew? Those I didn't lose would ask me to tell them what role to audition for. People would start asking me to fly to Vegas with them so I could tell them what number to bet at the roulette table."

"So you and Clarissa downplay your relationship and you block the rest off."

"That's right." She picked up her cold coffee and downed it. "After today, I guess that goes to hell."

"I told Sam I'd discussed what had happened in that room with you, that we'd talked about the murder and coming up there had upset you." He rose to fetch the pot and freshen her coffee. "The crew may mumble about overimaginative women, but that's all."

She shut her eyes. She hadn't expected sensitivity from him, much less understanding. "Thanks."

"It's your secret if you feel it's necessary to keep it, A.J."

"It's very necessary. How did you feel when you realized?" she demanded. "Uncomfortable? Uneasy? Even now, you're tiptoeing around me."

"Maybe I am." He started to pull out a cigarette, then shoved it back into the pack. "Yeah, it makes me uneasy. It's not something I've ever had to deal with before. A man has to wonder if he'll have any secrets from a woman who can look inside him."

"Of course." She rose, back straight. "And a man's entitled to protect himself. I appreciate what you've done, David. I'm sure my clothes are dry now. I'll change if you'll call me a cab."

"No." He was up and blocking her way before she could walk out of the kitchen.

"Don't make this any more difficult for me, or for yourself."

"Damned if I want to," he muttered, and found he'd already reached for her. "I can't seem to help it. You make me uneasy," he repeated. "You've made me uneasy all along. I still want you, Aurora. That's all that seems to matter at the moment."

"You'll think differently later."

He drew her closer. "Reading my mind?"

"Don't joke."

"Maybe it's time someone did. If you want to look into my head now, you'll see that all I can think about is taking you upstairs, to my bed."

Her heart began to beat, in her chest, in her throat. "And tomorrow?"

"The hell with tomorrow." He brought his lips down to hers with a violence that left her shaken. "The hell with everything but the fact that you and I have a need for each other. You're not going home tonight, Aurora."

She let herself go, let herself risk. "No, I'm not."

Chapter 7

There was moonlight, streaks of it, glimmering. She could smell the hyacinths, light and sweet, through the open windows. The murmur of a stream winding its way through the woods beside the house was quiet, soothing. Every muscle in A.J.'s body tensed as she stepped into David's bedroom.

The painting hung on the wall as she had known it would, vivid, sensual streaks on a white canvas. The first shudder rolled through her as she turned her head and saw her own vague reflection, not in a mirror, but in a tall glass door.

"I dreamed this." The words were barely audible as she took a step back. But was she stepping back into the dream or into reality? Were they somehow both the same? Panicked, she stood where she was. Didn't she have a choice? she asked herself. Was she just following a pattern already set, a pattern that had begun the moment David Brady had walked into her office?

"This isn't what I want," she whispered, and turned—for escape, for freedom—in denial, she couldn't have said. But he was there, blocking her way, drawing her closer, drawing her in just as she'd known he would be.

She looked up at him as she knew she had done before. His face was in shadows, as indistinct as hers had been in the glass. But his eyes were clear, highlighted by moonlight. His words were clear, highlighted by desire.

"You can't keep running, Aurora, not from yourself, not from me."

There was impatience in his voice, impatience that became all the sharper when his mouth closed over hers. He wanted, more desperately than he had allowed himself to believe. He needed, more intensely than he could afford to admit. Her uncertainty, her hesitation, aroused some deep, primitive part of him. Demand, take, possess. The thoughts twined together into one throbbing pulsebeat of desire. He didn't feel the pleasant anticipation he had with other women, but a rage, burning, almost violent. As he tasted the first hint of surrender, he nearly went mad with it.

His mouth was so hungry, his hands were so strong. The pressure of his body against hers was insistent. He held her as though she were his to take with or without consent. Yet she knew, had always known, the choice was ultimately hers. She could give or deny. Like a stone tossed into clear water, her decision now would send ripples flowing out into her life. Where they ended, how they altered the flow, couldn't be foretold. To give, she knew, was always a risk. And risk always held its own excitement, its own fear. With each second that passed, the pleasure grew more bold and ripe, until with a moan of acceptance, she brought her hands to his face and let herself go.

It was only passion, A.J. told herself while her body strained and ached. Passion followed no patterns, kept to no course. The need that grew inside her had nothing to do with dreams or hopes or wishes. It was her passion she couldn't resist, his passion she couldn't refuse. For tonight, this one night, she'd let herself be guided by it.

He knew the instant she was his. Her body didn't weaken, but strengthened. The surrender he'd expected became a hunger as urgent as his. There would be no slow seduction for either of them, no gentle persuasion. Desire was a razor's edge that promised as much pain as pleasure. They both understood it; they both acknowledged; they both accepted. Together they fell onto the bed and let the fire blaze.

His robe tangled around her. With an impatient oath, he yanked it down from her shoulder so that the tantalizing slope was exposed. His lips raced over her face, leaving hers unfulfilled while he stoked a line of heat down her throat. She felt the rasp of his cheek and moaned in approval. He sought to torment, he sought to dominate, but she met each move with equal strength. She felt the warm trace of his tongue and shivered in anticipation. Unwilling to leave the reins in his hands, she tugged at the buttons of his shirt, unfastening, tearing, until with her own patience ended, she ripped it from his back.

His flesh was taut under her palms, the muscles a tight ridge to be explored and exploited. Male, hard, strong. His scent wound its way into her senses, promising rough demands and frantic movement. She tasted furious demands, hot intentions, then her excitement bounded upward when she felt his first tremble. Painful, urgent, desperate needs poured from him into her.

It was what she wanted. As ruthless as he, she sought to drag him away from his control.

The bed was like a battlefield, full of fire and smoke and passions. The spread was soft, smooth, the air touched with spring, but it meant nothing to them. Warm flesh and sharp needs, rippling muscle and rough hands. That was their world. Her breath caught, not in fear, not in protest, but in excitement, as he pulled the robe down her body. When her arms were pinned she used her mouth as a weapon to drive him beyond reason. Her hips arched, pressing against him, tormenting, tempting, thrilling. As his hands moved over her, her strength seemed to double to race with her needs.

But here in this fuming, incendiary world there would be no winner and no loser. The fire sprinted along her skin, leaving dull, tingling aches wherever his hands or lips had touched. She wanted it, reveled in it, even while she burned for more. Not content to leave the control in his hands for long, A.J. rolled on top of him and began her own siege.

He'd never known a woman could make him shudder. He'd never known a woman could make him hurt from desire alone. She was long and limber and as ravenous as he. She was naked but not vulnerable. She was passionate but not pliant. He could see her in the moonlight, her hair pale and tumbled around her face, her skin glowing from exhilaration and needs not yet met. Her hands were soft as they raked over him, but demanding enough, bold enough, to take his breath away. The lips that followed them did nothing to soothe. She yanked his slacks down with a wild impatience that had his mind spinning and his body pounding. Then before he could react, she was sprawled across him, tasting his flesh.

It was madness. He welcomed it. It was torment. He could have begged for more. Once he'd thought he had discovered a simmering, latent passion in her, but nothing had prepared him for this. She was seduction, she was lust, she was greed. With both hands in her hair, he dragged her mouth to his so that he could taste them all.

It wasn't a dream, she thought dazedly as his mouth clung to hers and his hands again took possession. No dream had ever been so tempestuous. Reality had never been so mad. Tangled with her, he rolled her to her back. Even as she gasped for air, he plunged into her so that her body arched up, taut with the first uncontrollable climax. She reached up, too stunned to realize how badly she needed to hold on to him. Wrapped tight, their strengths fed each other as surely as their hungers did.

They lay together, weak, sated, both of them vanquished.

Gradually sanity returned. A.J. saw the moonlight again. His face was buried in her hair, but his breathing had steadied, as hers had. Her arms were still around him, her body locked tight to his. She told herself to let go, to reestablish distance, but lacked the will to obey.

It had only been passion, she reminded herself. It had only been need. Both had been satisfied. Now was the time to draw away, to move apart. But she wanted to nuzzle her cheek against his, to murmur something foolish and stay just as she was until the sun came up. With her eyes closed tight she fought the urge to soften, to give that which, once given, was lost.

No, he'd never known a woman could make him shudder. He'd never known a woman could make him weak. Yes, once he'd thought he'd discovered a simmering, latent passion in her, but he hadn't expected this. He shouldn't still feel so dazed. So involved.

He hadn't been prepared for the intensity of feeling. He hadn't planned on having the need grow and multiply even after it was satisfied. That was the reason he'd lost some part of himself to her. That was, had to be, the only reason.

But when she trembled, he drew her closer.

"Cold?"

"The air's cooled." It sounded reasonable. It sounded true. How could she explain that her body was still pumping with heat, and would be as long as he was there?

"I can shut the windows."

"No." She could hear the stream again, just smell the hyacinths. She didn't want to lose the sensations.

"Here, then." He drew away to untangle the sheets and pull them over her. It was then, in the dim light, that he noticed the pale line of smudges along her arm. Taking her elbow, he looked closer.

"Apparently I wasn't careful enough with you."

A.J. glanced down. There was regret in his voice, and a trace of a kindness she would have little defense against. If she hadn't been afraid, she would have longed to hear him speak just like that again, she would have rested her head on his shoulder. Instead, with a shrug she shifted and drew her arm away. "No permanent damage." She hoped. "I wouldn't be surprised if you found a few bruises on yourself."

He looked at her again and grinned in a way that was completely unexpected and totally charming. "It seems we both play rough."

It was too late to hold back a response to the grin. On impulse, A.J. leaned over and took a quick, none-too-gentle nip at his shoulder. "Complaining?"

She'd surprised him again. Maybe it was time for a

few surprises in his life. And in hers. "I won't if you won't." Then, in a move too abrupt to evade, he rolled over her again, pinning her arms above her head with one hand.

"Look, Brady—"

"I like the idea of going one-on-one with you, A.J." He lowered his head just enough to nibble on her earlobe, until she squirmed under him.

"As long as you have the advantage." Her voice was breathy, her cheeks flushed. With his hands on her wrists he could feel the gradual acceleration of her pulse. With his body stretched full length, he could feel the dips, the curves, the fluid lines of hers. Desire began to rise again as though it had never been quenched.

"Lady, I think I might enjoy taking advantage of you on a regular basis. I know I'm going to enjoy it for the rest of the night."

She twisted one way, twisted the other, then let out a hissing breath, as he only stared down at her. Being outdone physically was nearly as bad as being outdone intellectually. "I can't stay here tonight."

"You are here," he pointed out, then took his free hand in one long stroke from her hip to her breast.

"I can't stay."

"Why?"

Because reliving pent-up passion with him and spending the night with him were two entirely different things. "Because I have to work tomorrow," she began lamely. "And—"

"I'll drop you by your apartment in the morning so you can change." The tip of her breast was already hard against his palm. He ran his thumb over it and watched passion darken her eyes.

"I have to be in the office by eight-thirty."

"We'll get up early." He lowered his head to brush kisses at either side of her mouth. "I'm not planning on getting much sleep, anyway."

Her body was a mass of nerve endings waiting to be exploited. Exploitation led to weakness, she reminded herself. And weakness to losses. "I don't spend the night with men."

"You do with this one." He brought his hand up, tracing as he went until he cupped her throat.

If she was going to lose, she'd lose with her eyes open. "Why?"

He could have given her quiet, persuasive answers. And they might have been true. Perhaps that's why he chose another way. "We haven't nearly finished with each other yet, Aurora. Not nearly."

He was right. The need was screaming through her. That she could accept. But she wouldn't accept being pressured, being cajoled or being seduced. Her terms, A.J. told herself. Then she could justify this first concession. "Let go of my hands, Brady."

Her chin was angled, her eyes direct, her voice firm. She wasn't a woman, he decided, who could be anticipated. Lifting a brow, he released her hands and waited.

With her eyes on his, she brought them to his face. Slowly her lips curved. Whether it was challenge or surrender he didn't care. "I wouldn't plan to sleep at all tonight," she warned just before she pulled his mouth to hers.

The room was still dark when A.J. roused from a light doze to draw the covers closer. There was an ache, more pleasant than annoying, in her muscles. She stretched, then shifted to glance at the luminous dial of her clock. It wasn't there. With her mind fogged with sleep, she rubbed a hand over her eyes and looked again.

Of course it wasn't there, she remembered. She wasn't there. Her clock, her apartment and her own bed were miles away. Turning again, she saw that the bed beside her was empty. Where could he have gone? she wondered as she pushed herself up. And what time was it?

She'd lost time. Hours, days, weeks, it hadn't mattered. But now she was alone, and it was time for reality again.

They'd exhausted each other, depleted each other and fed each other. She hadn't known there could be anything like the night they'd shared. Nothing real had ever been so exciting, so wild or desperate. Yet it had been very real. Her body bore the marks his hands had made while he'd been lost in passion. His taste still lingered on her tongue, his scent on her skin. It had been real, but it hadn't been reality. Reality was now, when she had to face the morning.

What she'd given, she'd given freely. She would have no regrets there. If she'd broken one of her own rules, she'd done so consciously and with deliberation. Not coolly, perhaps, but not carelessly. Neither could she be careless now. The night was over.

Because there was nothing else, A.J. picked his robe up off the floor and slipped into it. The important thing was not to be foolish, but mature. She wouldn't cuddle and cling and pretend there had been anything more between them than sex. One night of passion and mutual need.

She turned her cheek into the collar of the robe and let it linger there for a moment where his scent had permeated the cloth. Then, securing the belt, she walked out of the bedroom and down the stairs.

The living room was in shadows, but the first tongues of light filtered through the wide glass windows. David stood there, looking out, while a fire, freshly kindled, crackled beside him. A.J. felt the distance between them was like a crater, deep, wide and jagged. It took her too long to remind herself that was what she'd expected and wanted. Rather than speak, she walked the rest of the way down the stairs and waited.

"I had the place built with this window facing east so I could watch the sun rise." He lifted a cigarette and drew deep so that the tip glowed in the half-light. "No matter how many times I see it, it's different."

She wouldn't have judged him as a man drawn to sunrises. She hadn't judged him as a man who would choose a secluded house in the hills. Just how much, A.J. wondered, did she know about the man she'd spent the night with? Thrusting her hands into the pockets of the robe, her fingers brushed cardboard. A.J. curled them around the matchbook he'd stuck in there and forgotten. "I don't take much time for sunrises."

"If I happen to be right here at the right time, I usually find I can handle whatever crises the day has planned a little better."

Her fingers closed and opened, opened and closed on the matchbook. "Are you expecting any particular crisis today?"

He turned then to look at her, standing barefoot and a bit hollow-eyed in his robe. It didn't dwarf her; she was only inches shorter than he. Still, somehow it made her appear more feminine, more...accessible, he decided, than anything else he remembered. It wouldn't be possible to tell her that it had just occurred to him that he was already in the middle of a crisis. Its name was Aurora J. Fields. "You know…" He tucked his hands in the back pockets of well-broken-in jeans before he took a step closer. "We didn't spend too much time talking last night."

"No." She braced herself. "It didn't seem that conversation was what either of us wanted." Nor was it conversation she'd prepared herself to deal with. "I'm going to go up and change. I do have to be in the office early."

"Aurora." He didn't reach out to stop her this time. He only had to speak. "What did you feel that first day with me in your office?"

After letting out a long breath, she faced him again. "David, I talked about that part of my life more than I cared to last night."

He knew that was true. He'd spent some time wondering why without finding any answers. She had them. If he had to probe and prod until she gave them up, he would. "You talked about it in connection with other people, other things. This happens to involve me."

"I'm going to be late for work," she murmured, and started up the landing.

"You make a habit of running away, Aurora."

"I'm not running." She whirled back, both hands clenched into fists in the pockets. "I simply don't see any reason to drag this all up again. It's personal. It's mine."

"And it touches me," he added calmly. "You walked into my bedroom last night and said you'd dreamed it. Had you?"

"I don't—" She wanted to deny it, but she had never been comfortable with direct lies. The fact that she couldn't use one had anger bubbling through.

"Yes. Dreams aren't as easily controlled as conscious thought."

"Tell me what you dreamed."

She wouldn't give him all. A.J.'s nails dug into her palms. She'd be damned if she'd give him all. "I dreamed about your room. I could have described it for you before I'd ever gone in. Would you like to put me under a microscope now or later?"

"Self-pity isn't attractive." As her breath hissed out he stepped onto the landing with her. "You knew we were going to be lovers."

Her expression became cool, almost disinterested. "Yes."

"And you knew that day in your office when you were angry with me, frustrated with your mother, and our hands met, like this." He reached out, uncurled her fist and pressed their hands palm to palm.

Her back was against the wall, her hand caught in his. She was tired, spitting tired, of finding herself in corners. "What are you trying to prove, a theory for your documentary?"

What would she say if he told her he'd come to understand she showed her fangs only when she was most vulnerable? "You knew," he repeated, letting the venom spill off of him. "And it frightened you. Why was that?"

"I'd just had a strong, physical premonition that I was going to be the lover of a man I'd already decided was detestable. Is that reason enough?"

"For annoyance, even anger. Not for fear. You were afraid that night in the back of the limo, and again last night when you walked into the bedroom."

She tried to jerk her arm aside. "You're exaggerating."

"Am I?" He stepped closer and touched a hand to her cheek. "You're afraid now."

"That's not true." Deliberately she unclenched her other hand. "I'm annoyed because you're pressing me. We're adults who spent the night together. That doesn't give you the right to pry into my personal life or feelings."

No, it didn't. That was his own primary rule and he was breaking it. Somehow he'd forgotten that he had no rights, could expect none. "All right, that's true. But I saw the condition you were in yesterday afternoon after walking into that room."

"That's done," she said quickly, maybe too quickly. "There's no need to get into it again."

Though he was far from convinced, he let it ride. "And I listened to you last night. I don't want to be responsible for anything like that happening to you again."

"You're not responsible—I am." Her voice was calmer now. Emotions clouded things. She'd spent years discovering that. "You don't cause anything, I do, or if you like, circumstances do. David, I'm twenty-eight, and I've managed to survive this—something extra all my life."

"I understand that. You should understand that I'm thirty-six. I haven't been personally exposed to any of this up until a few weeks ago."

"I do understand." Her voice chilled, just a little. "And I understand the natural reaction is to be wary, curious or skeptical. The same way one looks at a sideshow in the circus."

"Don't put words in my mouth." His anger came as a surprise to both of them. So much of a surprise, that when he grabbed A.J. by the shoulders, she offered no protest at all. "I can't help what reaction other people have had to you. They weren't me. Damn it, I've just spent the night making love to you and I don't even know who you are. I'm afraid to touch you, thinking I might set something off. I can't keep my hands off you. I came down here this morning because if I'd lain beside you another minute I'd have taken you again while you were half-asleep."

Before she'd had a chance to weigh her own reaction, she lifted her hands up to his. "I don't know what you want."

"Neither do I." He caught himself and relaxed his grip on her. "And that's a first. Maybe I need some time to figure it out."

Time. Distance. She reminded herself that was for the best. With a nod, she dropped her hands again. "That's reasonable."

"But what isn't is that I don't want to spend that time away from you."

Chills, anxiety or excitement, rushed up her spine. "David, I—"

"I've never had a night like the one I had with you."

The weakness came quickly, to be just as quickly fought back. "You don't have to say that."

"I know I don't." With a half laugh he rubbed his hands over the shoulders he'd just clenched. "In fact, it isn't very easy to admit it. It just happens to be true, for me. Sit down a minute." He drew her down to sit on the step beside him. "I didn't have a lot of time to think last night because I was too busy being…stunned," he decided. She didn't relax when he put his arm around her, but she didn't draw away. "I've packed a lot of thinking into the past hour. There's more to you, A.J., than there is to a lot of other women. Even without the something extra. I think what I want is to have a chance to get to know the woman I intend to spend a lot of time making love with."

She turned to look at him. His face was close, his arm more gentle than she'd come to expect. He didn't look like a man who had any gentleness in him, only power and confidence. "You're taking a lot for granted."

"Yeah, I am."

"I don't think you should."

"Maybe not. I want you—you want me. We can start with that."

That was simpler. "No promises."

The protest sprang to his mind so quickly it stunned him. "No promises," he agreed, reminding himself that had always been rule number two.

She knew she shouldn't agree. The smart thing, the safe thing to do, was to cut things off now. One night, passion only. But she found herself relaxing against him. "Business and personal relationships completely separate."

"Absolutely."

"And when one of us becomes uncomfortable with the way things are going, we back off with no scenes or bad feelings."

"Agreed. Want it in writing?"

Her lips curved slightly as she studied him. "I should. Producers are notoriously untrustworthy."

"Agents are notoriously cynical."

"Cautious," she corrected, but lifted a hand to rub it along the stubble on his cheek. "We're paid to be the bad guys, after all. And speaking of which, we never finished discussing Clarissa."

"It isn't business hours," he reminded her, then turned her hand palm up and pressed his lips to it.

"Don't try to change the subject. We need to iron this out. Today."

"Between nine and five," he agreed.

"Fine, call my office and… Oh, my God."

"What?"

"My messages." Dragging both hands through her hair, she sprang up. "I never called in for my messages."

"Sounds like a national emergency," he murmured as he stood beside her.

"I was barely in the office two hours. As it was I had to reschedule appointments. Where's the phone?"

"Make it worth my while."

"David, I'm not joking."

"Neither am I." Smiling down at her, he slipped his hand into the opening of the robe and parted it. She felt her legs liquefy from the knees down.

"David." She turned her head to avoid his lips, then found herself in deeper trouble, as her throat was undefended. "It'll only take me a minute."

"You're wrong." He unfastened the belt. "It's going to take longer than that."

"For all I know I might have a breakfast meeting."

"For all you know you don't have an appointment until noon." Her hands were moving down his back, under his shirt. He wondered if she was aware. "What we both know is that we should make love. Right now."

"After," she began, but sighed against his lips.

"Before."

The robe fell to the floor at her feet. Negotiations ended.

Chapter 8

A.J. should have been satisfied. She should have been relaxed. In the ten days following her first night with David, their relationship had run smoothly. When her schedule and his allowed, they spent the evening together. There were simple evenings walking the beach, elegant evenings dining out and quiet evenings dining in. The passion that had pulled them together didn't fade. Rather, it built and intensified, driving them to quench it. He wanted her, as completely, as desperately, as a man could want a woman. Of the multitude of things she was uncertain of, she could be absolutely certain of that.

She should have been relaxed. She was tied up in knots.

Each day she had to rebuild a defense that had always been like a second skin. Each night David ripped it away again. She couldn't afford to leave her emotions unprotected in what was, by her own description, a casual, physical affair. They would continue seeing each other as long as both of them enjoyed it. No promises, no commitments. When he decided to pull away, she needed to be ready.

It was, she discovered, like waiting for the other shoe to drop. He would undoubtedly break things off sooner or later. Passions that flamed too hot were bound to burn themselves out, and they had little else. He read thick, socially significant novels and informative nonfiction. A.J. leaned toward slim, gory mysteries and glitzy bestsellers. He took her to a foreign film festival full of symbolism and subtitles. She'd have chosen the Gene Kelly–Judy Garland classic on late-night TV.

The more they got to know each other, the more distance A.J. saw. Passion was the magnet that drew them together, but she was very aware its power would fade. For her own survival, she intended to be prepared when it did.

On a business level she had to be just as prepared to deal with David Brady, producer. A.J. was grateful that in this particular relationship she knew every step and every angle. After listening to David's ideas for expanding Clarissa's role in the documentary, she'd agreed to the extra shoots. For a price. It hadn't been money she'd wanted to wheedle out of him, but the promise of promotion for Clarissa's next book, due out in midsummer.

It had taken two days of heated negotiations, tossing the ball back and forth, refusals, agreements and compromises. Clarissa would have her promotion directly on the program, and a review on *Book Talk*, the intellectual PBS weekly. David would have his extra studio shoots and his interview with Clarissa and Alice Van

Camp. Both had walked away from the negotiating table smug that they had outdone the other.

Clarissa couldn't have cared less. She was busy with her plants, her recipes and, to A.J.'s mounting dismay, her wedding plans. She took the news of the promotions A.J. had sweated for with an absent "That's nice, dear," and wondered out loud if she should bake the wedding cake herself.

"Momma, a review on *Book Talk* isn't just nice." A.J. swung into the studio parking lot frustrated from the forty-minute drive during which she and Clarissa had talked at cross purposes.

"Oh, I'm sure it's going to be lovely. The publisher said they were sending advance copies. Aurora, do you think a garden wedding would be suitable? I'm afraid my azaleas might fade."

Brows lowered, she swung into a parking spot. "How many advance copies?"

"Oh, I'm really not sure. I probably wrote it down somewhere. And then it might rain. The weather's so unpredictable in June."

"Make sure they send at least three. One for the—June?" Her foot slipped off the clutch, so that the car bucked to a halt. "But that's next month."

"Yes, and I have dozens of things to do. Just dozens."

A.J.'s hands were very still on the wheel as she turned. "But didn't you say something about a fall wedding?"

"I suppose I did. You know my mums are at their best in October, but Alex is…" She flushed and cleared her throat. "A bit impatient. Aurora, I know I don't drive, but I think you've left your key on."

Muttering, she pulled it out. "Momma, you're talking about marrying a man you'll have known for less than two months."

"Do you really think time's so important?" she asked with a sweet smile. "It's more a matter of feelings."

"Feelings can change." She thought of David, of herself.

"There aren't any guarantees in life, darling." Clarissa reached over to cover her daughter's hand with her own. "Not even for people like you and me."

"That's what worries me." She was going to talk to Alex Marshall, A.J. promised herself as she pushed her door open. Her mother was acting like a teenager going steady with the football hero. Someone had to be sensible.

"You really don't have to worry," Clarissa told her as she stepped onto the curb. "I know what I'm doing— really, I do. But talk to Alex by all means."

"Momma." With a long sigh, A.J. linked arms. "I do have to worry. And mind reading's not allowed."

"I hardly have to when it's written all over your face. Is my hair all right?"

A.J. turned to kiss her cheek. "You look beautiful."

"Oh, I hope so." Clarissa gave a nervous laugh as they approached the studio doors. "I'm afraid I've become very vain lately. But Alex is such a handsome man, isn't he?"

"Yes," A.J. agreed cautiously. He was handsome, polished smooth and personable. She wouldn't be satisfied until she found the flaws.

"Clarissa." They'd hardly stepped inside, when Alex came striding down the hall. He looked like a man approaching a lost and valued treasure. "You look beautiful."

He had both of Clarissa's hands and looked to A.J.

as though he would scoop her mother up and carry her off. "Mr. Marshall." She kept her voice cool and deliberately extended her own hand.

"Ms. Fields." With obvious reluctance, he released one of Clarissa's hands to take A.J.'s. "I have to say you're more dedicated than my own agent. I was hoping to bring Clarissa down myself today."

"Oh, she likes to fuss," Clarissa put in, hoping to mollify them both. "And I'm afraid I'm so scatterbrained she has to remind me of all the little things about television interviews."

"Just relax," A.J. told her. "I'll go see if everything's set." Checking her watch as she went, she reached out to push open the thick studio doors, when David walked through.

"Good morning, Ms. Fields." The formal greeting was accompanied by the trail of his fingers over her wrist. "Sitting in again today?"

"Looking after my client, Brady. She's..." When she glanced casually over her shoulder, the words slipped back down her throat. There in the middle of the hallway was her mother caught up in a close and very passionate embrace. Stunned, she stared while dozens of feelings she couldn't identify ran through her.

"Your client appears to be well looked after," David murmured. When she didn't reply, he pulled her into a room off the hall. "Want to sit down?"

"No. No, I should—"

"Mind your own business."

Anger replaced shock very quickly. "She happens to be my mother."

"That's right." He walked to a coffee machine and poured two plastic cups. "Not your ward."

"I'm not going to stand by while she, while she—"

"Enjoys herself?" he suggested, and handed her the coffee.

"She isn't thinking." A.J. downed half the coffee in one swallow. "She's just riding on emotion, infatuation. And she's—"

"In love."

A.J. drank the rest of the coffee, then heaved the cup in the direction of the trash. "I hate it when you interrupt me."

"I know." And he grinned at her. "Why don't we have a quiet evening tonight, at your place? We can start making love in the living room, work our way through to the bedroom and back out again."

"David, Clarissa is my mother and I'm very concerned about her. I should—"

"Be more concerned with yourself." He had his hands on her hips. "And me." They slid firm and strong up her back. "You should be very concerned with me."

"I want you to—"

"I'm becoming an expert on what you want." His mouth brushed hers, retreated, then brushed again. "Do you know your breath starts trembling whenever I do that." His voice lowered, seductive, persuading. "Then your body begins to tremble."

Weak, weaker than she should have been, she lifted both hands to his chest. "David, we have an agreement. It's business hours."

"Sue me." He kissed her again, tempting, teasing as he slipped his hands under her jacket. "What are you wearing under here, A.J.?"

"Nothing important." She caught herself swaying forward. "David, I mean it. We agreed." His tongue traced her bottom lip. "No mixing—ah—no mixing business and...oh, damn." She forgot business and agreements and responsibilities, dragging his mouth to hers.

They filled her, those wild, wanton cravings only he could bring. They tore at her, the needs, the longings, the wishes she knew could never be met. In a moment of abandon she tossed aside what should be and groped blindly for what might be.

His mouth was as hard, as ravenous, as if it were the first time. Desire hadn't faded. His hands were as strong, as possessive and demanding, as ever. Passion hadn't dimmed. It didn't matter that the room was small and smelled of old coffee and stale cigarettes. Their senses were tangled around each other. Perfume was strong and sweet; tastes were dark and exotic.

Her arms were around his neck; her fingers were raking through his hair. Her mouth was hungry and open on his.

"Oh, excuse me." Clarissa stood in the doorway, eyes lowered as she cleared her throat. It wouldn't do to look too pleased, she knew. Just as it wouldn't be wise to mention that the vibrations bouncing around in the little room might have melted lead. "I thought you'd like to know they're ready for me."

Fumbling for dignity, A.J. tugged at her jacket. "Good. I'll be right in." She waited until the door shut, then swore pungently.

"You're even," David said lightly. "You caught her— she caught you."

Her eyes, when they met his, were hot enough to sear off a layer of skin. "It's not a joke."

"Do you know one thing I've discovered about you these past few days, A.J.? You take yourself too seriously."

"Maybe I do." She scooped her purse from the sofa,

then stood there nervously working the clasp. "But has it occurred to you what would have happened if a member of the crew had opened that door?"

"They'd have seen their producer kissing a very attractive woman."

"They would have seen you kissing me during a shoot. That's totally unprofessional. Before the first coffee break, everyone in the studio would be passing around the gossip."

"So?"

"So?" Exasperated, she could only stare at him. "David, that's precisely what we agreed we didn't want. We don't want your crew or our associates speculating and gossiping about our personal relationship."

Brow lifted, eyes narrowed attentively, he listened. "I don't recall discussing that in detail."

"Of course we did." She tucked her purse under her arm, then wished she still had something in her hands. "Right at the beginning."

"As I recall, the idea was to keep our personal and professional lives separate."

"That's just what I've said."

"I didn't take that to mean you wanted to keep the fact that we're lovers a secret."

"I don't want an ad in *Variety*."

He stuck his hands in his pockets. He couldn't have said why he was angry, only that he was. "You don't leave much middle ground, do you?"

She opened her mouth to spit at him, then subsided. "I guess not." On a long breath, she took a step forward. "I want to avoid the speculation, just as I want to avoid the looks of sympathy when things change."

It didn't require telepathy to understand that she'd been waiting for the change—no, he corrected, for the end—since the beginning. Knowledge brought an unexpected, and very unwelcome, twinge of pain. "I see. All right, then, we'll try it your way." He walked to the door and held it open. "Let's go punch in."

No, he couldn't have said why he was angry. In fact, he knew he shouldn't have been. A.J.'s ground rules were logical, and if anything, they made things easier for him. Or should have made things easier for him. She made absolutely no demands and accepted none. In other relationships he'd insisted on the same thing. She refused to allow emotions to interfere with her business or his. In the past he'd felt precisely the same way.

The problem was, he didn't feel that way now.

As the shoot ground to a halt because of two defective bulbs David reminded himself it was his problem. Once he accepted that, he could work on the solution. One was to go along with the terms. The other was to change them.

David watched A.J. cross the room toward Alex. Her stride was brisk, her eyes were cool. In the conservative suit she looked like precisely what she was—a successful businesswoman who knew where she was going and how to get there. He remembered the way she looked when they made love—slim, glowing and as dangerous as a neutron bomb.

David took out a cigarette then struck a match with a kind of restrained violence. He was going to have to plan out solution number two.

"Mr. Marshall." A.J. had her speech prepared and her determination at its peak. With a friendly enough smile, she interrupted Alex's conversation with one of the grips. "Could I speak with you for a minute?"

"Of course." Because he'd been expecting it, Alex

took her arm in his innate old-style manner. "Looks like we'll have time for a cup of coffee."

Together they walked back to the room where A.J. had stood with David a few hours before. This time she poured the coffee and offered the cup. But before she could start the prologue for the speech she'd been rehearsing, Alex began.

"You want to talk about Clarissa." He pulled out one of his cigars, then held it out. "Do you mind?"

"No, go ahead. Actually, Mr. Marshall, I would very much like to talk to you about Clarissa."

"She told me you were uneasy about our marriage plans." He puffed comfortably on his cigar until he was satisfied it was well started. "I admit that puzzled me a bit, until she explained that besides being her agent, you happen to be her daughter. Shall we sit down?"

A.J. frowned at the sofa, then at him. It wasn't going at all according to plan. She took her place on one end, while he settled himself on the other. "I'm glad that Clarissa explained things to you. It simplifies things. You'll understand now why I'm concerned. My mother is very important to me."

"And to me." As he leaned back, A.J. studied his profile. It wasn't difficult to see why her mother was infatuated. "You of all people can understand just how easy Clarissa is to love."

"Yes." A.J. sipped at her coffee. What was it she'd planned to say? Taking a deep breath, she moved back on track. "Clarissa is a wonderfully warm and very special person. The thing is, you've known each other for such a short time."

"It only took five minutes." He said it so simply, A.J. was left fumbling for words. "Ms. Fields," he continued, then smiled at her. "A.J.," he corrected. "It doesn't seem right for me to call you 'Ms. Fields.' After all, I'm going to be your stepfather."

Stepfather? Somehow that angle had bypassed her. She sat, coffee cup halfway to her lips, and stared at him.

"I have a son your age," he began again. "And a daughter not far behind. I think I understand some of what you're feeling."

"It's, ah, it's not a matter of my feelings."

"Of course it is. You're as precious to Clarissa as my children are to me. Clarissa and I will be married, but she'd be happier if you were pleased about it."

A.J. frowned at her coffee, then set it down. "I don't know what to say. I thought I did. Mr. Marshall, Alex, you've been a journalist for over a quarter of a century. You've traveled all over the world, seen incredible things. Clarissa, for all her abilities, all her insights, is a very simple woman."

"An amazingly comfortable woman, especially for a man who's lived on the edge, perhaps too long. I had thought of retiring." He laughed then, but comfortably, as he remembered his own shock when Clarissa had held his hand and commented on it. "That wasn't something I'd discussed with anyone, not even my own children. I'd been looking for something more, something other than deadlines and breaking stories. In a matter of hours after being with Clarissa, I knew she was what I'd been looking for. I want to spend the rest of my life with her."

A.J. sat in silence, looking down at her hands. What more could a woman ask for, she wondered, than for a man to love her with such straightforward devotion? Couldn't a woman consider herself fortunate to have a man who accepted who she was, what she was, and loved her because of it, not in spite of?

Some of the tension dissolved and as she looked up at him she was able to smile. "Alex, has my mother fixed you dinner?"

"Why, yes." Though his tone was very sober, she caught, and appreciated, the gleam in his eyes. "Several times. In fact, she told me she's left a pot of spaghetti sauce simmering for tonight. I find Clarissa's cooking as—unique as she is."

With a laugh, A.J. held out her hand again. "I think Momma hit the jackpot." He took her hand, then surprised her by leaning over to kiss her cheek.

"Thank you."

"Don't hurt her," A.J. whispered. She clung to his hand a moment, then composing herself rose. "We'd better get back. She'll wonder where we are."

"Being Clarissa, I'm sure she has a pretty good idea."

"That doesn't bother you?" She stopped by the door to look up at him again. "The fact that she's a sensitive?"

"Why should it? That's part of what makes Clarissa who she is."

"Yes." She tried not to think of herself, but didn't bite back the sigh in time. "Yes, it is."

When they walked back into the studio Clarissa looked over immediately. It only took a moment before she smiled. In an old habit, A.J. kissed both her cheeks. "There is one thing I have to insist on," she began without preamble.

"What is it?"

"That I give you the wedding."

Pleasure bloomed on Clarissa's cheeks even as she protested. "Oh, darling, how sweet, but it's too much trouble."

"It certainly is for a bride. You pick out your wedding dress and your trousseau and worry about looking terrific. I'll handle the rest." She kissed her again. "Please."

"If you really want to."

"I really want to. Give me a guest list and I'll handle the details. That's what I'm best at. I think they want you." She gave Clarissa a last quick squeeze before urging her back on set. A.J. took her place in the background.

"Feeling better?" David murmured as he came up beside her.

"Some." She couldn't admit to him that she felt weepy and displaced. "As soon as the shoot's finished, I start making wedding plans."

"Tomorrow's soon enough." When she sent him a puzzled look, he only smiled. "I intend to keep you busy this evening."

He was a man of his word. A.J. had barely arrived home, shed her jacket and opened the phone book to Caterers, when the bell rang. Taking the book with her, she went to answer. "David." She hooked her finger in the page so as not to lose her place. "You told me you had some things to do."

"I did them. What time is it?"

"It's quarter to seven. I didn't think you'd be by until around eight."

"Well after business hours, then." He toyed with, then loosened the top button of her blouse.

She had to smile. "Well after."

"And if you don't answer your phone, your service will pick it up after four rings?"

"Six. But I'm not expecting any calls." She stepped closer to slide her arms up his chest. "Hungry?"

"Yeah." He tested himself, seeing how long he could hold her at arm's length. It appeared to be just over thirty seconds.

"There's nothing in the kitchen except a frozen fish dinner." She closed her eyes as his lips skimmed over her jaw.

"Then we'll have to find another way to satisfy the appetite." He unhooked her skirt and, as it fell to the floor, drew his hands down her hips.

She yanked his sweater over his head and tossed it aside. "I'm sure we'll manage."

His muscles were tight as she ran her hands over him. Taut, tense all the way from his neck to his waist. With her blouse half-open, her legs clad in sheer stockings that stopped just at her thighs, A.J. pressed against him. She wanted to make him burn with just the thought of loving her. Then she was gasping for air, her fingers digging into his back as his hands took quick and complete possession.

When her legs buckled and she went limp against him, he didn't relent. For hours and hours he'd held back, watching her sit primly in the back of the studio, looking at her make her precise notes in her book. Now he had her, alone, hot, moist and, for the first time in their lovemaking, weak.

Holding her close, he slid with her to the floor.

Unprepared, she was helpless against a riot of sensation. He took her on a desperate ride, driving her up where the air was thin, plunging her down where it was heavy and dark. She tried to cling to him but lacked the strength.

She trembled for him. That alone was enough to drive him mad. His name came helplessly through her lips. He wanted to hear it, again and again, over and over. He wanted to know she thought of nothing else. And when he pulled the remaining clothes from both of them, when he entered her with a violence neither of them could fight, he knew he thought of nothing but her.

She shuddered again and again, but he held himself back from ultimate release. Even as he drove into her, his hands continued to roam, bringing unspeakable pleasures to every inch of her body. The carpet was soft at her back, but even when her fingers curled into it she could only feel the hard thrust of her lover. She heard him say her name, once, then twice, until her eyes fluttered open. His body rose above hers, taut with muscle, gleaming from passion. His breath was heaving even as hers was. She heard it, then tasted it when his mouth crushed down to devour. Then she heard nothing but her own sobbing moan as they emptied themselves.

"I like you naked." When he'd recovered enough, David propped himself on his elbow and took a long, long look. "But I have to admit, I'm fascinated by those little stockings you wear that stop right about here." To demonstrate, he ran his fingertip along her upper thigh.

Still dazed, A.J. merely moved against his touch. "They're very practical."

With a muffled laugh, he nuzzled the side of her neck. "Yes, that's what fascinates me. Your practicality."

She opened her eyes but kept them narrowed. "That's not what I meant." Because she felt too good to make an issue of it, she curled into him.

It was one of the things that charmed him most. David wondered if he told her how soft, how warm and open to affection she was after loving, if she would pull back. Instead he held her close, stroking and pleasing them both. When he caught himself half dozing, he pulled her up.

"Come on, let's have a shower before dinner."

"A shower?" She let her head rest on his shoulder. "Why don't we just go to bed?"

"Insatiable," he decided, and scooped her up.

"David, you can't carry me."

"Why not?"

"Because." She groped. "Because it's silly."

"I always feel silly carrying naked women." In the bathroom, he stood her on her feet.

"I suppose you make a habit of it," she commented dryly, and turned on the taps with a hard twist.

"I have been trying to cut down." Smiling, he pulled her into the shower with him so that the water rained over her face.

"My hair!" She reached up once, ineffectually, to block the flow, then stopped to glare at him.

"What about it?"

"Never mind." Resigned, she picked up the soap and began to rub it lazily over her body as she watched him. "You seem very cheerful tonight. I thought you were annoyed with me this morning."

"Did you?" He'd given some thought to strangling her. "Why would I be?" He took the soap from her and began to do the job himself.

"When we were talking…" The soap was warm and slick, his touch very thorough. "It doesn't matter. I'm glad you came by."

That was more than he'd come to expect from her. "Really?"

She smiled, then wrapped her arms around him and kissed him under the hot, steamy spray. "Yes, really. I like you, David. When you're not being a producer."

That, too, was more than he'd come to expect from her. And less than he was beginning to need. "I like you, Aurora. When you're not being an agent."

When she stepped out of the shower and reached for towels, she heard the bell ring again. "Damn." She gripped a towel at her breasts.

"I'll get it." David hooked a towel at his hips and strode out before A.J. could protest. She let out a huff of breath and snatched the robe from its hook on the door. If it was someone from the office, she'd have a lovely time explaining why David Brady, producer, was answering her door in a towel. She decided discretion was the better part of valor and stayed where she was.

Then she remembered the clothes. She closed her eyes on a moan as she imagined the carelessly strewn articles on her living room floor. Bracing herself, she walked down the hall back into the living room.

There was candlelight. On the ebony table she kept by the window, candles were already burning in silver holders on a white cloth. She saw the gleam of china, the sparkle of crystal, and stood where she was as David signed a paper handed to him by a man in a black suit.

"I hope everything is satisfactory, Mr. Brady."

"I'm sure it will be."

"We will, of course, be back for pickup at your convenience." With a bow to David, then another to A.J., he let himself out the door.

"David…" A.J. walked forward as if she weren't sure of her steps. "What is this?"

He lifted a silver cover from a plate. "It's coq au vin."

"But how did you—"

"I ordered it for eight o'clock." He checked his watch before he walked over to retrieve his pants. "They're very prompt." With the ease of a totally unselfconscious man, he dropped the towel and drew on his slacks.

She took another few steps toward the table. "It's lovely. Really lovely." There was a single rose in a vase. Moved, she reached out to touch it, then immediately brought her hand back to link it with her other. "I never expected anything like this."

He drew his sweater back over his head. "You said once you enjoyed being pampered." She looked stunned, he realized. Had he been so unromantic? A little uncertain, he walked to her. "Maybe I enjoy doing the pampering now and then."

She looked over, but her throat was closed and her eyes were filling. "I'll get dressed."

"No." Her back was to him now, but he took her by the shoulders. "No, you look fine."

She struggled with herself, pressing her lips together until she thought she could speak. "I'll just be a minute." But he was turning her around. His brows were already knit together before he saw her face.

"What's this?" He lifted a fingertip and touched a tear that clung to her lashes.

"It's nothing. I—I feel foolish. Just give me a minute."

He brushed another tear away with his thumb. "No, I don't think I should." He'd seen her weep before, but that had been a torrent. There was something soft in these tears, something incredibly sweet that drew him. "Do you always cry when a man offers you a quiet dinner?"

"No, of course not. It's just—I never expected you to do anything like this."

He brought her hand to his lips and smiled as he

kissed her fingers. "Just because I'm a producer doesn't mean I can't have some class."

"That's not what I meant." She looked up at him, smiling down at her, her hands still close to his lips. She was losing. A.J. felt her heart weaken, her will weaken and her wishes grow. "That's not what I meant," she said again in a whisper, and tightened her fingers on his. "David, don't make me want too much."

It was what he thought he understood. If you wanted too much, you fell too hard. He'd avoided the same thing, maybe for the same reasons, until one late afternoon on a beach. "Do you really think either of us can stop now?"

She thought of how many times she'd been rejected, easily, coolly, nervously. Friendship, affection, love could be turned off by some as quickly as a faucet. He wanted her now, A.J. reminded herself. He cared now. It had to be enough. She touched a hand to his cheek.

"Maybe tonight we won't think at all."

Chapter 9

"**I**tem fifteen, clause B. I find the wording here too vague. As we discussed, my client feels very strongly about her rights and responsibilities as a new mother. The nanny will accompany the child to the set, at my client's expense. However, she will require regular breaks in order to feed the infant. The trailer provided by you must be equipped with a portable crib and...'" For the third time during her dictation, A.J. lost her train of thought.

"Diapers?" Diane suggested.

"What?" A.J. turned from the window to look at her secretary.

"Just trying to help. Want me to read it back to you?"

"Yes, please."

While Diane read the words back, A.J. frowned down at the contract in her hand. "'And a playpen,'" A.J. finished, and managed to smile at her secretary. "I've never seen anyone so wrapped up in motherhood."

"Doesn't fit her image, does it? She always plays the heartless sex bomb."

"This little movie of the week should change that. Okay, finish it up with 'Once the above changes are made, the contract will be passed along to my client for signing.'"

"Do you want this out today?"

"Hmm?"

"Today, A.J.?" With a puzzled smile, Diane studied her employer. "You want the letter to go right out?"

"Oh. Yes, yes, it'd better go out." She checked her watch. "I'm sorry, Diane, it's nearly five. I hadn't realized."

"No problem." Closing her notebook, Diane rose. "You seem a little distracted today. Big plans for the holiday weekend?"

"Holiday?"

"Memorial Day weekend, A.J." With a shake of her head, Diane tucked her pencil behind her ear. "You know, three days off, the first weekend of summer. Sand, surf, sun."

"No." She began rearranging the papers on her desk. "I don't have any plans." Shaking off the mood, she looked up again. Distracted? What she was was a mess. She was bogged down in work she couldn't concentrate on, tied up in knots she couldn't loosen. With a shake of her head, she glanced at Diane again and remembered there were other people in the world beside herself. "I'm sure you do. Let the letter wait. There's no mail delivery Monday, anyway. We'll send it over by messenger Tuesday."

"As a matter of fact, I do have an interesting three days planned." Diane gave her own watch a check. "And he's picking me up in an hour."

"Go home." A.J. waved her off as she shuffled through papers. "Don't get sunburned."

"A.J.—" Diane paused at the door and grinned "—I don't plan to see the sun for three full days."

When the door shut, A.J. slipped off her glasses and rubbed at the bridge of her nose. What was wrong with her? She couldn't seem to concentrate for more than five minutes at a stretch before her attention started wandering.

Overwork? she wondered as she looked down at the papers in her hand. That was an evasion; she thrived on overwork. She wasn't sleeping well. She was sleeping alone. One had virtually nothing to do with the other, A.J. assured herself as she unstacked and restacked papers. She was too much her own person to moon around because David Brady had been out of town for a few days.

But she did miss him. She picked up a pencil to work, then ended up merely running it through her fingers. There wasn't any crime in missing him, was there? It wasn't as though she were dependent on him. She'd just gotten used to his company. Wouldn't he be smug and self-satisfied to know that she'd spent half her waking hours thinking about him? Disgusted with herself, A.J. began to work in earnest. For two minutes.

It was his fault, she thought as she tossed the pencil down again. That extravagantly romantic dinner for two, then that silly little bouquet of daisies he'd sent the day he'd left for Chicago. Though she tried not to, she reached out and stroked the petals that sat cheerful and out of place on her desk. He was trying to make a giddy, romantic fool out of her—and he was succeeding.

It just had to stop. A.J. adjusted her glasses, picked up her pencil and began to work again. She wasn't going to give David Brady another thought. When the knock sounded at her door a few moments later, she was staring into space. She blinked herself out of the daydream, swore, then called out. "Come in."

"Don't you ever quit?" Abe asked her when he stuck his head in the door.

Quit? She'd barely made a dent. "I've got a couple of loose ends. Abe, the Forrester contract comes up for renewal the first of July. I think we should start prodding. His fan mail was two to one last season, so—"

"First thing Tuesday morning I'll put the squeeze on. Right now I have to go marinate."

"I beg your pardon?"

"Big barbecue this weekend," Abe told her with a wink. "It's the only time my wife lets me cook. Want me to put a steak on for you?"

She smiled, grateful that he'd brought simpler things to her mind. Hickory smoke, freshly cut grass, burned meat. "No, thanks. The memory of the last one's a little close."

"The butcher gave me bad quality meat." He hitched up his belt and thought about spending the whole weekend in bathing trunks.

"That's what they all say. Have a good holiday, Abe. Just be prepared to squeeze hard on Tuesday."

"No problem. Want me to lock up?"

"No, I'll just be a few more minutes."

"If you change your mind about that steak, just come by."

"Thanks." Alone again, A.J. turned her concentration back to her work. She heard the sounds of her staff leaving for the day. Doors closing, scattered laughter.

David stood in the doorway and watched her. The rest of her staff was pouring out of the door as fast as they could, but she sat, calm and efficient, behind her desk. The fatigue that had had him half dozing on the plane washed away. Her hair was tidy, her suit jacket trim and smooth over her shoulders. She held the pencil in long, ringless fingers and wrote in quick, static bursts. The daisies he'd sent her days before sat in a squat vase on her desk. It was the first, the only unbusinesslike accent he'd ever seen in her office. Seeing them made him smile. Seeing her made him want.

He could see himself taking her there in her prim, organized office. He could peel that tailored, successful suit from her and find something soft and lacy beneath. With the door locked and traffic rushing by far below, he could make love with her until all the needs, all the fantasies, that had built in the days he'd been away were satisfied.

A.J. continued to write, forcing her concentration back each time it threatened to ebb. It wasn't right, she told herself, that her system would start to churn this way for no reason. The dry facts and figures she was reading shouldn't leave room for hot imagination. She rubbed the back of her neck, annoyed that tension was building there out of nothing. She would have sworn she could feel passion in the air. But that was ridiculous.

Then she knew. As surely as if he'd spoken, as surely as if he'd already touched her. Slowly, her hand damp on the pencil, she looked up.

There was no surprise in her eyes. It should have made him uneasy that she'd sensed him there when he'd made no sound, no movement. The fact that it didn't was something he would think of later. Now he could only think of how cool and proper she looked behind the desk. Of how wild and wanton she was in his arms.

She wanted to laugh, to spring up from the desk and

rush across the room. She wanted to be held close and swung in dizzying circles while the pleasure of just seeing him again soared through her. Of course she couldn't. That would be foolish. Instead she lifted a brow and set her pencil on her blotter. "So you're back."

"Yeah. I had a feeling I'd find you here." He wanted to drag her up from her chair and hold her. Just hold her. He dipped his hands into his pockets and leaned against the jamb.

"A feeling?" This time she smiled. "Precognition or telepathy?"

"Logic." He smiled, too, then walked toward the desk. "You look good, Fields. Real good."

Leaning back in her chair, she gave herself the pleasure of a thorough study. "You look a little tired. Rough trip?"

"Long." He plucked a daisy from the vase and spun it by the stem. "But it should be the last one before we wrap." Watching her, he came around the desk, then, resting a hip on it, leaned over and tucked the daisy behind her ear. "Got any plans for tonight?"

If she'd had any, she would have tossed them out the window and forgotten them. With her tongue caught in her teeth, A.J. made a business out of checking her desk calender. "No."

"Tomorrow?"

She flipped the page over. "Doesn't look like it."

"Sunday?"

"Even agents need a day of rest."

"Monday?"

She flipped the next page and shrugged. "Offices are closed. I thought I'd spend the day reading over some scripts and doing my nails."

"Uh-huh. In case you hadn't noticed, office hours are over."

Her heart was drumming. Already. Her blood was warming. So soon. "I'd noticed."

In silence he held out his hand. After only a slight hesitation, A.J. put hers into it and let him draw her up. "Come home with me."

He'd asked her before, and she'd refused. Looking at him now, she knew the days of refusal were long past. Reaching down, she gathered her purse and her briefcase.

"Not tonight," David told her, and took the briefcase to set it back down.

"I want to—"

"Not tonight, Aurora." Taking her hand again, he brought it to his lips. "Please."

With a nod, she left the briefcase and the office behind.

They kept their hands linked as they walked down the hall. They kept them linked still as they rode down in the elevator. It didn't seem foolish, A.J. realized, but sweet. He hadn't kissed her, hadn't held her, and yet the tension that had built so quickly was gone again, just through a touch.

She was content to leave her car in the lot, thinking that sometime the next day, they'd drive back into town and arrange things. Pleased just to be with him again, she stopped at his car while he unlocked the doors.

"Haven't you been home yet?" she asked, noticing a suitcase in the back seat.

"No."

She started to smile, delighted that he'd wanted to see her first, but she glanced over her shoulder again as she stepped into the car. "I have a case just like that."

David settled in the seat, then turned on the ignition. "That is your case."

"Mine?" Baffled, she turned around and looked closer. "But—I don't remember you borrowing one of my suitcases."

"I didn't. Mine are in the trunk." He eased out of the lot and merged with clogged L.A. weekend traffic.

"Well, if you didn't borrow it, what's it doing in your car?"

"I stopped by your place on the way. Your housekeeper packed for you."

"Packed…" She stared at the case. When she turned to him, her eyes were narrowed. "You've got a lot of nerve, Brady. Just where do you come off packing my clothes and assuming—"

"The housekeeper packed them. Nice lady. I thought you'd be more comfortable over the weekend with some of your own things. I had thought about keeping you naked, but that's a little tricky when you take walks in the woods."

Because her jaw was beginning to ache, she relaxed it. "You thought? *You* didn't think at all. You drop by the office and calmly assume that I'll drop everything and run off with you. What if I'd had plans?"

"Then that would've been too bad." He swung easily off the ramp toward the hills.

"Too bad for whom?"

"For the plans." He punched in the car lighter and sent her a mild smile. "I have no intention of letting you out of my sight for the next three days."

"You have no intention?" The fire was rising as she shifted in her seat toward him. "What about my intention? Maybe you think it's very male and macho to just—just bundle a woman off for a weekend without asking, without any discussion, but I happen to prefer being consulted. Stop the car."

"Not a chance." David had expected this reaction. Even looked forward to it. He touched the lighter to the tip of his cigarette. He hadn't enjoyed himself this much for days. Since the last time he'd been with her.

Her breath came out in a long, slow hiss. "I don't find abductions appealing."

"Didn't think I did, either." He blew out a lazy stream of smoke. "Guess I was wrong."

She flopped back against her seat, arms folded. "You're going to be sorry."

"I'm only sorry I didn't think of it before." With his elbow resting lightly on the open window, he drove higher into the hills, with A.J. fuming beside him. The minute he stopped the car in his drive, A.J. pushed open her door, snatched her purse up and began to walk. When he grabbed her arm, she spun around, holding the pastel-dyed leather like a weapon.

"Want to fight?"

"I wouldn't give you the satisfaction." She yanked her arm out of his hold. "I'm walking back."

"Oh?" He look a quick look at the slim skirt, thin hose and fragile heels. "You wouldn't make it the first mile in those shoes."

"That's my problem."

He considered a minute, then sighed. "I guess we'll just carry through with the same theme." Before she realized his intention, he wrapped an arm around her waist and hauled her over his shoulder.

Too stunned to struggle, she blew hair out of her eyes. "Put me down."

"In a few minutes," he promised as he walked toward the house.

"Now." She whacked him smartly on the back with her purse. "This isn't funny."

"Are you kidding?" When he stuck his key in the lock, she began to struggle. "Easy, A.J., you'll end up dropping on your head."

"I'm not going to tolerate this." She tried to kick out and found her legs pinned behind the knee. "David, this is degrading. I don't know what's gotten into you, but if you get hold of yourself now, I'll forget the whole thing."

"No deal." He started up the steps.

"I'll give you a deal," she said between her teeth as she made a futile grab for the railing. "If you put me down now, I won't kill you."

"Now?"

"Right now."

"Okay." With a quick twist of his body, he had her falling backward. Even as her eyes widened in shock, he was tumbling with her onto the bed.

"What the hell's gotten into you?" she demanded as she struggled to sit up.

"You," he said, so simply she stopped in the act of shoving him away. "You," he repeated, cupping the back of her neck. "I thought about you the whole time I was gone. I wanted you in Chicago. I wanted you in the airport, and thirty thousand feet up I still wanted you."

"You're—this is crazy."

"Maybe. Maybe it is. But when I was on that plane flying back to L.A. I realized that I wanted you here, right here, alone with me for days."

His fingers were stroking up and down her neck, soothing. Her nerves were stretching tighter and tighter. "If you'd asked," she began.

"You'd have had an excuse. You might have spent the

night." His fingers inched up into her hair. "But you'd have found a reason you couldn't stay longer."

"That's not true."

"Isn't it? Why haven't you spent a weekend with me before?"

Her fingers linked and twisted. "There've been reasons."

"Yeah." He put his hand over hers. "And the main one is you're afraid to spend more than a few hours at a time with me." When she opened her mouth, he shook his head to cut her off. "Afraid if you do, I might just get too close."

"I'm not afraid of you. That's ridiculous."

"No, I don't think you are. I think you're afraid of us." He drew her closer. "So am I."

"David." The word was shaky. The world was suddenly shaky. Just passion, she reminded herself again. That's what made her head swim, her heart pound. Desire. Her arms slid up his back. It was only desire. "Let's not think at all for a while." She touched her lips to his and felt resistance as well as need.

"Sooner or later we're going to have to."

"No." She kissed him again, let her tongue trace lightly over his lips. "There's no sooner, no later." Her breath was warm, tempting, as it fluttered over him. "There's only now. Make love with me now, in the light." Her hands slipped under his shirt to tease and invite.

Her eyes were open and on his, her lips working slowly, steadily, to drive him to the edge. He swore, then pulled her to him and let the madness come.

"It's good for you."

"So's calves' liver," A.J. said breathlessly, and paused to lean against a tree. "I avoid that, too."

They'd taken the path behind his house, crossed the

stream and continued up. By David's calculations they'd gone about three-quarters of a mile. He walked back to stand beside her. "Look." He spread his arm wide. "It's terrific, isn't it?"

The trees were thick and green. Birds rustled the leaves and sang for the simple pleasure of sound. Wildflowers she'd never seen before and couldn't name pushed their way through the underbrush and battled for the patches of sunlight. It was, even to a passionately avowed city girl, a lovely sight.

"Yes, it's terrific. You tend to forget there's anything like this when you're down in L.A."

"That's why I moved up here." He put an arm around her shoulders and absently rubbed his hand up and down. "I was beginning to forget there was any place other than the fast lane."

"Work, parties, meetings, parties, brunch, lunch and cocktails."

"Yeah, something like that. Anyway, coming up here after a day in the factory keeps things in perspective. If a project bombs in the ratings, the sun's still going to set."

She thought about it, leaning into him a bit as he stroked her arm. "If I blow a deal, I go home, lock the doors, put on my headset and drown my brain in Rachmaninoff."

"Same thing."

"But usually I kick something first."

He laughed and kissed the top of her head. "Whatever works. Wait till you see the view from the top."

A.J. leaned down to massage her calf. "I'll meet you back at the house. You can draw me a picture."

"You need the air. Do you realize we've barely been out of bed for thirty-six hours?"

"And we've probably logged about ten hours' sleep." Straightening a bit, she stretched protesting muscles. "I think I've had enough health and nature for the day."

He looked down at her. She wasn't A. J. Fields now, in T-shirt and jeans and scuffed boots. But he still knew how to play her. "I guess I'm in better shape than you are."

"Like hell." She pushed away from the tree.

Determined to keep up, she strode along beside him, up the winding dirt path, until sweat trickled down her back. Her leg muscles whimpered, reminding her she'd neglected her weekly tennis games for over a month. At last, aching and exhausted, she dropped down on a rock.

"That's it. I give up."

"Another hundred yards and we start circling back."

"Nope."

"A.J., it's shorter to go around this way than to turn around."

Shorter? She shut her eyes and asked herself what had possessed her to let him drag her through the woods. "I'll just stay here tonight. You can bring me back a pillow and a sandwich."

"I could always carry you."

She folded her arms. "No."

"How about a bribe?"

Her bottom lip poked out as she considered. "I'm always open to negotiations."

"I've got a bottle of cabernet sauvignon I've been saving for the right moment."

She rubbed at a streak of dirt on her knee. "What year?"

"Seventy-nine."

"A good start. That might get me the next hundred yards or so."

"Then there's that steak I took out of the freezer this morning, the one I'm going to grill over mesquite."

"I'd forgotten about that." She brought her tongue over her top lip and thought she could almost taste it. "That should get me halfway back down."

"You drive a hard bargain."

"Thank you."

"Flowers. Dozens of them."

She lifted a brow. "By the time we get back, the florist'll be closed."

"City-oriented," he said with a sigh. "Look around you."

"You're going to pick me flowers?" Surprised, and foolishly pleased, she lifted her arms to twine them around his neck. "That should definitely get me through the front door."

Smiling, she leaned back as he stepped off the path to gather blossoms. "I like the blue ones," she called out, and laughed as he muttered at her.

She hadn't expected the weekend to be so relaxed, so easy. She hadn't known she could enjoy being with one person for so long. There were no schedules, no appointments, no pressing deals. There were simply mornings and afternoons and evenings.

It seemed absurd that something as mundane as fixing breakfast could be fun. She'd discovered that spending the time to eat it instead of rushing into the morning had a certain appeal. When you weren't alone. She didn't have a script or a business letter to deal with. And she had to admit, she hadn't missed them. She'd done nothing more mind-teasing in two days than a crossword puzzle. And even that, she remembered happily, had been interrupted.

Now he was picking her flowers. Small, colorful

wildflowers. She'd put them in a vase by the window where they'd be cozy and bright. And deadly.

For an instant, her heart stopped. The birds were silent and the air was still as glass. She saw David as though she were looking through a long lens. As she watched, the light went gray. There was pain, sharp and sudden, as her knuckles scraped over the rock.

"No!" She thought she shouted, but the word came out in a whisper. She nearly slipped off the rock before she caught herself and stumbled toward him. She gasped for his name twice before it finally ripped out of her. "David! No, stop."

He straightened, but only had time to take a step toward her before she threw herself into his arms. He'd seen that blank terror in her eyes before, once before, when she'd stood in an old empty room watching something no one else could see.

"Aurora, what is it?" He held her close while she shuddered, though he had no idea how to soothe. "What's wrong?"

"Don't pick any more. David, don't." Her fingers dug hard into his back.

"All right, I won't." Hands firm, he drew her away to study her face. "Why?"

"Something's wrong with them." The fear hadn't passed. She pressed the heel of her hand against her chest as if to push it out. "Something's wrong with them," she repeated.

"They're just flowers." He showed her what he held in his hands.

"Not them. Over there. You were going to pick those over there."

He followed the direction of her gaze to a large sunny rock with flowers around the perimeter. He remembered he'd just been turning in their direction when her shouts had stopped him. "Yes, I was. Let's have a look."

"No." She grabbed him again. "Don't touch them."

"Calm down," he said quietly enough, though his own nerves were starting to jangle. Bending, he picked up a stick. Letting the flowers he'd already picked fall, he took A.J.'s hand in his and dragged the end of the stick along the edge of the rock through a thick clump of bluebells. He heard the hissing rattle, felt the jolt of the stick he held as the snake reared up and struck. A.J.'s hand went limp in his. David held on to the stick as he pulled her back to the path. He wore boots, thick and sturdy enough to protect against the snakes scattered through the hills. But he'd been picking flowers, and there had been nothing to protect the vulnerable flesh of his hands and wrists.

"I want to go back," she said flatly.

She was grateful he didn't question, didn't probe or even try to soothe. If he had, she wasn't sure what idiotic answers she'd have given him. A.J. had discovered more in that one timeless moment than David's immediate danger. She'd discovered she was in love with him. All her rules, her warnings, her precautions hadn't mattered. He could hurt her now, and she might never recover.

So she didn't speak. Because he was silent, as well, she felt the first pang of rejection. They entered through the kitchen door. David took a bottle of brandy and two water glasses out of a cupboard. He poured, handed one to A.J., then emptied half the contents of his own glass in one swallow.

She sipped, then sipped again, and felt a little steadier. "Would you like to take me home now?"

He picked up the bottle and added a dollop to his glass. "What are you talking about?"

A.J. wrapped both hands around her glass and made herself speak calmly. "Most people are uncomfortable after—after an episode. They either want to distance themselves from the source or dissect it." When he said nothing, only stared at her, she set her glass down. "It won't take me long to pack."

"You take another step," he said in a voice that was deadly calm, "and I don't know what the hell I'll do. Sit down, Aurora."

"David, I don't want an interrogation."

He hurled his glass into the sink, making her jolt at the sudden violence. "Don't we know each other any better than that by now?" He was shouting. She couldn't know it wasn't at her, but himself. "Can't we have any sort of discussion, any sort of contact, that isn't sex or negotiations?"

"We agreed—"

He said something so uncharacteristically vulgar about agreements that she stopped dead. "You very possibly saved my life." He stared down at his hand, well able to imagine what might have happened. "What am I supposed to say to you? Thanks?"

When she found herself stuttering, A.J. swallowed and pulled herself back. "I'd really rather you didn't say anything."

He walked to her but didn't touch. "I can't. Look, I'm a little shaky about this myself. That doesn't mean I've suddenly decided you're a freak." He saw the emotion come and go in her eyes before he reached out to touch her face. "I'm grateful. I just don't quite know how to handle it."

"It's all right." She was losing ground. She could feel it. "I don't expect—"

"Do." He brought his other hand to her face. "Do expect. Tell me what you want. Tell me what you need right now."

She tried not to. She'd lose one more foothold if she did. But his hands were gentle, when they never were, and his eyes offered. "Hold me." She closed her eyes as she said it. "Just hold me a minute."

He put his arms around her, drew her against him. There was no passion, no fire, just comfort. He felt her hands knead at his back until both of them relaxed. "Do you want to talk about it?"

"It was just a flash. I was sitting there, thinking about how nice it had been to do nothing. I was thinking about the flowers. I had a picture of them in the window. All at once they were black and ugly and the petals were like razors. I saw you bending over that clump of blue-bells, and it all went gray."

"I hadn't bent over them yet."

"You would have."

"Yeah." He held her closer a moment. "I would have. Looks like I reneged on the last part of the deal. I don't have any flowers for you."

"It doesn't matter." She pressed her lips against his neck.

"I'll have to make it up to you." Drawing back, he took both of her hands. "Aurora…" He started to lift one, then saw the caked blood on her knuckles. "What the hell have you done to yourself?"

Blankly she looked down. "I don't know. It hurts," she said as she flexed her hand.

"Come on." He led her to the sink and began to clean off dried blood with cool water.

"Ow!" She would have jerked her hand away if he hadn't held it still.

"I've never had a very gentle touch," he muttered.

She leaned a hip against the sink. "So I've noticed."

Annoyed at seeing the rough wound on her hand, he began to dab it with a towel. "Let's go upstairs. I've got some Merthiolate."

"That stings."

"Don't be a baby."

"I'm not." But he had to tug her along. "It's only a scrape."

"And scrapes get infected."

"Look, you've already rubbed it raw. There can't be a germ left."

He nudged her into the bathroom. "We'll make sure."

Before she could stop him, he took out a bottle and dumped medicine over her knuckles. What had been a dull sting turned to fire. "Damn it!"

"Here." He grabbed her hand again and began to blow on the wound. "Just give it a minute."

"A lot of good that does," she muttered, but the pain cooled.

"We'll fix dinner. That'll take your mind off it."

"You're supposed to fix dinner," she reminded him.

"Right." He kissed her forehead. "I've got to run out for a minute. I'll start the grill when I get back."

"That doesn't mean I'm going to be chopping vegetables while you're gone. I'm going to take a bath."

"Fine. If the water's still hot when I get back, I'll join you."

She didn't ask where he was going. She wanted to, but there were rules. Instead A.J. walked into the bedroom and watched from the window as he pulled out of the drive. Weary, she sat on the bed and pulled off her boots. The afternoon had taken its toll, physically, emotionally. She didn't want to think. She didn't want to feel.

Giving in, she stretched out across the bed. She'd rest for a minute, she told herself. Only for a minute.

David came home with a handful of asters he'd begged from a neighbor's garden. He thought the idea of dropping them on A.J. while she soaked in the tub might bring the laughter back to her eyes. He'd never heard her laugh so much or so easily as she had over the weekend. It wasn't something he wanted to lose. Just as he was discovering she wasn't something he wanted to lose.

He went up the stairs quietly, then paused at the bedroom door when he saw her. She'd taken off only her boots. A pillow was crumpled under her arm as she lay diagonally across the bed. It occurred to him as he stepped into the room that he'd never watched her sleep before. They'd never given each other the chance.

Her face looked so soft, so fragile. Her hair was pale and tumbled onto her cheek, her lips unpainted and just parted. How was it he'd never noticed how delicate her features were, how slender and frail her wrists were, how elegantly feminine the curve of her neck was?

Maybe he hadn't looked, David admitted as he crossed to the bed. But he was looking now.

She was fire and thunder in bed, sharp and tough out of it. She had a gift, a curse and ability she fought against every waking moment, one that he was just beginning to understand. He was just beginning to see that it made her defensive and defenseless.

Only rarely did the vulnerabilities emerge, and then with such reluctance from her he'd tended to gloss over them. But now, just now, when she was asleep and unaware of him, she looked like something a man should protect, cherish.

The first stirrings weren't of passion and desire, but of a quiet affection he hadn't realized he felt for her. He hadn't realized it was possible to feel anything quiet for Aurora. Unable to resist, he reached down to brush the hair from her cheek and feel the warm, smooth skin beneath.

She stirred. He'd wanted her to. Heavy and sleep-glazed, her eyes opened. "David?" Even her voice was soft, feminine.

"I brought you a present." He sat on the bed beside her and dropped the flowers by her hand.

"Oh." He'd seen that before, too, he realized. That quick surprise and momentary confusion when he'd done something foolish or romantic. "You didn't have to."

"I think I did," he murmured, half to himself. Almost as an experiment, he lowered his mouth to hers and kissed her softly, gently, with the tenderness she'd made him feel as she slept. He felt the ache move through him, sweet as a dream.

"David?" She said his name again, but this time her eyes were dark and dazed.

"Shh." His hands didn't drag through her hair now with trembles of passion, but stroked, exploring the texture. He could watch the light strike individual strands. "Lovely." He brought his gaze back to hers. "Have I ever told you how lovely you are?"

She started to reach for him, for the passion that she could understand. "It isn't necessary."

His lips met hers again, but they didn't devour and demand. This mood was foreign and made her heart pound as much with uncertainty as need. "Make love with me," she murmured as she tried to draw him down.

"I am." His mouth lingered over hers. "Maybe for the first time."

"I don't understand," she began, but he shifted so that he could cradle her in his arms.

"Neither do I."

So he began, slowly, gently, testing them both. Her mouth offered darker promises, but he waited, coaxing. His lips were patient as they moved over hers, light and soothing as they kissed her eyes closed. He didn't touch her, not yet, though he wondered what it would be like to stroke her while the light was softening, to caress as though it were all new, all fresh. Gradually he felt the tension in her body give way, he felt what he'd never felt from her before. Pliancy, surrender, warmth.

Her body seemed weightless, gloriously light and free. She felt the pleasure move through her, but sweetly, fluidly, like wine. Then he was the wine, heady and potent, drugging her with the intoxicating taste of his mouth. The hands that had clutched him in demand went lax. There was so much to absorb—the flavor of his lips as they lingered on hers; the texture of his skin as his cheek brushed hers; the scent that clung to him, part man, part woods; the dark, curious look in his eyes as he watched her.

She looked as she had when she'd slept, he thought. Fragile, so arousingly fragile. And she felt... At last he touched, fingertips only, along skin already warm. He heard her sigh his name in a way she'd never said it before. Keeping her cradled in his arms, he began to take her deeper, take himself deeper, with tenderness.

She had no strength to demand, no will to take control. For the first time her body was totally his, just as for the first time her emotions were. He touched, and she yielded. He tasted, and she gave. When he shifted her, she felt as though she could float. Perhaps she was. Clouds of pleasure, mists of soft, soft delight. When he began to undress her, she opened her eyes, needing to see him again.

The light had gone to rose with sunset. It made her skin glow as he slowly drew off her shirt. He couldn't take his eyes off her, couldn't stop his hands from touching, though he had no desire to be quick. When she reached up, he helped her pull off his own shirt, then took her injured hand to his lips. He kissed her fingers, then her palm, then her wrist, until he felt her begin to tremble. Bending, he brushed her lips with his again, wanting to hear her sigh his name. Then, watching her, waiting until she looked at him, he continued to undress her.

Slowly. Achingly slowly, he drew the jeans down her legs, pausing now and then to taste newly exposed skin. Pulses beat at the back of her knees. He felt them, lingered there, exploited them. Her ankles were slim, fragile like her wrists. He traced them with his tongue until she moaned. Then he waited, letting her settle again as he stripped off his own jeans. He came to her, flesh against flesh.

Nothing had been like this. Nothing could be like this. The thoughts whirled in her brain as he began another deliciously slow assault. Her body was to be enjoyed and pleasured, not worshiped. But he did so now, and enticed her to do the same with his.

So strong. She'd known his strength before, but this was different. His fingers didn't grip; his hands didn't press. They skimmed, they traced, they weakened. So intense. They'd shared intensity before, but never so quietly.

She heard him say her name. Aurora. It was like a dream, one she'd never dared to have. He murmured promises in her ear and she believed them. Whatever tomorrow might bring, she believed them now. She could smell the flowers strewn over the bed and taste the excitement that built in a way it had never done before.

He slipped into her as though their bodies had never been apart. The rhythm was easy, patient, giving.

Holding himself back, he watched her climb higher. That was what he wanted, he realized, to give her everything there was to give. When she arched and shuddered, the force whipped through him. Power, he recognized it, but was driven to leash it. His mouth found hers and drew on the sweetness. How could he have known sweetness could be so arousing?

The blood was pounding in his head, roaring in his ears, yet his body continued to move slowly with hers. Balanced on the edge, David said her name a last time.

"Aurora, look at me." When her eyes opened, they were dark and aware. "I want to see where I take you."

Even when control slipped away, echoes of tenderness remained.

Chapter 10

Alice Robbins had exploded onto the screen in the sixties, a young, raw talent. She had, like so many girls before her and after her, fled to Hollywood to escape the limitations of small-town life. She'd come with dreams, with hopes and ambitions. An astrologer might have said Alice's stars were in the right quadrant. When she hit, she hit big.

She had had an early, turbulent marriage that had ended in an early, turbulent divorce. Scenes in and out of the courtroom had been as splashy as anything she'd portrayed on the screen. With her marriage over and her career climbing, she'd enjoyed all the benefits of being a beautiful woman in a town that demanded, then courted, beauty. Reports of her love affairs sizzled on the pages of glossies. Glowing reviews and critical praise heaped higher with each role. But in her late twenties, when her career was reaching its peak, she found something that fulfilled her in a way success and reviews never had. Alice Robbins met Peter Van Camp.

He'd been nearly twenty years her senior, a hardbitten, well-to-do business magnate. They'd married after a whirlwind two-week courtship that had kept the gossip columns salivating. Was it for money? Was it for power? Was it for prestige? It had been, very simply, for love.

In an unprecedented move, Alice had taken her husband's name professionally as well as privately. Hardly more than a year later, she'd given birth to a son and had, without a backward glance, put her career on hold. For nearly a decade, she'd devoted herself to her family with the same kind of single-minded drive she'd put into her acting.

When word leaked that Alice Van Camp had been lured back into films, the hype had been extravagant. Rumors of a multimillion-dollar deal flew and promises of the movie of the century were lavish.

Four weeks before the release of the film, her son, Matthew, had been kidnapped.

David knew the background. Alice Van Camp's triumphs and trials were public fodder. Her name was legend. Though she rarely consented to grace the screen, her popularity remained constant. As to the abduction and recovery of her son, details were sketchy. Perhaps because of the circumstances, the police had never been fully open and Clarissa DeBasse had been quietly evasive. Neither Alice nor Peter Van Camp had ever, until now, granted an interview on the subject. Even with their agreement and apparent cooperation, David knew he would have to tread carefully.

He was using the minimum crew, and a wellseasoned one. "Star" might be an overused term, but

David was aware they would be dealing with a woman who fully deserved the title and the mystique that went with it.

Her Beverly Hills home was guarded by electric gates and a wall twice as tall as a man. Just inside the gates was a uniformed guard who verified their identification. Even after they had been passed through, they drove another half a mile to the house.

It was white, flowing out with balconies, rising up with Doric columns, softened by tall, tall trellises of roses in full bloom. Legend had it that her husband had had it built for her in honor of the last role she'd played before the birth of their son. David had seen the movie countless times and remembered her as an antebellum tease who made Scarlett O'Hara look like a nun.

There were Japanese cherry trees dripping down to sweep the lawn in long skirts. Their scent and the citrus fragrance of orange and lemon stung the air. As he pulled his car to a halt behind the equipment van, he spotted a peacock strutting across the lawn.

I wish A.J. could see this.

The thought came automatically before he had time to check it, just as thoughts of her had come automatically for days. Because he wasn't yet sure just how he felt about it, David simply let it happen.

And how did he feel about her? That was something else he wasn't quite sure of. Desire. He desired her more, even more now after he'd saturated himself with her. Friendship. In some odd, cautious way he felt they were almost as much friends as they were lovers. Understanding. It was more difficult to be as definite about that. A.J. had an uncanny ability to throw up mirrors that reflected back your own thoughts rather than hers. Still, he had come to understand that beneath the confidence and drive was a warm, vulnerable woman.

She was passionate. She was reserved. She was competent. She was fragile. And she was, David had discovered, a tantalizing mystery to be solved, one layer at a time.

Perhaps that was why he'd found himself so caught up in her. Most of the women he knew were precisely what they seemed. Sophisticated. Ambitious. Well-bred. His own taste had invariably drawn him to a certain type of woman. A.J. fit. Aurora didn't. If he understood anything about her, he understood she was both.

As an agent, he knew, she was pleased with the deal she'd made for her client, including the Van Camp segment. As a daughter, he sensed, she was uneasy about the repercussions.

But the deal had been made, David reminded himself as he walked up the wide circular steps to the Van Camp estate. As a producer, he was satisfied with the progress of his project. But as a man, he wished he knew of a way to put A.J.'s mind at rest. She excited him; she intrigued him. And as no woman had ever done before, she concerned him. He'd wondered, more often than once, if that peculiar combination equaled love. And if it did, what in hell he was going to do about it.

"Second thoughts?" Alex asked as David hesitated at the door.

Annoyed with himself, David shrugged his shoulders, then pushed the bell. "Should there be?"

"Clarissa's comfortable with this."

David found himself shifting restlessly. "That's enough for you?"

"It's enough," Alex answered. "Clarissa knows her own mind."

The phrasing had him frowning, had him searching. "Alex—"

Though he wasn't certain what he had been about to say, the door opened and the moment was lost. A formally dressed, French-accented maid took their names before leading them into a room off the main hall. The crew, not easily impressed, spoke in murmurs.

It was unapologetically Hollywood. The furnishings were big and bold, the colors flashy. On a baby grand in the center of the room was a silver candelabra dripping with crystal prisms. David recognized it as a prop from *Music at Midnight*.

"Not one for understatement," Alex commented.

"No." David took another sweep of the room. There were brocades and silks in jewel colors. Furniture gleamed like mirrors. "But Alice Van Camp might be one of the few in the business who deserves to bang her own drum."

"Thank you."

Regal, amused and as stunning as she had been in her screen debut, Alice Van Camp paused in the doorway. She was a woman who knew how to pose, and who did so without a second thought. Like others who had known her only through her movies, David's first thought was how small she was. Then she stepped forward and her presence alone whisked the image away.

"Mr. Marshall." Hand extended, Alice walked to him. Her hair was a deep sable spiked around a face as pale and smooth as a child's. If he hadn't known better, David would have said she'd yet to see thirty. "It's a pleasure to meet you. I'm a great admirer of journalists—when they don't misquote me."

"Mrs. Van Camp." He covered her small hand with both of his. "Shall I say the obvious?"

"That depends."

"You're just as beautiful face-to-face as you are on the screen."

She laughed, the smoky, sultry murmur that had made men itch for more than two decades. "I appreciate the obvious. And you're David Brady." Her gaze shifted to him and he felt the unapologetic summing up, strictly woman to man. "I've seen several of your productions. My husband prefers documentaries and biographies to films. I can't think why he married me."

"I can." David accepted her hand. "I'm an avid fan."

"As long as you don't tell me you've enjoyed my movies since you were a child." Amusement glimmered in her eyes again before she glanced around. "Now if you'll introduce me to our crew, we can get started."

David had admired her for years. After ten minutes in her company, his admiration grew. She spoke to each member of the crew, from the director down to the assistant lighting technician. When she'd finished, she turned herself over to Sam for instructions.

At her suggestion, they moved to the terrace. Patient, she waited while technicians set up reflectors and umbrellas to exploit the best effect from available light. Her maid set a table of cold drinks and snacks out of camera range. Though she didn't touch a thing, she indicated to the crew that they should enjoy. She sat easily through sound tests and blocking. When Sam was satisfied, she turned to Alex and began.

"Mrs. Van Camp, for twenty years you've been known as one of the most talented and best-loved actresses in the country."

"Thank you, Alex. My career has always been one of the most important parts of my life."

"One of the most. We're here now to discuss another

part of your life. Your family, most specifically your son. A decade ago, you nearly faced tragedy."

"Yes, I did." She folded her hands. Though the sun shone down in her face, she never blinked. "A tragedy that I sincerely doubt I would have recovered from."

"This is the first interview you've given on this subject. Can I ask you why you agreed now?"

She smiled a little, leaning back in her weathered rattan chair. "Timing, in life and in business, is crucial. For several years after my son's abduction I simply couldn't speak of it. After a time, it seemed unnecessary to bring it up again. Now, if I watch the news or look in a store window and see posters of missing children, I ache for the parents."

"Do you consider that this interview might help those parents?"

"Help them find their children, no." Emotion flickered in her eyes, very real and very brief. "But perhaps it can ease some of the misery. I'd never considered sharing my feelings about my own experience. And I doubt very much if I would have agreed if it hadn't been for Clarissa DeBasse."

"Clarissa DeBasse asked you to give this interview?"

After a soft laugh, Alice shook her head. "Clarissa never asks anything. But when I spoke with her and I realized she had faith in this project, I agreed."

"You have a great deal of faith in her."

"She gave me back my son."

She said it with such simplicity, with such utter sincerity, that Alex let the sentence hang. From somewhere in the garden at her back, a bird began to trill.

"That's what we'd like to talk about here. Will you tell us how you came to know Clarissa DeBasse?"

Behind the cameras, behind the crew, David stood

with his hands in his pockets and listened to the story. He remembered how A.J. had once told him of her mother's gradual association with celebrities. Alice Van Camp had come to her with a friend on a whim. After an hour, she'd gone away impressed with Clarissa's gentle style and straightforward manner. On impulse, she'd commissioned Clarissa to do her husband's chart as a gift for their anniversary. When it was done, even the pragmatic and business-oriented Peter Van Camp had been intrigued.

"She told me things about myself," Alice went on. "Not about tomorrow, you understand, but about my feelings, things about my background that had influenced me, or still worried me. I can't say I always liked what she had to say. There are things about ourselves we don't like to admit. But I kept going back because she was so intriguing, and gradually we became friends."

"You believed in clairvoyance?"

Alice's brows drew together as she considered. "I would say I first began to see her because it was fun, it was different. I'd chosen to lead a secluded life after the birth of my son, but that didn't mean I wouldn't appreciate, even need, little touches of flash. Of the unique." The frown smoothed as she smiled. "Clarissa was undoubtedly unique."

"So you went to her for entertainment."

"Oh, yes, that was definitely the motivation in the beginning. You see, at first I thought she was simply very clever. Then, as I began to know her, I discovered she was not simply clever, she was special. That certainly doesn't mean I endorse every palmist on Sunset Boulevard. I certainly can't claim to understand the testing and research that's done on the subject. I do believe, however, that there are some of us who are more sensitive, or whose senses are more finely tuned."

"Will you tell us what happened when your son was abducted?"

"June 22. Almost ten years ago." Alice closed her eyes a moment. "To me it's yesterday. You have children, Mr. Marshall?"

"Yes, I do."

"And you love them."

"Very much."

"Then you have some small glimmer of what it would be like to lose them, even for a short time. There's terror and there's guilt. The guilt is nearly as painful as the fear. You see, I hadn't been with him when he'd been taken. Jenny was Matthew's nanny. She'd been with us over five years and was very devoted to my son. She was young, but dependable and fiercely protective. When I made the decision to go back into films, we leaned on Jenny heavily. Neither my husband nor myself wanted Matthew to suffer because I was working again."

"Your son was nearly ten when you agreed to do another movie."

"Yes, he was quite independent already. Both Peter and I wanted that for him. Very often during the filming, Jenny would bring him to the studio. Even after the shooting was complete, she continued in her habit of walking to the park with him in the afternoon. If I had realized then how certain habits can be dangerous, I would have stopped it. Both my husband and myself had been careful to keep Matthew out of the limelight, not because we were afraid for him physically, but because we felt it was best that his upbringing be as normal and natural as possible. Of course he was recognized, and now and then some enterprising photographer would get a shot in."

"Did that sort of thing bother you?"

"No." When she smiled, the sultry glamour came through. "I suppose I was accustomed to such things. Peter and I didn't want to be fanatics about our privacy. And I wonder, and always have, if we'd been stricter would it have made any difference? I doubt it." There was a little sigh, as though it were a point she'd yet to resolve. "We learned later that Matthew's visits to the park were being watched."

"For a time the police suspected Jennifer Waite, your son's nanny, of working with the kidnappers."

"That was, of course, absurd. I never for a minute doubted Jenny's loyalty and devotion to Matthew. Once it was over, she was completely cleared." A trace of stubbornness came through. "She's still in my employ."

"The investigators found her story disjointed."

"The afternoon he was abducted, Jenny came home hysterical. We were the closest thing to family she had, and she blamed herself. Matthew had been playing ball with several other children while she watched. A young woman had come up to her asking for directions. She'd spun a story about missing her bus and being new in town. She'd distracted Jenny only a few moments, and that's all it took. When she looked back, Jenny saw Matthew being hustled into a car at the edge of the park. She ran after him, but he was gone. Ten minutes after she came home alone the first ransom call came in."

She lifted her hands to her lips a moment, and they trembled lightly. "I'm sorry. Could we stop here a moment?"

"Cut. Five minutes," Sam ordered the crew.

David was beside her chair before Sam had finished

speaking. "Would you like something, Mrs. Van Camp? A drink?"

"No." She shook her head and looked beyond him. "It isn't as easy as I thought it would be. Ten years, and it still isn't easy."

"I could send for your husband."

"I told Peter to stay away today because he's always so uncomfortable around cameras. I wish I hadn't."

"We can wrap for today."

"Oh, no." She took a deep breath and composed herself. "I believe in finishing what I start. Matthew's a sophomore in college." She smiled up at David. "Do you like happy endings?"

He held her hand. For the moment she was only a woman. "I'm a sucker for them."

"He's bright, handsome and in love. I just needed to remember that. It could have been..." She linked her hands again and the ruby on her finger shone like blood. "It could have been much different. You know Clarissa's daughter, don't you?"

A bit off-balance at the change of subject, David shifted. "Yes."

She admired the caution. "I meant it when I said Clarissa and I are friends. Mothers worry about their children. Do you have a cigarette?"

In silence he took one out and lit it for her.

Alice blew out smoke and let some of the tension fade. "She's a hell of an agent. Do you know, I wanted to sign with her and she wouldn't have me?"

David forgot his own cigarette in simple astonishment. "I beg your pardon?"

Alice laughed again and relaxed. She'd needed a moment to remember life went on. "It was a few months after the kidnapping. A.J. figured I'd come to her out of gratitude to Clarissa. And maybe I had. In any case, she turned me down flat, even though she was scrambling around trying to rent decent office space. I admired her integrity. So much so that a few years ago I approached her again." Alice smiled at him, enjoying the fact that he listened very carefully. Apparently, she mused, Clarissa was right on target, as always. "She was established, respected. And she turned me down again."

What agent in her right mind would turn down a top name, a name that had earned through sheer talent the label of "megastar"? "A.J. never quite does what you expect," he murmured.

"Clarissa's daughter is a woman who insists on being accepted for herself, but can't always tell when she is." She crushed out the cigarette after a second quick puff. "Thanks. I'd like to continue now."

Within moments, Alice was deep into her own story. Though the camera continued to roll, she forgot about it. Sitting in the sunlight with the scent of roses strong and sweet, she talked about her hours of terror.

"We would have paid anything. Anything. Peter and I fought bitterly about calling in the police. The kidnappers had been very specific. We weren't to contact anyone. But Peter felt, and rightly so, that we needed help. The ransom calls came every few hours. We agreed to pay, but they kept changing the terms. Testing us. It was the worst kind of cruelty. While we waited, the police began searching for the car Jenny had seen and the woman she'd spoken with in the park. It was as if they'd vanished into thin air. At the end of forty-eight hours, we were no closer to finding Matthew."

"So you decided to call in Clarissa DeBasse?"

"I don't know when the idea of asking Clarissa to help came to me. I know I hadn't slept or eaten. I just kept waiting for the phone to ring. It's such a helpless feeling. I remembered, God knows why, that Clarissa had once told me where to find a diamond brooch I'd misplaced. It wasn't just a piece of jewelry to me, but something Peter had given me when Matthew was born. A child isn't a brooch, but I began to think, maybe, just maybe. I needed some hope.

"The police didn't like the idea. I don't believe Peter did, either, but he knew I needed something. I called Clarissa and I told her that Matthew had been taken." Her eyes filled. She didn't bother to blink the tears away. "I asked her if she could help me and she told me she'd try.

"I broke down when she arrived. She sat with me awhile, friend to friend, mother to mother. She spoke to Jenny, though there was no calming the poor girl down even at that point. The police were very terse with Clarissa, but she seemed to accept that. She told them they were looking in the wrong place." Unselfconsciously she brushed at the tears on her cheek. "I can tell you that didn't sit too well with the men who'd been working around the clock. She told them Matthew hadn't been taken out of the city, he hadn't gone north as they'd thought. She asked for something of Matthew's, something he would have worn. I brought her the pajamas he'd worn to bed the night before. They were blue with little cars across the top. She just sat there, running them through her hands. I remember wanting to scream at her, plead with her, to give me something. Then she started to speak very quietly.

"Matthew was only miles away, she said. He hadn't been taken to San Francisco, though the police had traced one of the ransom calls there. She said he was still in Los Angeles. She described the street, then the house. A white house with blue shutters on a corner lot. I'll never forget the way she described the room in which he was being held. It was dark, you see, and Matthew, though he always tried to be brave, was still afraid of the dark. She said there were only two people in the house, one man and the woman who had spoken to Jenny in the park. She thought there was a car in the drive, gray or green, she said. And she told me he wasn't hurt. He was afraid—" her voice shuddered, then strengthened "—but he wasn't hurt."

"And the police pursued the lead?"

"They didn't have much faith in it, naturally enough, but they sent out cars to look for the house she'd described. I don't know who was more stunned when they found it, Peter and myself or the police. They got Matthew out without a struggle because the two kidnappers with him weren't expecting any trouble. The third accomplice was in San Fransico, making all the calls. The police also found the car he'd been abducted in there.

"Clarissa stayed until Matthew was home, until he was safe. Later he told me about the room he'd been held in. It was exactly as she'd described it."

"Mrs. Van Camp, a lot of people claimed that the abduction and the dramatic rescue of your son was a publicity stunt to hype the release of your first movie since his birth."

"That didn't matter to me." With only her voice, with only her eyes, she showed her complete contempt. "They could say and believe whatever they wanted. I had my son back."

"And you believe Clarissa DeBasse is responsible for that?"

"I know she is."

"Cut," Sam mumbled to his cameraman before he

walked to Alice. "Mrs. Van Camp, if we can get a few reaction shots and over-the-shoulder angles, we'll be done."

He could go now. David knew there was no real reason for him to remain during the angle changes. The shoot was essentially finished, and had been everything he could have asked for. Alice Van Camp was a consummate actress, but no one watching this segment would consider that she'd played a part. She'd been a mother, reliving an experience every mother fears. And she had, by the telling, brought the core of his project right back to Clarissa.

He thought perhaps he understood a little better why A.J. had had mixed feelings about the interview. Alice Van Camp had suffered in the telling. If his instincts were right, Clarissa would have suffered, too. It seemed to him that empathy was an intimate part of her gift.

Nevertheless he stayed behind the camera and restlessly waited until the shoot was complete. Though he detected a trace of weariness in her eyes, Alice escorted the crew to the door herself.

"A remarkable woman," Alex commented as they walked down the circular steps toward the drive.

"And then some. But you've got one yourself."

"I certainly do." Alex pulled out the cigar he'd been patiently waiting for for more than three hours. "I might be a little biased, but I believe you have one, as well."

Frowning, David paused by his car. "I haven't got A.J." It occurred to him that it was the first time he had thought of it in precisely those terms.

"Clarissa seems to think you do."

He turned back and leaned against his car. "And approves?"

"Shouldn't she?"

He pulled out a cigarette. The restlessness was growing. "I don't know."

"You were going to ask me something earlier, before we went in. Do you want to ask me now?"

It had been nagging at him. David wondered if by stating it aloud it would ease. "Clarissa isn't an ordinary woman. Does it bother you?"

Alex took a contented puff on his cigar. "It certainly intrigues me, and I'd be lying if I didn't admit I've had one or two uneasy moments. What I feel for her cancels out the fact that I have five senses and she has what we might call six. You're having uneasy moments." He smiled a little when David said nothing. "Clarissa doesn't believe in keeping secrets. We've talked about her daughter."

"I'm not sure A.J. would be comfortable with that."

"No, maybe not. It's more to the point what you're comfortable with. You know the trouble with a man your age, David? You consider yourself too old to go take foolish risks and too young to trust impulse. I thank God I'm not thirty." With a smile, he walked over to hitch a ride back to town with Sam.

He was too old to take foolish risks, David thought as he pulled his door open. And a man who trusted impulse usually landed flat on his face. But he wanted to see her. He wanted to see her now.

A.J.'s briefcase weighed heavily as she pulled it from the front seat. Late rush-hour traffic streamed by the front of her building. If she'd been able to accomplish more during office hours, she reminded herself as she lugged up her case, she wouldn't have to plow through papers tonight. She would have accomplished more if she hadn't been uneasy, thinking of the Van Camp interview.

It was over now, she told herself as she turned the key to lock both car doors. The filming of the documentary was all but over. She had other clients, other projects, other contracts. It was time she put her mind on them. Shifting her briefcase to her free hand, she turned and collided with David.

"I like running into you," he murmured as he slid his hands up her hips.

She'd had the wind knocked out of her. That's what she told herself as she struggled for breath and leaned into him. After a man and a woman had been intimate, after they'd been lovers, they didn't feel breathless and giddy when they saw each other. But she found herself wanting to wrap her arms around him and laugh.

"You might have cracked a rib," she told him, and contented herself with smiling up at him. "I certainly didn't expect to see you around this evening."

"Problem?"

"No." She let herself brush a hand through his hair. "I think I can work you in. How did the shoot go?"

He heard it, the barest trace of nerves. Not tonight, he told himself. There would be no nerves tonight. "It's done. You know, I like the way you smell up close." He lowered his mouth to brush it over her throat. "Up very close."

"David, we're standing in the parking lot."

"Mmm-hmm." He shifted his mouth to her ear and sent the thrill tumbling to her toes.

"David." She turned her head to ward him off and found her mouth captured by his in a long, lingering kiss.

"I can't stop thinking about you," he murmured, then

kissed her again, hard, until the breath was trembling from her mouth into his. "I can't get you out of my mind. Sometimes I wonder if you've put a spell on me. Mind over matter."

"Don't talk. Come inside with me."

"We don't talk enough." He put his hand under her chin and drew her away before he gave in and buried himself in her again. "Sooner or later we're going to have to."

That's what she was afraid of. When they talked, really talked, she was sure it would be about the end. "Later, then. Please." She rested her cheek against his. "For now let's just enjoy each other."

He felt the edge of frustration compete with the first flares of desire. "That's all you want?"

No, no, she wanted more, everything, anything. If she opened her mouth to speak of one wish, she would speak of dozens. "It's enough," she said almost desperately. "Why did you come here tonight?"

"Because I wanted you. Because I damn well can't keep away from you."

"And that's all I need." Was she trying to convince him or herself? Neither of them had the answer. "Come inside, I'll show you."

Because he needed, because he wasn't yet sure of the nature of his own needs, he took her hand in his and went with her.

Chapter 11

"Are you sure you want to do this?" A.J. felt it was only fair to give David one last chance before he committed himself.

"I'm sure."

"It's going to take the better part of your evening."

"Want to get rid of me?"

"No." She smiled but still hesitated. "Ever done anything like this before?"

He took the collar of her blouse between his thumb and forefinger and rubbed. The practical A.J. had a weakness for silk. "You're my first."

"Then you'll have to do what you're told."

He skimmed his finger down her throat. "Don't you trust me?"

She cocked her head and gave him a long look. "I haven't decided. But under the circumstances, I'll take a chance. Pull up a chair." She indicated the table behind her. There were stacks of paper, neatly arranged. A.J. picked up a pencil, freshly sharpened, and handed it to him. "The first thing you can do is mark off the names I give you. Those are the people who've sent an acceptance. I'll give you the name and the number of people under that name. I need an amount for the caterer by the end of the week."

"Sounds easy enough."

"Just shows you've never dealt with a caterer," A.J. mumbled, and took her own chair.

"What's this?" As he reached for another pile of papers, she waved his hand away.

"People who've already sent gifts, and don't mess with the system. When we finish with this, we have to deal with the guests coming in from out of town. I'm hoping to book a block of rooms tomorrow."

He studied the tidy but extensive arrangement of papers spread between them. "I thought this was supposed to be a small, simple wedding."

She sent him a mild look. "There's no such thing as a small, simple wedding. I've spent two full mornings haggling with florists and over a week off and on struggling with caterers."

"Learn anything?"

"Elopement is the wisest course. Now here—"

"Would you?"

"Would I what?"

"Elope."

With a laugh, A.J. picked up her first stack of papers. "If I ever lost a grip on myself and decided on marriage, I think I'd fly to Vegas, swing through one of those drive-in chapels and have it over with."

His eyes narrowed as he listened to her, as if he were trying to see beyond the words. "Not very romantic."

"Neither am I."

"Aren't you?" He put a hand over hers, surprising her. There was something proprietary in the gesture, and something completely natural.

"No." But her fingers linked with his. "There's not a lot of room for romance in business."

"And otherwise?"

"Otherwise romance tends to lead you to see things that aren't really there. I like illusions on the stage and screen, not in my life."

"What do you want in your life, Aurora? You've never told me."

Why was she nervous? It was foolish, but he was looking at her so closely. He was asking questions he'd never asked. And the answers weren't as simple as she'd once thought. "Success," she told him. Hadn't it always been true?

He nodded, but his thumb moved gently up and down the side of her hand. "You run a successful agency already. What else?" He was waiting, for one word, one sign. Did she need him? For the first time in his life he wanted to be needed.

"I…" She was fumbling for words. He seemed to be the only one who could make her fumble. What did he want? What answer would satisfy him? "I suppose I want to know I've earned my own way."

"Is that why you turned down Alice Van Camp as a client?"

"She told you that?" They hadn't discussed the Van Camp interview. A.J. had purposely talked around it for days.

"She mentioned it." She'd pulled her hand from his. David wondered why every time they talked, really talked, she seemed to draw further away from him.

"It was kind of her to come to me when I was just getting started and things were…rough." She shrugged her shoulders, then began to slide her pencil through her fingers. "But it was out of gratitude to my mother. I couldn't sign my first big client out of gratitude."

"Then later you turned her down again."

"It was too personal." She fought the urge to stand up, walk away from the table, and from him.

"No mixing business with personal relationships."

"Exactly. Do you want some coffee before we get started?"

"You mixed a business and personal relationship with me."

Her fingers tightened on the pencil. He watched them. "Yes, I did."

"Why?"

Though it cost her, she kept her eyes on his. He could strip her bare, she knew. If she told him she had fallen in love with him, had started the tumble almost from the first, she would have no defense left. He would have complete and total control. And she would have reneged on the most important agreement in her life. If she couldn't give him the truth, she could give him the answer he'd understand. The answer that mirrored his feelings for her.

"Because I wanted you," she said, and kept her voice cool. "I was attracted to you, and wisely or not, I gave in to the attraction."

He felt the twinge, a need unfulfilled. "That's enough for you?"

Hadn't she said he could hurt her? He was hurting her now with every word. "Why shouldn't it be?" She gave him an easy smile and waited for the ache to pass.

"Why shouldn't it be?" he murmured, and tried

to accept the answer for what it was. He pulled out a cigarette, then began carefully. "I think you should know we're shooting a segment on the Ridehour case." Though his eyes stayed on hers, he saw her tense. "Clarissa agreed to discuss it."

"She told me. That should wrap the taping?"

"It should." She was holding back. Though no more than a table separated them, it might have been a canyon. "You don't like it."

"No, I don't, but I'm trying to learn that Clarissa has to make her own decisions."

"A.J., she seems very easy about it."

"You don't understand."

"Then let me."

"Before I convinced her to move, to keep her residence strictly confidential, she had closets full of letters." She took her glasses off to rub at a tiny ache in her temple. "People asking for her to help them. Some of them involved no more than asking her to locate a ring, and others were full of problems so heartbreaking they gave you nightmares."

"She couldn't help everyone."

"That's what I kept telling her. When she moved down to Newport Beach, things eased up. Until she got the call from San Francisco."

"The Ridehour murders."

"Yes." The ache grew. "There was never a question of her listening to me on that one. I don't believe she heard one argument I made. She just packed. When I saw there was no stopping her from going, I went with her." She kept her breathing even with great effort. Her hands were steady only because she locked them so tightly together. "It was one of the most painful experiences of her life. She saw." A.J. closed her eyes and spoke to him what she'd never spoken to anyone. "I saw."

When he covered her hand with his, he found it cold. He didn't have to see her eyes to know the baffled fear would be there. Comfort, understanding. How did he show them? "Why didn't you tell me before?"

She opened her eyes. The control was there, but teetering. "It isn't something I like to remember. I've never before or since had anything come so clear, so hideously clear."

"We'll cut it."

She gave him a blank, puzzled look. "What?"

"We'll cut the segment."

"Why?"

Slowly he drew her hands apart and into his. He wanted to explain, to tell her so that she'd understand. He wished he had the words. "Because it upsets you. That's enough."

She looked down at their hands. His looked so strong, so dependable, over hers. No one except her mother had ever offered to do anything for her without an angle. Yet it seemed he was. "I don't know what to say to you."

"Don't say anything."

"No." She gave herself a moment. For reasons she couldn't understand, she was relaxed again. Tension was there, hovering, but the knots in her stomach had eased. "Clarissa agreed to this segment, so she must feel as though it should be done."

"We're not talking about Clarissa now, but you. Aurora, I said once I never wanted to be responsible for your going through something like this. I mean it."

"I think you do." It made all the difference. "The fact that you'd cut the segment because of me makes me feel very special."

"Maybe I should have told you that you are before now."

Longings rose up. She let herself feel them for only a moment. "You don't have to tell me anything. I realize that if you cut this part because of me I'd hate myself. It was a long time ago, David. Maybe it's time I learned to deal with reality a little better."

"Maybe you deal with it too well."

"Maybe." She smiled again. "In any case I think you should do the segment. Just do a good job of it."

"I intend to. Do you want to sit in on it?"

"No." She glanced down at the stacks of papers. "Alex will be there for her."

He heard it in her voice, not doubt but resignation. "He's crazy about her."

"I know." In a lightning change of mood, she picked up her pencil again. "I'm going to give them one hell of a wedding."

He grinned at her. Resiliency was only one of the things that attracted him to her. "We'd better get started."

They worked side by side for nearly two hours. It took half that time for the tension to begin to fade. They read off lists and compiled new ones. They analyzed and calculated how many cases of champagne would be adequate and argued over whether to serve salmon mousse or iced shrimp.

She hadn't expected him to become personally involved with planning her mother's wedding. Before they'd finished, she'd come to accept it to the point where she delegated him to help seat guests at the ceremony.

"Working with you's an experience, A.J."

"Hmm?" She counted the out-of-town guests one last time.

"If I needed an agent, you'd head the list."

She glanced up, but was too cautious to smile. "Is that a compliment?"

"Not exactly."

Now she smiled. When she took off her glasses, her face was abruptly vulnerable. "I didn't think so. Well, once I give these figures to the caterer, that should be it. Everyone who attends will have me to thank that they aren't eating Clarissa's Swedish meatballs. And you." She set the lists aside. "I appreciate all the help."

"I'm fond of Clarissa."

"I know. I appreciate that, too. Now I think you deserve a reward." She leaned closer and caught her tongue in her teeth. "Anything in mind?"

He had plenty in mind every time he looked at her. "We can start with that coffee."

"Coming right up." She rose, and out of habit glanced at her watch. "Oh, God."

He reached for a cigarette. "Problem?"

"*Empire*'s on."

"A definite problem."

"No, I have to watch it."

As she dashed over to the television, he shook his head. "All this time, and I had no idea you were an addict. A.J., there are places you can go that can help you deal with these things."

"Shh." She settled on the sofa, relieved she'd missed no more than the opening credits. "I have a client—"

"It figures."

"She has a lot of potential," A.J. continued. "But this is the first real break we've gotten. She's only signed for four episodes, but if she does well, they could bring her back through next season."

Resigned, he joined her on the sofa. "Aren't these repeats, anyway?"

"Not this one. It's a teaser for a spin-off that's going to run through the summer."

"A spin-off?" He propped his feet on an issue of *Variety* on the coffee table. "Isn't there enough sex and misery in one hour a week?"

"Melodrama. It's important to the average person to see that the filthy rich have their problems. See him?" Reaching over, she dug into a bowl of candied almonds. "That's Dereck, the patriarch. He made his money in shipping—and smuggling. He's determined that his children carry on his business, by his rules. That's Angelica."

"In the hot tub."

"Yes, she's his second wife. She married him for his money and power and enjoys every minute of them. But she hates his kids."

"And they hate her right back."

"That's the idea." Pleased with him, A.J. patted his leg. "Now the setup is that Angelica's illegitimate daughter from a long-ago relationship is going to show up. That's my client."

"Like mother like daughter?"

"Oh, yes, she gets to play the perfect bitch. Her name's Lavender."

"Of course it is."

"You see, Angelica never told Dereck she had a daughter, so when Lavender shows up, she's going to cause all sorts of problems. Now Beau—that's Dereck's eldest son—"

"No more names." With a sigh, he swung his arm over the back of the sofa. "I'll just watch all the skin and diamonds."

"Just because you'd rather watch pelicans migrate— Here she is."

A.J. bit her lip. She tensed, agonizing with her client over each line, each move, each expression. And she would, David thought with a smile, fluff him off if he mentioned she had a personal involvement. Just business? Not by a long shot. She was pulling for her ingenue and ten percent didn't enter into it.

"Oh, she's good," A.J. breathed at the commercial break. "She's really very good. A season—maybe two—of this, and we'll be sifting through offers for feature films."

"Her timing's excellent." He might consider the show itself a glitzy waste of time, but he appreciated talent. "Where did she study?"

"She didn't." Smug, A.J. sat back. "She took a bus from Kansas City and ended up in my reception area with a homemade portfolio and a handful of high school plays to her credit."

He gave in and tried the candied almonds himself. "You usually sign on clients that way?"

"I usually have Abe or one of the more maternal members of my staff give them a lecture and a pat on the head."

"Sensible. But?"

"She was different. When she wouldn't budge out of the office for the second day running, I decided to see her myself. As soon as I saw her I knew. Not that way," she answered, understanding his unspoken question. "I make it a policy not to sign a client no matter what feelings might come through. She had looks and a wonderful voice. But more, she had the drive. I don't know how many auditions I sent her on in the first few weeks. But I figured if she survived that, we were going to roll." She watched the next glittery set of *Empire* appear on the screen. "And we're rolling."

"It took guts to camp out in one of the top agencies in Hollywood."

"If you don't have guts in this town, you'll be flattened in six months."

"Is that what keeps you on top, A.J.?"

"It's part of it." She found the curve of his shoulder an easy place to rest her head. "You can't tell me you think you're where you are today because you got lucky."

"No. You start off thinking hard work's enough, then you realize you have to take risks and shed a little blood. Then just when everything comes together and a project's finished and successful, you have to start another and prove yourself all over again."

"It's a lousy business." A.J. cuddled against him.

"Yep."

"Why do you do it?" Forgetting the series, forgetting her client, A.J. turned her head to look at him.

"Masochism."

"No, really."

"Because every time I watch something I did on that little screen, it's like Christmas. And I get every present I ever wanted."

"I know." Nothing he could have said could have hit more directly home. "I attended the Oscars a couple of years ago and two of my clients won. Two of them." She let her eyes close as she leaned against him. "I sat in the audience watching, and it was the biggest thrill of my life. I know some people would say you're not asking for enough when you get your thrills vicariously, but it's enough, more than enough, to know you've had a part in something like that. Maybe your name isn't a household word, but you were the catalyst."

"Not everyone wants his name to be a household word."

"Yours could be." She shifted again to look at him. "I'm not just saying that because—" *Because I love you.* The phrase was nearly out before she checked it. When he lifted his brow at her sudden silence, she continued quickly. "Because of our relationship. With the right material, the right crew, you could be one of the top ten producers in the business."

"I appreciate that." Her eyes were so earnest, so intense. He wished he knew why. "I don't think you throw around compliments without thinking about them first."

"No, I don't. I've seen your work, and I've seen the way you work. And I've been around long enough to know."

"I don't have any desire, not at this point, anyway, to tie myself up with any of the major studios. The big screen's for fantasies." He touched her cheek. It was real; it was soft. "I prefer dealing in reality."

"So produce something real." It was a challenge— she knew it. By the look in his eyes, he knew it, as well.

"Such as?"

"I have a script."

"A.J.—"

"No, hear me out. David." She said his name in frustration when he rolled her under him on the sofa. "Just listen a minute."

"I'd rather bite your ear."

"Bite it all you want. After you listen."

"Negotiations again?" He drew himself up just to look down at her. Her eyes were lit with enthusiasm, her cheeks flushed with anticipation of excitement to come. "What script?" he asked, and watched her lips curve.

"I've done some business with George Steiger. You know him?"

"We've met. He's an excellent writer."

"He's written a screenplay. His first. It just happened to come across my desk."

"Just happened?"

She'd done him a few favors. He was asking for another. Doing favors without personal gain at the end didn't fit the image she'd worked hard on developing. "We don't need to get into that. It's wonderful, David, really wonderful. It deals with the Cherokees and what they called the Trail of Tears, when they were driven from Georgia to reservations in Oklahoma. Most of the point of view is through a small child. You sense the bewilderment, the betrayal, but there's this strong thread of hope. It's not your 'ride off into the sunset' Western, and it's not a pretty story. It's real. You could make it important."

She was selling, and doing a damn good job of it. It occurred to him she'd probably never pitched a deal while curled up on the sofa before. "A.J., what makes you think that if I were interested, Steiger would be interested in me?"

"I happened to mention that I knew you."

"Happened to again?"

"Yes." She smiled and ran her hands down to his hips. "He's seen your work and knows your reputation. David, he needs a producer, the right producer."

"And so?"

As if disinterested, she skimmed her fingertips up his back. "He asked if I'd mention it to you, all very informally."

"This is definitely informal," he murmured as he fit his body against hers. "Are you playing agent, A.J.?"

"No." Her eyes were abruptly serious as she took his face in her hands. "I'm being your friend."

She touched him, more deeply, more sweetly, than any of their loving, any of their passion. For a moment he could find nothing to say. "Every time I think I've got a track on you, you switch lanes."

"Will you read it?"

He kissed one cheek, then the other, in a gesture he'd seen her use with her mother. It meant affection, devotion. He wondered if she understood. "I guess that means you can get me a copy."

"I just happened to have brought one home with me." With a laugh, she threw her arms around him. "David, you're going to love it."

"I'd rather love you."

She stiffened, but only for a heartbeat. Their loving was physical, she reminded herself. Deeply satisfying but only physical. When he spoke of love, it didn't mean the emotions, but the body. It was all she could expect from him, and all he wanted from her.

"Then love me now," she murmured, and found his mouth with hers. "Love me now."

She drew him to her, tempting him to take everything at once, quickly, heatedly. But he learned that pleasure taken slowly, given gently, could be so much more gratifying. Because it was still so new, she responded to tenderness with hesitation. Her stomach fluttered when he skimmed her lips with his, offering, promising. She heard her own sigh escape, a soft, giving sound that whispered across his lips. Then he murmured her name, quietly, as if it were the only sound he needed to hear.

No rush. His needs seemed to meld with her own. No hurry. Content, she let herself enjoy easy kisses that aroused the soul before they tempted the body. Relaxed, she allowed herself to thrill to the light caresses that made her strong enough to accept being weak.

She wanted to feel him against her without boundaries. With a murmur of approval, she pulled his shirt over his head, then took her hands on a long stroke down his back. There was the strength she'd understood from the beginning. A strength she respected, perhaps even more now that his hands were gentle.

When had she looked for gentleness? Her mind was already too clouded to know if she ever had. But now that she'd found it, she never wanted to lose it. Or him.

"I want you, David." She whispered the words along his cheek as she drew him closer.

Hearing her say it made his heart pound. He'd heard the words before, but rarely from her and never with such quiet acceptance. He lifted his head to look down at her. "Tell me again." As he took her chin in his hand, his voice was low and husky with emotion. "Tell me again, when I'm looking at you."

"I want you."

His mouth crushed down on hers, smothering any more words, any more thoughts. He seemed to need more; she thought she could feel it, though she didn't know what to give. She offered her mouth, that his might hungrily meet it. She offered her body, that his could greedily take it. But she held back her heart, afraid he would take that, as well, and damage it.

Clothes were peeled off as patience grew thin. He wanted to feel her against him, all the long length of her. He trembled when he touched her, but he was nearly used to trembling for her now. He ached, as he always ached. Light and subtle along her skin was the path of scent. He could follow it from her throat, to the hollow of her breasts, to the pulse at the inside of her elbows.

She shuddered against him. Her body seemed to pulse, then sigh, with each touch, each stroke. He knew where the brush of a fingertip would arouse, or the nip of his teeth would inflame. And she knew his body just as intimately. Her lips would find each point of pleasure; her palms would stroke each flame higher.

He grew to need. Each time he loved her, he came to need not only what she would give, but what she could. Each time he was more desperate to draw more from her, knowing that if he didn't find the key, he'd beg. She could, simply because she asked for nothing, bring him to his knees.

"Tell me what you want," he demanded as she clung to him.

"You. I want you."

She was hovering above the clouds that shook with lightning and thunder. The air was thick and heavy, the heat swirling. Her body was his; she gave it willingly. But the heart she struggled so hard to defend lost itself to him.

"David." All the love, all the emotion she felt, shimmered in his name as she pressed herself against him. "Don't let me go."

They dozed, still wrapped together, still drowsily content. Though most of his weight was on her, she felt light, free. Each time they made love, the sense of her own freedom came stronger. She was bound to him, but more liberated than she had ever been in her life. So she lay quietly as his heart beat slowly and steadily against hers.

"TV's still on," David murmured.

"Uh-huh." The late-night movie whisked by, sirens blaring, guns blasting. She didn't care.

She linked her hands behind his waist. "Doesn't matter."

"A few more minutes like this and we'll end up sleeping here tonight."

"That doesn't matter, either."

With a laugh, he turned his face to kiss her neck where the skin was still heated from excitement. Reluctantly he shifted his weight. "You know, with a few minor changes, we could be a great deal more comfortable."

"In the bed," she murmured in agreement, but merely snuggled into him.

"For a start. I'm thinking more of the long term."

It was difficult to think at all when he was warm and firm against her. "Which long term?"

"Both of us tend to do a lot of running around and overnight packing in order to spend the evening together."

"Mmmm. I don't mind."

He did. The more content he became with her, the more discontent he became with their arrangement. *I love you.* The words seemed so simple. But he'd never spoken them to a woman before. If he said them to her, how quickly would she pull away and disappear from his life? Some risks he wasn't ready to take. Cautious, he approached in the practical manner he thought she'd understand.

"Still, I think we could come up with a more logical arrangement."

She opened her eyes and shifted a bit. He could see

there was already a line between her brows. "What sort of arrangement?"

He wasn't approaching this exactly as he'd planned. But then he'd learned that his usual meticulous plotting didn't work when he was dealing with A.J. "Your apartment's convenient to the city, where we both happen to be working at the moment."

"Yes." Her eyes had lost that dreamy softness they always had after loving. He wasn't certain whether to curse himself or her.

"We only work five days a week. My house, on the other hand, is convenient for getting away and relaxing. It seems a logical arrangement might be for us to live here during the week and spend weekends at my place."

She was silent for five seconds, then ten, while dozens of thoughts and twice as many warnings rushed through her mind. "A logical arrangement," he called it. Not a commitment, an "arrangement." Or more accurately, an amendment to the arrangement they'd already agreed on. "You want to live together."

He'd expected more from her, anything more. A flicker of pleasure, a gleam of emotion. But her voice was cool and cautious. "We're essentially doing that now, aren't we?"

"No." She wanted to distance herself, but his body kept hers trapped. "We're sleeping together."

And that was all she wanted. His hands itched to shake her, to shake her until she looked, really looked, at him and saw what he felt and what he needed. Instead he sat up and, in the unselfconscious way she always admired, began to dress. Feeling naked and defenseless, she reached for her blouse.

"You're angry."

"Let's just say I didn't think we'd have to go to the negotiating table with this."

"David, you haven't even given me five minutes to think it through."

He turned to her then, and the heat in his eyes had her bracing. "If you need to," he said with perfect calm, "maybe we should just drop it."

"You're not being fair."

"No, I'm not." He rose then, knowing he had to get out, get away from her, before he said too much. "Maybe I'm tired of being fair with you."

"Damn it, David." Half-dressed, she sprang up to face him. "You casually suggest that we should combine our living arrangements, then blow up because I need a few minutes to sort it through. You're being ridiculous."

"It's a habit I picked up when I starting seeing you." He should have left. He knew he should have already walked out the door. Because he hadn't, he grabbed her arms and pulled her closer. "I want more than sex and breakfast. I want more than a quick roll in the sheets when our schedules make it convenient."

Furious, she swung away from him. "You make me sound like a—"

"No. I make us both sound like it." He didn't reach for her again. He wouldn't crawl. "I make us both sound like precisely what we are. And I don't care for it."

She'd known it would end. She'd told herself she'd be prepared when it did. But she wanted to shout and scream. Clinging to what pride she had left, she stood straight. "I don't know what you want."

He stared at her until she nearly lost the battle with

the tears that threatened. "No," he said quietly. "You don't. That's the biggest problem, isn't it?"

He left her because he wanted to beg. She let him go because she was ready to.

Chapter 12

Nervous as a cat, A.J. supervised as folding chairs were set in rows in her mother's garden. She counted them—again—before she walked over to fuss with the umbrella-covered tables set in the side yard. The caterers were busy in the kitchen; the florist and two assistants were putting the finishing touches on the arrangements. Pots of lilies and tubs of roses were placed strategically around the terrace so that their scents wafted and melded with the flowers of Clarissa's garden. It smelled like a fairy tale.

Everything was going perfectly. With her hands in her pockets, she stood in the midmorning sunlight and wished for a crisis she could dig her teeth into.

Her mother was about to marry the man she loved, the weather was a blessing and all of A.J.'s preplanning was paying off. She couldn't remember ever being more miserable. She wanted to be home, in her own apartment, with the door locked and the curtains drawn, with her head buried under the covers. Hadn't it been David who'd once told her that self-pity wasn't attractive?

Well, David was out of her life now, A.J. reminded herself. And had been for nearly two weeks. That was for the best. Without having him around, confusing her emotions, she could get on with business. The agency was so busy she was seriously considering increasing her staff. Because of the increased work load, she was on the verge of canceling her own two-week vacation in Saint Croix. She was personally negotiating two multimillion-dollar contracts and one wrong move could send them toppling.

She wondered if he'd come.

A.J. cursed herself for even thinking of him. He'd walked out of her apartment and her life. He'd walked out when she'd kept herself in a state of turmoil, struggling to keep strictly to the terms of their agreement. He'd been angry and unreasonable. He hadn't bothered to call and she certainly wasn't going to call him.

Maybe she had once, she thought with a sigh. But he hadn't been home. It wasn't likely that David Brady was mooning and moping around. A. J. Fields was too independent, and certainly too busy, to do any moping herself.

But she'd dreamed of him. In the middle of the night she'd pull herself out of dreams because he was there. She knew, better than most, that dreams could hurt.

That part of her life was over, she told herself again. It had been only an…episode, she decided. Episodes didn't always end with flowers and sunlight and pretty words. She glanced over to see one of the hired help knock over a line of chairs. Grateful for the distraction, A.J. went over to help set things to rights.

When she went back into the house, the caterers were busily fussing over quiche and Clarissa was sitting contentedly in her robe, noting down the recipe.

"Momma, shouldn't you be getting ready?"

Clarissa glanced up with a vague smile and petted the cat that curled in her lap. "Oh, there's plenty of time, isn't there?"

"A woman never has enough time to get ready on her wedding day."

"It's a beautiful day, isn't it? I know it's foolish to take it as a sign, but I'd like to."

"You can take anything you want as a sign." A.J. started to move to the stove for coffee, then changed her mind. On impulse, she opened the refrigerator and pulled out one of the bottles of champagne that were chilling. The caterers muttered together and she ignored them. It wasn't every day a daughter watched her mother marry. "Come on. I'll help you." A.J. swung through the dining room and scooped up two fluted glasses.

"I wonder if I should drink before. I shouldn't be fuzzy-headed."

"You should absolutely be fuzzy-headed," A.J. corrected. Walking into her mother's room, she plopped down on the bed as she had as a child. "We should both be fuzzy-headed. It's better than being nervous."

Clarissa smiled beautifully. "I'm not nervous."

A.J. sent the cork cannoning to the ceiling. "Brides have to be nervous. I'm nervous and all I have to do is watch."

"Aurora." Clarissa took the glass she offered, then sat on the bed beside her. "You should stop worrying about me."

"I can't." A.J. leaned over to kiss one cheek, then the other. "I love you."

Clarissa took her hand and held it tightly. "You've always been a pleasure to me. Not once, not once in your entire life, have you brought me anything but happiness."

"That's all I want for you."

"I know. And it's all I want for you." She loosened her grip on A.J.'s hand but continued to hold it. "Talk to me."

A.J. didn't need specifics to understand her mother meant David. She set down her untouched champagne and started to rise. "We don't have time. You need to—"

"You've had an argument. You hurt."

With a long, hopeless sigh, A.J. sank back down on the bed. "I knew I would from the beginning. I had my eyes open."

"Did you?" With a shake of her head, Clarissa set her glass beside A.J.'s so she could take both her hands. "Why is it you have such a difficult time accepting affection from anyone but me? Am I responsible for that?"

"No. No, it's just the way things are. In any case, David and I… We simply had a very intense physical affair that burned itself out."

Clarissa thought of what she had seen, what she had felt, and nearly sighed. "But you're in love with him."

With anyone else, she could have denied. With anyone else, she could have lied and perhaps have been believed. "That's my problem, isn't it? And I'm dealing with it," she added quickly, before she was tempted into self-pity again. "Today of all days we shouldn't be talking about anything but lovely things."

"Today of all days I want to see my daughter happy. How do you think he feels about you?"

It never paid to forget how quietly stubborn Clarissa could be. "He was attracted. I think he was a little intrigued because I wasn't immediately compliant, and in business we stood toe-to-toe."

Clarissa hadn't forgotten how successfully evasive her daughter could be. "I asked you how you think he feels."

"I don't know." A.J. dragged a hand through her hair and rose. "He wants me—or wanted me. We match very well in bed. And then I'm not sure. He seemed to want more—to get inside my head."

"And you don't care for that."

"I don't like being examined."

Clarissa watched her daughter pace back and forth in her quick, nervous gait. So much emotion bottled up, she thought. Why couldn't she understand she'd only truly feel it when she let it go? "Are you so sure that's what he was doing?"

"I'm not sure of anything, but I know that David is a very logical sort of man. The kind who does meticulous research into any subject that interests him."

"Did you ever consider that it was you who interested him, not your psychic abilities?"

"I think he might have been interested in one and uneasy about the other." She wished, even now, that she could be sure. "In any case, it's done now. We both understood commitment was out of the question."

"Why?"

"Because it wasn't what he—what we," she corrected herself quickly, "were looking for. We set the rules at the start."

"What did you argue about?"

"He suggested we live together."

"Oh." Clarissa paused a moment. She was old-fashioned enough to be anxious and wise enough to accept. "To some, a step like that is a form of commitment."

"No, it was more a matter of convenience." Was that what hurt? she wondered. She hadn't wanted to analyze it. "Anyway, I wanted to think it over and he got angry. Really angry."

"He's hurt." When A.J. glanced over, surprised protest on the tip of her tongue, Clarissa shook her head. "I know. You've managed to hurt each other deeply, with nothing more than pride."

That changed things. A.J. told herself it shouldn't, but found herself weakening. "I didn't want to hurt David. I only wanted—"

"To protect yourself," Clarissa finished. "Sometimes doing one can only lead to the other. When you love someone, really love them, you have to take some risks."

"You think I should go to him."

"I think you should do what's in your heart."

Her heart. Her heart was broken open. She wondered why everyone couldn't see what was in it. "It sounds so easy."

"And it's the most frightening thing in the world. We can test, analyze and research psychic phenomena. We can set up labs in some of the greatest universities and institutions in the world, but no one but a poet understands the terror of love."

"You've always been a poet, Momma." A.J. sat down beside her again, resting her head on her mother's shoulder. "Oh, God, what if he doesn't want me?"

"Then you'll hurt and you'll cry. After you do, you'll pick up the pieces of your life and go on. I have a strong daughter."

"And I have a wise and beautiful mother." A.J. leaned

over to pick up both glasses of wine. After handing one to Clarissa, she raised hers in a toast. "What shall we drink to first?"

"Hope." Clarissa clinked glasses. "That's really all there is."

A.J. changed in the bedroom her mother always kept prepared for her. It hadn't mattered that she'd spent only a handful of nights in it over nearly ten years; Clarissa had labeled it hers, and hers it remained. Perhaps she would stay there tonight, after the wedding was over, the guests gone and the newlyweds off on their honeymoon. She might think better there, and tomorrow find the courage to listen to her mother's advice and follow her heart.

What if he didn't want her? What if he'd already forgotten her? A.J. faced the mirror but closed her eyes. There were too many "what ifs" to consider and only one thing she could be certain of. She loved him. If that meant taking risks, she didn't have a choice.

Straightening her shoulders, she opened her eyes and studied herself. The dress was romantic because her mother preferred it. She hadn't worn anything so blatantly feminine and flowing in years. Lace covered her bodice and caressed her throat, while the soft blue silk peeked out of the eyelets. The skirt swept to a bell at her ankles.

Not her usual style, A.J. thought again, but there was something appealing about the old-fashioned cut and the charm of lace. She picked up the nosegay of white roses that trailed with ribbon and felt foolishly like a bride herself. What would it be like to be preparing to bond yourself with another person, someone who loved and wanted you? There would be flutters in your stomach.

She felt them in her own. Your throat would be dry. She lifted a hand to it. You would feel giddy with a combination of excitement and anxiety. She put her hand on the dresser to steady herself.

A premonition? Shaking it off, she stepped back from the mirror. It was her mother who would soon promise to love, honor and cherish. She glanced at her watch, then caught her breath. How had she managed to lose so much time? If she didn't put herself in gear, the guests would be arriving with no one to greet them.

Alex's children were the first to arrive. She'd only met them once, the evening before at dinner, and they were still a bit awkward and formal with one another. But when her future sister offered to help, A.J. decided to take her at her word. Within moments, cars began pulling up out front and she needed all the help she could get.

"A.J." Alex found her in the garden, escorting guests to chairs. "You look lovely."

He looked a little pale under his tan. The sign of nerves had her softening toward him. "Wait until you see your bride."

"I wish I could." He pulled at the knot in his tie. "I have to admit I'd feel easier if she were here to hold on to. You know, I talk to millions of people every night, but this…" He glanced around the garden. "This is a whole different ball game."

"I predict very high ratings." She brushed his cheek. "Why don't you slip inside and have a little shot of bourbon?"

"I think I might." He gave her shoulder a squeeze. "I think I just might."

A.J. watched him make his way to the back door before she turned back to her duties. And there was

David. He stood at the edge of the garden, where the breeze just ruffled the ends of his hair. She wondered, as her heart began to thud, that she hadn't sensed him. She wondered, as the pleasure poured through her, if she'd wished him there.

He didn't approach her. A.J.'s fingers tightened on the wrapped stems of her flowers. She knew she had to take the first step.

She was so lovely. He thought she looked like something that had stepped out of a dream. The breeze that tinted the air with the scents of the garden teased the lace at her throat. As she walked to him, he thought of every empty hour he'd spent away from her.

"I'm glad you came."

He'd told himself he wouldn't, then he'd been dressed and driving south. She'd pulled him there, through her thoughts or through his own emotions, it didn't matter. "You seem to have it all under control."

She had nothing under control. She wanted to reach out to him, to tell him, but he seemed so cool and distant. "Yes, we're nearly ready to start. As soon as I get the rest of these people seated, I can go in for Clarissa."

"I'll take care of them."

"You don't have to. I—"

"I told you I would."

His clipped response cut her off. A.J. swallowed her longings and nodded. "Thanks. If you'll excuse me, then." She walked away, into the house, into her own room, where she could compose herself before she faced her mother.

Damn it! He swung away, cursing her, cursing himself, cursing everything. Just seeing her again had made him want to crawl. He wasn't a man who could live on his knees. She'd looked so cool, so fresh and lovely, and for a moment, just a moment, he'd thought he'd seen the emotions he needed in her eyes. Then she'd smiled at him as though he were just another guest at her mother's wedding.

He wasn't going to go on this way. David forced himself to make polite comments and usher well-wishers to their seats. Today, before it was over, he and A. J. Fields were going to come to terms. His terms. He'd planned it that way, hadn't he? It was about time one of his plans concerning her worked.

The orchestra A.J. had hired after auditioning at least a half-dozen played quietly on a wooden platform on the lawn. A trellis of sweet peas stood a few feet in front of the chairs. Composed and clear-eyed, A.J. walked through the garden to take her place. She glanced at Alex and gave him one quick smile of encouragement. Then Clarissa, dressed in dusky rose silk, stepped out of the house.

She looks like a queen, A.J. thought as her heart swelled. The guests rose as she walked through, but she had eyes only for Alex. And he, A.J. noted, looked as though no one else in the world existed but Clarissa.

They joined hands, and they promised.

The ceremony was short and traditional. A.J. watched her mother pledge herself, and fought back a sense of loss that vied with happiness. The words were simple, and ultimately so complex. The vows were timeless, and somehow completely new.

With her vision misted, her throat aching, she took her mother in her arms. "Oh, be happy, Momma."

"I am. I will be." She drew away just a little. "So will you."

Before A.J. could speak, Clarissa turned away and was swept up in an embrace by her new stepchildren.

There were guests to feed and glasses to fill. A.J. found keeping busy helped put her emotions on hold. In a few hours she'd be alone. Then she'd let them come. Now she laughed, brushed cheeks, toasted and felt utterly numb.

"Clarissa." David had purposely waited until she'd had a chance to breathe before he approached her. "You're beautiful."

"Thank you, David. I'm so glad you're here. She needs you."

He stiffened and only inclined his head. "Does she?"

With a sigh, Clarissa took both of his hands. When he felt the intensity, he nearly drew away. "Plans aren't necessary," she said quietly. "Feelings are."

David forced himself to relax. "You don't play fair."

"She's my daughter. In more ways than one."

"I understand that."

It took her only a moment, then she smiled. "Yes, you do. You might let her know. Aurora's an expert at blocking feelings, but she deals well with words. Talk to her?"

"Oh, I intend to."

"Good." Satisfied, Clarissa patted his hand. "Now I think you should try the quiche. I wheedled the recipe out of the caterer. It's fascinating."

"So are you." David leaned down to kiss her cheek.

A.J. all but exhausted herself. She moved from group to group, sipping champagne and barely tasting anything from the impressive display of food. The cake with its iced swans and hearts was cut and devoured. Wine flowed and music played. Couples danced on the lawn.

"I thought you'd like to know I read Steiger's script." After stepping beside her, David kept his eyes on the dancers. "It's extraordinary."

Business, she thought. It was best to keep their conversation on business. "Are you considering producing it?"

"Considering. That's a long way from doing it. I have a meeting with Steiger Monday."

"That's wonderful." She couldn't stop the surge of pleasure for him. She couldn't help showing it. "You'll be sensational."

"And if the script ever makes it to the screen, you'll have been the catalyst."

"I like to think so."

"I haven't waltzed since I was thirteen." David slipped a hand to her elbow and felt the jolt. "My mother made me dance with my cousin, and at the time I felt girls were a lower form of life. I've changed my mind since." His arm slid around her waist. "You're tense."

She concentrated on the count, on matching her steps to his, on anything but the feel of having him hold her again. "I want everything to be perfect for her."

"I don't think you need to worry about that anymore."

Her mother danced with Alex as though they were alone in the garden. "No." She sighed before she could prevent it. "I don't."

"You're allowed to feel a little sad." Her scent was there as he remembered, quietly tempting.

"No, it's selfish."

"It's normal," he corrected. "You're too hard on yourself."

"I feel as though I've lost her." She was going to cry. A.J. steeled herself against it.

"You haven't." He brushed his lips along her temple. "And the feeling will pass."

When he was kind, she was lost. When he was gentle, she was defenseless. "David." Her fingers tightened on his shoulder. "I missed you."

It cost her to say it. The first layer of pride that covered all the rest dissolved with the words. She felt his hand tense, then gentle on her waist.

"Aurora."

"Please, don't say anything now." The control she depended on wouldn't protect her now. "I just wanted you to know."

"We need to talk."

Even as she started to agree, the announcement blared over the mike. "All unmarried ladies, line up now for the bouquet toss."

"Come on, A.J." Her new stepsister, laughing and eager, grabbed her arm and hustled her along. "We have to see who's going to be next."

She wasn't interested in bouquets or giddy young women. Her life was on the line. Distracted, A.J. glanced around for David. She looked back in time to throw up her hands defensively before her mother's bouquet landed in her face. Embarrassed, A.J. accepted the congratulations and well-meaning teasing.

"Another sign?" Clarissa commented as she pecked her daughter's cheek.

"A sign that my mother has eyes in the back of her head and excellent aim." A.J. indulged herself with burying her face in the bouquet. It was sweet, and promising. "You should keep this."

"Oh, no. That would be bad luck and I don't intend to have any."

"I'm going to miss you, Momma."

She understood—she always had—but she smiled and gave A.J. another kiss. "I'll be back in two weeks."

She barely had time for another fierce embrace before her mother and Alex dashed off in a hail of rice and cheers.

Some guests left, others lingered. When the first streaks of sunset deepened the sky she watched the orchestra pack up their instruments.

"Long day."

She turned to David and reached out a hand before she could help it. "I thought you'd gone."

"Just got out of the way for a while. You did a good job."

"I can't believe it's done." She looked over as the last of the chairs were folded and carted away.

"I could use some coffee."

She smiled, trying to convince herself to be light. "Do we have any left?"

"I put some on before I came back out." He walked with her to the house. "Where were they going on their honeymoon?"

The house was so empty. Strange, she'd never noticed just how completely Clarissa had filled it. "Sailing." She laughed a little, then found herself looking helplessly around the kitchen. "I have a hard time picturing Clarissa hoisting sails."

"Here." He pulled a handkerchief out of his pocket. "Sit down and have a good cry. You're entitled."

"I'm happy for her." But the tears began to fall. "Alex is a wonderful man and I know he loves her."

"But she doesn't need you to take care of her anymore." He handed her a mug of coffee. "Drink."

Nodding, she sipped. "She's always needed me."

"She still does." He took the handkerchief and dried her cheeks himself. "Just in a different way."

"I feel like a fool."

"The trouble with you is you can't accept that you're supposed to feel like a fool now and again."

She blew her nose, unladylike and indignant. "I don't like it."

"Not supposed to. Have you finished crying?"

She sulked a moment, sniffled, then sipped more coffee. "Yes."

"Tell me again that you missed me."

"It was a moment of weakness," she murmured into the mug, but he took it away from her.

"No more evasions, Aurora. You're going to tell me what you want, what you feel."

"I want you back." She swallowed and wished he would say something instead of just staring at her.

"Go on."

"David, you're making this difficult."

"Yeah, I know." He didn't touch her, not yet. He needed more than that. "For both of us."

"All right." She steadied herself with a deep breath. "When you suggested we live together, I wasn't expecting it. I wanted to think it through, but you got angry. Well, since you've been away, I've had a chance to think it through. I don't see why we can't live together under those terms."

Always negotiating, he thought as he rubbed a hand over his chin. She still wasn't going to take that last step. "I've had a chance to think it through, too. And I've changed my mind."

He could have slapped her and not have knocked the wind from her so successfully. Rejection, when it came, was always painful, but it had never been like this. "I see." She turned away to pick up her coffee, but her hands weren't nearly steady enough.

"You did a great job on this wedding, A.J."

Closing her eyes, she wondered why she felt like laughing. "Thanks. Thanks a lot."

"Seems to me like you could plan another standing on your head."

"Oh, sure." She pressed her fingers to her eyes. "I might go into the business."

"No, I was thinking about just one more. Ours."

The tears weren't going to fall. She wouldn't let them. It helped to concentrate on that. "Our what?"

"Wedding. Aren't you paying attention?"

She turned slowly to see him watching her with what appeared to be mild amusement. "What are you talking about?"

"I noticed you caught the bouquet. I'm superstitious."

"This isn't funny." Before she could stalk from the room he had caught her close.

"Damn right it's not. It's not funny that I've spent eleven days and twelve nights thinking of little but you. It's not funny that every time I took a step closer, you took one back. Every time I'd plan something out, the whole thing would be blown to hell after five minutes with you."

"It's not going to solve anything to shout at me."

"It's not going to solve anything until you start listening and stop anticipating. Look, I didn't want this any more than you did. I liked my life just the way it was."

"That's fine, then. I liked my life, too."

"Then we both have a problem, because nothing's going to be quite the same again."

Why couldn't she breathe? Temper never made her breathless. "Why not?"

"Guess." He kissed her then, hard, angry, as if he wanted to kick out at both of them. But it only took an instant, a heartbeat. His lips softened, his hold gentled and she was molded to him. "Why don't you read my mind? Just this once, Aurora, open yourself up."

She started to shake her head, but his mouth was on hers again. The house was quiet. Outside, the birds serenaded the lowering sun. The light was dimming and there was nothing but that one room and that one moment. Feelings poured into her, feelings that once would have brought fear. Now they offered, requested and gave her everything she'd been afraid to hope for.

"David." Her arms tightened around him. "I need you to tell me. I couldn't bear to be wrong."

Hadn't he needed words? Hadn't he tried time and again to pry them out of her? Maybe it was time to give them to her. "The first time I met your mother, she said something to me about needing to understand or discover my own tenderness. That first weekend you stayed with me, I came home and found you sleeping on the bed. I looked at you, the woman who'd been my lover, and fell in love. The problem was I didn't know how to make you fall in love with me."

"I already had. I didn't think you—"

"The problem was you did think. Too much." He drew her away, only to look at her. "So did I. Be civilized. Be careful. Wasn't that the way we arranged things?"

"It seemed like the right way." She swallowed and moved closer. "It didn't work for me. When I fell in love with you, all I could think was that I'd ruin everything by wanting too much."

"And I thought if I asked, you'd be gone before the words were out." He brushed his lips over her brow. "We wasted time thinking when we should have been feeling."

She should be cautious, but there was such ease, such

quiet satisfaction, in just holding him. "I was afraid you'd never be able to accept what I am."

"So was I." He kissed one cheek, then the other. "We were both wrong."

"I need you to be sure. I need to know that it doesn't matter."

"Aurora. I love you, who you are, what you are, how you are. I don't know how else to tell you."

She closed her eyes. Clarissa and she had been right to drink to hope. That was all there was. "You just found the best way."

"There's more." He held her, waiting until she looked at him again. And he saw, as he'd needed to, her heart in her eyes. "I want to spend my life with you. Have children with you. There's never been another woman who's made me want those things."

She took his face in her hands and lifted her mouth to his. "I'm going to see to it there's never another."

"Tell me how you feel."

"I love you."

He held her close, content. "Tell me what you want."

"A lifetime. Two, if we can manage it."

* * * * *

DUAL IMAGE

Chapter 1

Balancing a bag of groceries in one arm, Amanda let herself into the house. She radiated happiness. From outside came the sound of birds singing in the spring sunshine. The gold of her wedding ring caught the light. As a newlywed of three months, she was anxious to prepare a special, intimate dinner as a surprise for Cameron. Her demanding hours at the hospital and clinic often made it impossible for her to cook, and as a new bride she found pleasure in it. This afternoon, with two appointments unexpectedly canceled, she intended to fix something fancy, time-consuming and memorable. Something that went well with candlelight and wine.

As she entered the kitchen she was humming, a rare outward show of emotion for she was a reserved woman. With a satisfied smile, she drew a bottle of Cameron's favorite Bordeaux from the bag. As she studied the label, a smile lingered on her face while she remembered the first time they'd shared a bottle. He'd been so romantic, so attentive, so much what she'd needed at that point in her life.

A glance at her watch told her she had four full hours before her husband was expected home. Time enough to prepare an elaborate meal, light the candles and set out the crystal.

First, she decided, she was going upstairs to get out of her practical suit and shoes. There was a silk caftan upstairs, sheer, in misty shades of blue. Tonight, she wouldn't be a psychiatrist, but a woman, a woman very much in love.

The house was scrupulously neat and tastefully decorated. Such things came naturally to Amanda. As she walked toward the stairs, she glanced at a vase of Baccarat crystal and wished fleetingly she'd remembered fresh flowers. Perhaps she'd call the florist and have something extravagant delivered. Her hand trailed lightly over the polished banister as she started up. Her eyes, usually serious or intent, were dreamy. Carelessly, she pushed open the bedroom door.

Her smile froze. Utter shock replaced it. As she stood in the doorway, all color seemed to drain out of her cheeks. Her eyes grew huge before pain filled them. Out of her mouth came one anguished word.

"Cameron."

The couple in bed, locked in a passionate embrace, sprang apart. The man, smoothly handsome, his sleek hair disheveled, stared up in disbelief. The woman—feline, sultry, stunning—smiled very, very slowly. You could almost hear her purr.

"Vikki." Amanda looked at her sister with anguished eyes.

"You're home early." There was a hint, only a suspicion of a laugh in her sister's voice.

Cameron put a few more inches between himself and his sister-in-law. "Amanda, I…"

In one split second, Amanda's face contorted. With her eyes locked on the couple in bed, she reached in her jacket pocket and drew out a small, lethal revolver. The lovers stared at it in astonishment, and in silence. Coolly, she aimed and fired. A puff of confetti burst out.

"Ariel!"

Dr. Amanda Lane Jamison, better known as Ariel Kirkwood, turned to her harassed director as the couple in bed and members of the television crew dissolved into laughter.

"Sorry, Neal, I couldn't help myself. Amanda's *always* the victim," she said dramatically while her eyes danced. "Just think what it might do for the ratings if she lost her cool just once and murdered someone."

"Look, Ariel—"

"Or even just seriously injured them," she went on rapidly. "And who," she continued, flinging her hand toward the bed, "deserves it more than her spineless husband and scheming sister?"

At the hoots and applause of the crew, Ariel took a bow, then reluctantly turned over her weapon to her director when he held out his hand.

"You," he said with a long-suffering sigh, "are a certified loony, and have been since I've known you."

"I appreciate that, Neal."

"This time the tape's going to be running," he warned and tried not to grin. "Let's see if we can shoot this scene before lunch."

Agreeably, Ariel went down to the first floor of the set. She stood patiently while her hair and makeup were touched up. Amanda was always perfection. Organized, meticulous, calm—all the things Ariel herself wasn't.

She'd played the character for just over five years on the popular daytime soap opera *Our Lives, Our Loves*.

In those five years, Amanda had graduated with honors from college, had earned her degree in psychiatric medicine and had gone on to become a respected therapist. Her recent marriage to Cameron Jamison appeared to be made in heaven. But, of course, he was a weak opportunist who'd married her for her money and social position, while lusting after her sister—and half the female population of the fictional town of Trader's Bend.

Amanda was about to be confronted with the truth. The story line had been leading up to this revelation for six weeks, and the letters from viewers had poured in. Both they and Ariel thought it was about time Amanda found out about her louse of a husband.

Ariel liked Amanda, respected her integrity and poise. When the cameras rolled, Ariel *was* Amanda. While in her personal life she would much prefer a day at an amusement park to an evening at the ballet, she understood all the nuances of the woman she portrayed.

When this scene was aired, viewers would see a neat, slender woman with pale blond hair sleeked back into a sophisticated knot. The face was porcelain, stunning, with an icy kind of beauty that sent out signals of restrained sexuality. Class. Style.

Lake-blue eyes, high curved cheekbones added to the look of polished elegance. A perfectly shaped mouth tended toward serious smiles. Finely arched brows that were shades darker than the delicate blond of her hair accented luxurious lashes. A flawless beauty, perfectly composed—that was Amanda.

Ariel waited for her cue and wondered vaguely if she'd turned off her coffeepot that morning.

They ran through the scene again, from cue to cut,

then a second time when it was discovered that Vikki's strapless bathing suit could be seen when she shifted in bed. Then came reaction shots—the camera zoomed in close on Amanda's pale, shocked face and held for several long, dramatic seconds.

"Lunch."

Response was immediate. The lovers bounded out of either side of the bed. In his bathing trunks, J. T. Brown, Ariel's on-screen husband, took her by the shoulders and gave her a long hard kiss. "Look, sweetie," he began, staying in character, "I'll explain about all this later. Trust me. I gotta call my agent."

"Wimp," Ariel called after him with a very un-Amandalike grin before she hooked her arm through that of Stella Powell, her series sister. "Pull something over that suit, Stella. I can't face the commissary food today."

Stella tossed back her tousled mass of auburn hair. "You buying?"

"Always sponging off your sister," Ariel mumbled. "Okay, I'll spring, but hurry up. I'm starving."

On her way to her dressing room, Ariel walked off the set, then through two more—the fifth floor of Doctors Hospital and the living room of the Lanes, Trader's Bend's leading family. It was tempting to shed her costume and take down her hair, but it would only mean fooling with wardrobe and makeup after lunch. Instead, she just grabbed her purse, an outsize hobo bag that looked a bit incongruous with Amanda's elegant business suit. She was already thinking about a thick slice of baklava soaked in honey.

"Come on, Stella." Ariel stuck her head in the adjoining dressing room as Stella zipped up a pair of snug jeans. "My stomach's on overtime."

"It always is," her coworker returned as she pulled on a bulky sweatshirt. "Where to?"

"The Greek deli around the corner." More than ready, Ariel started down the hall in her characteristically long, swinging gait while Stella hurried to keep up. It wasn't that Ariel rushed from place to place, but simply that she wanted to see what was next.

"My diet," Stella began.

"Have a salad," Ariel told her without mercy. She turned her head to give Stella a quick up-and-down glance. "You know, if you weren't always wearing those skimpy outfits on camera, you wouldn't have to starve yourself."

Stella grinned as they came to the street door. "Jealous."

"Yeah. I'm always elegant and *always* proper. You have all the fun." Stepping outside, Ariel took a deep breath of New York. She loved it—had always loved it in a way usually reserved for tourists. Ariel had lived on the long thin island of Manhattan all of her life, and yet it remained an adventure to her. The sights, the smells, the sounds.

It was brisk for mid-April, and threatening to rain. The air was damp and smelled of exhaust. The streets and sidewalks were clogged with lunchtime traffic— everyone hurrying, everyone with important business to attend to. A pedestrian swore and banged a fist on the hood of a cab that had clipped too close to the curb. A woman with spiked orange hair hustled by in black leather boots. Somone had written something uncomplimentary on a poster for a hot Broadway play. But Ariel saw a street vendor selling daffodils.

She bought two bunches and handed one to Stella.

"You can never pass up anything, can you?" Stella mumbled, but buried her face in the yellow blooms.

"Think of all I'd miss," Ariel countered. "Besides, it's spring."

Stella shivered and looked up at the leaden sky. "Sure."

"Eat." Ariel grabbed her arm and pulled her along. "You always get cranky when you miss meals."

The deli was packed with people and aromas. Spices and honey. Beer and oil. Always a creature of the senses, Ariel drew in the mingled scents before she worked her way to the counter. She had an uncanny way of getting where she was going through a throng without using her elbows or stepping on toes. While she moved, she watched and listened. She wouldn't want to miss a scent, or the texture of a voice, or the clashing colors of food. As she looked behind the glass-fronted counter, she could already taste the things there.

"Cottage cheese, a slice of pineapple and coffee—black," Stella said with a sigh. Ariel sent her a brief, pitying look.

"Greek salad, a hunk of that lamb on a hard roll and a slice of baklava. Coffee, cream and sugar."

"You're disgusting," Stella told her. "You never gain an ounce."

"I know." Ariel moved down the counter to the cashier. "It's a matter of mental control and clean living." Ignoring Stella's rude snort she paid the bill then made her way through the crowded deli toward an empty table. She and a bull of a man reached it simultaneously. Ariel simply held her tray and sent him a stunning smile. The man straightened his shoulders, sucked in his stomach and gave way.

"Thanks," Stella acknowledged and dismissed him at the same time, knowing if she didn't Ariel would invite him to join them and upset any chance of a private conversation. The woman, Stella thought, needed a keeper.

Ariel did all the things a woman alone should know better than to do. She talked to strangers, walked alone at night and answered her door without the security chain attached. It wasn't that she was daring or careless, but simply that she believed in the best of people. And somehow, in a bit more than twenty-five years of living, she'd never been disillusioned. Stella marveled at her, even while she worried about her.

"The gun was one of your best stunts all season," Stella remarked as she poked at her cottage cheese. "I thought Neal was going to scream."

"He needs to relax," Ariel said with her mouth full. "He's been on edge ever since he broke up with that dancer. How about you? Are you still seeing Cliff?"

"Yeah." Stella lifted her shoulder. "I don't know why, it's not going anywhere."

"Where do you want it to go?" Ariel countered. "If you have a goal in mind, just go for it."

With a half laugh, Stella began to eat. "Not everyone plunges through life like you, Ariel. It always amazes me that you've never been seriously involved."

"Simple." Ariel speared a fork into her salad then chewed slowly. "I've never met anyone who made my knees tremble. As soon as I do, that'll be it."

"Just like that?"

"Why not? Life isn't as complicated as most people make it." She added a dash of pepper to the lamb. "Are you in love with Cliff?"

Stella frowned—not because of the question, she was used to Ariel's directness. But because of the answer. "I don't know. Maybe."

"Then you're not," Ariel said easily. "Love's a very definite emotion. Sure you don't want any of this lamb?"

Stella didn't bother to answer the question. "If you've never been in love, how do you know?"

"I've never been to Turkey, but I'm sure it's there."

With a laugh, Stella picked up her coffee. "Damn, Ariel, you've always got an answer. Tell me about the script."

"Oh, God." Ariel put down her fork, and leaning her elbows on the table, folded her hands. "It's the best thing I've ever read. I want that part. I'm going to get that part," she added with something that was apart from confidence. It was simple fact. "I swear, I've been waiting for the character of Rae to come along. She's heartless," Ariel continued, resting her chin on her folded hands. "Complex, selfish, cold, insecure. A part like that…" She trailed off with a shake of her head. "And the story," she added on a long breath as her mind jumped from one aspect to the next. "It's nearly as cold and heartless as she is, but it gets to you."

"Booth DeWitt," Stella mused. "It's rumored that he based the character of Rae on his ex-wife."

"He didn't gloss it over either. If he's telling it straight, she put him through hell. In any case," she said, as she began to eat again, "it's the best piece of work that's come my way. I'm going to read for it in a couple of days."

"TV movie," Stella said thoughtfully. "Quality television with DeWitt writing and Marshell producing. You'd have our own producer at your feet if you got it. Boy, what a boost for the ratings."

"He's already playing politics." With a small frown, Ariel broke off a chunk of baklava. "He got me an invitation to a party tonight at Marshell's condo. DeWitt's supposed to be there. From what I hear, he's got the last say on casting."

"He's got a reputation for wanting to push his own buttons," Stella agreed. "So why the frown?"

"Politics're like rain in April—you know it's got to happen, but it's messy and annoying." Then she shrugged the thought away as she did anything unavoidable. In the end, from what she knew of Booth DeWitt, she'd earn the part on her own merit. If there was one thing Ariel had an abundance of, it was confidence. She'd always needed it.

Unlike Amanda, the character she played on the soap, Ariel hadn't grown up financially secure. There'd been a great deal more love than money in her home. She'd never regretted it, or the struggle to make ends meet. She'd been sixteen when her mother had died and her father had gone into a state of shock that had lasted nearly a year. It had never occurred to her that she was too young to take on the responsibilities of running a home and raising two younger siblings. There'd been no one else to do it. She'd sold powder and perfume in a department store to pay her way through college, while managing the family home and taking any bit part that came her way.

They'd been busy, difficult years, and perhaps that in itself had given her the surplus of energy and drive she had today. And the sense that whatever had to be done, could be done.

"Amanda."

Ariel glanced up to see a small, middle-aged woman carrying a take-out bag that smelled strongly of garlic. Because she was called by her character's name almost as often as she was by her own, she smiled and held out her hand. "Hello."

"I'm Dorra Wineberger and I wanted to tell you you're just as beautiful as you are on TV."

"Thank you, Dorra. You enjoy the show?"

"I wouldn't miss it, not one single episode." She beamed at Ariel then leaned closer. "You're wonderful, dear, and so kind and patient. I just feel someone ought to tell you that Cameron— He's not good for you. The best thing for you to do is send him packing before he gets his hands on your money. He's already pawned your diamond earrings. And this one…" Dorra folded her lips and glared at Stella. "Why you bother with this one, after all the trouble she's caused you… If it hadn't been for her, you and Griff would be married like you should be." She sent Stella an affronted glare. "I know you've got your eyes on your sister's husband, Vikki."

Stella struggled with a grin and, playing the role, tossed her head and slanted her eyes. "Men are interested in me," she drawled. "And why not?"

Dorra shook her head and turned back to Ariel. "Go back to Griff," she advised kindly. "He loves you, he always has."

Ariel returned the quick squeeze of her hand. "Thanks for caring."

Both women watched Dorra walk away before they turned back to each other. "Everyone loves Dr. Amanda," Vikki said with a grin. "She's practically sacred."

"And everyone loves to hate Vikki." With a chuckle, Ariel finished off her coffee. "You're so rotten."

"Yeah." Stella gave a contented sigh. "I know." She chewed her pineapple slowly, with a wistful look at Ariel's plate. "Anyway, it always strikes me as kind of weird when people get me confused with Vikki."

"It just means you're doing your job," Ariel corrected. "If you go into people's homes every day and don't draw emotion out of them, you better look for another line of work. Nuclear physics, log rolling. Speaking of work," she added with a glance at her watch.

"I know… Hey, are you going to eat the rest of that?"

Laughing, Ariel handed her the baklava as they rose.

It was well after nine when Ariel paid off the cab in front of P. B. Marshell's building on Madison Avenue. She wasn't concerned with being late because she wasn't aware of the time. She'd never missed a cue or a call in her life, but when it wasn't directly concerned with work, time was something to be enjoyed or ignored.

She overtipped the cabbie, stuffed her change in her bag without counting it, then walked through the light drizzle into the lobby. She decided it smelled like a funeral parlor. Too many flowers, too much polish. After giving her name at the security desk, she slipped into an elevator and pushed the penthouse button. It didn't occur to her to be nervous at the prospect of entering P. B. Marshell's domain. A party to Ariel was a party. She hoped he served champagne. She had a hankering for it.

The door was opened by a stiff-backed, stone-faced man in a dark suit who asked Ariel's name in a discreet British accent. When she smiled, he accepted her offered hand before he realized it. Ariel walked past the butler, leaving him with the impression of vitality and sex—a combination that left him disconcerted for several minutes. She lifted a glass of champagne from a tray, and spotting her agent, crossed the room to her.

Booth saw Ariel's entrance. For an instant, he was reminded of his ex-wife. The coloring, the bone structure. Then the impression was gone, and he was looking at a young woman with casually curling hair that flowed past her shoulders. It seemed misted with fine drops of rain. A stunning face, he decided. But the look of an ice goddess vanished the moment she laughed. Then there was energy and verve.

Unusual, he thought, as vaguely interested in her as he was in the drink he held. He let his eyes skim down her and decided she'd be slim under the casual pleated pants and boxy blouse. Then again, if she was, she would have exploited her figure rather than underplaying it. From what Booth knew of women, they accented whatever charms at their disposal and concealed the flaws. He'd come to accept this as a part of their innate dishonesty.

He gave Ariel one last glance as she rose on her toes to kiss the latest rage in an off-Broadway production. God, he hated these long, crowded pseudoparties.

"…If we cast the female lead."

Booth turned back to P. B. Marshell and lifted his glass. "Hmm?"

Too used to Booth's lapses of attention to be annoyed, Marshell backtracked. "We can get this into production and wrapped in time for the fall sweeps if we cast the female lead. That's virtually all that's holding us back now."

"I'm not worried about the fall sweeps," Booth returned dryly.

"The network is."

"Pat, we'll cast Rae when we find Rae."

Marshell frowned into his Scotch, then drank it. At two hundred and fifty pounds, he needed several glasses to feel any effect. "You've already turned down three top names."

"I turned down three actresses who weren't suitable," Booth corrected. He drank from his own glass as a man who knew liquor and maintained a cautious relationship with it. "I'll know Rae when I see her." His lips moved into a cool smile. "Who'd know better?"

A free, easy laugh had Marshell glancing across the room. For a moment his eyes narrowed in concentration. "Ariel Kirkwood," he told Booth, gesturing with his empty glass. "The network execs would like to push her your way."

"An actress." Booth studied Ariel again. He wouldn't have pegged her as such. Her entrance had caught his attention simply because it hadn't been an *entrance*. There was something completely unselfconscious about her that was rare in the profession. She'd been at the party long enough to have wangled an introduction to him and Marshell, yet she seemed content to stay across the room sipping champagne and flirting with an up-and-coming actor.

She stood easily, in a relaxed manner that wasn't a pose but would photograph beautifully. She made an unattractive face at the actor. The contrast of the ice-goddess looks and the freewheeling manner piqued his curiosity.

"Introduce me," Booth said simply and started across the room.

Ariel couldn't fault Marshell's taste. The condo was stylishly decorated in elegant golds and creams. The carpet was thick, the walls lacquered. She recognized the signed lithograph behind her. It was a room she knew Amanda would understand and appreciate. Ariel enjoyed visiting it. She'd never have lived there. She laughed up at Tony as he reminisced about the improvisation class they'd taken together a few years before.

"And you started using gutter language to make sure everyone was awake," she reminded him and tugged on the goatee he wore for his current part.

"It worked. What cause is it this week, Ariel?"

Her brows lifted as she sipped her champagne. "I don't have weekly causes."

"Biweekly," he corrected. "Friends of Seals, Save the Mongoose. Come on, what are you into now?"

She shook her head. "There's something that's taking up a lot of my time right now. I can't really talk about it."

Tony's grin faded. He knew that tone. "Important?"

"Vital."

"Well, Tony." Marshell clapped the young actor on the back. "Glad to see you could make it."

Though it was very subtly done, Tony came to attention. "It was nice that you were having this on a night when the theater's dark, Mr. Marshell. Do you know Ariel Kirkwood?" He laid a hand on her shoulder. "We go back a long way."

"I've heard good things about you." Marshell extended his hand.

"Thank you." Ariel left her hand in his a moment as she sorted her impressions. Successful—fond of food from the bulk of him—amiable when he chose to be. Shrewd. She liked the combination. "You make excellent films, Mr. Marshell."

"Thank you," he returned and paused, expecting her to do some campaigning. When she left it at that, he turned to Booth. "Booth DeWitt, Ariel Kirkwood and Tony Lazarus."

"I've seen your play," Booth told Tony. "You know your character very well." He shifted his gaze to Ariel. "Ms. Kirkwood."

Disconcerting eyes, she thought, so clear and direct

a green in such a remote face. He gave off signals of aloofness, traces of bitterness, waves of intelligence. Obviously he didn't concern himself overmuch with trends or fashion. His hair was thick and dark and a bit long for the current style. Yet she thought it suited his face. She thought the face belonged to the nineteenth century. Lean and scholarly with a touch of ruggedness and a harshness in the mouth that kept it from being smooth.

His voice was deep and appealing, but he spoke with a clipped quality that indicated impatience. He had the eyes of an observer, she thought. And the air of a man who wouldn't tolerate interference or intimacies. She wasn't certain she'd like him, but she did know she admired his work.

"Mr. DeWitt." Her palm touched his. Strength— she'd expected that. It was in his build, long, rangy— and in his face. Distance—she'd expected that as well. "I enjoyed *The Final Bell*. It was my favorite film of last year."

He passed this off as he studied her face. She exuded sex, in her scent, in her looks—not flagrant or elusive, but light and free. "I don't believe I'm familiar with your work."

"Ariel plays Dr. Amanda Lane Jamison on *Our Lives, Our Loves*," Tony put in.

Good God, a soap opera, Booth thought. Ariel caught the faint disdain on his face. It was something else she'd expected. "Do you have a moral objection to entertainment, Mr. DeWitt?" she said easily as she sipped champagne. "Or are you just an artistic snob?" She smiled as she spoke, the quick, dashing smile that took any sting from the words.

Beside her, Tony cleared his throat. "Excuse me a

minute," he said and exited stage left. Marshell mumbled something about freshening his drink.

When they were alone, Booth continued to study her face. She was laughing at him. He couldn't remember the last time anyone had had the courage, or the occasion, to do so. He wasn't certain if he was annoyed or intrigued. But at the moment he wasn't what he'd been for the past hour. Bored.

"I haven't any moral objections to soap operas, Ms. Kirkwood."

"Oh." She sipped her champagne. A sliver of sapphire on her finger winked in the light and seemed to reflect in her eyes. "A snob then. Well, everyone's entitled. Perhaps there's something else we can talk about. How do you feel about the current administration's foreign policy?"

"Ambivalent," he murmured. "What sort of character do you play?"

"A sterling one." Her eyes continued to dance. "How do you feel about the space program?"

"I'm more concerned about the planet I'm on. How long have you been on the show?"

"Five years." She beamed a smile at someone across the room and raised her hand.

He looked at her again, carefully, and for the first time since he'd come into the party, he smiled. It did something attractive to his face, though it didn't make him quite as approachable as it indicated. "You don't want to talk about your work, do you?"

"Not particularly." Ariel returned his smile with her own open one. Something stirred faintly in him that he'd thought safely dormant. "Not with someone who considers it garbage. In a moment, you'd ask me if I'd ever considered doing any serious work, then I'd probably get nasty. My agent tells me I'm supposed to charm you."

Booth could feel the friendliness radiating from her and distrusted it. "Is that what you're doing?"

"I'm on my own time," Ariel returned. "Besides—" she finished off her champagne "—you aren't the type to be charmed."

"You're perceptive," Booth acknowledged. "Are you a good actress?"

"Yes, I am. It would hardly be worth doing something if you weren't good at it. What about sports?" She twirled her empty glass. "Do you think the Yankees stand a chance this year?"

"If they tighten up the infield." Not your usual type, he decided. Any other actress up for a prime part in one of his scripts would've been flooding him with compliments and mentioning every job she'd ever had in front of the camera. "Ariel…" Booth plucked a fresh glass of champagne from a passing waiter and handed it to her. "The name suits you. A wise choice."

She felt a pull, a quick, definite pull, that seemed to come simply from the way he'd said her name. "I'll tell my mother you said so."

"It's not a stage name?"

"No. My mother was reading *The Tempest* when she went into labor. She was very superstitious. I could have been Prospero if I'd been a boy." With a little shudder, she sipped. "Well, Booth," she began, deciding she'd been formal long enough. "Shouldn't we just come out with the fact that we both know I'll be reading for the part of Rae in a couple of days? I intend to have it."

He nodded in acknowledgment. Though she was refreshingly direct, this was more what he'd expected.

"Then I'll be frank enough to tell you that you're not the type I'm looking for."

She lifted a brow without any show of discomfort. "Oh? Why?"

"For one thing, you're too young."

She laughed—a free, breezy sound that seemed completely unaffected. He didn't trust that either. "I think my line is I can be older."

"Maybe. But Rae's a tough lady. Hard as a rock." He lifted his own drink but never took his eyes off her. "You've got too many soft points. They show in your face."

"Because this is me. And I've yet to play myself in front of a camera." She paused a moment as the idea worked around in her head. "I don't think I'd care to."

"Is any actress ever herself?"

Her eyes came back to his. He was watching her again with that steady intenseness most would have found unnerving. Though the pull came again, Ariel accepted the look because it was part of him. "You don't care for us much as a breed, do you?"

"No." For some reason he didn't question, Booth felt compelled to test her. He lifted a strand of her hair. Soft—surprisingly soft. "You're a beautiful woman," he murmured.

Ariel tilted her head as she studied him. His eyes had lost nothing of their directness. She might have felt pleasure in the compliment if she hadn't recognized it as calculated. Instead she felt disappointment. "And?"

His brows drew together. "And?"

"That line usually leads to another. As a writer I'm sure you have several tucked away."

He let his fingers brush over her neck. She felt the

strength in them, and the carelessness of the gesture. "Which one would you like?"

"I'd prefer one you meant," Ariel told him evenly. "But since I wouldn't get it, why don't we skip the whole thing? You know, your character, Phil, is narrow-minded, cool blooded and rude. I believe you portrayed yourself very well." She lifted her glass one last time and decided it was a shame that he thought so little of women, or perhaps of people in general. "Good night, Booth."

When she walked away, Booth stood looking after her for several moments before he started to laugh. At the time, it didn't occur to him that it was the first easy laugh he'd had in almost two years. It didn't even occur to him that he was laughing at himself.

No, she wasn't his Rae, he mused, but she was good. She was very, very good. He was going to remember Ariel Kirkwood.

Chapter 2

Booth stood by the wide expanse of window in Marshell's office and watched New York hustle by. From that height, he felt removed from it, and the rush and energy radiating up from the streets and sidewalks. He was satisfied to be separate. Connections equaled involvement.

None of the actresses they'd auditioned in the past two weeks came close to what he was after. He knew what he wanted for the part of Rae—who better?

When he'd first started the script it had been an impulse—therapy, he mused with a grim smile. Cheaper than a psychiatrist and a lot more satisfying. He'd never expected to do any more than finish it, purge his system and toss it in a drawer. That was before he'd realized it was the best work he'd ever done. Perhaps anger was the tenth Muse. In any case, he was first and foremost a writer. However painful it was to expose himself and his mistakes to the public, there was no tossing his finest work in a drawer. And since he was going to have it performed, he was going to have it performed well.

He'd thought it would be difficult to cast the part of Phil, the character who was essentially himself. And yet that had been surprisingly simple. The core of the story wasn't Phil, but Rae, a devastatingly accurate mirror of his ex-wife, Elizabeth Hunter. A superb actress, a gracious celebrity—a woman without a single genuine emotion.

Their marriage had started with a whirlwind and ended in disaster. Booth didn't consider himself blameless, though he placed most of the blame on his own gullibility. He'd believed in her image, fallen hard for the perfection of face and body. He could have forgiven the faults, the flaws soon discovered. But he could never, would never, forgive being used. And yet, Booth was still far from sure whether he blamed Liz for using him, or himself for allowing it to happen.

Either way, the tempestuous five-year marriage had given him grist for a clean, hard story that was going to be an elaborate television movie. And more, it had given him a firm distrust of women, particularly actresses. Two years before, when the break had finally come, he'd promised himself that he'd never become involved with another woman who could play roles that well. Honesty, if it truly existed, was what he'd look for when he was ready.

His thoughts came back to Ariel. Perhaps she was centered in his mind because of her surface resemblance to Liz, but he wasn't certain. There was no similarity in mannerisms, voice cadence or style of dress. And the biggest contrast seemed to be in personality. She hadn't put herself out to charm him or to hold his attention.

And she'd done both. Perhaps she'd simply used a different angle on an old game.

While he hadn't trusted it, he'd enjoyed her lack of artifice. The breezy laugh, the unaffected gestures, the candid looks. It had been a long time since a woman had lingered in his mind. A pity, Booth mused, that she was unsuitable for the part. He could have used the distraction. Instinct told him that Ariel Kirkwood would be nothing if she wasn't a distraction.

"I'm still leaning toward this Julie Newman." Chuck Tyler, the director, tossed an eight-by-ten glossy on Marshell's desk. "A lot of camera presence and her first reading was very good."

With the photo in one hand, Marshell tipped back in his deep leather chair. The sun at his back streamed over both the glossy and the gold he wore on either hand. "An impressive list of credits, too."

"No." Booth didn't bother to turn around, but stood watching the traffic stream. For some odd reason he visualized himself on his boat in Long Island Sound, sailing out to sea. "She lacks the elegance. Too much vulnerability."

"She can act, Booth," Marshell said with a now familiar show of impatience.

"She's not the one."

Marshell automatically reached in his pocket for the cigars he'd given up a month before. He swore lightly under his breath. "And we're running out of time and options."

Booth gave an unconcerned shrug. Yes, he'd like to be sailing, stripped to the waist with the sun on his back and the water so blue it hurt the eyes. He'd like to be alone.

When the buzzer on his desk rang, Marshell heaved

a sigh and leaned forward to answer. "Ms. Kirkwood's here for her reading, Mr. Marshell."

With a grunt, Marshell flipped open the portfolio Ariel's agent had sent him, then passed it to Chuck. "Send her in."

"Kirkwood," Chuck mused, frowning over Ariel's publicity shot. "Kirkwood... Oh, yeah, I saw her last summer in an off-Broadway production of *Streetcar*."

Vaguely interested, Booth looked over his shoulder. "Stella?"

"Blanche," Chuck corrected, skimming over her list of credits.

"Blanche DuBois?" Booth gave a short laugh as he turned completely around. "She's fifteen to twenty years too young for that part."

Chuck merely lifted his eyes. "She was good," he said simply. "Very good. And from what I'm told, she's very good on the soap. I don't have to tell you how many of our top stars started that way."

"No, you don't." Booth sat negligently on the arm of a chair. "But if she's stuck with the same part for five years, she's either not good enough for a major film or major theater, or she's completely without ambition. Because she's an actress, I'd have to go with the former."

"Keep sharpening your cynicism," Marshell said dryly. "It's good for you."

Booth's grin flashed—that rare one that came and went so quickly it left the onlooker dazzled and unsure why. Ariel caught a glimpse of it as she entered the room. It went a long way toward convincing her to change her initial opinion of him. It passed through her mind, almost as quickly as Booth's grin, that perhaps he had some redeeming personal qualities after all. She was always ready to believe it.

"Ms. Kirkwood." Marshell heaved his bulk from the chair and extended his hand.

"Mr. Marshell, nice to see you again." She took a brief scan of the room, her gaze lingering only fleetingly on Booth as he remained seated on the arm of the chair. "Your office is just as impressive as your home."

Booth waited while she was introduced to Chuck. She'd dressed very simply, he noticed. Deceptively so if you considered the bold scarves she'd twisted at the waist of the demure blue dress. Violets and emeralds and wild pinks. A daring combination, and stunningly effective. Her hair was loose again, giving her an air of youth and freedom he would never equate with the character she wanted to portray. Absently, he took out a cigarette and lit it.

"Booth." Ariel gave him an easy smile before her gaze flicked over the cigarette. "They'll kill you."

He took a drag and let out a lazy stream of smoke. "Eventually." She wore the same carelessly sexy scent he'd noticed the night of the party. Booth wondered why it was that it suited her while contrasting at the same time. She fascinated. It seemed to be something she did effortlessly. "I'm going to cue you," he continued and reached for a copy of the script. "We'll use the confrontation scene in the third act. You're familiar with it?"

All business, Ariel noted curiously. Does he ever relax? Does he ever choose to? Though she was rarely tense herself, she recognized tension in him and wondered why he was nervous. What nerves she felt herself were confined to a tiny roiling knot in the center of her stomach. She always acknowledged it and knew, if anything, it would help to push her through the reading.

"I'm familiar with it," she told him, accepting another copy of the script.

Booth took a last drag on his cigarette then put it out. "Do you want a lead-in?"

"No." Now her palms were damp. Good. Ariel knew better than to want to be relaxed when twinges of emotions would sharpen her skills. Taking deep, quiet breaths she flipped through the bound script until she found the right scene. It wasn't a simple one. It stabbed at the core of the character—selfish ambition and icy sex. She took a minute.

Booth watched her. She looked more like the guileless ingenue than the calculating leading lady, he mused and was almost sorry there wasn't a part for her in the film. Then she looked up and pinned him with a cold, bloodless smile that completely stunned him.

"You always were a fool, Phil, but a successful one and so rarely boring, it's hardly worth mentioning."

The tone, the mannerisms, even the expression was so accurate, he couldn't respond. For a moment, he completely lost Ariel in the character and the woman he'd fashioned her after. He felt a twist in his stomach, not of attraction or even admiration, but of anger—totally unexpected and vilely real. Booth didn't have to look at the script to remember the line.

"You're so transparent, Rae. It amazes me that you could deceive anyone into believing in you."

Ariel laughed, rather beautifully, so that all three men felt a chill race up their spine. "I make my living at deception. Everyone wants illusions, so did you. And that's what you got."

With a long, lazy stretch, she ran a hand through her hair, then let it fall, pale gold in the late-morning sunlight. It was one of Liz Hunter's patented gestures. "I acted my way out of that miserable backwater town in Missouri where I had the misfortune to be born, and

I've acted my way right up to the top. You were a great help." She walked over to him with the small, cool smile still on her lips, in her eyes. With an eloquent gesture, she brushed her hand down his cheek. "And you were compensated. Very, very well."

Phil grabbed her wrist and tossed it aside. Ariel merely lifted a brow at the violence of the movement. "Sooner or later you're going to slip," he threatened.

She tilted her head and spoke very softly. "Darling, I never slip."

Slowly, Booth rose. The expression on his face might have had any woman trembling, would have had any woman making some defensive move. Ariel merely looked up at him with the same coldly amused expression. It was he who had to force himself to calm.

"Very good, Ariel Kirkwood." Booth tossed the script aside.

She grinned, because every instinct told her she'd won. With the long expelled breath, she could almost feel Rae drain out of her. "Thanks. It's a tremendous part," she added as her stomach unknotted. "Really a tremendous part."

"You've done your research," Marshell murmured from behind his desk. Because he knew Elizabeth Hunter, Ariel's five-minute read had left him uncomfortable and impressed. And he knew Booth. There was little doubt in his mind as to what Rae's creator was feeling. "You'll be available for a callback?"

"Of course."

"I saw your Blanche DuBois, Ms. Kirkwood," Chuck put in. "I was very impressed then, and now."

She flashed him an unaffected smile though she was aware Booth was still staring at her. If he was moved, she thought, then the reading had gone better than she could have hoped. "It was my biggest challenge, up until now." She wanted to get out, walk, breathe the air, savor the almost-victory while she could. "Well, thank you." She pushed her hair from her shoulder as she scanned the three men again. "I'll look forward to hearing from you."

Ariel walked toward the elevator too frightened to believe she was right, too terrified to believe she was wrong. Up until that moment, she hadn't let herself dwell on just how much she wanted the part, and just what it could mean in her life.

She wasn't without ambition, but she had chosen acting and had continued with it for the love of it. And the challenge. Playing the part of Rae would hand her all three needs on a silver platter. As she stepped into the elevator, her palms were dry and her heart was pounding. She didn't hear Booth approach.

"I'd like to talk to you." He stepped in with her and punched the button for the lobby.

"Okay." A long sigh escaped as she leaned back against the side of the car. "God, I'm glad that's over. I'm starving. Nothing makes me hungrier than a reading."

He tried to relate the woman who was smiling at him with eyes warm and alive with the woman who had just exchanged lines with him. He couldn't. She was a better actress than he'd given her credit for, and therefore, more dangerous. "It was an excellent reading."

She eyed him curiously. "Why do I feel I've just been insulted?"

After the doors slid open Booth stood for a moment, then nodded. "I think I said before that you were perceptive."

Her slim heels clicked over the tile as she crossed the

lobby with him. Booth noticed a few heads turn, both male and female, to look after her. She was either unaware or unconcerned. "Why are you on daytime TV?"

Ariel slanted him a look before she began to walk north. "Because it's a good part on a well-written, entertaining show. That's number one. Number two is that it's steady work. When actors are between jobs, they wait tables, wash cars, sell toasters and generally get depressed. While I might not mind the first three too much, I hate the fourth. Have you ever seen the show?"

"No."

"Then you shouldn't turn your nose up." She stopped by a sidewalk vendor and drew in the scent of hot pretzels. "Want one?"

"No," Booth said again and tucked his hands in his pockets. Sexuality, sensuality—both seemed to pour out of her as she stood next to a portable pretzel stand on a crowded sidewalk. He continued to watch her as she took the first generous bite.

"I could live off them," she told him with her mouth full and her eyes laughing. "Good nutrition's so admirable and so hard to live with. I like to ignore it for long stretches of time. Let's walk," she suggested. "I have to when I'm keyed up. What do you do?"

"When?"

"When you're keyed up," Ariel explained.

"Write." He matched her casually swinging pace while the bulk of pedestrian traffic bustled by them.

"And when you're not keyed up you write," Ariel added as she took another bite of her pretzel. "Have you always been so serious?"

"It's steady work," he countered and she laughed.

"Very quick. I didn't think I'd like you, but you've got a nice sense of cautious humor." Ariel stopped at another vendor and bought a bunch of spring violets. She closed her eyes and breathed deep. "Wonderful," she murmured. "I always think spring's the best until summer. Then I'm in love with the heat until fall. Then fall's the best until winter." Laughing, she looked over the blooms into his eyes. "And I also tend to ramble when I'm keyed up."

When she lowered the flowers, Booth took her wrist, not with the same violence as he had during the reading, but with the same intensity. "Who are you?" he demanded. "Who the hell are you?"

Her smile faded but she didn't draw away. "Ariel Kirkwood. I can be a lot of other people when there's a stage or a camera, but when it's over, that's who I am. That's all I am. Are you looking for complications?"

"I don't have to look for them—they're always there."

"Strange, I rarely run into any." She studied him, all frank eyes and creamy beauty. Booth didn't care for the stir it brought him. "Come with me," she invited, then took his hand before he'd thought to object.

"Where?"

She threw back her head and pointed up the magnificently sheer surface of the Empire State Building. "To the top." Laughing, she pulled him inside. "All the way to the top."

Booth looked around impatiently as she bought tickets for the observation deck. "Why?"

"Does there always have to be a reason?" She slipped the violets into the twisted scarves at her waist, then tucked her arm through his. "I love things like this. Ellis Island, the Staten Island ferry, Central Park. What's the use of living in New York if you don't enjoy it? When's the last time you did this?" Her shoulder rested against his upper arm as they crowded into an elevator.

"I think I was ten." Even with the press of bodies and mingling scents he could smell her, wild and sweet.

"Oh." Ariel laughed up at him. "You grew up. Too bad."

Booth said nothing for a moment as he studied her. She seemed to always be laughing—at him or at some private joke she was content to keep to herself. Was she really that easy with herself and her life? Was anyone? Then he asked, "Don't we all?"

"Of course not. We all get older, but the rest is a personal choice." They herded off one elevator and onto another that would take them to the top.

This was a man she could enjoy, Ariel mused as she stood beside Booth. She could enjoy that serious, high-minded streak and the dry, almost reluctant humor. Still, there was the part in the film to think of. Ariel would have to be very careful to keep her feelings for one separate from her feelings for the other. But then, she'd never been a person who'd had any trouble separating the woman and the actress.

For now, the reading was over and the afternoon was free. Her mood was light, and there was a man with her who'd be fascinating to explore. The day could hardly offer anything more.

The souvenir stands were crowded with people—different countries, different voices. Ariel decided she'd buy something foolish on her way out. She caught Booth looking around him with his eyes slightly narrowed. An observer, she thought with a slight nod of approval. She was one herself, though perhaps on a different level. He'd dissect, analyze and file. She just enjoyed the show.

"Come on outside," she invited and took his hand in a characteristic gesture. "It's wonderful." Pushing open the heavy door, Ariel welcomed the first slap of wind with a laugh. With her hand still firmly gripping Booth's, she hurried to the wall to take in New York.

She never saw it as a toy board as many did from that height, but as something real enough to touch and smell from any distance. It never failed to excite and fascinate her. Ariel rarely asked more of anything or anyone. When she was here, she always believed she could accomplish whatever she needed to.

"I love heights." She leaned out as far as she could and felt the frantic current of air swirl around her. "Staggering heights. And wind. If I could, I'd come here every day. I'd never get tired of it."

Though it was normally an intimacy he would have shunned, Booth allowed his hand to stay in hers. Her skin was smooth and elegant; her face was flushed in the brisk air while her hair blew wildly. The eyes, he thought, the eyes were too alive, too full of everything. A woman like this would demand spectacular emotions from everyone she touched. The stir he felt wasn't as easily suppressed this time. Deliberately, he looked away from her and down.

"Why not the World Trade Center?" he asked and let his gaze skim over the island he lived on.

Ariel shook her head. "It doesn't have the same feeling as this, nothing does. Just like there's only one Eiffel Tower, one Grand Canyon and one Olivier." She didn't bother to brush her hair back from her face as she tilted toward him. "They're all spectacular and unique. What do you like, Booth?"

A family walked by laughing, the mother holding her skirts, the father carrying a toddler. He watched them pause nearby and look over the wall. "In what way?"

"In any way," Ariel told him. "If you could've spent

today doing anything you wanted, what would you have done?"

"Gone sailing," he said, remembering that moment in Marshell's office. "I'd've been sailing on the sound."

Interest flickered in her eyes as it seemed every emotion or thought she had did. "You have a boat?"

"Yes. I don't have much time for it."

Don't take much time for it, she corrected silently. "A solitary pursuit. That's admirable." She turned, leaning back against the wall so that she could watch the people circle the deck. The wind plastered her dress against her, revealing the slenderness, the elegance of the woman. "I don't often like to be solitary," she murmured. "I need people, the contacts, the contrasts. I don't have to know them. I just like knowing they're there."

"Is that why you act?" They were face-to-face now, their bodies casually close—as if they were friends. It struck Booth as odd, but he had no desire to back away. "So you can have an audience?"

Her expression become thoughtful, but when she smiled, it was easy. "You're a very cynical man."

"That's the second time today that's been mentioned."

"It's all right. It probably comes in handy with your writing. Yes, I act for an audience," she continued. "I won't deny my own ego, but I think I act for myself first." She lifted her face so that the air could race over it. "It's a marvelous profession. How else can you be so many people? A princess, a tramp, a victim, a loser. You write to be read, but don't you first write to express yourself?"

"Yes." He felt something odd, almost unfamiliar—a loosening of muscles, an easing of thought. It took him a moment to realize he was relaxing, and only a moment longer to draw back. When you relaxed, you got burned. That much he was certain of. "But then writers have egos that nearly rival actors'."

Ariel made a sound that was somewhere between a sigh and an expulsion of air. "She really put you through the mill, didn't she?"

His eyes frosted, his voice chilled. "That's none of your business."

"You're wrong." Though she felt a twinge of regret when she sensed his withdrawal, Ariel went on. "If I'm going to play Rae, it's very much my business. Booth…" She laid a hand on his arm, wishing she understood him well enough to get past the wall of reserve, the waves of bitterness. "If you'd wanted to keep this part of your life private, you wouldn't have written it out."

"It's a story," he said flatly. "I don't put myself on display."

"In most cases, no," she agreed. "I've always felt a certain sense of distance in your work, though it's always excellent. And for someone so successful, you kept a fairly low profile, even when you were married to Liz Hunter. But you've let something out in this script. It's too late to pull it back now."

"I've written a story about two people who are totally unsuited to each other, who used each other. The man is a bit of an idealist, and just gullible enough to fall for an exquisite face. Before the story ends, he learns that appearances mean little and that trust and loyalty are illusions. The woman is cold, ambitious and gifted, but she'll never be satisfied with her own talents. She's a vampire in the pure sense of the word, and she sucks him dry. There may be similarities between the story and actuality, but my life is still my life."

"No trespassing." Ariel turned to look back down into the city, the world she understood. "All right, the signs are posted." She listened to the sound of the wind, the sound of voices. Someone reeked of a drugstore cologne. An empty bag of potato chips skimmed and rustled along the concrete. "I'm not a very good businesswoman. I won't apologize for my lifestyle or my personality, but I will do my best to keep our conversations very professional."

She took a deep breath and turned back to him. Some of the warmth had left her eyes, and he felt a momentary regret. "I'm a good actress, an excellent craftsman. I've known since the first moment I picked up the script that I could play Rae. And I'm astute enough to know how well my reading went."

"No, you're not a fool." Even with the regret, Booth felt more comfortable on this level. He understood her now—an actress in search of that prime part. "I wouldn't have said you were what I was looking for— until this afternoon. No one's come even close to the core of that character before you."

She felt the tickling dryness down in her throat, the sudden lurch of her heart rate. "And?" she managed.

"And I want you to come back and read with Jack Rohrer. He's cast as Phil. If the chemistry's there, you've got the part."

Ariel took a deep breath. She leaned against the sturdy observation glass and tried to take it calmly. She'd told him she'd be professional. No good, she realized as the pleasure bubbled up inside her. It simply wasn't any use. With a shout of laughter, she threw her arms around his neck and clung. The touching was vital, the sharing essential.

Ariel Kirkwood—the skinny dreamer from West

185th Street—was going to star in a DeWitt script, a
P. B. Marshell production opposite Jack Rohrer. Would
life never stop amazing her? As she clung to Booth,
Ariel dearly hoped it wouldn't.

His hands had come to her waist in reflex, but he left
them there as her laughter warmed his ear. He found
it odd that he was sharply reminded of two things—
his young niece's boundless pleasure when he'd given
her an elaborate dollhouse one Christmas, and the first
time, as a man, he'd ever held a woman. The softness
was there—that unique strength and give only a woman's body has. The childlike pleasure was there—with
the innocence only the young possess.

He could have held her. It moved in him to do so,
just to hold something soft and sweet and without shadows. She fit so well against him. The curve of her cheek
against his, the alignment of bodies. She fit too well,
so that he stood perfectly still and drew her no closer.

Something drifted through her pleasure and excitement. He smelt of soap—solid—as his body felt. There
was nothing casual about him, nothing easy. He was
all intensity and intellect. The strength drew her; his
reserve drew her. He was a man who would be there
to pick you up, however reluctantly, if you stumbled.
Who would demand that you keep pace with him, and
who would expect you to give him exactly the amount
of room he wanted when he wanted it. He was a man
whom a woman who ran on her emotions and her senses
would do well to avoid. She wished almost painfully
that his arms would come around her, even while she
knew they wouldn't.

Ariel drew away but kept their faces close so that
she might have a hint of what it would be like to have
that serious, unsmiling mouth lowered to hers. She was

breathless, and her eyes made no secret of her attraction or her surprise in feeling it.

"I'm sorry," she said quietly. "Physical displays come naturally to me. I have a feeling you don't care for them."

Had there ever been a woman he'd wanted to kiss more than this one? Almost, almost, he could taste the mouth inches from his own. Nearly, very nearly, he could feel its texture against his own. When he spoke, his voice was indifferent, his eyes remote. "There's a time and a place."

Ariel let out a long breath and decided she'd set herself up for a backhanded slap. "You're a tough man, Booth DeWitt," she murmured.

"I'm a realist, Ariel." He took out a cigarette, cupping his lighter against the wind with hands that amazed him because they weren't steady.

"What a hard thing to be." Consciously, she relaxed—shoulder muscles, stomach muscles, hands. A moment's awareness didn't equal trouble. She'd felt it before; it was a blessing and a curse in a woman like herself. Ariel didn't understand indifference to people or to things. Everything you saw, touched, heard, triggered some emotion. "But then, you're stuck with it." More at ease, she smiled at him. "I'm going to enjoy working with you, Booth, though I know it's not going to be a picnic. I'm going to give your script my very best shot, and we'll both benefit."

He nodded as the smoke whipped up and away. "I don't accept anything less than the best."

"Fine, you won't be disappointed." It was in her nature to reach out and touch, to add something personal. But one slap was enough for one day.

"Good."

With a laugh, she shook her head. "You're attractive, Booth. I haven't the least idea why because I don't think you're a very nice person."

He blew out another stream of smoke and watched her lazily. "I'm not," he agreed.

"In any case, we'll give each other what's needed professionally."

Then because she rarely resisted impulses of any kind, she kissed his cheek before thrusting the violets at him and walking away. Booth stood in the wind on top of New York with a handful of spring flowers and stared after her.

Chapter 3

Booth had been on and around sets most of his professional life. There were eighteenth-century drawing rooms, twentieth-century bedrooms, bars and restaurants and department stores. Spaceships and log cabins. With props and backdrops and ingenuity, anything could be created.

When you came to the bottom line, one set was the same as another—technicians, lights, cameras, booms, miles of cable. It was an industry of illusion and image. What looked glamorous outside the business was ultimately only a job, and often a tedious and exacting one. Long hours, lengthy delays, lights that made a studio into a furnace, bitter coffee.

From the outset of his career, he'd never been content to be isolated with his typewriter and ideas. He'd insisted from his very first screenplay on being involved with the production end. He understood the practicality and the creativity of the right camera angle, the proper lighting. It appealed to the realistic part of him. Still, he had the ability to see the set and the people while blocking out the crowding equipment. To watch as an outsider, to see as a viewer. This appealed to the dreamer he'd always kept under strict control.

Booth wasn't sure what had motivated him to visit the set of *Our Lives, Our Loves.* He knew that the script he was currently working on had hit a snag, and that he wanted to see Ariel again. Perhaps it was the scent of violets that continued to drift to him as he tried to work. Twice he'd started to throw them away…but he hadn't. Part of him, deep, long repressed, needed such things, however much he disliked acknowledging it.

So he had come to see Ariel, telling himself he simply wanted to watch her work before he committed himself to choosing her for the part of Rae. It was logical, practical. It was something he'd tried very hard to resist.

Ariel sat at the kitchen table with her bare feet propped in a chair while Jack Shapiro, who played Griff Martin, Amanda's college sweetheart, mulled over a hand of solitaire. On another part of the soundstage, her television parents were discussing their offspring. After they'd finished, she and Jack would tape their scene.

"Black six on the red seven," she mumbled, earning herself a glare from Jack.

"Solitaire," he reminded her. "As in alone."

"It's an antisocial game."

"You think headphones are antisocial."

"They are." Smiling sweetly, she moved the six herself.

"Why don't you go call the Committee for the Salvation of Three-legged Land Mammals? They probably want you at their next luncheon."

The timing wasn't quite right, she decided, to ask

him to contribute to the Homes for Kittens fund she was currently involved with. "Don't get snotty," she said mildly. "You're supposed to adore me."

"Should've had my head examined after you threw me over for Cameron."

"It's your own fault for not explaining what you were doing alone in that hotel room with Vikki."

Jack sniffed and turned over another card. "You should've trusted me. A man has his pride."

"Now I'm stuck in a disastrous marriage *and* I might be pregnant."

Glancing up, he grinned. "Great for the ratings. Did you see them posted this week? We're up a whole point."

She leaned her elbows on the table. "Wait until things start heating up between Amanda and Griff again." She put a black ten on the jack of diamonds. "Sizzle, spark, smolder."

He smacked her hand. "You're a great smolderer." Unable to resist, he leered. "I haven't kissed you in six months."

"Then when you get your chance, big guy, make it good. Amanda's no pushover." Rising, she strolled away for a last-minute check with makeup.

The hospital set had already been prepared for the brief but intense meeting between the former lovers, Amanda and Griff. Some subtle dark smudges were added under her eyes to give the appearance of a sleepless night. The rest of her makeup gave her a slight pallor.

By the time the cameras rolled, Amanda was in her office, going through her patient files. She seemed very calm, very much in control. Her expression was totally serene. Abruptly, she slammed the drawer back in the cabinet and whirled around to pace. When the tape was edited, it would flash back to her discovery of her husband and sister. Amanda grabbed a china cup from her desk and hurled it against the wall. With the back of her hand to her mouth, she stared at the broken pieces. The knock at her office door had her balling her fists and making a visible struggle for control. Deliberately, she walked around her desk and sat down.

"Come in."

The camera focused on Jack as Dr. Griff Martin, rough-and-ready looks, rough-and-ready temper—Amanda's first and only lover before her marriage. Ariel knew what the director would edit in a reaction shot later, but now, with the tape running on Jack's entrance, she screwed up her face and stuck out her tongue. Jack gave her one of his character's patented lengthy looks designed to make the female heart flutter.

"Amanda, have you got a minute?"

When the lens was focused on her again, her face was properly composed with just a hint of strain beneath the serenity. "Of course, Griff." For a subtle sign of nerves, she gripped her hands together on the desktop.

"I've got a case of wife beating," he began in the clipped, almost surly tone of his character. Both Amanda and several million female viewers had found his diamond-in-the-rough style irresistible. "I need your help."

They went through the scene, laying the groundwork for a story line that would throw them together again and again over the next few weeks, building the sexual tension. When the camera was briefly at Jack's back he crossed his eyes at Ariel and bared his teeth. As she went back to her patient file, she made certain she walked over his foot. Neither of them lost the rhythm of the scene.

"You look tired." As Griff, Jack started to touch her shoulder, then stopped himself. Frustration radiated from his eyes. "Is everything all right?"

Amanda turned and gave him a soulful eye-locking look. Her mouth trembled open, then closed again. Slowly, she turned back to the file and shut the drawer quietly. "Everything's fine. I have a heavy workload right now. And I have a patient due in a few minutes."

"I'll get out of here then." He started for the door and paused. With his hand on the knob, he stared at her. "Mandy..."

Amanda kept her back to him. The camera came in close as she shut her eyes and fought for control. "I'll see your patient tomorrow, Griff." There was the faintest of tremors in her voice.

He waited five humming seconds. "Yeah, fine."

When she heard the door close, Amanda pressed her hands to her face.

"Cut."

"I'm going to get you for that," Jack said as he pushed the prop door open again. "I think you broke one of my toes."

Ariel fluttered her lashes at him. "You're such a baby."

"All right, children," the director said mildly. "Let's get the reaction shots."

Agreeably, Ariel moved behind Amanda's desk again. It was then she saw Booth. Surprise and pleasure showed on her face, though his expression wasn't welcoming. He was frowning at her, his arms crossed over a casual black sweater. He didn't return her smile, nor did she expect him to. Booth DeWitt wasn't a man who smiled often or easily. It only made her more determined to nudge him into it.

She'd thought about him—surprisingly often. At the moment, she had enough on her mind, both personally and professionally, yet she'd found herself wondering about Booth DeWitt and what went on inside that aloof exterior. She'd seen flashes of something warm, something approachable. For Ariel, it was enough to make her dig for more.

And there'd been that pull—the pull she remembered with perfect clarity. She wanted to feel it again, to enjoy it, to understand it.

She finished the taping and had an hour before she and Stella would play out their confrontation scene on the Lane living-room set. "Jerry, I found a kitten for your daughter," she told one of the technicians as she rose. "It's a little calico, I can bring it in on Friday."

"Been to the pound again," Jack said with a sigh. Ignoring him, Ariel stepped over some cable and walked to Booth.

"Hi, want some coffee?"

"All right."

"I keep a Mr. Coffee in my dressing room. The stuff at the commissary's poison." She led the way, not bothering to ask why he was there. Her door was open, as she usually left it. Walking in, she went directly to the coffeemaker. "You have to make do with powdered milk."

"Black's fine."

Her dressing room was chaos. Clothes, magazines, pamphlets were tossed over all available space. Her dressing table was littered with jars and bottles and framed photographs of the cast. It smelled of fresh flowers, makeup and dust.

On the wall was a calendar that read February though it was midway through April. An electric clock was unplugged and stuck on 7:05. Booth counted three and one-half pairs of shoes on the floor.

In the midst of it, Ariel stood in a raw-silk suit the color of apricots with her hair pale and glowing in a so-phisticated knot. She smelled like a woman should at sunset—soft, with a hint of anticipation. As the coffee began to drip, she turned back to him.

"I'm glad to see you again."

The simplicity of the statement made Booth almost believe it. Cautiously, he kept half the room between them as he watched her. "The taping was interesting. You're very good, Ariel. You milked that five-minute scene for everything there was."

Again she had the impression more of criticism than flattery. "It's important in a soap. You're working in lit-tle capsules. Some people only tune in a couple times a week. Then there are those who turn it on as a whim. You hope to grab them."

"Your character." He eyed the suit, approving the subdued style. "I'd say she's a very controlled profes-sional woman who's currently going through some per-sonal crisis. There were a lot of sexual sparks bouncing around between her and the young doctor."

"Very good." With a smile, Ariel picked up two cups, mismatched. "That's neatly tied up. Want some M&M's? I keep a stash in my drawer."

"No. Do you always play around on set when you're not on camera?"

She stirred powdered milk into her coffee, added a generous spoon of sugar, then handed Booth his. "Jack and I have a running contest on who can make who blow their lines. Actually, it makes us sharper and lowers the tension level." Carelessly, she took magazines from a chair and left them stacked on the floor. "Sit down."

"How many pages of dialogue do you have to learn a week?"

"Varies," she said and sipped. "We run about eighty-five pages of script a day now that we've gone to an hour. Some days I might have twenty or thirty where my character's involved. But for the most part, I tape about three days a week—we don't do a lot of takes." Opening the drawer on her dressing table, she took a handful of candies and began to eat them one at a time. "I'm told it's the closest thing to live TV you can get."

Watching her, he drank. "You really enjoy it."

"Yes, I've been very comfortable with Amanda. Which is why I want to do other things as well. Ruts are monotonous places, but so easy to stay in."

He glanced around the room. "I can't imagine you in one."

Ariel laughed and sat on the edge of her dressing table. "A great compliment. You're frugal with them." Something in his aloof, cool expression made her smile. "Would you like to have dinner?" she asked on impulse.

For an instant surprise flickered over his face—the first time she'd seen it. "It's a bit early for dinner," he said mildly.

"I like the way you do that," she said with a nod. "Conversations with you are never boring. If you're free tonight, I could pick you up at seven."

She was asking him for a date, he thought, very simply, very smoothly, in a manner more friendly than flirtatious. As he had often since the first time he'd met her, Booth wondered what made her tick. "All right, seven." Reaching in his pocket, he pulled out a note pad and scrawled on it. "Here's the address."

Taking it, Ariel scanned the words with a small sound of approval. "Mmm, you've got a great view of the park." She looked up and grinned in the way that always made him think she'd just enjoyed a little private joke. "I'm a sucker for views."

"I've gathered that already."

Booth walked over to set down his mug and stood close enough so that his legs brushed hers. She didn't back away but watched him with clear, curious eyes. There was something deadly in that face, she thought. Something any woman would recognize and a wary one would retreat from. Fascinated, she counted the beat of her own rapid pulse.

"I'll let you get back to work."

With the slightest move on his part, the contact was broken. Ariel stayed exactly where she was. "I'm glad you stopped by," she said, though she was no longer sure it was precisely the truth.

With a nod, he was gone. Ariel sat on the edge of her cluttered dressing table and wondered if for the first time in her life she'd bitten off more than she could chew.

Because the sun was setting and it was a huge red ball, Ariel paid off the cab two blocks from Booth's apartment building. She wanted some time to think about a phone call she'd received about Scott, her brother's child.

Poor little guy, she thought. So vulnerable, so grown-up. She wondered how much longer it would be before the courts decided his fate. Because she wanted him with her so badly, Ariel refused to believe anything else would happen. Her brother's son, so suddenly orphaned, so miserably unhappy with his maternal grandparents.

They didn't want him, she reflected. Not really. There was such a world of difference between love and duty. Once everything was arranged, she'd be able to give him the kind of easy, unfettered childhood she'd had—with the financial advantages she hadn't known.

She wouldn't think of the complications now. To think of them would make her start doubting the outcome, and she couldn't bear it. She and her lawyers were taking all the possible steps.

Because she wanted no publicity to touch her nephew, Ariel had kept the entire matter to herself—something she rarely did. Perhaps because she had no one to speak to about it, she worried. Every day she told herself Scott would be with her permanently before the end of summer. As long as she kept telling herself, she was able to believe it. Now it was evening, and there was no more she could do.

It was only a little past seven o'clock when she pushed the button of the elevator for Booth's floor in the sleek building on Park Avenue. She'd already set aside that one flash of nerves she felt about him and had decided to enjoy the evening. The idea that he'd been able to make her nervous at all was intriguing enough.

She liked men, the basic personality differences between them and women. Of her closest friends, many were men, in and out of the business. The key word remained *friends*—she was very cautious about lovers. She ran on emotion, and knowing it, had always been careful of physical relationships.

She was a romantic, unashamedly. Ariel had never doubted that there was one great love waiting for everyone. She had no intention of settling for less—with hearts and flowers and skyrockets included. When she found the right man, she'd know. Whether it was tomorrow or twenty years from tomorrow didn't matter, as long as she found him. In the meantime, she filled her life with work, her friends and her causes. Ariel Kirk-wood simply didn't believe in boredom.

She approved of the quiet, carpeted hallway as she strolled down to Booth's apartment. It was wainscoted and elegant. But as she lifted her hand to press the button on his door, she felt that odd flutter of nerves again.

Inside, Booth was standing by the high wide window that looked out over Central Park. He was thinking of her, had been thinking of her for most of the day. And he didn't care for it.

Twice, he'd nearly called to cancel the dinner, telling himself he had work to do. Telling himself he didn't have the time or the inclination to spend an evening with an actress he hardly knew. But he hadn't canceled because he could still see the way her eyes warmed, the way her whole face moved when she smiled.

A professional trick. Liz had had a bagful of them, and unless his perception was very, very wrong, this woman was as skilled an actress as Liz Hunter. That's what he told himself, and yet... And yet he hadn't canceled.

When the buzzer rang, Booth looked over his shoulder at the closed door. It was simply an evening, he decided. A few hours out of the day in which he could study the woman being considered for a major part in an important film. He had little doubt that she would make a pitch for the part before the night was over. With a shrug, Booth walked to the door. That was the business, and she was entitled.

Then, when he opened the door, she smiled at him. He realized he wanted her with an intensity he hadn't felt in years. "Hi. You look nice," she said.

The struggle with desire only made him more remote, made his voice more scrupulously polite. "Come in."

Ariel walked through the door then studied the room with open curiosity. Neat. Her first impression was one of meticulous order. Style. Who could fault a gleaming mix of Chippendale and Hepplewhite? The colors were muted, easy on the eyes. The furniture was arranged in such a way as to give a sense of balance. She could smell neither dust nor polish. It was as though the room was perpetually clean and rarely lived in. Somehow, she didn't think it really suited that harsh, nineteenth-century face. No, there was too much formality here for a man who looked like Booth, for a man who moved like him.

Though she felt no sense of welcome, she could appreciate the rather stationary beauty and respect the organized taste.

"A very fastidious man," she murmured, then walked over to study his view of the city.

She wore a dress with yards of skirt and whirls of color. Booth wondered if that was why he suddenly felt life jump into the room. He preferred the quiet, the settled, even the isolated. Yet somehow, for the first time, he felt the appeal of having warmth in his home.

"I was right about this," Ariel said and put her hands into the deep pockets of her skirt. "It's lovely. Where do you work?"

"I have an office set up in another room."

"I'd probably have put my desk right here." Laughing, she turned to him so that the mix of colors in her dress seemed to vibrate. "Then again, I wouldn't get much work done." His eyes were very dark and very steady, his face so expressionless he might have been thinking of anything or nothing. "Do you stare at everyone that way?"

"I suppose I do. Would you like a drink?"

"Yes, some dry vermouth if you have it." She wandered over to a cherrywood breakfront and studied his collection of Waterford. No one chose something so lovely, or so capable of catching light and fire if they lacked warmth. Where was his, she wondered. Buried so deep that he'd forgotten it, or simply dormant from lack of use?

Booth paused beside her and offered a glass. "You like crystal?"

"I like beautiful things."

What woman didn't? he thought brittlely. A Russian lynx, a pear-shaped diamond. Yes, women liked beautiful things, particularly when someone else was providing them. He'd already done more than his share of that.

"I watched your show today," Booth began, deciding to give her the opening for her pitch and see what she did with it. "You come across very well as the competent psychiatrist."

"I like Amanda." Ariel sipped her vermouth. "She's a very stable woman with little hints of vulnerability and passion. I like seeing how subtle I can make them without hiding them completely. What did you think of the show?"

"A mass of complication and intrigue. I was surprised that the bulk of the plots didn't concern fatal diseases and bed hopping."

"You're out of step." She smiled over the rim. "Of course, every soap has some of those elements, but we've done a lot of expanding. Murder, politics, social issues, even science fiction. We do quite a bit of location shooting now in the race for ratings." She drank again. This time it was an opal, milky blue, that gleamed on her hand. "Last year we shot in Greece and Venice. I've never eaten so much in my life. Griff and Amanda had a lovers' rendezvous in Venice that was sabotaged. You must've noticed Stella—she plays my sister Vikki."

"The barracuda." Booth nodded. "I recognized the type."

"Oh, Vikki's that all right. Plotting, scheming, being generally nasty. Stella has a marvelous time with her. Vikki's had a dozen affairs, broken up three marriages, destroyed a senator's career. Just last month she pawned our mother's emerald brooch to pay off gambling debts." With a sigh, Ariel drank again. "She has all the fun."

Booth's grin flashed, lingering in his eyes as they met Ariel's. "Are you talking about Stella or Vikki?"

"Both, I suppose. I wondered if I'd be able to do that."

"What?"

"Make you smile. You don't very often, you know."

"No?"

"No." She felt the tug again, sharp and very physical. Indulging herself, she let her gaze lower briefly to his mouth and enjoyed the sensation it brought to her own. "I guess you're too busy picking up parts of people and filing them away."

Finishing off his drink, he set the glass aside. "Is that what I do?"

"Always. It's natural, I suppose, in your line of work, but I decided I was going to pull one out of you before the evening was over." He was still watching her, and though the smile was only a hint now, it was still lurking. It suited him, she thought, that trace of amusement—a cautious, even reluctant amusement. And again, she felt the tug of attraction. With her brows slightly drawn together, she stepped closer. It wasn't something she could or would walk away from.

"Aren't you curious?" she asked quietly, then went

on when he didn't answer. "The thing is, I'm not certain I can go through the evening wondering what it would be like."

She put one hand on his shoulder and leaned forward just until their lips touched. There was no pressure, no demand on either side, and yet she felt that slightest of contacts through her whole system. There was a twinge deep inside her, a soft rushing sound in her ears. The mouth against hers was warmer than she'd expected and its taste more potent. Their bodies weren't touching, and the kiss remained a mere meeting of lips. Ariel felt herself open and was mildly surprised. Then, she felt her knees tremble and was stunned.

Slowly, she backed up, unaware that her eyes were wide with shock. Desire had ripped through him at the taste of her mouth, but Booth knew how to conceal his emotions. He wanted her—in the part of Rae and in his bed. To his thinking it wouldn't be long before she offered him one to ensure the other. He'd been much younger when Liz had lured him into bed for a part. He was older now and knew the game. And somehow, he felt Ariel would be more honest in her playing.

"Well…" Ariel let out a long breath while her mind raced. She wished she had five minutes alone to think this through. Somehow she'd always expected she'd fall in love in the blink of an eye, but she wasn't idealistic enough to believe it would be handed back to her. She needed to work out her next move. "And now that the pressure's off—" she set her glass aside "—why don't we go eat?"

Before she could step away, Booth took her arm. If they were going to play out the scene, he wanted to do it then and there. "What do you want?"

There was none of the quiet warmth in his voice that

she'd felt in the kiss. Ariel looked into his eyes and saw nothing but a reflection of herself. An unwise man to love, she thought. And, of course, she should have expected that was what would happen to her when the time came. "To go to dinner," she told him.

"I've given you the opportunity to mention the part, you haven't. Why?"

"That's business. This isn't."

He gave a quick laugh. "In this business, it's all business," he countered. "You want to play Rae."

"I wouldn't have read for it if I didn't want it. And once I finish the next reading I'll have it." It frustrated her that she couldn't read him. "Booth, why don't you tell me what you're getting at? It'd be easier for both of us."

He inclined his head, and with his hand on her arm drew her an inch closer. "Just how much are you willing to do for it?"

His meaning was like a slap in the face. Outrage didn't come, but a piercing hurt that made her face pale and her eyes darken. "I'm willing to give the very best performance I'm capable of." Jerking out of his hold, she started for the door.

"Ariel..." He hadn't expected to call her back, but the look in her eyes had made him feel foul. When she didn't pause, he was going across the room before he could stop himself. "Ariel." Taking her arm again, he turned her around.

The hurt radiating from her was so sharp and real he couldn't convince himself not to believe it. The strength of the need to draw her against him was almost painful. "I'll apologize for that."

She stared at him, wishing it was in her to tell him to go to hell. "I'll accept it," she said instead, "since I'm sure you don't make a habit of apologizing for anything. She took a few pieces out of you, didn't she?"

His hand dropped away from her arm. "I don't discuss my private life."

"Maybe that's part of the problem. Is it women in general, or just actresses you detest?"

His eyes narrowed so that she could only see a glint of the anger. It wasn't necessary to see what you could feel. "Don't push me."

"I doubt anyone could." Though she felt the anger was a promising sign, Ariel didn't feel capable of dealing with it, or her own feelings at the moment. "It's a pity," she continued as she turned for the door again. "When whatever's frozen inside you thaws, I think you'll be a remarkable man. In the meantime, I'll stay out of your way." She opened the door, then turned back. "About the part, Booth, please deal with my agent." Quietly, she closed the door behind her.

Chapter 4

"No, Scott, if you eat any more cotton candy your teeth're going to fall right out. And then—" Ariel hauled her nephew up for one fierce hug "—you'd be stuck with stuff like smashed bananas and strained spinach."

"Popcorn," he demanded, grinning at her.

"Bottomless pit." She nuzzled into his neck and let the love flow over her.

Sunday was precious, not only because of the sunshine and balmy spring temperatures, not only because there were hours and hours of leisure time left to her, but because she had the afternoon to spend with the most important person in her life.

He even smells like his father, Ariel thought and wondered if it were possible to inherit a scent. Still holding him, with his sturdy legs wrapped around her waist, she studied his face.

Essentially, it was like looking in a mirror. There'd

only been ten months between Ariel and her brother, Jeremy, and they'd often been taken for twins. Scott had pale curling hair, clear blue eyes and a face that promised to be lean and rather elegant once it had fined down from childhood. At the moment, it was sticky with pink spun sugar. Ariel kissed him firmly and tasted the sweetness.

"Yum-yum," she murmured, kissing him again when he giggled.

"What about your teeth?"

Arching a brow, she shifted his weight to a more comfortable position. "It doesn't count when it's secondhand."

He gave her a crooked smile that promised to be a heartbreaker in another decade. "How come?"

"It's scientific," Ariel claimed. "Probably the sugar evaporates after being exposed to air and skin."

"You're making that up," he told her with great approval.

Struggling with a smile, she tossed her long smooth braid behind her back. "Who me?"

"You're the best at making up."

"That's my job," she answered primly. "Let's go look at the bears."

"They better have big ones," Scott stated as he wriggled down. "*Great* big ones."

"I hear they're enormous," she told him. "Maybe even big enough to climb right out of the cages."

"Yeah?" His eyes lit up at the idea. Ariel could almost see him writing out the scenario in his mind. The escape, the panic and screams of the crowd and his ultimate heroism in driving the giant, drooling bears back behind the bars. Then, of course, his humbleness in accepting the gratitude of the zookeepers. "Let's go!"

Ariel allowed herself to be dragged along at Scott's dashing pace, winding through the stream of people who'd come to spend their day at the Bronx Zoo. This she could give him, she thought. The fun, the preciousness of childhood. It was such a short time, so concentrated. So many years were passed as an adult—with obligations, responsibilities, worries, timetables. She wanted to give him the freedom, to show him what boundaries you could leap over and the ones you had to respect. Most of all, she wanted to give him love.

She loved and wanted him, not only for the memories he brought back of her brother, but for himself—his uniqueness and odd stability. Though she was a woman who ran her life on a staggered routine that wasn't a routine at all, who enjoyed coming and going on the impulse of the moment, she'd always needed stability—someone to care for, to nurture, to give her back some portion of the emotion she spent. There was nothing like a child, with its innocence and lack of restrictions, to give and take of love. Even now, while he raced and laughed and pointed, caught up in the day and the animals, Scott was feeding her.

If Ariel had believed Scott was happy living with his grandparents, she could have accepted it. But she knew that they were smothering all the specialness that radiated from him.

They weren't unkind people, she mused, but simply set in their thinking. A child was to be formed along certain lines, and that was that. A child was a duty, a solemn one. While she understood the duty, it was joy that came first. They would raise him to be responsible, polite and well-read. And they'd forget the wonder of it.

Perhaps it would have been easier if Scott's grandparents hadn't disapproved of Ariel's brother so strongly or if Scott hadn't been conceived in youthful defiance and passion...and out of wedlock. Marriage and Scott's birth hadn't eased over the strain in the relationship, nor had the tragic and sudden accident that had taken her brother and young sister-in-law. Scott's grandparents would look at the boy and be reminded that their daughter had married against their wishes and was dead. Ariel looked at him and saw life at its best.

He needs me, she thought, and ruffled his hair as he stood staring wide-eyed at a lumbering bear. Even when her heart wasn't involved, she'd never been able to resist a need. With Scott, her heart had been lost the first time she'd seen him—red and scrawny behind a hospital glass wall.

And she understood that she needed him. To have someone receive her love was vital. She thought of Booth.

He needed her, too, she thought, as a small secret smile touched her lips. Though he didn't know it. A man like that needed the ease that love could bring to his life, and the laughter. And she wanted to give it to him.

Why? Leaning against the barrier, Ariel shook her head. She had no solid reason, and that was enough to convince her it was right. When you could dissect something and find all the answers, you could find all the wrong ones. She trusted instincts and emotions much more than she trusted the intellect. She loved—quickly, unwisely and completely. When she thought about it, Ariel decided she should never have expected it to be otherwise.

If she told him now, he'd think she was lying or insane. She could hardly blame him. It wouldn't be easy to win the confidence of a man as wary or as cynical as Booth DeWitt. With a smile, Ariel nibbled on some of Scott's popcorn. Challenges kept the excitement in life, after all. Whether Booth realized it or not, she was about to add some excitement to his.

"Why're you laughing, Ariel?"

She grinned down at Scott, then scooped him up. He laughed as he always did at her quick, physical shows of affection. "Because I'm happy. Aren't you? It's a happy day."

"I'm always happy with you." His arms went tight around her neck. "Can't I stay with you? Can't I live at your house—all the time?"

She buried her face in the curve of his shoulder—a tender place—knowing she couldn't tell him how hard she was trying to give him that. "We have today," she said instead. "All day."

Holding him, she could smell the scent of his soap and shampoo, the scent of roasted popcorn, the hot, pungent scent of the sun. With another laugh, she set her nephew down. Today, she told herself, that was what she'd show him.

"Let's go see the snakes. I like to watch them slither."

Booth couldn't understand why she kept crowding his mind. He should have been able to push Ariel into a corner of his brain and keep her there while he worked. Instead, she kept filling it.

He could have accepted it if he'd been able to keep her in her slot—the actress he was all but certain would play his Rae. He could have rationalized his obsession if it had remained a professional one. But Booth kept seeing her as she'd been on top of New York, with her hair blowing frantically and her eyes filled with the wonder of it. That woman had nothing in common with the character of Rae.

And he could see her as she'd looked in his apartment. Vital, fresh—with energy and integrity shimmering from her. He could remember her hurt when he'd been deliberately cruel, and his own guilt—a sensation he'd sworn he'd never feel again. He hardly knew her, and yet she was drawing things out of him he'd promised himself he wouldn't feel again. He was perceptive enough to know she was a woman who could draw out more. For that reason, he'd decided to keep a safe, professional distance between them.

Still, as Booth watched Ariel talk with Jack Rohrer before the reading, he couldn't keep the established lines firmly in place. Was it because she was beautiful and he had always been susceptible to beauty? Was it because she was just unique enough to catch the attention and hold it?

As a writer he couldn't suppress his fascination with the unusual. But he got something from her—some feeling of absolute stability despite the fact that she dressed somewhere between a Gypsy and a teenager. He'd already asked her who she was and had been far from satisfied with her answer. Perhaps, just perhaps he should find out for himself.

"They look good together," Marshell murmured.

The sound Booth made might have been agreement or disinterest, but he didn't take his eyes from Ariel. If he hadn't remembered her first reading so well, he'd have sworn he was making a mistake even considering her for the part. Her smile was much too open, her gestures too fluid. You could look at her and feel the warmth. He found it disconcerting to realize she made him nervous.

Desire. Yes, he felt desire. Booth weighed and measured it. Strong, hard and very nearly urgent—and that with only a look. Of course, she was a woman a man had to want. He wasn't worried about the desire, or even his interest, but about the niggling sensation that something was being slipped out of him without his knowledge and against his will.

Pulling out a cigarette, he watched her through the blue-tinted smoke. It might be worth his while, both as a man and as a writer, to see how many faces she could wear, and how easily she wore them. He sat on the edge of Marshell's desk.

"Let's get started."

At the brief, quiet order, Ariel turned her head and met Booth's gaze. *He's different today,* she thought, but couldn't quite pigeonhole the reason. He still looked at her with that intrusive, serious stare that bordered on the brooding. The distance was still there; she was sensitive enough to recognize the wall he kept erected between himself and the rest of the world. But there was something...

Ariel smiled at him. When he didn't respond, she picked up her copy of the script. She was going to give the best damn reading of her career. For herself and— for some odd reason—for Booth.

"All right, I'd like you to start at the top of the scene where they've come home from the party." Absently Booth tapped his cigarette in a gold-etched ashtray. Behind him, Marshell nibbled on a stomach mint. "Do you want to read it over first?"

Ariel glanced up from the script. *He still thinks I'm going to blow it,* she realized, and was grateful for the hard knot in her stomach. "It isn't necessary," she told him, then turned to Jack.

For the second time, Booth witnessed the transformation. How was it that even her eyes seemed to go paler, icier when she spoke as Rae? He could feel the old sexual pull and intellecutal abhorrence his ex-wife had always brought to him. With the cigarette smoldering between his fingertips, Booth listened to Rae's scorn and Phil's anger—and remembered all too clearly.

A vampire. He'd called her that and accurately. Bloodless, heartless, alluring. Ariel slipped into the character as if it were a second skin. Booth knew he should admire her for it, even be grateful that she'd made his search for the right actress end. But her chameleon skill annoyed him.

The chemistry was right. Ariel and Jack hurled their lines at each other while the anger and sexual sparks flew. There wasn't any escaping it and no logical reason to try. Without knowing why, Booth was certain that giving Ariel the part was good professional judgment and a serious personal error. He'd just have to deal with the latter as he went.

"That'll do."

The moment Booth cut the scene, Ariel threw her head back and let out breathless laughter. The release— the sudden absence of tension—was tremendous. It would always be that way, she realized, with a part as tough and as cold as this one.

"Oh, God, she's so utterly hateful, so completely self-consumed." Eyes alight, face flushed, she whirled to Booth. "You despise her, and yet she pulls you in. Even when you see the knife she's going to slide under your ribs, it's hard to step away."

"Yes." Watching the scene had disturbed him more than he'd expected. Rising, Booth left his hands in his pockets. "I want you for the part. We'll contact your agent and negotiate the details."

She sighed, but the smile lingered around her mouth.

"I can see I've overwhelmed you," Ariel said dryly. "But the bottom line is the part. You won't regret it. Mr. Marshell, Jack, it'll be a pleasure working with you."

"Ariel..." Marshell rose and accepted her offered hand. It had been a long time since he'd watched a scene that had left him as shaken as this one. "Unless I miss my guess—and I never do—you're going to hit it big with this."

She flashed him a grin and felt like flying. "I don't suppose I'll complain. Thank you."

Booth had her elbow before she could turn around, and before he'd realized he intended to touch her. He wanted to vent fury on something, someone, but reasoned it away. "I'll walk you out."

Feeling the tension in his fingers, she had to resist the urge to soothe it. This wasn't a man who'd appreciate stroking. "All right."

They followed the same route they'd taken the week before, but this time in silence. Ariel sensed he needed it. When they came to the street door, she waited for him to say whatever he intended to say.

"Are you free?" he asked her.

A bit puzzled, she tilted her head.

"For an early dinner," he elaborated. "I feel I owe you a meal."

"Well." She brushed the hair back from her face. His invitation, such as it was, pleased her—something she took no trouble to hide. "Technically that's the other way around. Why do you want to have dinner with me?"

Just looking at her—the laughing eyes, the generous mouth—pulled him in two directions. Get closer before you lose it. Back off before it's too late. "I'm not completely sure."

"Good enough." She took his hand and lifted her free one for a cab. "Do you like grilled pork chops?"

"Yes."

She laughed over her shoulder before pulling him into the cab. "An excellent start." After giving the driver an address in Greenwich Village, she settled back. "I think the next move is to have a conversation without a word, one single word, that has to do with business. We might just make it in each other's company for more than an hour."

"All right." Booth nodded. He'd made the decision to get to know her and get to know her he would. "But we'll steer away from politics, too."

"Deal."

"How long have you lived in New York?"

"I was born here. A native." She grinned and crossed her legs. "You're not. I read somewhere that you're from Philadelphia and very top-drawer. Lots of influential relatives." She didn't even glance around when the cab skidded and swerved. "Are you happy in New York?"

He'd never thought about equating it with happiness, but now that he did, the answer came easily. "Yes. I need the demands and the movement for long periods of time."

"And then you need to go away," she finished. "And be alone—on your boat."

Before he could be uncomfortable with her accuracy, he'd accepted it. "That's right. I relax when I'm sailing and I like to relax alone."

"I paint," she told him. "Terrible paintings." With a laugh, she rolled her eyes. "But it helps me work the kinks out when I get them. I keep threatening people with an original Kirkwood as a Christmas present, but I haven't the heart to do it."

"I'd like to see one," he murmured.

"The problem seems to be that I splatter my mood on the canvas. Here we are." Ariel hopped out of the cab and stood on the curb.

Booth glanced around at the tiny storefronts. "Where're we going?"

"To the market." In her easy manner, she hooked her arm through his. "I don't have any pork chops at home."

He looked down at her. "Home?"

"Most of the time I'd rather cook than eat out. And tonight I'm too wired to deal with a restaurant. I have to be busy."

"Wired?" After studying her profile, Booth shook his head. His hair was dark in the lowering sun, and the movement sent it settling carelessly around his face. A contrast, Ariel mused, to the rather formal exterior. "I'd have said you look remarkably calm."

"Uh-uh. But I'm trying to save the full explosion until after my agent calls and tells me everything's carved in granite. Don't worry—" she smiled up at him "—I'm a fair cook."

If a man judged only by that porcelain face, he'd never have believed she'd know one end of the stove from the other. But Booth knew about surfaces. Maybe, just maybe, there'd be a surprise under hers. Despite all the warnings he'd given himself, he smiled. "Only fair?"

Her eyes lit in appreciation. "I hate to brag, but actually, I'm terrific." She steered him into a small, cluttered market that smelled heavily of garlic and pepper, and began a haphazard selection for the evening meal. "How're the avocados today, Mr. Stanislowski?"

"The best." The grocer looked over her head to study

Booth out of the corner of his eye. "Only the best for you, Ariel."

"I'll have two then, but you pick them out." She poked at a head of romaine. "How did Monica do on her history quiz?"

"Ninety-two percent." His chest swelled a bit under his apron, but he continued to speculate on the dark, brooding man who'd come in with Ariel.

"Terrific. I need four really nice center-cut chops." While he selected them, she studied the mushrooms, well aware that he was bursting with curiosity over Booth. "You know, Mr. Stanislowski, Monica would love a kitten."

As he started to weigh the meat, the grocer sent her an exasperated glance. "Now, Ariel…"

"She's certainly old enough to care for one on her own," Ariel continued and pinched a tomato. "It'd be company for her, and a responsibility. And she did get ninety-two on that quiz." Looking over, she sent him a dashing, irresistible smile. He flushed and shifted his feet.

"Maybe if you were to bring one by, we could think about it."

"I will." Still smiling, she reached for her wallet. "How much do I owe you?"

"That was smoothly done," Booth murmured when they stepped outside. "And it's the second time I've heard you palming off a kitten. Did your cat have a litter?"

"No, I just happen to know about a number of home-less kittens." She tilted her face toward him. "If you're interested…"

"No." The answer was firm and brief as he took the bag from her.

Ariel merely smiled and decided she could work on him later. Now, she breathed in the scent of spices and baking from the open doorways. Some children raced along the sidewalk, laughing. A few old men sat out on the stoops to gossip. After the dinner hour, Ariel knew other members of the family would come out to talk and exchange news and enjoy the spring weather. Through a screened window she heard some muted snatches of Beethoven's Ninth, and farther down the pulse of top forty rock.

Two years before, Ariel had moved to the Village for the neighborhood feel, and had never been disappointed. She could sit outside and listen to the elderly reminisce, watch the children play, hear about the latest teenage heartthrob or the newest baby. It had been exactly what she'd needed when her family had gone its separate ways.

"Hi, Mr. Miller, Mr. Zimmerman."

The two old men who sat on the steps of the converted brownstone eyed Booth before they looked at Ariel. "Don't think you should give that Cameron another chance," Mr. Miller told her.

"Boot him out." Mr. Zimmerman gave a wheeze that might have been a chuckle. "Get yourself a man with backbone."

"Is that an offer?" She kissed his cheek before climbing the rest of the steps.

"I'll have a dance at the block party," he called after her.

Ariel winked over her shoulder. "Mr. Zimmerman, you can have as many as you want." As they started up the inside steps, Ariel began to fish in her bag for her keys. "I'm crazy about him," she told Booth. "He's a retired music instructor and still teaches a few kids on the side. He sits on the stoop so he can watch the women go by." She located the keys attached to a large, plastic, grinning sun. "He's a leg man."

Automatically, Booth glanced over his shoulder. "He told you?"

"You just have to watch the direction his eyes take when a skirt passes."

"Yours included?"

Her eyes danced. "I fit into the category of niece. He thinks I should be married and raising large quantities of babies."

She fit a single key into a single lock, something Booth thought almost unprecedented for New York, then pushed open the door. He'd been expecting the unusual. And he wasn't disappointed.

The focal point of the living room was a long oversize hammock swinging from brass ceiling hooks. One end of it was piled with pillows and beside it was a washstand holding one thick candle, three-quarters burned down. There was color—he'd known there'd be an abundance of it—and a style that was undefinable.

The sofa was a long, curved French antique upholstered with faded rose brocade, while a long wicker trunk served as a coffee table. As in Ariel's dressing room, the entire area was cluttered with books, papers and scents. He caught the fragrance of candle wax, potpourri and fresh flowers. Bunches of spring blossoms were spilling from a collection of vases that ran from dime-store pottery to Meissen.

There was an umbrella stand in the shape of a stork that was filled with ostrich and peacock feathers. A pair of boxing gloves hung in the corner behind the door.

"I guess you'd class as a featherweight," Booth mused.

Ariel followed his gaze and smiled. "They were my

brother's. He boxed in high school. Want a drink?" Before he could answer, she took the bag from him, then headed down a hallway.

"A little Scotch and water." When he turned, his attention and his senses were struck by a wall of paintings. They were hers, of course. Who else would paint with that kind of kinetic energy, verve and disregard for rules? There were splotches of color, lines of it, zigzags. Moving closer, Booth decided that while he wouldn't call them terrible, he wasn't quite sure what he'd call them. Vivid, eccentric, disturbing. Certainly they weren't paintings to relax by. They showed both flair and heedlessness, and whether she'd intended them to or not they suited the room to perfection.

As he continued to study the paintings, three cats came into the room. Two were hardly more than kittens, coal black and amber eyed. They dashed around his legs once before they made a beeline for the kitchen. The other was a huge tiger who managed to walk with stiff dignity on three legs. Booth could hear Ariel laugh and say something to the two cats who had found her. The tiger watched Booth with quiet patience.

"Scotch and water." Ariel came back in, barefoot, carrying two glasses.

Booth accepted the glass, then gestured with it. "Those must be some kinks you work out."

Ariel glanced toward her paintings. "Looks like it, doesn't it? Saves money on a therapist—though I shouldn't say that since I play the role of one."

"You've quite a place here."

"I learned I thrive on confusion." Laughing up at him, she sipped. "You've met Butch, I see." She bent and slid one hand over the tiger's back. He arched, letting out a grumble of a purr. "Keats and Shelley were the rude ones. They're having their dinner."

"I see." Booth glanced down to see Butch rub against Ariel's leg before he waddled over to the sofa and leaped onto a cushion. "Don't you find it difficult tending three cats in a city apartment while dealing with a demanding profession?"

She only smiled. "No. I'm going to start the grill."

Booth lifted a brow. "Where?"

"Why, on the terrace." Ariel walked over and slid open a door. Outside was a postage-stamp balcony more along the lines of a window ledge. On it she'd crammed pots of geraniums and a tiny charcoal grill.

"The terrace," Booth murmured over her shoulder. Only an incurable optimist or a hopeless dreamer would have termed it so. He found himself grateful she had. Laughing, he leaned against the doorjamb.

After straightening from the grill, Ariel stared at him. The sound of his laughter whispered along her skin and eased her mind. "Well, well. That's very nice. Do you know that's the first time since I've met you that you've laughed and meant it?"

Booth shrugged and sipped at his Scotch. "I suppose I'm out of practice."

"We'll soon fix that," Ariel said. She smiled, holding her hand out, palm up. "Got a match?"

Booth reached in his pocket, but something— perhaps the humor in her eyes—changed his mind. Stepping forward, he took her shoulders and lowered his mouth to hers.

He'd caught her off guard. Ariel hadn't expected him to do anything on impulse, and he'd given no sign of his intention. Before she had time to prepare, the power of the kiss whipped through her, touching the emotions, the senses, then taking over.

It wasn't a mere touching of lips this time, but a hard, thorough demand that had her wrapped in his arms and trapped against the side of the door. She reached up to take his face in her hands as she gave, unquestioningly, what he sought from her.

There was no gradual smoldering, no experimentation, but a leap of flame so intense and quick it seemed they were already lovers. She felt the instant intimacy and understood it. Her heart was already his, she couldn't deny him her body.

He felt the need churn and was relieved. It had been long, too long, since he'd more than indifferently wanted a woman. There was nothing indifferent about the passion he felt now. It was hard and clear, like the wind that buffeted him when he sailed. It spelled freedom. Drawing her closer, Booth absorbed it.

He could smell her—that warm, teasing fragrance that seemed to pulse out of her skin. How often had that scent come to him when he'd only thought of her? He remembered her taste. Alluring, giving and again warm. And the feel of her body—slender, soft, with still more warmth. It was that that touched every aspect of her, that promised to fill him. He needed it, though he'd gone for years without knowing it. Perhaps he needed her.

And it was that that had him pulling back when he wanted more and more of what she had an abundance of.

Her eyes opened slowly when her mouth was free. Ariel looked directly, unblinkingly at him. This time she saw more than a reflection of self. She saw longings and caution and a glimpse of emotion that stirred her.

"I've wanted you to do that," she murmured.

Booth forced himself to level, forced himself to think

past the senses she sent swimming. "I haven't got anything for you."

That hurt, but Ariel knew love wasn't painless. "I think you're wrong. But then, I have a tendency to rush into things. You don't." She took a deep breath and a step back. "Why don't you light this and I'll go make a salad?" Without waiting for his answer she turned and walked into the kitchen.

Steady, she ordered herself. She knew she had to be steady to deal with Booth and the feelings he brought to her. He wasn't a man who would accept a flood of emotion all at once, or the demands that went with it. If she wanted him in her life, she'd have to tread carefully, and at his pace.

He wasn't nearly as hard and cool as he tried to be, Ariel mused. With a half smile, she began to wash the fresh vegetables. She could tell from his laugh, and from those flickers of amusement in his eyes. And, of course, she was certain she couldn't have fallen in love with a man without a sense of humor. It pleased her to be able to draw it out of him. The more they were together, the easier it was. She wondered if he knew. Humming, she began to slice an avocado.

Booth watched her from the doorway. A smile lingered on her lips, and her eyes held that light he was growing too used to. She used the kitchen knife with the careless confidence of one who was accustomed to domestic chores. In one easy movement she tossed her hair behind her back.

Why should such a simple scene hold so much appeal for him, he wondered. Just looking at her standing at the sink, her hands full, the water running, he could feel himself relaxing. What was it about her that made him want to put his feet up and his head back?

At that moment, he could see himself going to her to wrap his arms around her waist and nuzzle. He must be going mad.

She knew he was there. Her senses were keen, and sharper still where Booth was involved. Keeping her back to him, she continued preparing the salad. "Have any trouble lighting it?"

He lifted a brow. "No."

"Well, it doesn't take long to heat up. Hungry?"

"A bit." He crossed the room to her. He wouldn't touch her, but he'd get just a little closer.

Smiling, she held up a thin slice of avocado, offering him a bite. Ariel could see the wariness in his eyes as he allowed her to feed him. "I'm never a bit hungry," she told him, finishing off the slice herself. "I'm always starving."

He'd told himself he wouldn't touch her, yet he found that the back of his hand was sliding over the side of her face. "Your skin," he murmured. "It's beautiful. It looks like porcelain, feels like satin." His gaze skimmed over her face, over her mouth before it locked on hers. "I should never have touched you."

Her heart was pounding. Gentleness. That was unexpected and would undermine her completely. "Why?"

"It leads to more." His fingers ran slowly down the length of her hair before he dropped his hands. "I haven't any more. You want something from me," he murmured.

Her breath trembled out. She'd never realized what a strain it was to hold in your emotions. She'd never tried. "Yes, I do. For now, just some companionship at dinner. That should be easy."

When she started to turn back to the sink, Booth stopped her. "Nothing about this is going to be easy. If

I continue to see you, like this, I'm going to take you to bed."

It would be easy, so easy, just to go into his arms. But he'd never accept the generosity, and she'd never survive the emptiness. "Booth, I'm a grown woman. If I go to bed with you, it's my choice."

He nodded. "Perhaps. I just want to make sure I have one." He turned and left her alone in the room.

Ariel took a deep breath. She wasn't going to have it, she decided. No, not any of it. He'd simply have to learn how to cope without the moodiness and tension. Lifting the platter of chops, she went back into the living room.

"Lighten up, DeWitt," she ordered and caught a glimpse of surprise on his face as she went to the grill. "I have to deal with melodrama and misery in every episode. I don't let it into my personal life. Fix yourself another drink, sit down and relax." Ariel set the chops on the grill, added some freshly ground pepper, then walked to the stereo. She switched on jazz, bluesy and mellow.

When she turned around he was still standing, looking at her. "I mean it," she told him. "I have a firm policy about worrying about what complications might come up. They're going to happen if you think about it or if you don't. So why waste your time?"

"Is it that easy for you?"

"Not always. Sometimes I have to work at it."

Thoughtfully, he drew out a cigarette. "We won't be good together," he said after he'd lit it. "I don't want anyone in my life."

"Anyone?" She shook her head. "You're too intelligent to believe a person can live without anyone. Don't you need friendship, companionship, love?"

Blowing out a stream of smoke, he tried to ignore the

twinge the question brought him. He'd spent more than two years convincing himself he didn't. Why should he just now, so suddenly, realize the fruitlessness of it? "Each one of those things requires something in return that I no longer want to give."

"Want to give." Her gaze was thoughtful, her mouth unsmiling. "At least you're honest in your phrasing. The more I'm around you, the more I realize you never lie to anyone—but yourself."

"You haven't been around me enough to know who or what I am." He crushed out his cigarette and thrust his hands in his pockets. "And you're much better off that way."

"I or you?" she countered, then shook her head when he didn't answer. "You're letting her make a victim out of you," Ariel murmured. "I'm surprised."

His eyes narrowed; the green frosted. "Don't open closets unless you know what's inside, Ariel."

"Too safe." She preferred the simple anger she felt from him now. With a half laugh, she crossed to him and put her hands on his upper arms. "There's no fun in life without risks. I can't function without fun." Her fingers squeezed, gently. "Look, I enjoy being with you. Is that all right?"

"I'm not sure." She was pulling him in again, with the lightest of touches. "I'm not sure it is for either of us."

"Do yourself a favor," she suggested. "Don't worry about it for a few days and see what happens." Rising on her toes, she brushed his mouth in a gesture that was both friendly and intimate. "Why don't you fix that drink?" she added, grinning. "Because I'm burning the chops."

Chapter 5

"No, Griff, I won't discuss my marriage." Amanda picked up a delft-blue watering can and meticulously tended the plants in her office window. The sun, a product of the sweltering stage lights, poured through the glass.

"Amanda, you can't keep secrets in small towns. It's already common knowledge that you and Cameron aren't living together any longer."

Beneath the trim, tailored jacket, her shoulders stiffened. "Common knowledge or not, it's my business." Keeping her back to him, she examined a bloom on an African violet.

"You're losing weight, there are shadows under your eyes. Damn it, Mandy, I can't stand to see you this way."

She waited a beat, then turned slowly. "I'm fine. I'm capable of handling what needs to be handled."

Griff gave a short laugh. "Who'd know that better than I do?"

Something flared in her eyes, but her voice was cool and final. "I'm busy, Griff."

"Let me help you," he said with sudden, characteristic passion. "It's all I've ever wanted to do."

"Help?" Her voice chilled as she set down the can. "I don't need any help. Do you think I should confide in you, trust you after what you did to me?" As she tilted her head, the tiny sapphires in her ears glinted. She shifted on her mark. "The only difference between you and Cameron is that I let you tear up my life. I won't make the same mistake again."

Fury burst from him as he grabbed her arm. "You never asked me what Vikki was doing in my room. Not then, and not in all these months. You bounced back quick, Mandy, and ended up with another man's ring on your finger."

"It's still there," she said quietly. "So you'd better take your hands off me."

"Do you think that's going to stop me now that I know you don't love him?" Passion, rage, desire—all emanated from his eyes, his voice, his body. "I can look at you and see it," he went on before she could deny it. "I know what's inside you like no one else does. So handle it." He dragged his hands through her hair and dislodged pins. The camera dollied closer. "And handle this."

Pulling her against him, Griff crushed her mouth with his. She nearly tore away. Nearly. For a heartbeat, she was still. Amanda lifted her hands to his shoulders to push away, but clung instead. A soft, muffled moan escaped as passion flared. For a moment, they were locked together as they'd once been. Then, he dragged her away, keeping his hands tight on her arms. Desire and anger sparked between them. His tangible, hers restrained.

"You're not going to back away from me this time," he told her. "I'll wait, but I won't wait long. You come to me, Mandy. That's where you belong."

Releasing her, Griff stormed out of the office. Amanda lifted an unsteady hand to her lips and stared at the closed door.

"Cut."

Ariel marched around the prop wall of her office. "You ate those onions on purpose."

Jack tugged on her disheveled hair. "Just for you, sweetie."

"Swine."

"God, I love it when you call me names." Dramatically, Jack gathered her in his arms and bent her backward in an exaggerated dip. "Let me take you to bed and show you the true meaning of passion."

"Not until you chew a roll of breath mints, fella." Giving him a firm push, Ariel freed herself, then turned to her director. The furnace of stage lights had already been dimmed. "Neal, if that's it for today, I've got an appointment across town."

"Take off. See you at seven on Monday."

In the dressing room, Ariel stripped Amanda's elegant facade away and replaced it with slim cotton pants and a billowy, tailored man's shirt. After slipping on flat shoes she left the studio and went outside. There was a small group of fans waiting, hoping that someone recognizable would appear. They clustered around Amanda, autograph books in hand, as they chattered about the show and tossed questions.

"Are you going to go back with Griff?"

Ariel looked over at the sparkling-eyed teenager and grinned. "I don't know…he's awfully hard to resist."

"He's super! I mean, his eyes are just so *green*." She tucked her gum into the corner of her mouth and sighed. "I'd die if he looked at me the way he looks at you."

Ariel thought of another pair of green eyes and nearly sighed herself. "We'll have to wait to see what develops, won't we? I'm glad you like the show." Easing away from the crowd, she hailed a cab. The minute she gave the address, she slumped back against the seat.

She wasn't sure why she felt so tired. She supposed it was the prospect of the meeting that made her so bone weary. True, she hadn't been sleeping as well as was her habit, but she'd gone through wakeful phases before without any strain.

Booth. If Booth were the only thing on her mind, she could have dealt with it well enough. She hoped she would. But there was Scott.

The idea of confronting his grandparents didn't frighten her, but it did weary her. Ariel had spoken with them before. There was no reason to believe this session would be any different.

She remembered the way Scott had beamed and glowed at the zoo. Such a simple thing. Such a vital thing. The way he'd clung to her—it tore at her heart. If there were just some other way…

Closing her eyes, she sighed. She didn't believe there would be another way, not even with all her natural optimism. In the end, they'd come to a complicated, painful custody suit with Scott caught in the middle.

What was best? What was right? Ariel wanted someone to tell her, to advise and comfort her. But for the first time in her life she felt it impossible to confide in anyone. The more private she kept this affair, the less chance there was of Scott being hurt by it. She would just have to follow her instincts, and hope.

With her mind on a dozen other things, Ariel paid the cabbie and walked into the sleek steel building that housed her lawyer's offices. On the way from the lobby to the thirtieth floor, she gathered all her confidence together. This would be perhaps the last time she'd have the opportunity to speak with Scott's grandparents on an informal basis. She needed to give it her best shot.

The little tremor in her stomach wasn't so different from stage fright. Comfortable with it, Ariel walked into Bigby, Liebowitz and Feirson.

"Good afternoon, Ms. Kirkwood." The receptionist beamed a smile at Ariel and wondered if she could get away with a similar outfit. Not slim enough, she decided wistfully. Instead of looking dashing, she'd just look frumpy. "Mr. Bigby's expecting you."

"Hello, Marlene. How's the puppy working out?"

"Oh, he's so smart. My husband couldn't believe that a mutt could learn so many tricks. I really want to thank you for arranging it for me."

"I'm glad he's got a good home." She caught herself lacing her fingers together—a rare outward sign of tension. Deliberately Ariel dropped her hands to her sides as the receptionist rang through.

"Ms. Kirkwood's here, Mr. Bigby. Yes, sir." She rose as she replaced the receiver. "I'll take you back. If you have time before you leave, Ms. Kirkwood, my sister'd love your autograph. She never misses your show."

"I'd be happy to." Ariel's fingers groped for each other and she restrained them. *Save the nerves for later,* she told herself, *when you can afford them.* For once, she'd apply some of Amanda's steady calm to her personal life.

"Well, Ariel." The spindly, bearded man behind the

massive desk rose as she entered. The room carried a vague scent of peppermint and polish. "Right on time."

"I never miss a cue." Ariel crossed the plush carpet with both hands extended. "You look good, Charlie."

"I feel good since you talked me into giving up smoking. Six months," he said with a grin. "Three days and—" he checked his watch "—four and a half hours."

She squeezed his hands. "Keep counting."

"We've got about fifteen minutes before the Andersons are due. Want some coffee?"

"Oh, yeah." On the words, Ariel sunk into a creamy leather chair.

Bigby pushed his intercom. "Would you bring some coffee back, Marlene? So…" He set down the receiver and folded his neat, ringless hands. "How're you holding up?"

"I'm a wreck, Charlie." She stretched out her legs and ordered herself to relax. First the toes, then the ankles, then all the way up. "You're practically the only one I can talk to about this. I'm not used to holding things in."

"If things go well you won't have to much longer."

She sent him a level look. "What chance do we have?"

"A fair one."

With a small sigh, Ariel shook her head. "Not good enough."

After a brief knock, Marlene entered with the coffee tray. "Cream and sugar, Ms. Kirkwood?"

"Yes, thank you." Ariel accepted the cup then immediately rose and began to pace. Maybe if she could turn some of the nerves to energy she wouldn't burst. Maybe. "Charlie, Scott needs me."

And you need him, he thought as he watched her.

"Ariel, you're a responsible member of your community with a good reputation. You have a steady job with an excellent income, though it can and will be argued that it's not necessarily stable. You put your brother through college and have some sort of an involvement with every charity known to man." He saw her smile at that and was pleased. "You're young, but not a child. The Andersons are both in their midsixties. That should have some bearing on the outcome, and you'll have the emotion on your side."

"God, I hate to think of there being sides," she murmured. "There're sides in arguments, in wars. This can't be a war, Charlie. He's just a child."

"As difficult as it is, you're going to have to think practically about this."

With a nod, she sipped uninterestedly at her coffee. Practical. "But I'm single, and I'm an actress."

"There're pros and cons. This last-ditch meeting was your idea," he continued. "I don't like to see you get churned up this way."

"I have to try just once more before we find ourselves in court. The idea that Scotty might have to testify…"

"Just an easy talk with the judge in chambers, Ariel. It's not traumatic, I promise you."

"Not to you, maybe not to him, but to me…" She whirled around, her eyes dark with passion. "I'd give it up, Charlie. I swear I'd give it up this minute if I could believe he'd be happy with them. But when he looks at me…" Breaking off, she shook her head. Both hands were clenched on the coffee cup and she concentrated on relaxing them. "I know I'm being emotional about this, but it's the only way I've ever been able to judge what was right and what was wrong. If I look at it practically, I know they'll feed him and shelter him and educate him. But nurturing…" She turned to stare out of the window. "I keep coming back to the nurturing. Am I doing the best for him, Charlie? I just want to be sure."

For a moment, he sat fondling the gold pen on his desk. She asked hard questions. In the law, it wasn't a matter of best, but of justice. The two weren't always synonymous. "Ariel, you know the boy. At the risk of sounding very unlawyerlike, I say you have to do what your heart tells you."

Smiling, she turned back. "You say the right things. That's all I've ever been able to do." For a moment, she hesitated, then plunged. Since she was here for advice, she'd go all the way with it. "Charlie, if I told you I'd fallen in love with a man who thinks relationships are to be avoided at all costs and actresses are the least trustworthy individuals on the planet, what would you say?"

"I'd say it was typical of you. How long do you figure it'll take you to change his mind?"

Laughing, she dragged a hand through her hair. "Always the right thing," she said again.

"Sit down and drink your coffee, Ariel," he advised. "You're the one who says if something's meant to happen, it happens."

"When have I ever said anything so trite?" she demanded but did as he said. "All right, Charlie." She heaved a long sigh. "Do you want to give me the lecture on what I should expect and what I shouldn't say?"

"For what good it'll do." He toyed with the edge of Ariel's file. "You'll meet the Andersons' lawyer, Basil Ford. He's very painstaking and very conservative. I've dealt with him before."

"Did you win?"

Bigby grinned at her as he leaned back in his chair. "I'd say we're about even. Since this is a voluntary, informal meeting, there won't be that much for either Ford or me to do. But if he asks you a question you shouldn't answer, I'll take care of it." Meticulously, Bigby settled the English bone-china cup back in its saucer. "Otherwise, say what you want, but don't elaborate more than necessary. Above all, don't lose your temper or your grip. If you want to yell or cry, wait until they've gone."

"You've gotten to know me very well," she murmured. "All right, I'll be calm and lucid." When the buzzer sounded on his desk, Ariel balled her hands into fists.

"Yes, Marlene, bring them in. And we'll need more coffee." He looked across at Ariel, measuring the strain in her eyes against the strength. "It's a discussion," he reminded her. "It's doubtful anything will be decided here today."

She nodded and concentrated on relaxing her hands.

When the door opened, Bigby rose, all joviality. "Basil, good to see you." He stretched his hand out to meet that of the erect, gray-suited man with thinning hair. "Mr. and Ms. Anderson, please have a seat. We'll have coffee in a moment. Basil Ford, Ariel Kirkwood."

Ariel nearly let out a tense giggle at the cocktail introduction. "Hello, Mr. Ford." She found his handshake firm and his gaze formidable.

"Ms. Kirkwood." He sat smoothly with his briefcase by his side.

"Hello, Mr. Anderson, Ms. Anderson."

Ariel received a nod from the woman and a brief formal handshake from her husband. Attractive peo-

ple. Solid people. She'd always felt that from them—
along with their rigidity. Both stood straight, a product
of their military training. Anderson had retired from
active service as a full colonel ten years before, and in
her youth, his wife had been an Army nurse.

They'd met during the war, had served together and
married. You could sense their closeness—the intimacy
of thoughts and values. Perhaps, Ariel mused, that was
why they had trouble seeing anyone else's viewpoint.

Together, the Andersons sat on a cushy two-seater
sofa. Both were conservatively dressed: her iron-gray
hair was skimmed back and his snowy white was
cropped close. Feeling the waves of their disapproval,
Ariel bit back a sigh. Instinct and experience told her
she'd never get through to them on an emotional level.

While coffee was served, Bigby steered the conversation into generalities. The Andersons answered politely and ignored Ariel as much as possible. Because
they spoke around her, she took care not to ask them any
direct questions. She'd antagonize them soon enough.

She recognized the signal when Bigby sat behind his
desk and folded his hands on the surface.

"I believe we can all agree that we have one mutual
concern," he began. "Scott's welfare."

"That's why we're here," Ford said easily.

Bigby skimmed his gaze over Ford and concentrated
on the Andersons. "Since that's the case, an informal
meeting like this where we can exchange points of view
and options should be to everyone's benefit."

"Naturally, my clients' main concern is their grandchild's well-being." Ford spoke in his beautiful orator's
voice before he sipped his coffee. "Ms. Kirkwood's interest is understood, of course. As to the matter of cus-

tody, there's no question as to the rights and capability of Mr. and Ms. Anderson."

"Nor of Ms. Kirkwood's," Bigby put in mildly. "But it isn't rights and capabilities we're discussing today. It's the child himself. I'd like to make it clear that, at this point, we're not questioning your intentions or your ability to raise the child." He spoke to the Andersons again, skillfully bypassing his colleague. "The issue is what's best for Scott as an individual."

"My grandson," Anderson began in his deep, raspy voice, "belongs where he is. He's well fed, well dressed and well disciplined. His upbringing will have a sense of order. He'll be sent to the best schools available."

"What about well loved?" Ariel blurted out before she could stop herself. "What money can't buy…" Leaning forward she focused her attention on Scott's grandmother. "Will he be well loved?"

"An abstract question, Ms. Kirkwood," Ford put in briskly. "If we could—"

"No, it isn't," Ariel interrupted, sparing him a glance before she turned back to the Andersons. "There's nothing more solid than love. Nothing more easily given or withheld. Will you hold him at night if he's frightened of shadows? Will you understand how important it is to pretend that he's protecting you? Will you always listen when he needs to talk?"

"He won't be coddled if that's what you mean." Anderson set down his coffee and rested a hand on one knee. "A child's values are molded early. These fantasies—that you encourage—aren't healthy. I have no intention of allowing my grandson to live in a dreamworld."

"A dreamworld." Ariel stared at him and saw a solid

rock wall of resistance. "Mr. Anderson, Scott has a beautiful imagination. He's full of life, and visions."

"Visions." Anderson's lips thinned. "Visions will do nothing but make him look for what isn't there, expect what he can't have. The boy needs a firm basis in reality. In what *is*. You make your living from pretending, Ms. Kirkwood. My grandson won't live his life in a storybook."

"There're twenty-four hours in every day, Mr. Anderson. Isn't there enough reality in that so we can put a small portion of time aside for wishing? All children need to believe in wishes, especially Scott after so much has been taken away from him. Please..." Her gaze shifted to the stiff-backed woman on the sofa. "You've known grief. Scott lost the two people in the world who meant love and security and normality. All of those things have to be given back to him."

"By you?" Ms. Anderson sat very still, her eyes remained very level. In them Ariel saw remnants of pain. "My daughter's child will be raised by me."

"Ms. Kirkwood." Ford interrupted smoothly, then crossed his legs. "To touch on more practical matters, I'm aware that you currently have a key role in a— Daytime drama, I believe is the word. This equals a regular job with a steady income. But to be down-to-earth for a moment, it's habitual for these things to change. How would you support a child if your income was interrupted?"

"My income won't be interrupted." Bigby caught her eye, so with an effort Ariel held on to her temper. "I'm under contract. I'm also signed to do a film with P. B. Marshell." Noticing the flicker of speculation, Ariel blessed fate for throwing the part her way.

"That's very impressive," Ford told her. "However,

I'm sure you'd be the first to admit that your profession is renowned for its ups and downs."

"If we're talking financial stablity, Mr. Ford, I assure you that I'm capable of giving Scott all the material requirements necessary. If my career should take a downswing, I'd simply supplement it. I've experience in both the retail and the restaurant business." A half smile teased her mouth as she thought of her days selling perfume and powder, and waiting tables. Oh, yes, *experience* was the right word. "But I can't believe any of us would put a bank statement first when we're discussing a child." It was said calmly, with only a hint of disdain.

"I'm sure we all agree that the child's monetary well-being is of primary importance," Bigby put in. The subtle tone of his voice was his warning to Ariel. "There's no question that both the Andersons and my client are capable of providing Scott with food, shelter, education, etc."

"There's also the matter of marital status." Ford stroked a long finger down the side of his nose. "As a single woman, a single professional woman, Ms. Kirkwood, just how much time would you be able to spare for Scott?"

"Whatever he needs," Ariel said simply. "I recognize my priorities, Mr. Ford."

"Perhaps." He nodded, resting a hand on the arm of his chair. "And perhaps you haven't thought this through completely. Having never raised a child, you might not be fully aware of the time involved. You have an active social life, Ms. Kirkwood."

His words and tone were mild, his meaning clear. Any other time, in any other place, she would have been amused. "Not as active as it reads in print, Mr. Ford."

Again, he nodded. "You're also a young woman, attractive. I'm sure it's reasonable to assume that marriage is highly likely at some time in the future. Have you considered how a potential husband might feel about the responsibility of raising someone else's child?"

"No." Her fingers laced together. "If I loved a man enough to marry him, he'd accept Scott as part of me, of my life. Otherwise, he wouldn't be the kind of man I'd love."

"If you had to make a choice—"

"Basil." Bigby held up a hand, and though he smiled, his eyes were hard. "We shouldn't get bogged down in this sort of speculation. No one expects us to solve this custody issue here today. What we want is to get a clear picture of everyone's feelings. What your clients and mine want for Scott."

"His well-being," Anderson said tersely.

"His happiness," Ariel murmured. "I want to believe they're the same thing."

"You're no different from your brother." Anderson's voice was sharp and low, like the final snap of a whip. "Happiness. He preached happiness at all costs to my daughter until she tossed aside all her responsibilities, her education, her values. Pregnant at eighteen, married to a penniless student who put more effort into flying a kite than keeping a decent job."

Ariel's mouth trembled open as the pain struck. No, she wouldn't waste her breath defending her brother. He needed no defense. "They loved each other," she said instead.

"Loved each other." Color rose in Anderson's cheeks, the first and only sign of emotion Ariel had seen from him. "Can you honestly believe that's enough?"

"Yes. They were happy together. They had a beautiful child together. They had dreams together." Ariel swallowed as the urge to weep pounded at her. "Some people never have that much."

"Barbara would still be alive if we'd kept her away from him."

Ariel looked over at the older woman and saw more than pain now. The strong, bony hands shook slightly, the voice broke. It was a combination of grief and fury that Ariel recognized and understood. "Jeremy's gone, too, Ms. Anderson," she said quietly. "But Scott's here."

"He killed my daughter." The woman's eyes glowed against a skin gone abruptly pale.

"Oh, no." Ariel reached out, shocked by the words, drawn by the pain. "Ms. Anderson, Jeremy adored Barbara. He'd never have done anything to hurt her."

"He took her up in that plane. Barbara had no business being up in one of those small planes. She wouldn't have been if he hadn't taken her."

"Ms. Anderson, I know how you feel—"

She jerked away from Ariel's offer of comfort, her breath suddenly coming fast and shallow. "Don't you tell me you know how I feel. She was my only child. My only child." Rising, she sent Ariel an icy stare that shimmered with tears. "I won't discuss Barbara with you, or Barbara's son." She walked from the office in quick, controlled steps that were silent on the carpet.

"I won't have you upsetting my wife." Mr. Anderson stood, erect and unyielding. "We've known nothing but misery since the first time we heard the name Kirkwood."

Though her knees had begun to shake, Ariel rose to face him. "Scott's name is Kirkwood, Mr. Anderson."

Without a word, he turned and strode out of the room.

"My clients are understandably emotional on this

issue." Ford's voice was so calm Ariel barely heard it. With the slightest nod of agreement, she wandered to stare out the window.

She didn't register the subdued conversation the attorneys carried on behind her. Instead, she concentrated on the flow of traffic she could see but not quite hear thirty floors below. She wanted to be down there, surrounded by cars and buses and people.

Strange how she'd nearly convinced herself she was resigned to her brother's death. Now, the helpless anger washed over her again until she could have screamed with it. Screamed just one word. *Why?*

"Ariel." Bigby put a hand on her shoulder and repeated her name before Ariel turned her head. Ford and his clients had left. "Come sit down."

She lifted a hand to his. "No, I'm all right."

"Like hell you are."

With a half laugh, she rested her forehead against the glass. "I will be in a minute. Why is it, Charlie, I never believe how hard or how ugly things can be until they happen? And even then— Even then I can't quite understand it."

"Because you look for the best. It's a beautiful talent of yours."

"Or an escape mechanism," she murmured.

"Don't start coming down on yourself, Ariel." His voice was sharper then he'd intended, but he had the satisfaction of seeing her shoulders straighten. "Another of your talents is being able to pull in other people's emotions. Don't do it with the Andersons."

Letting out a long sigh, she continued to stare down to the street. "They're hurting. I wish there was a way we could share the grief instead of hurling it at one another. But there's nothing I can do about them," she whispered and closed her eyes briefly, tightly. "Charlie, Scott doesn't belong with them. He's all I care about. Not once, not one single time did either of them call him by name. He was always the boy, or my grandchild, never Scott. It's as though they can't give him his own identity, maybe because it's too close to Jeremy's." For an extra moment she rested her palms against the window ledge. "I only want what's right for Scott—even if it's not me."

"It's going to go to court, Ariel, and it's going to be very, very hard on you."

"You've explained all that before. It doesn't matter."

"I can't give you any guarantees on the outcome."

She moistened her lips and turned to face him. "I understand that, too. I have to believe that whatever happens will be what's best for Scott. If I lose, I was meant to lose."

"At the risk of being completely unprofessional—" he touched the tips of her hair "—what about what's best for you?"

With a smile, she cupped his face in her hand and kissed his cheek. "I'm a survivor, Charlie, and a whole hell of a lot tougher than I look. Let's worry about Scott."

He was capable of worrying about more than one thing at a time, and she was still pale, her eyes still a bit too bright. "Let me buy you a drink."

Ariel rubbed her knuckles against his beard. "I'm fine," she said definitely. "And you're busy." Turning, she picked up her purse. Her stomach was quivering. All she wanted to do was to get out in the air and clear her head. "I just need to walk for a bit," she said half to herself. "After I think it all the way through again I'll feel better."

At the door she paused and looked back. Bigby was still standing by the window, a frown of concern on his face. "Can you tell me we have a chance of winning?"

"Yes, I can tell you that. I wish I could tell you more."

Shaking her head, Ariel pulled open the door. "It's enough. It has to be enough."

Chapter 6

Booth considered taking everything he'd written that day and ditching it. That's what sensible people did with garbage. Leaning back in his chair, he scowled at the half-typed sheet staring back at him, and at the stack of completed pages beside his machine. Then again, to-morrow it might not seem quite so much like garbage and he could salvage something.

He couldn't remember the last time he'd hit a wall like this in his work. It was like carving words into granite—slow, laborious, and the finished product was never perfectly clear and sharp. You got sweaty, your muscles and eyes ached, and you barely made a dent. He'd given the script ten hours that day, and perhaps half of that with his full concentration. It was out of character. It was frustrating.

It was Ariel.

What the hell was he going to do about it? Booth ran

his hands over his face with a weariness that came from lack of production rather than lack of energy. There'd never been a woman he couldn't block out of his mind for long periods of time—even Liz at the height of their disastrous marriage. But this woman... With a sound of annoyance, Booth pushed away from the typewriter. This woman was breaking all the rules. His rules—the ones he'd formed for personal survival.

The worst of it was he just wanted to be with her. Just to see her smile, hear her laugh, listen to her talk about something that didn't have to make sense.

And the hardest of it was the desire. It shifted and rippled continually under the surface of his thoughts. He had the blessing-curse of a writer's imagination. No effort was needed for Booth to feel the way her skin would heat under his hands, the way her mouth would give and take. And it took no effort to project mentally how she could foul up his life.

Because they'd be working together, he could only avoid her so much. Making love with her was inevitable—so inevitable he knew he'd have to weigh the consequences. But for now, with his rooms quiet around him and thoughts of Ariel crowding his mind, Booth couldn't think beyond having her. Prices always had to be paid... Who would know that better than he?

Glancing down at his work, Booth admitted that he was already paying. His writing was suffering because he couldn't control his concentration. His pace, usually smooth, was erratic and choppy. What he was producing lacked the polish so integral to his style.

Too often, he caught himself staring into space—something writers do habitually. But it wasn't his characters who worked in his mind. Too often, he found himself awake before dawn after a restless night. But it wasn't his plot that kept him from sleep.

It was Ariel.

He thought of her too much, too exclusively for comfort. And he was a man who hoarded his comfort. His work was always, had always been, of paramount importance to him. He intended it to continue to be. Yet he was allowing someone to interfere, intrude.

Allowing? Booth shook his head as he lit a cigarette. He was a man of words, of shades of meanings, and knew that wasn't the proper one. He hadn't allowed Ariel into his mind—she'd invaded it.

The smoke seared his throat. Too many cigarettes, he admitted as he took another drag. Too many long days and nights. He was pushing it—and there were moments, a few scattered moments when he took the time to wonder why.

Ambition wasn't the issue. Not if ambition equaled the quest for glory and money. Glory had never concerned him, and money had never been a prime motivation. Success perhaps, in that he had always sought then insisted on quality when anything was associated with his name. But it was more a matter of obsession— that was what his writing had been since he'd first put pen to paper.

When a man had one obsession, it was easy to have two. Booth stared at the half-typed page and thought of Ariel.

The doorbell rang twice before he roused himself to answer it. If his work had been flowing at all, he would have ignored it completely. Interruptions, he thought ruefully as he left the littered desk behind, sometimes had their advantages.

"Hi." Ariel smiled at him and kept her hands in her

pockets. It was the only way she could keep them from lacing together. "I know I should've called, but I was walking and took the chance that you wouldn't be frantically writing some monumental scene." *You're babbling,* she warned herself and clenched both hands.

"I haven't written a monumental scene in hours." He studied her a moment, perceptive enough to know that beneath the smile and animated voice there was trouble. A week before, perhaps even days before, he'd have made an excuse and shut her out. "Come in."

"I must've caught you at a good time," Ariel commented as she crossed the threshold. "Otherwise you'd've growled at me. Were you working?"

"No, I'd stopped." She looked ready to burst, he mused. The casualness, the glib remarks didn't mask the outpouring of emotion. It showed in her eyes, in her movements. A quick glance showed him that her hands were fists in her pockets. Tension? One didn't associate the word with her. He wanted to touch her, to soothe, and had to remind himself that he didn't need anyone else's problems. "Want a drink?"

"No— Yes," she amended. Perhaps it would calm her more than the two-hour walk had done. "Whatever's handy. It's a beautiful day." Ariel paced to the window and found herself reminded too much of standing in Bigby's office. She turned her back on the view. "Warm. Flowers are everywhere. Have you been out?"

"No." He handed her a dry vermouth without offering her a chair. In this mood he knew she'd never sit still.

"Oh, you shouldn't miss it. Perfect days're rare." She drank, then waited for her muscles to loosen. "I was going to walk through the park, then found myself here."

He waited a moment as she stared down into her glass. "Why?"

Slowly, Ariel lifted her eyes to his. "I needed to be with someone—it turned out to be you. Do you mind?"

He should have. God knows he wanted to. "No." Without thinking, Booth took a step closer—physically, emotionally. "Do you want to tell me about it?"

"Yes." The word came out on a sigh. "But I can't." Turning away, she set down her glass. She wasn't going to level. Why had she been so sure she would? "Booth, it isn't often I can't handle things or find myself so scared that running away looks like the best out. When it happens, I need someone."

He was touching her hair before he could stop himself, was turning her to face him before he'd weighed the pros and cons. And he was holding her before either of them could be surprised by the simplicity of it.

Ariel clung as relief flowed over her. He was strong—strong enough to accept her strength and understand the moments of weakness. She needed that very basic human support, without question, without demands. His chest was hard and firm against her. Over her back his hands ran gently. He said nothing. For the first time in hours, Ariel felt her balance return. Kindness gave her hope; she was a woman who'd always been able to survive on that alone.

What's troubling her, Booth wondered. He could feel the panic in the way her hands gripped him. Even when he felt her begin to relax he remembered that first frantic grip. Her work, he thought. Or something more personal? Either way, it had nothing to do with him. And yet... While she was soft and vulnerable in his arms he felt it had everything to do with him.

He should step back. His lips brushed through her hair as he breathed in her fragrance. It was never safe to lower the wall. His lips skimmed along her temple.

"I want to help you." The words ran through his mind and spilled out before he was aware of them.

Ariel's arms tightened around him. That phrase meant more, infinitely more, than I love you. Without knowing it, he'd just given her everything she needed. "You have." She tilted her head back so that she could see his face. "You are."

Lifting a hand, she ran her fingers over the long firm bones in his face, over the taut skin roughened by a day's growth of beard. Love was something that moved in her too strongly to be ignored. She needed to share it, if not verbally, then by touch.

Softly, slowly, she closed the distance and brushed his lips with hers. Her lids lowered, but through her lashes she watched his eyes as he watched hers. The intensity in his never altered. Ariel knew he was absorbing her mood, and testing it.

It was he who shifted the angle, without increasing the pressure. Easily he toyed with her mouth, nipping into the softness of her bottom lip, tracing the shape with just the tip of his tongue until the flutter in her stomach spread to her chest. He needed to draw in the sensation of her as a woman, as an individual. He wanted to know her physically; he needed to understand the subtleties of her mind. As she felt her body give, her mind yield, Ariel wondered how it was he didn't hear the love shouting out of her.

He was struck by the emotion that raced from her. He'd never held a woman capable of such feeling, or one who, by possessing it, demanded it in return. It wasn't a simple matter of response. Even as his senses began to swim, Booth understood that. He wanted to give to her. And though he wanted, he knew he couldn't. Risks were for the foolish, and he couldn't afford to play the fool a second time.

Compassion, however, touched off compassion. If nothing else, he could give her a few hours' relief from whatever plagued her mind. He ran his hands up her arms for the sheer pleasure of it. "How nice a day is it?" he asked.

Ariel smiled. Her fingers were still on his face, her lips only inches from his. "It's spectacular."

"Let's go out." Booth paused only long enough to take her hand before he headed for the door.

"Thank you." Ariel touched her head briefly to his shoulder in one more simple show of affection he wasn't accustomed to. It warmed him—and cautioned him.

"What for?"

"For not asking questions." Ariel stepped into the elevator, leaned back against the wall and sighed.

"I generally stay out of other people's business."

"Do you?" She opened her eyes and the smile lingered. "I don't. I'm an inveterate meddler—most of us are. We all like to get inside other people. You just do it more subtly than most."

Booth shrugged as the elevator reached lobby level. "It's not personal."

Ariel laughed as she stepped out. Swinging her purse over her shoulder, she moved in her habitual quick step. "Oh, yes, it is."

He stopped a moment and met the humor in her eyes. "Yes," he admitted. "It is. But then, as a writer I can observe, dissect, steal other people's thoughts and feelings without having to get involved enough to advise or comfort or even sympathize."

"You're too hard on yourself, Booth," Ariel murmured. "Much too hard."

His brow quirked in puzzlement. Of all the things he'd ever been accused of, that wasn't one of them. "I'm a realist."

"On one level. On another you're a dreamer. All writers are dreamers on some level—the same way all actors are children on one. It has nothing to do with how clever you are, how practical, how smart. It goes with the job." She stepped out into the warmth and the sun. "I like being a child, and you like being a dreamer. You just don't like to admit it."

Annoyance. He should've felt annoyance but felt pleasure instead. As long as he could remember, no one else had ever understood him. As long as he could remember, he'd never cared. "You've convinced yourself you know me very well."

"No, but I've made a few scratches in the surface." She sent him a saucy look. "And you've a very tough surface."

"And yours is very thin." Unexpectedly he cupped her face in his hand for a thorough study. His fingers were firm, as if he expected resistance and would ignore it. "Or seems to be." How could he be sure, he wondered. How could one person ever be sure of another?

Ariel was too used to being examined, and already too used to Booth to be disconcerted. "There's little underneath that doesn't show through."

"Perhaps that's why you're a good actress," he mused. "You absorb the character easily. How much is you, and how much is the role?"

He was far from ready to trust, she realized when

he dropped his hand. "I can't answer that. Maybe when the film's over, you'll be able to."

He inclined his head in acknowledgment. It was a good answer—perhaps the best answer. "You wanted to walk in the park."

Ariel tucked her arm companionably through his. "Yeah. I'll buy you an ice cream."

Booth turned his head as they walked. "What flavor?"

"Anything but vanilla," Ariel said expansively. "There's nothing remotely vanilla about today."

She was right, Booth decided. It was a spectacular day. The grass was green, the flowers vivid and pungent. He could smell the park smells. Peanuts and pigeons. Enthusiastic joggers pumped by in colorful sweatbands and running shorts, streaks of sweat down their backs.

Spring would soon give way to early summer. The trees were full, the leaves a hardy shade rather than the tender hue they'd been only weeks before. Shade spread in invitation while the sun baked the benches and paths. He knew Ariel would choose the sun. And he wondered, as he strolled along beside her, why he'd gone so long without seeking it himself.

As Ariel bit into an ice cream confection coated with chocolate and nuts, she thought of Scott. But this time, the apprehension was gone. She'd only needed to lean on someone for a moment, draw on someone else's emotional strength, to have her faith return. Her head was clear again, her nerves gone. With a laugh, she turned into Booth's arms and kissed him hard.

"Ice cream does that to me." She was still laughing as she dropped onto a swing. "And sunshine." She leaned way back and kicked her feet to give herself momentum. The tips of her hair nearly skimmed the ground. It was pale, exquisitely pale in the slanting sun. As it fell back, it left her face unframed and stunning. Her skin was flushed with color as she pushed off again and let herself glide.

"You seem to be an expert." Booth leaned against the frame of the swing as her legs flashed by him.

"Absolutely. Want to join me?"

"I'll just watch."

"It's one of your best things." Ariel threw out her legs again for more height and enjoyed the thrill that swept through her stomach. "When's the last time you were on one of these?"

A memory surged through his mind—of himself at five or six and his primly uniformed, round-faced nanny. She'd pushed him on a swing while he'd squealed and demanded to go higher. At the time he hadn't believed there was any more to life than that rushing pendulum ride. Abruptly, he appreciated Ariel's claim that she enjoyed being a child.

"A hundred years ago," he murmured.

"Too long." Skimming her feet on the ground, she slowed the swing. "Get on with me." She blew the hair out of her eyes and grinned at his blank expression. "You can stand, one foot on either side of me. It's sturdy enough—if you are," she added with just enough of a challenge in the tone to earn a scowl.

"Practicing your psychiatry?"

Her grin only widened. "Is it working?"

She was laughing at him again, and knowing it, Booth took the bait. "Apparently." He stepped behind her to grab the chain with his hands. "How high do you want to go?"

Ariel tipped back her head to give him an upside-down smile. "As high as I can."

"No crying uncle," Booth warned as he began to push her.

"Ha." Ariel tossed back her hair and shifted her grip. "Fat chance, DeWitt."

She felt him jump nimbly onto the swing as they began to fly, then threw her body into it until the rhythm steadied. The sky tilted over her, blue and dusted with clouds. The ground swayed, brown and green. She rested her head against a firm, muscled thigh and let the sensations carry her.

Grass. She could smell it, sun drenched and trampled, mixed with the dusty scent of dry earth. Children's laughter, cooing pigeons, traffic—Ariel could hear each separate sound individually and as a mixture.

The air tasted of spring—sweet, light. An image of a watermelon ran through her mind. Yes, that was what she thought of as the breeze fluttered over her cheeks. But overall, most of all, it was Booth who played with her senses. It was him she felt firmly against her back, his quiet breathing she heard beneath all the other sounds. She could smell him—salt and soap and tobacco. She had only to shift the angle of her head to see his strong, capable hands around the chain of the child's swing. Ariel closed her eyes and absorbed it all. It was like coming home. Content, she slid her hands higher on the chain so that they brushed his. The contact, warm flesh to warm flesh, was enough.

He'd forgotten what it was like to do something for no reason. And by forgetting it, Booth had forgotten the purity of pleasure. He felt it now, without the intellectual justifications he so often restricted himself with. Because he understood that freedom brought vulnerability, he'd doled it out to himself miserly. Only on those rare occasions when he was completely alone, away from responsibilities and his work, had he allowed his heart and mind to drift. Now, it happened so spontaneously he hardly realized it. Bypassing the dangers of relaxation, Booth enjoyed the ride.

"Higher!" Ariel demanded on a breathless laugh as she leaned into the arch. "Much higher!"

"Much higher and you'll land on your nose."

Her sound of pleasure rippled over the air. "Not me. I land on my feet. Higher, Booth!"

When she turned her head up to laugh into his face, he lost himself in her. Beauty—it was there, but not the cool, distant beauty he saw on camera. Looking at her now, he saw nothing of his Rae, nothing of her Amanda. There was only Ariel. For the first time in longer than he cared to remember, he felt a twinge of hope. It scared the hell out of him.

"Faster!" she shouted, not giving him any time to dwell on what was happening inside him. Her laughter was infectious, as was her enthusiasm. They soared together until his arms ached. When the swing began to slow, she leaped from it and left him wobbling.

"Oh, that was wonderful." Still laughing, Ariel turned in a circle, arms wide. "Now I'm starving. Absolutely starving."

"You just had ice cream." Booth leaped off the swing to find himself breathless and his blood pumping.

"Not good enough." Ariel whirled around to him and linked her hands behind his head. "I need a hot dog— really need a hot dog with everything."

"A hot dog." Because it seemed so natural, he bent

to kiss her. Her mouth was warm, the lips curved. "Do you know what they put in those things?"

"No. And I don't want to. I want to stuff myself with whatever nasty stuff it has in it and feel wonderful."

Booth ran his hands down her sides. "You do feel wonderful."

Her smile changed, softened. "That's about the nicest thing you've ever said to me. Kiss me again, right here, while I'm still flying."

Booth drew her closer as his lips tasted hers. Fleetingly he wondered why the gentle kiss moved him equally as much as the passion had yet somehow differently. He wanted her. And along with her body he wanted that energy, that verve, the joie de vivre. He wanted to explore and measure it, and to test it for its genuineness. Booth was still far from sure that anyone in the world he knew could be quite so real. And yet, he was beginning to want to believe it.

Drawing her away he watched her lashes flutter up, her lips curve. But he remembered that sense of panic he'd felt from her when he'd first opened his door. If her emotions were as vibrant as they seemed, she wouldn't be limited to joy and vivacity.

"A hot dog," he repeated and speculated on how much he would learn of her and how long it would take. "It's your stomach, but I'll spring for it."

"I knew you could be a sport, Booth." She slipped her arm around his waist as they walked. "I just might have two."

"Masochistic tendencies run in your family?"

"No, just gluttony. Tell me about yours."

"I don't have masochistic tendencies."

"Your family," she corrected, chuckling. "They must be very proud of you."

His brow lifted while a ghost of a smile played around his mouth. "That depends on your point of view. I was supposed to follow family tradition and go into law. Throughout most of my twenties I was the black sheep."

"Is that so?" Tilting her head, she studied him with fresh interest. "I can't imagine it. I've always had a fondness for black sheep."

"I would've made book on it," Booth said dryly. "But one might say I've been accepted back into the fold in the past few years."

"It was the Pulitzer that did it."

"The Oscar didn't hurt," Booth admitted, seeing the humor in something he'd barely noticed before. "But the Pulitzer had more clout with the DeWitts of Philadelphia."

Ariel scented the hot dog stand and guided him toward it. "You'll be adding an Emmy to the list next year."

He pulled out his wallet as Ariel leaned over the stand and breathed deeply. "You're very confident."

"It's the best way to be. Are you having one?"

The scent was too good to resist. When had he eaten last? What had he eaten? Booth shrugged the thoughts way. "I suppose."

Ariel grinned and held up two fingers to the concessionaire. When hers was in its bun she began to go through the condiments one at a time. "You know, Booth—" she piled on relish "—*The Rebellion* was brilliant, clean, hard-hitting, exquisite characterizations, but it wasn't as entertaining as your *Misty Tuesday*."

Booth watched her take the first hefty bite. "My purpose in writing isn't always to entertain."

"No, I understand that." Ariel chewed thoughtfully,

then accepted the soda Booth offered her. "It's just my personal preference. That's why I'm in the profession. I want to be entertained, and I need to entertain."

He added a conservative line of mustard to his hot dog. "That's why you've been satisfied with daytime drama."

She shot him a look as they began to walk again. "Don't get snide. Quality entertainment's the core of it. If I was handy juggling plates and riding a unicycle, that's what I'd do."

After the first bite, Booth realized the hot dog was the best thing he'd eaten in a week, perhaps in months. "You have a tremendous talent," he told her, but didn't notice the surprised lift of her brow at the ease of the compliment. "It's difficult for me to understand why you aren't doing major films or theater. A series, even a weekly series is dragging, backbreaking work. Being a major character in a show that airs five days a week has to be exhausting, impossible and frustrating."

"Exactly why I do it." She licked mustard from her thumb. "I was raised right here in Manhattan. The pace's in my blood. Have you ever considered why L.A. and New York are on opposite ends of the continent?"

"A lucky geographical accident."

"Fate," Ariel corrected. "Both might be towns where show business is of top importance, but no two cities could have more opposing paces. I'd go crazy in California—mellow isn't my speed. I like doing the soap because it's a daily challenge, it keeps me sharp. And when there's the time and the opportunity, I like doing things like *Streetcar*. But…" She finished off her hot dog with a sigh. "Doing the same play night after night becomes too easy, and you get too comfortable."

He drank down cola—a flavor he'd nearly forgotten. "You've been playing the same character for five years."

"Not the same thing." She crunched an ice cube and enjoyed the shock of cold. "Soaps're full of surprises. You never know what kind of angle they're going to throw at you to pump up ratings or lead in a fresh story line." She scooted around a middle-aged matron walking a poodle. "Right now Amanda's facing a crumbling marriage and a personal betrayal, the possibility of an abortion and a rekindling of an old affair. Not dull stuff. And though it's top secret, I'll tell you she's going to work with the police on a profile of the Trader's Bend Ripper."

"The what?"

"As in Son of Jack the Ripper," she said mildly. "Her former lover Griff's the number-one suspect."

"Doesn't it ever bother you that so much melodrama goes on in a small town with four or five connecting families?"

She stopped to look at him. "Do you know your Coleridge?"

"Passably."

"'The willing suspension of disbelief.'" Ariel crumpled her napkin, then tossed both it and her empty cup into a trash can. "It's all that's necessary to get along in this world. Believe it might happen, it could happen. Plausibility's all that's necessary. As a writer, you should know that."

"Perhaps I should. I've always leaned more toward reality."

"If it works for you." The lift of her shoulders seemed to indicate that all was accepted. "But sometimes it's easier to believe in coincidence, or magic or simple luck. Straight reality without any detours is a very hard road."

"I've had a few detours," he murmured. It occurred to him that Ariel Kirkwood had already led him off the paved road he'd adhered to for years. Booth began to wonder just where her twisting direction would lead them. Lost in thought, he didn't notice that they were in front of his building until she stopped. His work was waiting, his privacy, his solitude. He wanted none of it.

"Come up with me."

The request was simple, the meaning clear. And her need was huge. Shaking her head, Ariel touched the hair that had fallen over his forehead. "No, it's best that I don't."

He took her hand before she could drop it back to her side. "Why? I want you, you want me."

If it were only so simple, she thought as the desire to love him grew and grew. But she knew, instinctively, that it wouldn't be simple, not for either of them once begun. For him there was too much distrust, for her too many vulnerabilities.

"Yes, I want you." Ariel saw the change in his eyes and knew it would be much more difficult to walk away than to go with him. "And if I came upstairs, we'd make love. Neither of us is ready for that, Booth, not with each other."

"If it's a game you're playing to make me want you more, it's hardly necessary."

She drew her hand from his and stood on her own. "I like to play games," she said quietly. "And I'm very good at most of them. Not this kind."

Pulling out a cigarette, he lit it with a snap of his lighter. "I've no patience for the wine and candlelight routine, Ariel."

He saw the humor light in her eyes and could have cursed her. "How lucky that I don't have a need for them." Putting her hands on his shoulders, she leaned forward and kissed him. "Think of me," she requested and turned quickly to walk away.

As he stared after her, Booth knew he'd think of little else.

Chapter 7

It was going to be hard work, with long days, short nights and constant demands on both the body and the mind. Ariel was going to love every minute of it.

The producers of the soap were cooperating fully with Marshell; the network strategy was to everyone's advantage. The word, the big word, was always *ratings*. But it was Ariel who had to squeeze in the time for both projects, and Ariel who had to learn hundreds of pages of script as Amanda and as Rae.

Under different circumstances they might have simply written around her for a few weeks on *Our Lives, Our Loves,* but with Amanda and Griff's relationship heating up and the Ripper on the prowl, it wasn't possible. Amanda had a key role in too many vital scenes. So instead, Ariel had to shoot a backbreaking number of those scenes in a short period of time. This would give her three straight weeks to concentrate exclusively on the film. If that project ran behind schedule, she'd have to compensate by dividing her time and energies between Amanda and Rae.

The idea of eighteen-hour days and 5:00 a.m. calls couldn't dull her enthusiasm. The pace, merciless as it was, was almost natural to her in any case. And it helped keep her mind off the custody trial, which was set for the following month.

And there was Booth. Even the idea of working with him excited her. The daily contact would be stimulating. The professional competition and cooperation would keep her sharp. The preproduction stages had shown her that Booth would be as intimately involved with the film as any member of the cast and crew—and that he had unquestioned authority.

Throughout the sometimes hysterical meetings, he'd remained calm and had said little. But when he spoke, he was rarely questioned. It wasn't a matter of arrogance or overbearing, as Ariel saw it. Booth DeWitt simply didn't comment unless he knew he was right.

Perhaps, if it was meant to be, they'd move closer to each other as the film progressed. Emotion. It was what she wanted to give him, and what she needed from him. Time. She knew it was a major factor in whatever happened between them. Trust. This above all was needed—and this, above all, was missing.

There were times during the preproduction stages of the filming that Ariel felt Booth watching her too objectively, and distancing himself from her too successfully.

Ariel found herself at an impasse. The more skillfully she played Rae, the more firmly Booth stepped back from her. She understood it, and was helpless to change it.

The set was elegant, the lighting low and seductive.

Across a small rococo table, Rae and Phil shared lobster bisque and champagne. Ariel's costume was clinging midnight silk. Diamonds and sapphires winked at her ears and throat. An armed guard in the studio attested to the fact that paste wasn't used on a Marshell production.

The intimate late-night supper was actually taking place at 8:00 a.m. in the presence of a full crew. Sipping lukewarm ginger ale from a tulip glass, Ariel gave a husky laugh and leaned closer to Jack.

She knew what was needed here—sex, raw and primitive under a thin sheen of sophistication. It would have to leap onto the screen with a gesture, a look, a smile, rather than through dialogue. She was playing a role within a role. Rae was her character, and Rae was never without a mask. Tonight, she would project a warmth, a soft femininity that was no more than a facade. It was Ariel's job to show both this, and the skill with which Rae played the part. If the actress Ariel portrayed wasn't clever, the impact on the character of Phil would waver. The connection between the two was vital. They fed each other, and by doing so, the entire story.

Rae wanted Phil, and the viewer had to know that she wanted him physically nearly as much as she wanted the connections he could bring her professionally. To win him, she had to be what he wanted. Ambition and skill were a deadly combination when added to beauty. Rae had all three and the capacity to use them. It was Ariel's job to show the duality of her nature, but to show it subtly.

The scene would end in the bedroom; that portion of the film would be shot at a different time. Now, the tension and the sexuality had to be heightened to a point where both Phil and the audience were completely seduced.

"Cut!"

Chuck ran a hand over the back of his neck and lapsed into silence. Both the actors and crew recognized the gesture from their director and remained silent and alert. The scene wasn't pleasing him, and he was working out why. Keyed up, Ariel didn't allow the tension to drain out of her. She needed the nerves to maintain the image of Rae. The sight of the ginger ale and the scent of the food in front of her made her stomach roll uneasily. They were already on the fourth take. Objectively, she watched her glass being refilled, her plate replaced. When this was over, she thought, she'd never even look at a glass of ginger ale again.

"Disgusting, isn't it?"

Glancing over, Ariel saw Jack Rohrer grimace at her. She locked Rae in a compartment of her brain before she grinned at him. "I've never wanted a cup of coffee and a bagel so much in my life."

"Please." He leaned back from the table. "Don't mention real food."

"More feline," Chuck said abruptly and focused on Ariel. "That's how I see Rae—a sleek black cat with manicured claws."

Ariel smiled at the image. Yes, that was Rae.

"When you say the line, 'One night won't be enough, you make me greedy,' you should practically purr it."

Ariel nodded while she flexed her hands. Yes, Rae would purr that line, while she calculated every angle. Ariel had a mental image of a cat—glossy, seductive and just this side of evil.

Just before the clapper was struck for the next take, Ariel caught Booth's eye. He was frowning at her while he stood off camera. Though his hands were casually in his pockets and his expression was still and calm, she sensed the wall of tension around him. Unable to break it down, she used it and the eye contact to pull herself back into character.

As the scene unfolded, she forgot the flat, warm taste of the ginger ale, forgot the intrusion of cameras and crew. Her attention was completely focused on the man across from her, who was no longer a fellow actor but an intended victim. She smiled at something he said, a smile Booth recognized too well. Seductive as black lace, cold as ice. There wasn't a man alive who'd be immune to it.

When she reached the line Chuck had focused on, Ariel paused a beat, dipping her fingertip into Jack's glass, then slowly touched the dampened skin to her mouth, then his. The seductive ad lib had the temperature on the set soaring. Even while he mentally approved the gesture and Ariel's intuition, Booth felt his stomach muscles tighten.

She knew her character, he mused, almost as well as he did himself. So well, it was always an effort to separate them in his mind. This attraction that plagued him—at whom was it directed? That surge of jealousy he felt unexpectedly when the woman on set melted into another man's arms—for whom did he really feel it? He'd entwined reality and fiction so tightly in this script, then had chosen an actress skilled enough to blur those lines. Now, he found himself trapped between fiction and fact. Was the woman he wanted the shadow or the light?

"Cut! Cut and print! Fantastic." Grinning from ear to ear, Chuck walked over and kissed both Ariel and Jack. "We're lucky the camera didn't overload on that scene."

Jack flashed a white-toothed smile. "You're lucky I didn't. You're damn good." Jack laid a hand on Ariel's shoulder. "So damn good I'm going to have a cup of coffee and call my wife."

"Ten minutes," Chuck announced. "Set up for reaction shots. Booth, what'd you think?"

"Excellent." With his eyes on Ariel, Booth walked toward them. There was nothing of the cat about her now. If anything, she looked a bit weary. He found that while the knot in his stomach had loosened, he had to fight the urge to stroke her cheek. Booth was more accustomed to the first sensation. "You look like you could use some coffee yourself."

"Yeah." Again, Ariel forced herself to lock Rae's personality away. She wanted nothing more than to relax completely, but knew she could only allow herself a few degrees. "You buying?"

Nodding, he led her off set where a catering table was already set up with coffee, doughnuts and Danishes. Ariel's stomach revolted at the thought of food, but she took the steaming Styrofoam cup in both hands.

"This schedule's difficult," Booth commented.

"Mmm." She shrugged that off and let the coffee wash away the aftertaste of ginger ale. "No, the schedule's no tighter than the soap's—lighter in some ways. The scene was difficult."

He lifted a brow. "Why?"

The scent of the coffee was real and solid. Ariel could almost forget the spongy food she'd had to nibble on for the past two hours. "Because Phil's smart and cautious—not an easy man to seduce or to fool. Rae has to do both, and she's in a hurry." She glanced over the rim of her cup. "But then, you know that."

"Yes." He took her wrist before she could drink again. "You look tired."

"Only between takes." She smiled, touched by the reluctant concern. "Don't worry about me, Booth. Frantic's my natural pace."

"There's something else."

She thought of Scott. It's not supposed to show, she reminded herself. The minute you walk into the studio, it's not supposed to show. "You're perceptive," she murmured. "A writer's first tool."

"You're stalling."

Ariel shook her head. If she thought about it now, too deeply, her control would begin to slip. "It's something I have to deal with. It won't interfere with my work."

He took her chin firmly into his hand. "Does anything?"

For the first time, Ariel felt a threat of pure anger run through her. "Don't confuse me with a role, Booth—or another woman." She pushed his hand away, then turning her back on him, walked back onto the set.

The temper pleased him, perhaps because it was easier to trust negative emotions. Leaning back against the wall, Booth made a decision. He was going to have her—tonight. It would ease a portion of the tension in him and alleviate the wondering. Then both of them, in their own way, would have to deal with the consequences.

Ariel found the anger was an advantage. Rae, she mused, was a woman who had anger simmering just below the surface at all times. It added to the discontent, and the ambition. Instead of trying to rid herself of it—something she wasn't certain she could do in any case—Ariel used it to add more depth to an already complicated character. As long as she clung to Rae's mercurial, demanding personality, she didn't feel her own weariness or frustrations.

True, her senses were keen enough so that she knew exactly where Booth was and where his attention was focused even when she was in the middle of a scene. That was something to be dealt with later. The more he pushed at her—mentally, emotionally—the more she was determined to give a stellar performance.

By six and wrap time, Ariel discovered that Rae had drained her. Her body ached from the hours of standing under the lights. Her mind reeled from the repetition of lines, the drawing and releasing of emotions. It was only the first week of filming, and already she felt the strain of the marathon.

Nobody said it'd be easy, Ariel reminded herself as she slipped into her dressing room to change into her street clothes. And it wouldn't be nearly so important if it were. The trouble was, she was beginning to equate her success in the part with her success in her relationship with Booth. If she could pull one off, she could do the same with the other.

Shaking her head, Ariel stripped out of her costume, shedding Rae as eagerly as she did the silk. An idea like that, she reminded herself, had a very large trapdoor. Rae was a part to be acted, no matter how entangled it was with reality. Booth was real life—her life. No matter how willing she was to take risks or accept a challenge, that was something she couldn't afford to forget.

Gratefully, Ariel creamed off her stage makeup and let her skin breathe. She sat, propping her feet on her dressing table so that the short kimono she wore skimmed her thighs. Taking her time, letting herself come down, she undid the sleek knot the hairdresser had arranged and let her hair fall free. With a contented sigh, Ariel tipped her head back, shut her eyes and fell into a half doze.

That was how Booth found her.

The room was cluttered in her usual fashion so that she seemed to be a single island of calm. The air was assaulted with scents—powder, face cream, the same potpourri just hinting of lilac that she kept at home. The lights around her mirror were glaring. Her breathing was soft and even.

As he shut the door behind him, Booth let his gaze run up the long slender length of her legs, exposed from toe to thigh. The kimono was loosely, almost carelessly knotted, so that it gaped intriguingly down the center of her body nearly to the waist. Her hair fell behind the chair, mussed from her own hands so that the curve of neck and shoulder made an elegant contrast.

Her face seemed a bit pale without the color needed for the camera…fragile. Without it, the faintest of shadows could be seen under her eyes.

Booth wanted almost painfully to possess her, just as she was at that moment. With hardly a thought as to what he was doing, he turned the lock on the door. He sat on the arm of a chair, lit a cigarette and waited.

Ariel woke slowly. She tended to sleep quickly and wake gradually. Even before she'd drifted from that twilight world to consciousness, she knew she was refreshed. The nap had been no more than ten minutes. Any longer and she'd have been groggy, any shorter, tense. With a sigh, she started to stretch. Then she sensed she wasn't alone. Curious, she turned her head and looked at Booth.

"Hello."

He saw no remnants of the anger in her eyes, nor was there any coolness, that sign of resentment, in her voice. Even the weariness he'd sensed in her briefly had vanished. "You didn't sleep long." His cigarette had burned down nearly to the filter without his noticing. He crushed it out. "Though I don't know anyone who could've slept at all in that position."

"For a ten-minute session, I can sleep anywhere." She pointed her toes, tensing all her muscles, then released them. "I had to recharge."

"A decent meal would help."

Ariel put a hand to her stomach. "It wouldn't hurt."

"You barely touched anything at lunch."

It didn't surprise her that he'd noticed, only that he'd commented on it. "Normally I'd have gorged myself. Eating lobster bisque at dawn threw my whole system out of whack. A bagel's more my style. Or a bowl of Krispie Krinkies."

"Of what?"

"Eight essential vitamins," she said with a half grin. Reluctantly, she slid her feet to the floor. The gap in her robe shifted, and absently she tugged at the lapels. "We are wrapped for the day, aren't we? There isn't a problem?"

"We wrapped," he agreed. "And there's a problem."

The brush she'd lifted paused halfway to her hair. "What kind?"

"Personal." He rose and took the brush from her hand. "Every day this week I've watched you, listened to you, smelled you. And every day this week, I've wanted you." He took the brush through her hair in one long, smooth stroke while in the lighted mirror, his eyes met hers. When she didn't move, he drew the brush down again, cupping the curve of her shoulder with his free hand. "You asked me to think of you. I have."

Too close to the surface, Ariel warned herself. Her

emotions were always too close to the surface. There was nothing she could do about it. "Every day this week," she began in a voice that was already husky, "you've watched me and listened to me be someone else. You might be wanting someone else."

His eyes remained on hers as he lowered his mouth to her ear. "I'm not watching anyone else now."

Her heart lurched. Ariel would have sworn she felt the jerk of movement inside her breast. "Tomorrow—"

"The hell with tomorrow." Booth let the brush drop as he drew her to her feet. "And yesterday." His gaze was intense, a hot, hot green that had her throat going dry. She'd wondered what it would be like if he allowed any emotion freedom. This was his passion, and it was going to sweep her away.

If she hadn't loved him... But, of course, she did. All caution whipped away as her mouth met his. There was a time for thinking, and a time for feeling. There was a time for withholding, and a time for giving freely. There was a time for reason, and a time for romance.

All that Ariel had, all that she felt, thought, wished, went into the touch of mouth to mouth. And as her body followed her heart, she wrapped herself around him and offered unconditionally. She felt the floor tilt and the air freeze before she became lost in her own longings. Her lips parted, inviting; her tongue touched, arousing. Her breath fluttered, answering.

She was firm, as he was, yet softer. Feeling the hard length of man against her, she became completely, utterly feminine. The pleasure was liquid, passing through her as warmed wine. As his grip tightened, she melted further until she was as pliant as any man's fantasy. But she was very real.

He'd never known another woman like her, so utterly

free with emotions that flowed and crested until he was drowning in them. Passion had been expected and was there, but… More, infinitely more, was a range of feeling so intense, so sweet, it was irresistible.

As he'd watched her on the set, he'd wanted her. When he'd come into the room to see her sleeping, desire had assaulted him. Now, with her yielding, vibrating with emotions he could hardly name, Booth needed her as he'd never needed anyone. And had never wanted to.

Too late. The thought ran through his mind that it was too late for her—too late for him. Then his hands were buried in her hair, his thoughts a kaleidoscope of sensations.

She smelled faintly of lemon from the cream she'd used on her face, while her hair carried the familiar fragrance of light sexuality. The thin material of her kimono swished as his hands parted it to find her. And she was softer than a dream, but so small he had a moment's fear that he would hurt her. Then her body arched, pressing against his hand so that it was her strength that aroused him. With a sound that was more of surrender than triumph, he buried his face against her throat.

Even while her mind was floating, Ariel knew she had to feel the texture of his flesh against hers. Slowly, her hands ran up his sides, drawing up his sweater. She followed the movement, over his shoulders, until there was nothing barring her exploration—and nothing to stop her sensitized skin from meeting his.

When he drew her down she went willingly. As her back rested against the littered sofa, she cupped her hands behind his head and brought his mouth back to hers. The taste of his passion rippled through her and lit the next spark.

Not so passive now, not so pliant, she moved under him, sending off twinges of excitement to pulse through both of them. The sudden aggression of her lips was welcome. The kiss went on and on, deeper, moister, while two pairs of hands began to test and appreciate.

He could feel the frantic beat of her heart under his palm. When he pressed his lips against her breast, he felt her shudder. The outrageous desire to absorb her ran through him as he began to draw in her variety of tastes, now with his lips, now with the tip of his tongue. Sometimes, some places, it was hot, others sweet, but always it was Ariel.

The lights glared into the room, reflecting from the mirror as he began a thorough, intense journey over her. The curve of her shoulder held fascinations he'd never known before. The skin at the inside of her wrist was so delicate he almost thought he could hear the blood run through the veins. Everywhere he touched, he felt her pulse. She was so giving. That alone was enough to make his head swim.

And as he touched, tasted, took, so did she. If he became more demanding, she responded in kind, keeping pace with him. Or perhaps it was he who kept pace with her. She stroked with those long, elegant fingers so that he knew what it was to be on the verge of madness, and within sight of heaven.

She wanted nothing more than what she could find in him. Touches of tenderness that moved her. Flares of fires that tormented her. His hair brushed over her skin and that alone excited her. Flesh grew damp with passion and the struggle to control—the struggle to prolong. Ariel learned that pleasure alone was a shallow thing; but pleasure, when combined with love, was all.

Together, they understood that there could be no more waiting. The final barriers of clothing were tugged impatiently away. She opened for him. Madness and heaven became one.

Ariel felt as though she could run for miles. Her body was alive with so many sensations. Her mind leaped with them. She lay beneath Booth, tingling with an awareness that radiated down to her toes and finger-tips. With her eyes closed, her body still aligned with his, she counted his heartbeats as they thudded against her. In that private, liquid world they'd gone to, Booth hadn't been calm, he hadn't been detached. Letting her lashes flutter up, she smiled. His hand was laced with hers. She wondered if he were aware of it. He'd wanted her. Just her.

Contentment. Was that what he was feeling? Booth lay sated, drained, aware only of Ariel's warm, slim form beneath him. As far as he could remember, he'd never experienced anything remotely like this. Total relaxation...a complete lack of tension. He didn't even have the energy to dissect the feeling, and instead en-joyed it. With a sound of pure pleasure, he turned his face in to her throat. He felt as well as heard her gurgle of laughter.

"Funny?" he murmured.

Ariel ran her hands up the length of his back, then down again to his waist. "I feel good. So good." Her fingertips skimmed over his hips. "So do you."

Shifting slightly, Booth raised himself on one elbow so that he could look at her. Her eyes were laughing. With a fingertip he traced the spot just below her jaw where he'd discovered delectable, sensitive skin. "I still don't know what I'm doing with you."

She brushed the hair from his forehead and watched it fall back again. "Do you always have to have an intellectual reason?"

He frowned, but his fingers spread over her face as if he were blind and memorizing it. "I always have."

She wanted to sigh but smiled instead. Taking his face in her hands, Ariel brought him down for a hard kiss. "I defy the intellect."

That made him laugh, and because he was off balance, she was able to roll him over. With her body slanted across his, she stretched and nuzzled into his shoulder. Booth felt the crinkle of paper and the rumple of cloth beneath him. "What am I lying on?"

"Mmm. This and that."

Arching, he pulled a crumpled pamphlet from under his left hip. "Anyone ever mention that you're sloppy?"

"From time to time."

Absently, Booth glanced at the pamphlet about the plight of baby seals before he dropped it to the floor. He tugged at another paper stuck to his right shoulder. A halfway house for battered wives. Curiosity piqued, he twisted a bit and found another. ASPCA literature.

"Ariel, what is all this?"

She gave his shoulder a last nibble before she rested her cheek on it. He held several wrinkled leaflets. "I suppose you might call it my hobby."

"Hobby?" He put his free hand under her chin to lift it. "Which one?"

"All of them."

"All?" Booth looked at the leaflets in his hand again and wondered how many others were squashed beneath him. "You mean you're actively involved in all these organizations?"

"Yeah. More or less."

"Ariel, no one person would have the time."

"Oh, no." She shifted, folding her arms across his chest for support. "That's a cop-out. You make time." She tilted her head toward the papers he held. "Those baby seals, do you know what's done to them, how it's done?"

"Yes, but—"

"And those abused women. Most of them come into that shelter without any self-esteem, without any emotional or financial support. Then there's—"

"Wait a minute." He let the papers slide to the floor so he could take her shoulders. How slim they were, he realized abruptly. And how easily she could make him forget just how delicately she was formed. "I understand all that, but how can you be involved in all these causes, run your life and pursue your career?"

She smiled. "There're twenty-four hours in every day. I don't like to waste any of them."

Seeing that she was perfectly serious, Booth shook his head. "You're a remarkable woman."

"No." Ariel bent her head and kissed his chin. It dipped slightly in the center—not quite a cleft. "I just have a lot of energy. I need to put it somewhere."

"You could put all of it into furthering your career," he pointed out. "You'd be top box office within six months. There'd be no question of your success."

"Maybe. But I wouldn't be happy with it."

"Why?"

It was back; she felt it. The doubts, the distrust. With a sigh, Ariel sat up. In silence, she picked up her kimono and pulled it on. How quickly warmth could turn to chill. "Because I need more."

Dissatisfied, Booth took her arm. "More what?"

"More everything!" she said with a sudden passion that stunned him. "I need to know I've done my best, and not just in one area of my life. Do you really think I'm so limited?"

The fire in her eyes intrigued him. "I believe what I said indicated your lack of limitations."

"Professionally," she snapped. "I'm a person first. I need to know I touched someone, helped somehow." She dragged both hands through her hair in frustration. "I need to know I cared. Success isn't just a little gold statue for my trophy case, Booth." Whirling, she yanked open the door of her closet and pulled out her street clothes.

As Booth sat up, the papers beneath him rustled. "You're angry."

"Yes, yes, yes!" With her back to him, Ariel wriggled into her briefs. In the mirror, Booth could see the reflected temper on her face.

"Why?"

"Your favorite question." Ariel flung the kimono to the floor, then dragged a short-sleeved sweatshirt over her head. "Well, I'll give you the answer, and you're not going to like it. You still equate me with her." She flung the words at him; as they hit, he too began to dress. "Still," she continued, "even after what just happened between us, you still measure me by her."

"Maybe." He rose and drew his sweater over his head. "Maybe I do."

Ariel stared at him a moment, then stepped into her jeans. "It hurts."

Booth stood very still as the two words sliced into

him. He hadn't expected them—their simplicity, their honesty. He hadn't expected his own reaction to them. "I'm sorry," he murmured.

Stepping closer, he touched her arm and waited for her to look up at him. The hurt was in her eyes, and he knew it was the second time he'd put it there. "I've never been a particularly fair man, Ariel."

"No," she agreed. "But it's hard for me to believe that someone so intelligent could be so narrow-minded."

He waited for his own anger to rise, and when it didn't, shook his head. "Maybe it's simplest to say you weren't in my plans."

"I think that's clear." Turning away, she began to brush her hair methodically. Hurt pulsed from her still, laced with anger. It never occurred to her to rely on pride and conceal them both. "I told you before that I tend to rush into things. I also understand that not everyone keeps the same pace. But I'd think by this time you'd see that I'm not the character you created—or the woman who inspired her."

"Ariel." She stiffened when he took her shoulders. He could see her fingers flex on the brush handle. "Ariel," he said again and lowered his brow to the top of her head. Why did he want so much what he'd cut himself off from? "I'll hurt you again," he said quietly. "I'm bound to hurt you if I continue to see you."

Her body relaxed on a sigh. Why was she fighting the inevitable? "Yes, I know."

"And knowing that, knowing what you could do to my own life, I don't want to stop seeing you."

She reached up to cover the hand on her shoulder with her own. "But you don't know why."

"No, I don't know why."

Ariel turned in his arms and held him. For a moment

they stood close, her head on his shoulder, his hands at her waist. "Buy me dinner," she requested, then tipped back her head and smiled at him. "I'm starving. I want to be with you. Those are two definite facts. We'll just take the rest as it comes."

He'd been right to call her remarkable, Booth thought. He pressed his lips to her brow. "All right. What would you like to eat?"

"Pizza with mushrooms," she answered immediately. "And a cheap bottle of Chianti."

"Pizza."

"A huge one—with mushrooms."

With a half laugh he tightened his hold. He was no longer sure he could let go. "It sounds like a good start."

Chapter 8

At 7:00 a.m., Ariel sat in a makeup chair, with a huge white drop cloth covering her costume, going over her lines while a short, fussy-handed man with thinning hair slanted blusher over her cheekbones. She could hear, but paid no attention to, the buzz of activity around her. Someone shouted for gel for the lights. A coil of cable was dropped to the floor with a thud. Ariel continued to read.

The upcoming scene was a difficult one, with something perilously close to a soliloquy in the middle. If she didn't get the rhythm just right, the pitch perfect, the entire mood would be spoiled.

And her own mood wasn't helping her concentration.

She'd had another lovely Sunday with Scott, which had ended with a tense and tearful departure. Though she'd long ago resigned herself to the fact that she was a creature of emotional highs and lows, Ariel couldn't rid herself of the despondency or the nagging sense of guilt.

Scott had clung to her, with great, silent tears running down his cheeks, when she'd returned him to the Andersons' home in Larchmont. It was the first time in all the months since his parents' death that he'd created a scene at the end of their weekly visit. The Andersons had met his tears with grim, tight-lipped impatience while both had cast accusing glares at Ariel.

After she'd soothed him, Ariel had wondered all during the lengthy train ride home if she'd unconsciously brought on the scene. By wanting him so badly, was she encouraging him to want her? Did she spoil him? Was she overcompensating because of her love for his father and her pain in the loss?

She'd spent a sleepless night over it, and the questions had built and pressed on her. But there'd been no firm answers in the morning. Within a few weeks, she'd have to live with the decision of a judge who would see Scott as a minor rather than as a little boy who liked to play pretend games. Could a judge, however experienced, however fair, see the heart of a child? It was one more question that kept her awake at night.

Now, Ariel knew she had to put her personal business aside. Her part in the film was more than a job; it was a responsibility. Both the cast and the crew depended on her to do her best. Her name on the contract guaranteed she would give all her skill. And, she reminded herself as she rubbed an aching temple, worrying wasn't going to help Scott.

"My dear, if you continue to fidget, you'll spoil what I've already done."

Bringing herself back, Ariel smiled at the makeup man. "Sorry, Harry. Am I beautiful?"

"Almost exquisite." He pursed his lips as he touched up her brows. The natural arch, he thought with professional admiration, needed very little assistance from him. "For this scene, you should look like Dresden. Just a little more here..." Ariel sat obediently while he smoothed more color into her lips. "And I'll have to insist that there be no more frowning. You'll spoil my work."

Surprised, Ariel met his eyes. She'd been sure she'd had her expression, if not her thoughts, under control. Foolish, she decided, then reminded herself that problems were to be left on the other side of the studio door. That was the first rule of showmanship.

"No more frowns," she promised. "I can't be responsible for spoiling a masterpiece."

"Well, nothing changes. Still cramming before zero hour."

"Stella!" Ariel glanced up and broke into the first true smile of the day. "What're you doing here?"

"Taking a busman's holiday." Stella dropped into the chair beside Ariel, pulling up her legs, then folding them under her. "I used your name—and some charm," she added with a sweep of her lashes, "to get in. You don't mind if I watch the morning's shooting, do you?"

"Of course not. How're things at Trader's Bend?"

"Heating up, love, heating up." With a wicked smile, Stella tossed her thick mane of hair behind her shoulder. "Now that Cameron's trying to blackmail Vikki over her gambling debts, and the Ripper's claimed his third victim, *and* Amanda and Griff are starting to simmer, they can't keep up with the mail or the phone calls. Rumor is *Tube* wants to do a two-part spread on the cast. That's big time."

Ariel's brow quirked. "Cover story?"

"That's what I hear through the grapevine. Hey, I got stopped in the market the other day. A woman named

Ethel Bitterman gave me a lecture on moral standing and family loyalty over the cucumbers."

Laughing, Ariel drew off her protective drape to reveal a frothy, raspberry-colored sundress. This was what she'd needed, she realized. That sense of camaraderie and family. "I've missed you, Stella."

"Me, too. But tell me…" Stella's gaze skimmed up the dress that, while demure and feminine, reeked of sex. "How does it feel to be playing the bad girl for a change?"

Ariel's eyes lit up. "It's wonderful, but it's tough. It's the toughest part I've ever played."

Stella smiled and buffed her nails on her sleeve. "You always claimed I had all the fun."

"I might've been right," Ariel countered. "And I may've oversimplified. But I don't remember ever working harder than this."

Stella rested her chin on her hand. "Why?"

"I guess because Rae's always playing a part. It's like trying to get inside a half dozen personalities and make them one person."

"And you're eating it up," Stella observed.

"I guess I am." With a quick laugh she settled back. "Yeah, I am. One day I'll feel absolutely drained, and the next so wired…" She shrugged and set her script aside. If she didn't know her lines by now, she never would. "In any case, I know if I have a choice, when this is over, I'd like to do a comedy. A Judy Holliday type. Something full of fun and wackiness."

"What about Jack Rohrer?" Stella dug in her purse and found a dietary lemon drop. "What's he like to work with?"

"I like him." Ariel smiled ruefully. "But he doesn't

make it a picnic. He's a perfectionist—like everyone else on this film."

"And the illustrious Booth DeWitt?"

"Watches everything," Ariel murmured.

"Including you." Moving only her eyes, Stella changed the focus of her attention. "At least he has been for the past ten minutes."

Ariel didn't have to turn her head. She already knew. In her mind's eye she could see him, standing a bit apart from the grips and gaffers as they checked the lighting and the set. He'd remove himself from the activity so as not to interfere with the flow, but his presence would be felt by everyone. And that presence alone would make everyone just tense enough to be sharp.

She knew he'd be watching her, half-wary, half-accepting. More than anything else, she wanted to merge the two into trust. And trust into love.

Booth watched her laugh at something Stella said. He watched the animated hand movements, the slight tilt of her head that meant she was avidly interested. Then again, Ariel rarely did anything that wasn't done avidly. Whatever had been clouding her mood when she'd come in earlier had been smoothed over. As he remembered the trouble in her eyes, Booth wondered what problem plagued her and why, when she seemed so willing to share everything, she was unwilling to share that.

Lighting a cigarette, Booth told himself he should be grateful she kept it to herself. Why should he want to be involved? He knew very well that one of the quickest ways to become vulnerable to someone else was to become concerned with their problems.

Beside him a stagehand thoroughly sprayed an elegant arrangement of fresh flowers. The lighting director called for a final check on the candlepower. A mike boom was lowered into place. Booth wondered what Ariel had done over the weekend.

He'd wanted to spend it with her, but she'd put him off and he hadn't insisted. He wouldn't box her in, because by doing so he set limits on himself. That was a trap he wouldn't fall into. But he remembered the utter peace he'd felt lying with her in her dressing room after passion was spent.

He couldn't say she was a calming influence—too much energy crackled from her. Yet she had a talent for soothing the tension from his mind.

He wanted to talk to her again. He wanted to touch her again. He wanted to make love with her again. And he wanted to escape from his own needs.

"Places!" The assistant director called out as he paced the set, rechecking the blocking.

Booth leaned back against the wall, his thumbs hooked absently in his pockets. It never occurred to him, as it often had to Ariel, how seldom he sat.

They would shoot a section of an extensive scene that morning. The other parts would be filmed later on the lawns of a Long Island estate. The elegant lawn party they'd shoot on location was to be Rae's first full-scale attempt at entertaining since marrying Phil. And afterward, indoors and in private, would come their first full-scale argument.

She looked like something made of spun-sugar icing. Her words were as vicious as snake venom. And all the while, with the fury and the poison oozing from her, she hadn't a hair out of place. The fragile color in her cheeks never fluctuated. It was Ariel's job to keep the character cold-blooded, and the words smoldering.

She knew it was all in the eyes. Rae's gestures were a facade. Her smile was a lie. Both the ice and the fire had to come from the eyes. The scene had to be underplayed, understated from her end. It was a constant strain to keep her own emotions from bubbling out. If *she* were to fight with words, she'd shout them, hurl them—and fling off the ones tossed back at her. Rae drawled them, almost lazily. And Ariel ached.

This was Booth's life, she thought. Or a mirror image of what had been his life. This was his pain, his mistakes, his misery. She was caught up in it. If she hurt, how did he feel watching?

Rae gave Phil a bored look as he grabbed both her arms.

"I won't have it," he raged at her, eyes blazing while hers remained cool as a lake.

"Won't have it?" Rae repeated, transmitting utter disdain with the tone, with the movement of an eyebrow. "What is it you won't have?"

"I will not have you raying the pole." Jack closed his eyes and made a gargling sound.

"Raying the pole?" Ariel repeated. "Having a little trouble with your tongue?"

She felt the tension snap as the scene was cut, but wasn't certain if she was grateful or not. She wanted this one over.

"Playing the role," Jack enunciated carefully. "I will not have you *playing* the *role*. I got it." He held up both hands, mocking himself and his flubbed line.

"Fine, as long as you understand that I can and will ray the pole whenever I choose."

He grinned at Ariel. "Smart mouth."

She patted his cheek. "Aw, yours'll wise up, Jack. Give yourself a chance."

"Places. Take it from the entrance."

For the third time that morning, Ariel swung through the French doors with her skirts billowing behind her.

They moved through the scene again, immersing themselves in the characters even with the starts and stops and changes of camera angles.

To end the scene, Rae was to laugh, take the glass of Scotch from Phil's hand, sip, then toss the contents into his face. Caught up in character, Ariel took the glass, tasted the warm, weak tea, then with an icy smile, poured the contents over the elegant floral arrangement. Without missing a beat in the change of staging, Jack ripped the glass out of her hand and hurled it across the room.

"Cut!"

Snapping back, Ariel stared at her director. "Oh, God, Chuck, I don't know where that came from. I'm sorry." With a hand pressed to her brow, she looked down at the now drenched mixture of fragile hothouse blooms.

"No, no. Damn!" Laughing, he gave her a bear hug. "That was perfect. Better than perfect. I wish I'd thought of it myself." He laughed again and squeezed Ariel until she thought her bones might crack. "She'd have done that. She *would* have done just that." With his arm slung around Ariel's shoulder, Chuck turned to Booth. "Booth?"

"Yes." Without moving, Booth indicated a nod. "Leave it as it stands." He pinned Ariel with cool, green eyes. He should have written it that way, he realized. Throwing a drink in Phil's face was too obvious for Rae. Even too human. "You seem to know her better than I do now."

She let out an uneven breath, giving Chuck's hand

a squeeze before she walked toward Booth. "Is that a compliment?"

"An observation. They're setting up for the close-ups," he murmured, then brought his attention back to her. "I won't give you carte blanche, Ariel, but I'm willing to feed you quite a bit of rope in your characterization. And obviously so is Chuck. You understand Rae."

She could have been amused or annoyed. As always when she had a choice, Ariel chose amusement. "Booth, if I were playing a mushroom, I'd understand that mushroom. It's my job."

He smiled because she made it easy. "I believe you would."

"Didn't you catch the commercial where I played the ripe, juicy plum?"

"Must've been out of town."

"It was a classic. Over and above my shower scene for Fresh Wave shampoo—though, of course, sensuality was the basis in both spots."

"I want to come home with you tonight," he said quietly. "I want to stay with you tonight."

"Oh." When would she get used to the simple ways he had of saying monumental things?

"And when we're alone," Booth murmured as he watched the pulse in her throat begin to flutter, "I want to take off your clothes, little by little, so that I can touch every inch of you. Then I want to watch your face while we make love."

"Ariel, let's get these close-ups!"

"What?" A bit dazed, she mumbled the word while she continued to stare at Booth. Already she could feel his hands on her, taste his breath as it mixed with her own.

"They can have your face—for now," Booth told her,

more aroused by her reaction to his words than he would have thought possible. "Tonight, it's mine."

"Ariel!"

Flung back to the present, she turned to go back to the set. With a look that was amused and puzzled, she glanced back over her shoulder. "You're not predictable, Booth."

"Is that a compliment?" he countered.

She grinned. "My very best one."

Hour after hour, line after line, scene after scene, the morning progressed. Though the film was naturally shot out of sequence, Ariel could feel it beginning to jell. Because it was television, the pace was fast. Her pace. Because it was DeWitt and Marshell, the expectations were high. As were hers.

You sweltered under the lights; changed moods, costumes; were powdered, dusted and glossed. Again and again. You sat and waited during scene changes or equipment malfunctions. And somewhere between the tension and the tedium was your vocation.

Ariel understood all that, and she wanted all of that. She never lost the basic pleasure in performing, even after ten retakes of a scene where Rae rode an exercise bike while discussing a new script with her agent.

Muscles aching, she eased herself off the bike and dabbed at the sweat, which didn't have to be simulated, on her face.

"Poor baby." Stella grinned as a stagehand offered Ariel a towel. "Just remember, Ariel, we never work you this hard on *Our Lives*."

"Rae *would* have to be a fitness fanatic," she muttered, stretching her shoulders. "Body conscious. I'm conscious now." With a little moan, Ariel bent to ease a cramp in her leg. "Conscious of every muscle in my body that hasn't been used in five years."

"It's a wrap." Chuck gave her a companionable slap on the flank as he passed. "Go soak in a hot tub."

Ariel barely suppressed a less kind suggestion. She slung the towel over her shoulder, gripped both damp ends and stuck out her tongue.

"You never did have any respect for directors," Stella commented. "Come on, kid, I'll keep you company while you change. Then I've got a hot date."

"Oh, really?"

"Yeah. My new dentist. I went in for a checkup and ended up having a discussion on dental hygiene over linguine."

"Good God." Not bothering to hide a grin, Ariel pushed open her dressing-room door. "He works fast."

"Uh-uh, I do." With a laugh that held both pleasure and nerves, Stella walked into the room. "Oh, Ariel, he's so sweet—so serious about his work. And…" Stella broke off and dropped onto Ariel's cluttered sofa. "I remember something you said a few weeks ago about love—it being a definite emotion or something." She lifted her hands as if to wave away the exact phrase and grip the essence. "Anyway, I haven't come down to earth since I sat in that tilt-back chair and looked up into those baby-blue eyes of his."

"That's nice." For the moment Ariel forgot her sore muscles and the line of sweat dripping down her back. "That's really nice, Stella."

Stella searched for another lemon drop and found her supply depleted. Knowing Ariel, she walked to the dressing table, pulled open a drawer and succumbed to the stash of candy-coated chocolate. "I heard somewhere that people in love can spot other people in love."

She slanted her friend a look as Ariel stripped out of her leotard. "To test a theory, my guess is that you've fallen for Booth DeWitt."

"Right the first time." Ariel pulled on the baggy sweatpants and shirt she'd worn to the studio.

With a frown, Stella crunched candy between her teeth. "You always liked the tough roles."

"I seem to lean toward them."

"How's he feel about you?"

"I don't know." Gratefully, Ariel creamed off the last of her makeup. With a flourish, she dumped one more part of Rae into the waste can. "I don't think he does, either."

"Ariel…" Reluctance to give advice warred with affection and loyalty. "Do you know what you're doing?"

"No," she answered immediately, both brows lifting. "Why would I want to?"

Stella laughed as she headed for the door. "Stupid question. By the way—" she stopped with her hand on the knob "—I just thought I'd mention that you were brilliant today. I've worked with you week after week for five years, and today you blew me away. When this thing hits the screen, you're going to take off so fast even you won't be able to keep up."

Astonished, pleased and, perhaps for the first time, a bit frightened, Ariel sat on the edge of her dressing table. "Thanks—I think."

"Don't mention it." Slipping into the character of Vikki, Stella blew Ariel a cool kiss. "See you in a couple of weeks, big sister."

For several moments after the door shut, Ariel sat in silence. Did she, when push came to shove, want to take off and take off fast? She remembered that P. B. Marshell had said something similiar to her after her second reading for the part, but Ariel had seen that more as an overall view of the project itself. She knew Stella, and understood that the praise from her had been directed personally and individually. For the first time the ripple effect of the role of Rae struck her fully. However much a cliché it sounded, it could make her a star.

Wearing her baggy sweats, one hip leaning on her jumbled dressing table, Ariel explored the idea.

Money—she shrugged that away. Her upbringing had taught her to view money for what it was, a means to an end. In any case, her financial status for the past three years had been more than adequate for both her needs and her taste.

Fame. She grinned at that. No, she couldn't claim she was immune to fame. It still brought her a thrill to sign her name in an autograph book or talk to a fan. That was something she hoped would never change. But fame had degrees, and with each rise in height, the payment for it became greater. The more fans, the less privacy. That was something she'd have to think about carefully.

Artistic freedom. It was that, Ariel admitted on a deep breath, that was the clincher. To be able to *choose* a part rather than be chosen. Glory and a big bank account were nothing in comparison. If Rae could bring her that…

With a shake of her head, she rose. Daydreaming about the future couldn't change anything. For now, her career, and her life, would simply have to go a day at a time. Still, she was a woman who liked to expect everything. Ariel would much rather be disappointed than pessimistic. She was grinning when she opened the door and nearly collided with Booth.

"You look happy," he commented as he took her arms to balance her.

"I am happy." Ariel kissed him hard and firm on the mouth. "It's been a good day."

The kiss, casual as it was, shot straight through him. "You should be exhausted."

"No, you should be exhausted after running the New York Marathon. How do you feel about a giant hamburger and a glutton's portion of fries?"

He'd had a quiet restaurant in mind—something French and dimly lit. After a glance at her sweat suit and glowing face, Booth shook his head. "Sounds perfect. It's your turn to buy."

Ariel tucked her arm through his. "You got it. Do you like banana milk shakes?"

His expression stated his opinion clearly. "I don't believe I've ever had one."

"You're going to love it," Ariel promised.

It wasn't as bad as he'd imagined—and the hamburger had been hefty and satisfying. Dusk was settling over the city when they returned to Ariel's apartment. The moment she opened the door, the kittens dashed for her feet.

"Good grief, you'd think they hadn't been fed in a week." Bending, she scooped up both of them and nuzzled. "Did you miss me, you little pigs, or just your evening meal?"

Before Booth realized what she was up to, Ariel had thrust both kittens into his arms. "Hang on to them for me, will you?" she said easily. "I have to feed Butch, too." She sauntered toward the kitchen, with the three-legged Butch waddling behind. Booth was left with two mewing kittens and no choice but to follow. One—Keats or Shelley—climbed onto his shoulder as he went after Ariel.

"I'm surprised you don't have a litter of puppies, as well." He lifted a brow as the kitten sniffed at his ear.

Ariel laughed as the kitten batted playfully at Booth's hair. "I would if the landlord wasn't so strict. But I'm working on him. Meanwhile—" she set out three generous bowls of food "—it's chow time."

Chuckling, she took the kitten from Booth's shoulder while the other leaped to the floor. Within seconds all three cats were thoroughly involved. "See?" She brushed a few traces of cat hair from his shirt. "They're no trouble at all, hardly any expense and wonderful companions, especially for someone who works most often at home."

Booth gave her a steady look, cupped her face in his hands, then grinned despite himself. "No."

"No what?"

"No, I don't want a cat."

"Well, you can't have one of mine," she said amiably. "Besides, you look more like the dog type."

"Oh, really?" He slipped his arms around her waist.

"Mmm. A nice cocker spaniel that would sleep by your fire at night."

"I don't have a fireplace."

"You should have. But until you take care of that, the puppy could curl right up on a little braided rug by the window."

He caught her bottom lip between his teeth and nipped lightly. "No."

"No one should live alone, Booth. It's depressing."

He could feel her response in the quickening of her heartbeat, the quiet shudder of breath. "I'm used to living alone. I like it that way."

She liked the feel of his roughened cheek against

hers. "You must've had a pet when you were a child," Ariel murmured.

Booth remembered the golden Labrador with the lolling tongue that he'd adored—and that he hadn't thought of in years. Oh, no, he thought as he felt himself begin to weaken. She wasn't going to get to him on this. "As a child, I had the time and the temperament for a pet." Slowly, he slipped his hands under her sweatshirt and up her back. "Now I prefer other ways of spending my free time."

But she'd laid the groundwork, Ariel thought with a small smile. Advance and retreat was the secret of a successful campaign. "I have to shower," she told him, drawing back far enough to smile again. "I'm still sticky from that last scene."

"I enjoyed watching it. You've fascinating thigh muscles, Ariel."

Amused, she lifted both brows. "I have *aching* thigh muscles. And I'll tell you something, if I were to ride a bike for the three or four miles I did today, it wouldn't be anchored to the floor."

"No." He gathered her hair in his hand to draw her head back. "You wouldn't be content to stay in the same place." He touched his mouth teasingly to hers, retreating when she would have deepened the touch to a kiss. "I'll wash your back."

Thrills raced up her spine as if he already were. "Hmm, what a nice idea. I suppose I should warn you," she continued as they walked out of the kitchen, "I like the water in my shower hot—very hot."

When they stepped into the bathroom, he slipped his hands under the baggy sweatshirt. She was slim and warm beneath. "Don't you think I can take it?"

"I figure you're pretty tough." Eyes laughing up at

him, Ariel began to unbutton his shirt. "For a screen-writer."

In one surprising move, Booth whipped the sweat-shirt over her head and bit down on her shoulder. "I'd say you're pretty soft." He ran his hands down her rib cage, then banded her waist. "For an actress."

"Touché," Ariel murmured breathlessly as he tugged loose the drawstring of her pants.

"I like to feel you," he said, stroking his hands over her as she continued to undress him. "Though there isn't much of you. An elegant little body. Long boned, hipless." His hands journeyed down her back, and far-ther. "Very smooth."

By the time they were both naked, Ariel was shiver-ing. But not from cold. Drawing away, she turned the taps. Water rushed from the showerhead, striking por-celain and steaming toward the ceiling. Stepping in, Ariel closed her eyes to let her body soak up the heat and the sensuality.

That was one of the things that continued to fascinate him about her—her capacity for experiencing. Nothing was ever ordinary to her, Booth decided as he stepped behind her and drew the curtain closed. She wouldn't know the meaning of boredom. Everything she did or thought was unique, and being unique, exciting.

As the water coursed over them both, he wrapped his arms around her and drew her back against his chest. This was affection, he realized, the sort he'd felt very rarely in his life. Yet he felt it for her.

Ariel lifted her face to the spray. So many sensa-tions buffeted her at that moment, she couldn't keep up. So she stopped trying. It was enough to be close, to be held. And to love. Perhaps some people needed more—security, words, promises. Perhaps one day, she would, too. But now, just for now, she had all she wanted. Turning, she caught Booth close and fastened her mouth to his.

Passion flared in her quickly this time, as if it had been waiting for hours, days. Maybe years. It built so fast that the kiss alone had her gasping for air and fretting for more. Without being aware of it, she stood on her toes so that the curve of their bodies would be aligned. With desperate fingers, she combed through his hair and gripped, as if he might try to break away. But his arms were tight around her, and his mouth was as seeking as hers.

Reeling toward the crest, Ariel clung, and Ariel offered.

God, he'd never known anyone so giving. As he drank in all the flavors of her mouth, Booth wondered if it were possible for a woman to be so confident, so comfortable with herself that she could be this generous. Without any hesitation, her body was there for him. Her mind was tuned to him. Instinctively, Booth knew she thought more of his needs, his pleasures, than her own. And by doing so, she touched off a long dormant tenderness.

"Ariel…" Murmuring her name, he ran kisses over her face, which the water made incredibly soft, incredibly sweet. "You make me want things I'd forgotten— and almost believe in them again."

"Don't think." She rubbed her lips over his to soothe, to entice. "This time don't think at all."

But he would, Booth told himself. Or he'd take her too quickly, and perhaps too roughly. This time, he'd give her back a portion of what she'd already given him. Cupping the soap in his hand, he ran it over her back. He thought he heard her purr like one of her cats. It made him smile.

Her senses began to sharpen. She could hear the hiss of the spray as it struck tile, and feel the steam as it billowed in puffy clouds. Soapy hands slid over her—slick, soft, sensitive. His flesh was wet and warm where her mouth pressed. Through half-closed eyes she could see the lather cling to her, then him, before it was sluiced away.

His hand moved once between their slippery bodies to find her—stunningly—so that she cried out in surprise and rippling pleasure. Then it journeyed elsewhere while his lips traced hot and damp over her shoulder. The tang of citrus from the soap made her head reel.

"Do they still ache?" Booth asked her as his fingers kneaded the backs of her thighs.

"What?" Floating, Ariel leaned against him, her arms curved over his back, her hands firm on his shoulders. Water struck her back in soft, hissing spurts, then seemed to slither away. "No, no, nothing aches now."

With a laugh, Booth dipped his tongue into her ear and felt her shiver. "Your hair goes to gold when it's wet."

She smelled the shampoo, felt its cool touch on her scalp before he began to massage. Nothing, Ariel thought, had ever aroused her more.

Slowly, lingeringly, he washed her hair while the frothy bubbles of shampoo ran down his arms. The scent was familiar to him now, that fresh, inviting fragrance that caught at him every time he was near her. He enjoyed the intimacy of having the scent spill over him and cling—to her skin, to his. Shifting his weight, he moved them both under the gush of the shower so that water and lather raced down their bodies and away.

And while they stood, hot and wet and entangled, he slipped into her. It seemed natural, as if he'd been her lover for years. It was thrilling, as though he'd never touched her before.

He felt Ariel's nails dig into his shoulders, heard her moan of surrender and demand. He took her there, with more care than he'd ever shown a woman. And he felt a rush of freedom.

Chapter 9

Ariel rode a roller coaster for two weeks. Her time with Booth seemed like a ride with dips and curves and speed and surprises. Of course, she'd always loved them—the faster and wilder the better.

She'd been right when she'd told Booth he was unpredictable. Neither was he a simple man to deal with. Ariel decided she wanted it no other way.

There were times he was incredibly tender, showing her flashes of romance and affection that she'd never expected from him. A box of wildflowers delivered before an early studio call. A rainy-day picnic in his apartment with champagne in paper cups while thunder raged.

Then there were the times he pulled away, drew into himself so intensely that she couldn't reach him. And when she knew, instinctively, not to try.

The anger and impatience in him were ingrained. Perhaps it was that, contrasting with the glimpses of humor and gentleness, that had caused her to lose her heart. It was the whole man she loved, no matter how difficult. And it was the whole man she wanted to belong to. This man—brooding, angry, reluctantly sweet—was the man she'd been waiting for.

As the film progressed, their relationship grew closer, despite Booth's occasional stretches of isolation. Closer, yes, but without the simplicity she looked for. For love, in Ariel's mind, was a simple thing.

If he was resisting love, so much the better, Ariel told herself. When he accepted it—she wouldn't allow herself to doubt he would—it would be that much stronger. For she needed absolute love, the unconditional giving of heart and mind. She could wait a little longer to have it all.

If she had one regret, it was that she wasn't free to confide in him about Scott. The closer the trial came, the more she felt the need to talk to Booth about it, seek comfort, gain reassurance. Though it was tempting, Ariel never even considered it. This problem was hers, and hers alone. As Scott was hers to protect and defend.

When she thought of the future, it was still in sections. Booth, Scott, her career. She needed her own brand of absolute faith to believe that they'd all come together in the end.

After a long, hectic morning, Ariel considered the lengthy delay anticipated because of equipment breakdown a reward. It was the first time in weeks she'd be able to watch *Our Lives, Our Loves,* and catch up on Amanda's life with the people of Trader's Bend.

"You're not really going to watch television for the next hour," Booth protested as Ariel pulled him down the corridor.

"Yes, I am. It's like visiting home." She shook the bag of pretzels in her hand. "And I've got provisions."

"When they get the sound board fixed, you're going to have a hell of an afternoon ahead of you." He kneaded her shoulder as they walked. Though it didn't often show, he'd seen brief glimpses of strain in her eyes, isolated moments when she looked a bit lost. "You'd be better off putting your feet up and catching a nap."

"I never nap." When she pushed open her dressing room door, she upended a stack of magazines. Hardly sparing them a glance, she walked over to the small portable television set in the corner.

"I seem to recall coming in here one day and finding you with your feet up on the table and your eyes closed."

"That's different." She fiddled with a dial until she was satisfied with the color. "That was recharging. I'm not ready for recharging, Booth." Eyes wide and excited, she whirled around. "It's really going well, isn't it? I can feel it. Even after all these weeks, the edge is still on. That's a sure sign we're doing something special."

"I was a bit leery about doing a film for television." He took a few pamphlets from the sofa and dropped them onto a table. "Not anymore. Yes, it's going to be very special." He held out a hand to her. "You're very special."

As always, the subtle unexpected statement went straight to her heart. Ariel took the offered hand and brought it to her lips. "I'm going to enjoy watching you accept that Emmy."

He lifted a brow. "And what about yours?"

"Maybe," she said and laughed. "Just maybe." The lead-in music for the soap distracted her. "Ah, here we go. Back to Trader's Bend." Dropping onto the sofa, she pulled Booth with her. After ripping open the bag of pretzels, Ariel became totally absorbed.

She didn't watch as an actress or as a critic, but as a viewer. Relaxing her mind, she let herself become caught up in the connecting plot lines and problems. Even when she saw herself on the screen, she didn't look for flaws or perfection. She didn't consider she was looking at Ariel, but at Amanda.

"Don't tell me what I want," Amanda told Griff in a low, vibrating voice. "You have no business offering me unsolicited advice on my life, much less coming into my house uninvited."

"Now, you look." Griff took her arm when she would have turned away. "You're pushing yourself right to the edge. I can see it."

"I'm doing my job," she corrected coolly. "Why don't you concentrate on yours and leave me alone?"

"Leaving you alone's the last thing I'm going to do." As the camera zoomed in, the viewer was witness to his struggle for control. When Griff continued, his voice was calmer but edged with his familiar passion. "Damn it, Mandy, you're almost as close to this Ripper thing as the cops. You know better than to stay in this house by yourself. If you won't let me help you, at least go stay with your parents for a while."

"With my parents." Her composure began to crack as she dragged a hand through her hair. "Stay with my parents, while Vikki's there? Just how much do you think I can take?"

"All right, all right." Frustrated, he tried to draw her against him, only to have her jerk away. "Mandy, please, I'm worried about you."

"Don't be. And if you really want to help, leave me

alone. I need to go over the psychiatric profile before I meet with Lieutenant Reiffler in the morning."

Fisted hands were shoved in his pockets. "Okay, look, I'll sleep down here on the couch. I swear I won't touch you. I just can't leave you out here alone."

"I don't want you here!" she shouted, losing her tenuous grip on control. "I don't want anyone, can't you understand that? Can't you understand that I need to be alone?"

He stared at her while she fought back tears, shoulders heaving. "I love you, Mandy," he said so quietly it could barely be heard. But his eyes had already said it.

As the camera zoomed in on her, a single tear spilled out and rolled down Amanda's cheek. "No," she whispered, turning away. But Griff's arms came around her, drawing her back against him.

"Yes, you know I do. There's never been anyone for me but you. It killed me when you left me, Mandy. I need you in my life. I need what we'd planned to have together. We've got a second chance. All we have to do is take it."

Staring into nowhere, Amanda pressed a hand to her stomach where she knew Cameron's baby was sleeping—a baby Griff would never accept, and one she had to. "No, there aren't any second chances, Griff. Please leave me alone."

"We belong together," he murmured, burying his face in her hair. "Oh, God, Mandy, we've always belonged together."

For his sake, for her own, she had to make him leave. Pain flashed into her eyes before she controlled her expression. "You're wrong," she said flatly. "That was yesterday. Today I don't want you to touch me."

"I can't crawl anymore." Ripping himself away from her, Griff headed for the door. "I won't crawl anymore."

As the door slammed behind him, Amanda slumped down on the couch. Curling on her side, she buried her face in a pillow and wept. The camera panned slowly to the window to show a shadowy silhouette behind the closed curtains.

"Well, well," Booth murmured at the commercial break. "The lady has her problems."

"And then some." Ariel stretched and leaned back against the cushions. "That's the thing about soaps— one problem gets resolved and three more crop up."

"So, is she going to give Griff a break and take him back?"

Ariel grinned at the casualness of the question. He really wants to know, she mused, pleased. "Tune in tomorrow."

His eyes narrowed. "You know the story line."

"My lips are sealed," she said primly.

"Really?" Booth caught her chin in his hand. "Let's see." He pressed his to them firmly, and though hers curved, they remained shut. Challenged, he shifted closer and his fingers spread over her jawline, lightly stroking. With the barest of touches, he traced the shape of her mouth, wetting her lips, using no pressure. When he nibbled at one corner, then the other, he felt the tell-tale melting of her bones, heard the quiet sigh. Effortlessly, his tongue slipped between her lips to tease hers.

"Cheat," Ariel managed.

"Yeah." God, she made him feel so good. He'd almost stopped wondering how long it would last. The end, what he considered the inevitable end to what they brought each other, was becoming more blurred every day. "I've never believed in playing fair."

"No?" Her sudden aggression caught him off balance. Before he knew it, Booth was on his back, with her body pressed into his. "In that case, no holds barred."

The greedy kiss left him stunned, so that by the time he'd gripped some control again, she'd unbuttoned his shirt for her seeking hands. "Ariel…" Half-amused, half-protesting, he took her wrist, but her free hand skimmed down the center of his body to spread over his stomach.

Amusement, protests, reason, slipped away.

"I never get enough of you." He gripped her hair, destroying the sleek knot the hairdresser had tended so carefully hours before.

"I plan to see that you don't." With quick, open mouthed kisses she moved over his shoulder, drawing away the shirt as she went.

She took him over hills and into valleys with such speed and fury he could only follow. For as long as he could remember, Booth had led in every aspect of his life—not trusting enough to let another guide. But now he could barely keep pace with her. The energy, the verve he'd so long admired in her was in complete control. As he was swept along, Booth wondered why it was suddenly so easy to break yet another rule. Then, as she had once requested, he didn't think at all.

Feelings. Ariel drew them in as they radiated from him. This was what she'd been so patiently, so desperately waiting for. Emotions were finally overtaking him. As they merged with her own, she felt the bond, the link, and nearly wept with the wonder of it.

He loves me, she thought. Maybe he doesn't know it yet, maybe he won't for days and weeks to come. But it's there. The urge to weep altered to an urge to laugh. And it was with laughter and with joy that she took him into her.

Winded, Booth lay still while Ariel curled like a cat on his chest. "Was all that just to keep me from learning the story line?"

Her chuckle was muffled against his skin. "There're no lengths I won't go to to protect security." She snuggled against him. "No sacrifice too great."

"With that in mind, I think I'll ask about the identity of the Ripper—tonight." Drawing her up, he examined her. The silk blouse she'd been wearing was unbuttoned and trailing over one shoulder. The thin slacks lay in a heap on the floor. Her hair was a provocative tangle. "You're going to catch hell from wardrobe and makeup."

"It was worth it." Straightening her blouse, Ariel began to do up the buttons. "I'll tell them I took a nap."

With a laugh, he sat up and tugged on her tumbled hair. "There's no mistaking what you've been up to. Your eyes always give you away."

"Do they?" Carefully, she stepped into her slacks. "I wonder." Absently smoothing out the creases, she turned to him. "You haven't seen it in all these weeks." As she watched, his brows drew together. "You're a perceptive man, and I've never had a strong talent or a strong desire to hide my feelings." She smiled as he continued to frown at her. "I love you."

His face, his body—Ariel thought even his mind—went very still. He said nothing. "Booth, you don't have to look as though I've just pulled a gun on you." Stepping closer, she touched the back of her hand to his cheek. "Taking love's easy—giving it's a bit harder, for some people anyway. Please, take it as it's offered. It's free."

He wasn't at all certain what he was feeling—only

that he'd never felt anything like it before. The very novelty made him wary. "It's not wise to give things away, Ariel, especially to someone who isn't ready for them."

"And holding on to something when it needs to be given's even more foolish. Booth, can't you trust me even now, just enough to accept my feelings?"

"I don't know," he murmured. As he rose, conflicting emotions, conflicting desires tore at him. He wanted to distance himself as quickly and as completely as possible. He wanted to hold her and never let go. Panic, he felt the stab of it. Pleasure, the sweetness of it.

"They're there whether you can or can't. I've never been good at controlling my emotions, Booth. I'm not sorry for it."

Before he could speak there was a brisk knock on the door. "Ariel, you're needed on the set in fifteen minutes."

"Thank you."

He had to think, Booth told himself. Be logical... Be careful. "I'll send the hairdresser in."

"Okay." She smiled, and it almost reached her eyes. When he'd gone, Ariel stared at her reflection in the mirror. The lights around it were dull and dark. "So who expected it'd be easy?" she asked herself.

In just under fifteen minutes, Ariel walked back toward the set. She looked every bit as cool and as sleek as she had when she'd walked off over an hour before. Despite Booth's reaction, which she'd half expected, she felt lighter, easier, after telling Booth of her feelings. It was, after all, merely stating aloud what was, sharing what couldn't be changed. As a general rule, Ariel considered concealments a waste of time, and consequences a by-product of living. Her gait was free and easy as she crossed the studio.

She knew something was happening before she saw the thicket of people or heard the excited voices. Tension in the air. She felt it and thought instantly of Booth. But it wasn't Booth she saw when she passed the false wall of the living-room set.

Elizabeth Hunter.

Elegance. Ice. Smooth, smooth femininity. Outrageous beauty. Ariel saw her laugh lightly and lift a slender cigarette to her lips. She posed effortlessly, as if the cameras were on and focused on her. Her hair shimmered, pale, frosty. Her skin was so exquisite it might have been carved from marble.

On the screen, she was larger than life, desirable, unattainable. Ariel saw little difference in the flesh. There couldn't be a man alive who wouldn't dream of peeling off that layer of frost and finding something molten and wild inside. If she were truly like Rae, Ariel thought, that man—any man—would be disappointed. Curious, she walked closer.

"Pat, how could I stay away?" Liz lifted one graceful hand and touched Marshell's check. A fantasy of diamonds and sapphires winked on her ring finger. "After all, one might say I have a...vested interest in this film." The provocative pout—a Hunter trademark—touched her mouth. "Don't tell me you're going to chase me away."

"Of course not, Liz." Marshell looked uncomfortable and resigned. "None of us knew you were in town."

"I just wrapped the Simmeon film in Greece." She drew on the slender cigarette again and carelessly flicked ashes on the floor. "I flew right in." She shot a look over Marshell's shoulder. Not hostile, not grim, but simply predatory. It was then Ariel saw Booth.

He stood slightly apart from the circle of people

around Liz, as if he again sought distance without wholly removing himself. He met the look his ex-wife sent him without a flicker of expression. Even if Ariel had chosen to intrude, she doubted if she could have gauged his thoughts.

"I wasn't allowed to read the screenplay." Liz continued to talk to Marshell though her eyes remained on Booth. "But little dribbles leaked through to me. I must say, I'm fascinated. And a bit miffed that you didn't ask me to do the film."

Marshell's eyes hardened, but he stuck with diplomacy. "You were unavailable, Liz."

"And inappropriate," Booth added mildly.

"Ah, Booth, always the clever last word." Liz blew smoke in his direction and smiled.

It was a smile Ariel recognized. She'd seen it on the screen in countless Hunter movies. She'd mimicked it herself as Rae. It was the smile a witch wore before she cut the wings off a bat. Without realizing it, Ariel moved forward in direct defense of Booth. Liz's gaze shifted and locked.

It wasn't a pleasant survey. Again, not hostile but simply and essentially cold. Ariel studied Liz in turn and absorbed impressions. She was left with a sensation of emptiness. And what she felt was pity.

"Well…" Liz held out her cigarette for disposal. A small woman with a wrinkled face plucked it from her fingers. "It's easy to deduce that this is Rae."

"No." Unconsciously, Ariel smiled with the same cold glitter as Liz. "I'm Ariel Kirkwood. Rae's a character."

"Indeed." The haughty lift of brow had been used in a dozen scenes. "I always try to absorb the character I portray."

"And it works brilliantly for you," Ariel acknowledged with complete sincerity. "I limit that to when the lights are on, Miss Hunter."

Only the barest flicker in her eyes betrayed annoyance. "Would I have seen you do anything else, dear?"

There was no mistaking the patronizing tone. Again, Ariel felt a flash of sympathy. "Possibly."

He didn't like seeing them together. No, Booth thought violently, by God, he didn't. It had given him a wave of sheer pleasure to see Liz again and feel nothing. Absolutely nothing. No anger, no frustration. Not even disgust. The lack of feeling had been like a balm. Until Ariel had come on set.

Face-to-face, they could have been sisters. The resemblance was heightened by the fact that Ariel's hair, makeup and wardrobe were styled to Liz's taste. He saw too many similarities. And as he looked closer, too many contrasts. Booth wasn't sure which annoyed him more.

No matter how she was dressed, warmth flowed from Ariel. The inner softness edged through. He could feel the emotion from her even three feet away. And he saw…pity? Yes, it was pity in her eyes. Directed at Liz. Booth lit a cigarette with a jerk of his wrist. God, he'd rid himself of one and was being reeled in by another. Standing there, he could feel the quicksand sucking at his legs. Was there any closer analogy for love?

"Let's get started," he ordered briefly. Liz shot him another look.

"Don't let me hold things up. I'll stay out of the way." She glided to the edge of the set, sat in a director's chair and crossed her legs. A burly man, the small woman and what was hardly more than a boy settled behind her.

The audience had Ariel's adrenaline pumping. The

scene they were to shoot was the same one she'd auditioned with. More than any other, Ariel felt it encapsulated Rae's personality, her motives, her essence. She didn't think Liz Hunter would enjoy it, but... Ariel felt she'd be able to gauge just how successful her performance was by Liz's reaction to it.

With a faintly bored expression on her face, Liz sat back and watched the scene unfold. The dialogue was not precisely a verbatim account of what had occurred between her and Booth years before, but she recognized the tenor. Damn him, she thought with a flicker of anger that showed nowhere on her sculpted face. Damn him for his memory and his talent. So this was his revenge.

While she hoped the film fell flat, she was too shrewd to believe it would. She could shrug that off. Liz was clever enough, experienced enough to make the film work for her rather than against her. With the right angle, she could get miles and miles of publicity from Booth's work. That balanced things...to a point.

She was a woman of few emotions, but the most finely tuned of these was jealousy. It was this that ate at her as she sat, silent, watching. Ariel Kirkwood, she thought as one rose-tipped nail began to tap on the arm of the chair. Liz was vain enough to consider herself more beautiful, but there was no denying the difference in age. Years were something that haunted her.

And talent. Her teeth scraped against each other because she wanted to scream. Her own skill, the accolades and awards she'd received for it were never enough. Especially when she was faced with a beautiful, younger woman of equal ability. Damn them both. Her finger began to tap harder, staccato. The young man put a soothing hand on her shoulder and was shrugged away.

Liz could taste the envy that edged toward fury. The

part should have been hers, she thought as her lips tightened. If she had played Rae, she'd have added a dozen dimensions to the part—such as it was. She had more talent in the palm of her hand than this Ariel Kirkwood had in her whole body. More beauty, more fame, more sexuality. Her head began to pound as she watched Ariel skillfully weave sex and ice into the scene.

Then her eyes met Booth's, and she nearly choked on an oath. He was laughing at her, Liz realized. Laughing, though his mouth was sober and his expression calm. He'd pay for that, she told herself as her lids lowered fractionally. For that and for everything else. She'd see that he and this no-talent actress from nowhere both paid.

Booth knew his ex-wife well enough to know what was going on in her mind. It should have pleased him; perhaps it would have only a few weeks before. Now, it did little more than slightly disgust him.

Shifting his gaze from her, he focused his attention on Ariel. Of all the scenes in the screenplay, this was the hardest for him. He'd crystallized himself too well as Phil in these few sharp, hard lines. And his Rae was too real here. Ariel made her too real, he thought as he wished for a cigarette. In this short, seven-minute scene, which would take much, much longer to complete, it was almost impossible to separate Ariel from Rae—and Rae from Liz.

Ariel had said she loved him. Fighting discomfort that was laced with panic, Booth watched her. Was it possible? Once before he'd believed a woman who'd whispered those words to him. But Ariel...there was no one and nothing quite like Ariel.

Did he love her? Once before he'd believed himself in love. But whatever emotion it had been, it hadn't been love. And it had been smeared with a fascination for great beauty, great talent, cool, cool sex. No, he didn't understand love—if it existed in the way he believed Ariel thought of it. No, he didn't understand it, and he told himself he didn't want it. What he wanted was his privacy, his peace.

And while he stood there, watching his own scene being painstakingly reproduced on film, he had neither.

"Cut. Cut and print." Chuck ran a hand along the back of his neck to ease the tension. "Hell of a job." Letting out a long breath, he walked toward Ariel and Jack. "Hell of a job, both of you. We'll wrap for today. Nothing's going to top that."

Relieved, Ariel let her stomach relax, muscle by muscle. She glanced over idly at the sound of quiet applause.

Liz rose gracefully from her chair. "Marvelous job." She gave Jack her dazzling, practiced smile before she turned to Ariel. "You have potential, dear," Liz told her. "I'm sure this part will open a few doors for you."

Ariel recognized the swipe and took it on the chin. "Thank you, Liz." Deliberately, she drew the pins from her hair and let it fall free. She wanted badly to shed Rae. "It's a challenging part."

"You did your best with it." Smiling, Liz touched her lightly on the shoulder.

I must've been on the money, Ariel thought and grinned. *I must've been right on the money.*

Liz wanted to rip the thick, tumbled hair out by the roots. She turned to Marshell. "Pat, I'd love to have dinner. We've a lot to catch up on." She slipped her arm through his and patted his hand. "My treat, darling."

Mentally swearing, Marshell acquiesced. The best way to get her out without a scene was simply to get her out. "My pleasure, Liz. Chuck, I'll want a look at the dailies first thing in the morning."

"Oh, by the way." Liz paused beside Booth. "I really don't think this little film will do much harm to your career, darling." With an icy laugh she skimmed a finger down his shirt. "And I must say, I'm rather flattered, all in all. No hard feelings, Booth."

He looked down at the beautiful, heartless smile. "No feelings, Liz. No feelings at all."

Her fingers tightened briefly on Marshell's arm before she swept away. "Oh, Pat, I must tell you about this marvelous young actor I met in Athens…"

"Exit stage left," Jack murmured, then shrugged when Ariel raised a brow at him. "Must still be functioning as Phil. But let me tell you, that's one lady I wouldn't turn my back on."

"She's rather sad," Ariel said half to herself.

Jack gave a snort of laughter. "She's a tarantula." With another snort he cupped a hand on Ariel's shoulder. "Let me tell you something, kid. I've been in the business a lot of years, worked with lots of actresses. You're first class. And that just gripped her cookies."

"And that's sad," Ariel repeated.

"Better put a layer of something over that compassion, babe," he warned. "You'll get burned." Giving her shoulder a last squeeze, he walked off the set.

Gratefully, Ariel dropped into a chair. The lights were off now, the temperature cooling. Most of the stagehands were gone, except for three who huddled in a corner discussing a poker game. Tipping her head back, she waited as Booth approached.

"That was a tough one," she commented. "How do you feel?"

"I'm fine. You?"

"A little drained. I've only a few scenes left, none of them on this scale. Next week, I'll be back to Amanda."

"How do you feel about that?"

"The people on the soap are like family. I miss them."

"Children leave home," he reminded her.

"I know. So will I when the time's right."

"We both know you won't be signing another contract with the soap." He drew out a cigarette, lighting it automatically, drawing in smoke without tasting it. "Whether you're ready to admit it or not."

Feeling his tension, she tensed in turn. "You're mixing us again," she said quietly. "Just how much longer is it going to take you to see me for who I am, without the shadows?"

"I know who you are," Booth corrected. "I'm not sure what to do about it."

She rose. Maybe it was the lingering strain from the scene, or perhaps her sadness from watching Liz Hunter suffer in her own way. "I'll tell you what you don't want," she said with an edge to her voice he hadn't heard before. "You don't want me to love you. You don't want the responsibility of my emotions or of your own."

He could deal with this, Booth thought as he took another drag. A fight was something he could handle effortlessly. "Maybe I don't. I told you what I thought right up front."

"So you did." With a half laugh, she turned away. "Funny that you're the one who's always preaching change at me, and you're the one so unable to do so yourself. Let me tell you something, Booth." She whirled back, vibrantly glowing Ariel. "My feelings are mine. You can't dictate them to me. The only thing it's possible for you to do is dictate to yourself."

"It isn't a matter of dictating." He found he didn't

want the cigarette after all. It tasted foul. Booth left it smoldering, half-crushed, in an ashtray. "It's a matter of not being able to give you what you want."

"I haven't asked you for anything."

"You don't have to ask." He was angry, really angry, without being aware when he'd crossed the line. "You've pulled at me from the start—pulled at things I want left alone. I made a commitment once, I'll be damned if I'll do it again. I don't want to change my lifestyle. I don't want—"

"To risk failure again," Ariel finished.

His eyes blazed at her, but his voice was very, very calm. "You're going to have to learn to watch your step, Ariel. Fragile bones are easily broken."

"And they mend." Abruptly, she was too weary to argue, too weary to think. "You'll have to work out your own solution, Booth. The same as I'll work out mine. I'm not sorry I love you, or that I've told you. But I am sorry that you can't accept a gift."

When he'd watched her walk away, Booth slipped his hands in his pockets and stared at the darkened set. No, he couldn't accept it. Yet he felt as though he'd just tossed away something he'd searched for all of his life.

Chapter 10

The water was a bit choppy. Small whitecaps bounced up, were swallowed, then bounced back again. Directly overhead the sky was a hard diamond blue, but to the east, dark clouds were boiling and building. There was the threat of rain in the wind that blew in from the Atlantic. Booth estimated he had two hours before the storm caught up with him—an hour before he'd be forced to tack to shore to avoid it.

And on shore the heat would be staggering, the humidity thick enough to slice. On the water, the breeze smelled of summer and salt and storms. He could taste it as it whipped by him and billowed his sail. Exhilaration—he knew it for the sensation that could clear the mind and chill the skin. Holding lightly to the rigging, he let the wind take him.

Booth wore nothing but cutoffs and deck shoes. He hadn't bothered to shave for two days. His eyes had grown accustomed to squinting against the sun reflecting off the water, and his hands to the feel of rough rope against the palm. Both were harsh, both were challenging.

Exhilaration? This time it hadn't come with the force he'd expected. For days he'd sailed as long as the sun and the weather allowed. He'd worked at night until his mind was drained.

Escape? Was that a better word for what he'd come for? Perhaps, Booth mused as he sailed over the choppy water. Lifting a beer to his lips he let the taste race over his tongue. Perhaps he was escaping, but he was no longer needed on the set, and he had finally had to admit that he couldn't work in the city. He needed a few days away from the filming, from the pressure to produce, from his own standards of perfection.

That was all a lie.

None of those things had driven him out of Manhattan and onto Long Island. He'd needed to get away from Ariel—from what Ariel was doing to him. And perhaps most of all from his feelings for her. Yet the miles didn't erase her from his thoughts. It took no effort to think of her, and every effort not to. Though she haunted him, Booth was certain he'd been right to come away. If thinking of her ate at him, seeing her, touching her would have driven him mad.

He didn't want her love, he told himself savagely. He couldn't—wouldn't—be responsible for the range of emotions Ariel was capable of. Booth took another long pull from the beer can, then scowled at the water. He wasn't capable of loving her in return. He didn't possess those kinds of feelings. Whatever emotions he had were directed exclusively toward his work. He'd promised himself that. Inside, in the compartment that held the brighter feelings one person had for another, he was empty. He was void.

He ached for her—body, mind, soul.

Damn her, he thought as he jerked at the rigging. Damn her for pulling at him, for crowding him…for asking nothing of him. If she'd asked, demanded, pleaded, he could have refused. It was so simple to say no to an obligation. All she did was give until he was so full of her, he was losing himself.

He'd work, Booth told himself as he began to tack methodically back toward shore. The boat bucked beneath him as the wind kicked up. Adjusting the sails, he concentrated on the pure physicality of the task. Use your muscles, your back, not your brain. Don't think, he warned himself, until it's time to write again.

He'd bury himself in work for the rest of the afternoon. He'd pour himself into his writing through the evening, late into the night, until his mind was too jumbled to think of anything—anyone. He'd stay away from her physically until he could stay away from her mentally. Then he'd go back to New York and pick up his life as he'd left it. Before Ariel.

Thunder rumbled ominously as he docked the boat.

Ariel watched the lightning snake across the sky and burst. The night sky was like a dark mirror abruptly cracked then made whole again. Still no rain. The heat storm had been threatening all evening, building up in the east and traveling toward Manhattan. She'd looked forward to it. Wearing a long shirt and nothing else, she stood at the window to watch it come.

Earlier, her neighbors had been sitting on their stoops, fanning and sweating and complaining of the heat. She didn't mind it. Before the night was over the rain would wash away the stickiness. But at the moment, though her thin shirt was clinging damply to her back and thighs, she enjoyed the enervating quality of the heat, and the violence in the sky.

The storm was coming from the east, she thought again. Perhaps Booth was already watching the rain she still anticipated. She wondered if he was working, oblivious to the booming thunder. Or if, like her, he stood and watched the fury in the sky. She wondered when he'd come back—to her.

He would, Ariel affirmed staunchly. She only hoped he'd come back with an easy mind. She'd thrown him a curve. With a half smile, Ariel felt the first rippling breeze pass through the screen and over her skin. She wasn't sorry, though his reaction had hurt, then angered her. That was over. Perhaps, for a moment, she'd forgotten that to Booth love wasn't the open-ended gift it was to her. He'd see the restrictions, the risks, the pains.

The pains, she thought, resting her palms on the windowsill. Why was she always so surprised to find out she could hurt just as intensely as she could be happy? She wanted him, physically, but he was miles from her reach, emotionally, but he'd distanced himself from her feelings.

She hadn't been surprised when Booth had absented himself from the last few days of shooting. All the key scenes had been done. Nor was she surprised when Marshell had mentioned idly that Booth had gone to his secluded Long Island home to write and to sail. She missed him, she felt the emptiness; but Ariel was too independent to mourn the loss of him for a few days. He needed his solitude. A part of her understood that, enough to keep her from misery.

Hadn't she herself painted almost through the night after Liz Hunter had visited the set?

Ariel glanced around at the frantic canvas slashed with cobalt and scarlets. It wasn't a painting she'd keep in the living room for long. Too angry, too disturbing. As soon as she'd fully coped with those feelings, she'd stick the canvas in a closet.

Everyone had his or her own means of dealing with the darker emotions. Booth's was to draw into himself; hers was to let them lash out. Either way, any way, the resolution would come. She had only to hang on a little while longer.

And so she told herself when she thought of Scott. The hearing would begin at the end of the week. That, too, would be resolved, but Ariel refused to look at any more than one solution. Scott had to come to her. The doubts she'd once harbored about her right to claim him, his need to be with her, were gone. As time went on, he became more and more unhappy with the Andersons. His visits were punctuated by desperate hugs, and more and more by pleas that he be allowed to stay with her.

It wasn't a matter of abuse or neglect. It was a simple matter of love, unconditional love that came naturally from her, and didn't come at all from his grandparents. Whatever hardships she and Scott were facing now would be a thing of the past before long. It was a time to concentrate on whens instead of nows. That was how she got through the slowly moving days between the filming and the hearing. Without Booth.

Ariel closed her eyes as the rain began to gush out of the sky. Oh, God, if only the night were over.

The rain was just tapering off as Booth pushed away from his computer. He'd gotten more accomplished than he'd anticipated, but the juices were drying up. He knew better than to push himself when he got to this point. In another hour he'd try again perhaps, or maybe not for a day or two. But it would come back, and the story would flow again.

No, he couldn't write anything now, but it was still this side of midnight and he was restless. The storm had cleared the air, making him wish he were on the water again, under the burgeoning moonlight. He should eat. As he rubbed the stiffness from his neck, he remembered he hadn't bothered with dinner. A meal and an early night.

As he walked through the house into the kitchen, silence drummed around him. Strange, he'd never noticed just how thick silence could be, just how empty a house could be when it had only one occupant. And stranger still, how only a few months before he'd have appreciated both, even expected both. Again, before Ariel. His life seemed to have come down to two stages. Before Ariel and after Ariel. It wasn't an easy admission for a man to make.

Booth pulled a tray of cold cuts out of the refrigerator without any real interest. Mechanically, he fixed a sandwich, found a ripe peach and poured a glass of milk. The solitary meal had never seemed less appealing—so much so he considered tipping the entire mess down the sink.

Shaking off the feeling, he carried it into his bedroom and set the plate on the dresser. What he needed was some noise, he decided. Something to occupy his mind without straining the brain. Booth switched on the television, then flipped the channel selector without any particular goal in mind.

Normally he would have bypassed the late-night talk

show in favor of an old movie. When Liz's laughter flowed out at him, he paused. He might still have passed it by, but his curiosity was piqued. Thinking it might be an interesting diversion, Booth picked up his plate, set it on the bedside table and stretched out.

He'd been on the show himself a number of times. Though he wasn't overly fond of the format or the exposure, he knew the game well enough to understand the need to reach the public through the form. The show was popular, slickly run, and the host knew his trade. With boyish charm he could draw the unexpected out of celebrities and keep the audience from turning the channel or just flicking off the switch.

"Of course I was terribly excited to film on location in Greece, Bob." Liz leaned just a bit closer to her host while her ice-blue gown glistened coolly in the lights. "And working with Ross Simmeon was a tremendous experience."

"Didn't I hear you and Simmeon had a feud going?" Robert MacAllister tossed off the question with a grin. It said, come on, relax, you can tell me. It was a well-practiced weapon.

"A feud?" Liz fluttered her lashes ingenuously. She was much too sharp to be caught in that trap. She crossed her legs so that the gown shimmered over her body. "Why, no. I can't imagine where anyone would get that idea."

"It must have something to do with the three days you refused to come on set." With a little deprecating shrug, MacAllister leaned back in his chair. "A disagreement over the number of lines in a key scene."

"That's nonsense." *Damn Simmeon and all the rumormongers.* "I'd had too much sun. My physician put me on medication for a couple of days and recom-

mended a rest." She glittered a smile right back at him.
"Of course there were a few tense moments, as there
will be on any major film, but I'd work with Ross tomorrow..." or the devil himself, her tone seemed to say.
"If the right script came along."

"So, what're you up to now, Liz? You've had an un-
broken string of successes. It must be getting tough to
find just the right property."

"It's always hard to put together the right touch of
magic." She gestured gracefully so that the ring on her
hand caught the light and glittered. "The right script,
the right director, the right leading man. I've been so
lucky—particularly since *To Meet at Midnight*."

Booth set his half-eaten sandwich aside and nearly
laughed. *He'd* written it for her and had made her a
major star. Top box office. Luck had had nothing to
do with it.

"Your Oscar-winning performance," Bob acknowledged. "And of course a brilliant screenplay." He sent
her an off-center smile. "You'd agree with that?"

It was the opening she'd been waiting for. And ma-
neuvering toward. "Oh, yes. Booth DeWitt is possibly—
no, assuredly the finest screenwriter of the eighties.
Regardless of our, well, personal problems, we've always respected each other professionally."

"I know all about personal problems," Bob said ruefully and got the laugh. His three marriages had been
well publicized. And so had his alimony figures. "How
do you feel about his latest work?"

"Oh." Liz smiled and let one hand flutter to her
throat before it fell into her lap. "I don't suppose the
content's much of a secret, is it?"

Again the expected laugh, a bit more restrained.

"I'm sure Booth's script is wonderful, they all are. If

it's, ah, one-sided," she said carefully, "it's only natural. From what I'm told it's common for a writer to reflect some parts of his personal life…and in his own way," she added. "As a matter of fact, I visited the set just last week. Pat Marshell's producing, you know, and Chuck Tyler's directing."

"But…" Bob prompted, noting her obvious reluctance.

"As I said, it's so difficult to find that right brand of magic." She tossed out the first seeds with a smile. "And Booth's never done anything for the small screen before. A difficult transition for anyone."

"Jack Rohrer's starring." Obligingly, Bob fed her the next line.

"Yes, excellent casting there. I thought Jack was absolutely brilliant in *Of Two Minds*. That was a script he could really sink his teeth into."

"But this one…"

"Well, I happen to be a big Jack Rohrer fan," Liz said, apparently sidestepping the question. "I doubt there's any part he can't find some meat on."

"And his costar?" Bob folded his hands on his desk. Liz was out for the jugular, he decided. It wouldn't hurt his ratings.

"The female lead's a lovely girl. I can't quite think of her name, but I believe she has a part on a soap opera. Booth often likes to experiment rather than to go with experienced actors."

"As he did with you."

Her eyes narrowed fractionally. She didn't quite like that tone, or that direction. "You could put it that way." The haughtiness in her voice indicated otherwise. "But really, when one has the production rate this project has, one should shoot for the best talent available. Naturally, that's a personal opinion. I've always thought actors should pay their dues—God knows, I paid mine—rather than be cast in a major production because of a...shall we say personal whim?"

"Do you think Booth DeWitt has a personal whim going with Ariel Kirkwood? That's her name, isn't it?"

"Why, yes, I think it is. As to the other, I could hardly say." She smiled again, charmingly. "Especially on the air, Bob."

"Her physical resemblance to you is striking."

"Really?" Liz's eyes frosted. "I much prefer being one of a kind, though of course it's flattering to have someone attempt to emulate me. Naturally, I wish the girl the best of luck."

"That's gracious of you, Liz, particularly since the plot line's rumored to be less than kind to the character that some say mirrors you."

"Those that know me will pay little attention to a slanted view, Bob. All in all, I'll be fascinated to see the finished product." The statement was laced with boredom, almost as if she'd yawned. "That is, of course, if it's ever actually aired."

"Ever aired? You see some problem there?"

"Nothing I can talk about," she said with obvious reluctance. "But you and I know how many things can happen between filming and airing, Bob."

"No plans to sue, huh, Liz?"

She laughed, but it came off hollow. "That would give the film entirely too much importance."

Bob mugged at the camera. "Well, with that we'll take a little break here. When we come back, James R. Lemont will be joining us to tell us about his new book, *Hollywood Secrets*. We know about those, too, don't we, Liz?" After his wink, the screen switched to the first commercial.

Leaning back against the pillows, his meal forgotten, Booth drew on his cigarette and sent the smoke to the ceiling. He was angry. He could feel it in the hard knot in his stomach. The swipes she'd taken at the film hadn't even been subtle, he reflected. Oh, perhaps she'd fool a certain percentage of people, but no one remotely connected with the business, and no one with any perception. She'd done her best to toss a few poison darts and had ended up, in Booth's opinion, by making a fool of herself.

But he was angry. And the anger, he discovered, came from the slices she'd taken at Ariel. Quite deliberate, quite calculated, and unfortunately for Liz, quite obvious. She was a cat, and normally a clever one. Jealousy was essentially the only thing that could make her lose that edge.

Naturally she'd be jealous of Ariel, Booth mused. Of anyone young, beautiful and talented. Add that to the bile she'd have to swallow over the film itself, and Liz would be as close to rage as her limited range of emotions would allow. And this was her way of paying back.

Rising, Booth slammed off the set before he paced the room. She'd bring up the film—and Ariel—in every interview she gave, at every party she attended, in the hope to sabotage both. Of course, she wouldn't do any appreciable damage, but knowing that didn't ease his temper. No one had the right to take potshots at Ariel, and the fact that they were being taken through him, because of him, made it worse.

He could, if he chose, book himself on the circuit to promote the film and to counter Liz's campaign. That would only add fuel to the fire. He knew the best way to make the storm Liz was trying to brew fizzle was to keep silent. Frustrated, he walked to the window. He could hear the water from there. Just barely. He wondered if Ariel had watched the late-night talk show. And how she was dealing with it.

Stretched out in the hammock, plumped by pillows, with a bowl of fresh popcorn resting on her stomach, Ariel listened to Liz Hunter. Her brow lifted once as a reference was made to herself. Ariel crunched on popcorn and smiled as Robert MacAllister reminded Liz that *the girl's* name was Ariel Kirkwood.

Poor Liz, she thought. She was only making it worse for herself. Perhaps because Ariel had been inside Rae's skin for so many weeks, she noticed small things. The tapping of a fingertip on the arm of the chair, the brief tightening of the lips, the flash in the eyes that was a bit of anger, a bit of desperation. The more Liz talked, the shakier her support became.

She'd have been much better off if she'd said nothing, Ariel mused. A no-comment, a shrug of that haughty shoulder. Miscalculation, Ariel thought with a sigh. A foolish one.

I can't hurt her. Ariel shifted her gaze from the screen to the ceiling. No one can take her talent away from her. A pity she doesn't realize that. It's Booth she really wants to hurt, Ariel decided. She'd want to make him pay for using Rae to strip off a few masks. Yet didn't Liz realize he was just as bitterly honest with his own character?

Ariel glanced back at the television screen as Liz's face dominated the screen. There was a line of dissatisfaction between her brows, very faint. Ariel wondered if she were the only one who noticed it, because she was so intimately involved. I know you, Ariel told the image on the screen, I know you inside and out. And that made her swallow hard. It was just a little scary.

Ariel lay back, tuning out the sound of the set and tuning back into the rain. It was nearly over, only a patter now against the windowpane. Booth had probably seen it, she decided. And if he hadn't caught the show, he'd know of the content very soon. He'd be angry. Ariel could almost see his hard-eyed, grim-mouthed reaction. She herself had been fighting an edge of temper that threatened to dominate her other feelings.

Anger was useless; she wished she could tell him. He had to know that he'd opened the door for this when he'd written the script. She'd opened it a bit further when she'd taken the part. She hoped, when he'd calmed, that he'd see Liz Hunter had done the film more good than harm.

When the phone rang, Ariel leaned over. Years of experience kept her balanced rather than tumbling out of the hammock and onto the floor. Swinging a bit dangerously, she gripped the phone and hauled it up to her. "Hello."

"That witch."

With a half laugh, Ariel lay back on the pillows. "Hi, Stella."

"Did you catch the MacAllister show?"

"Yeah, I've got it on."

"Listen, Ariel, she's making a joke out of herself. Anyone with two brain cells will see that."

"Then why're you angry?"

She could hear Stella take a deep breath. "I've been sitting here listening to that woman talk, wishing you the *best* of luck." Stella muttered something under her breath, then began to talk so fast the words tumbled into each other. "The best of luck my foot. She'd like to see you drop off the face of the earth. She'd like to stick a knife in you."

"A nail file, maybe."

"How can you joke about it?" Stella demanded.

Because if I don't I might just start screaming. "How can you take it so seriously?" Ariel said instead.

"Listen, Ariel…" Stella's voice was barely controlled. "I know that kind of woman. I've been playing the type for the past five years. There's nothing she wouldn't do, nothing, if she thought she could get to you. Damn it, you trust everyone."

"Some less than others." Though the concern and the loyalty touched her, she laughed. "Stella, I'm not a complete fool."

"You're not a fool at all," Stella shot back, outraged. "But you're naive. You actually believe the kid who stops you on the street asking for a donation is really collecting for a foundling home."

"He might be," Ariel mumbled. "Besides, what does that have to do with—"

"Everything!" Stella cut her off with something close to a roar. "I care about you. I worry about you every time I think about you walking blithely down the street without a thought to the crazies in the world."

"Come on, Stella, if I thought about it too much I'd never go out at all."

"Well think about this: Liz Hunter's a powerful, vindictive woman who'd like to ruin you. You watch your back, Ariel."

Who'd know that better than I? Ariel thought with a quick shudder. I've been playing her character for weeks. "If I promise, will you stop worrying?"

"No." Slightly mollified, Stella sighed. "Promise anyway."

"You got it. Are you calm now?"

Stella made a quiet sound in her throat. "I don't understand why you're not angry."

"Why should I be when you're doing it for me—and so well?"

Stella heaved a long breath. "Good night, Ariel."

"Night, Stella… Thanks."

Ariel replaced the receiver and swung gently to and fro in the hammock. As she stared up at the ceiling, she marveled over how fortunate she was. Friendship was a precious thing. To have someone ready to leap to your defense, claws bared, was a comforting sensation. She had friends like that, and a job that paid her well for doing what she would gleefully have done for nothing. She had the unquestioning love of a little boy, and God willing, would have him to care for within a few weeks. She had so much.

As Ariel lay back, struggling to count her blessings, she thought of Booth. And ached for him.

Two days later, Ariel received a surprise visit. It was her first free day since resuming her role of Amanda. She was spending it doing something she rarely started, and more rarely finished. Housecleaning.

In tattered shorts and a halter, she sat on her windowsill two stories up, and leaning out, washed the outside of her windows. The volume on her radio was turned up so that the sinuous violins of *Scheherazade* all but shook the panes. Occasionally someone from the neighborhood would shout up at her. Ariel would stop working—something that took no effort at all—and shout back down.

The important thing was to keep busy, to keep occupied. If she gave herself more than a brief moment of spare time, time to think, she might go mad. The next day marked the beginning of the custody hearing. And a full two weeks since she'd last seen Booth. Ariel polished window glass until it shone.

She felt something like an itch between the shoulder blades, like a fingertip on the back of the neck. Twisting her head, she looked down and saw Booth on the sidewalk below. Relief came in waves. Even if she'd tried, even if she'd thought to try, she couldn't have stopped the smile that illuminated her whole face.

"Hi."

Looking up at her, he felt a need so great it buckled his knees. "What the hell are you doing?"

"Washing the windows."

"You could break your neck."

"No, I'm anchored." One of the kittens brushed against her ankles so that she jolted and braced herself with her knees. "Are you coming up?"

"Yeah." Without another word, he disappeared from view.

As he climbed the stairs Booth reminded himself of his promise. He wasn't going to touch her—not once. He would say what he'd come to say, do what he'd come to do, then leave. He wouldn't touch her and start that endless cycle of longings and desires and dreams all over again. Over the past two weeks he'd purged himself of her.

As he reached the landing he nearly believed it. Then she opened the door.

She still held a damp rag in one hand. She wore no makeup; the flush of color in her cheeks came from pleasure and exertion. Her hair was scooped back and tied with a bit of yarn. The scent of ammonia was strong.

His fingers itched for just one touch, just one. Booth curled them into his palms and stuck them in his pockets.

"It's good to see you." Ariel leaned against the door and studied him. People didn't change in two weeks, she reminded herself as she compared every angle and plane in his face with the memory she'd been carrying with her. He looked the same, a bit browner perhaps from the sun, but the same. Love washed over her.

"You've been sailing."

"Yes, quite a bit."

"It's good for you. I can see it." She stepped back, knowing from the tense way he was standing that he wouldn't accept her hand if she offered. "Come in."

He stepped into chaos. When Ariel cleaned, it was from the bottom up and nothing was safe. Drawers had been turned out, tables cleared off. Furniture and windows gleamed. There wasn't a clear place to stand, much less sit.

"Sorry," she said as she followed his survey. "I'm a bit behind on my spring cleaning." The pressure in her chest was increasing with every second they stood beside each other, and miles apart. "Want a drink?"

"No, nothing. I'll make this quick because you're busy." He'd make it quick because it hurt, physically, painfully, not to touch what he still wanted…and to still want what he'd convinced himself he couldn't have. "I'm assuming you saw the MacAllister show the other night."

"That's old news," Ariel countered. She sat on the hammock, legs dangling free, fingers locked tightly.

With his hands still in his pockets, Booth rocked back on his heels. "How'd you feel about it?"

With a shrug, Ariel crossed her ankles. "She took a couple stabs at the film, but—"

"She took a couple stabs at you," he corrected. His voice had tightened, his eyes narrowed.

Gauging his mood, Ariel decided to play it light. She smiled. "I'm not bleeding."

Booth frowned at her a moment, then judged she was a great deal less concerned than he. That was something he had to change. "She hasn't stopped there, Ariel." He walked closer, the better to study her face, the better to perhaps catch the drift of her scent. "She had quite a little session with the producer of your show, then with a few network executives."

"With my producer?" Puzzled, she tilted her head and tried to reason it out. "Why?"

"She wants them to fire you—or, ah, to let your contract lapse."

Stunned, she said nothing. But her face went pale. The rag slipped silently from her hand to the floor.

"She'd agree to do a series of guest spots for the show, if you were no longer on it. Your producer politely turned her down. So she went upstairs."

Ariel swallowed the panic. All she could think, all that drummed in her mind was, *not now, not during the hearing.* She needed the stability of that contract for Scott. "And?"

He hadn't expected this white-lipped, wide-eyed reaction. A woman with her temperament should have been angry, angry enough to rage, throw things, explode. He could even have understood amusement, a burst of laughter, a shake of the head and a shrug. She was confident enough for that. He'd thought she was. What he saw in her eyes was basic fear.

"Ariel, just how important do you think you are to the show?"

She found she had to swallow before she could form the first word. "Amanda's a popular character. I get the lion's share of mail, a lot of it addressed to Amanda rather than me. In my last contract, my scale was upgraded with the minimum amount of negotiation." She swallowed again and gripped her hands together. That was all very logical, all very practical. She wanted to scream. "Anyone can be replaced. On a soap, that's the number-one rule. Are they going to let me go?"

"No." Frowning at her, he stepped closer. "I'm surprised you'd think they would. You're already their biggest reason for the ratings lead. And with the film due in the fall, the show's bound to cash in on it. In a strictly practical way of thinking, you—day after day—are worth a great deal more to the network than Liz in a one-shot deal." When Ariel let out a long breath he had to fight the urge to take her into his arms. "Does the show mean that much to you?"

"Yes, it means that much to me."

"Why?"

"It's my show," she said simply. "My character." As the panic faded, the anger seeped in. "If I leave it, it'll be because it's what I want, or because I'm not good enough anymore." Giving in to rage she plucked up a little yellow vase from the table beside her and flung it and the baby's breath it held at the wall. Glass shattered, flowers spilled. "I've given five years of my life to that show." As her breathing calmed again, she stared at the shards of vase and broken blooms. "It's important to me," she continued, looking back up at Booth. "At the moment, for a lot of reasons, it's essential." Ariel gripped the side of the hammock and struggled to relax. "How did you hear about this?"

"From Pat. There's been quite a meeting of the minds as concerns you. We decided you should hear about this latest move privately."

"I appreciate it." The anger was fading. Relief made her light-headed. "Well, I'm sorry she feels so pressured that she'd try to do me out of a job, but I imagine she'll back off now."

"You're smarter than that."

"There's nothing she can do to me, not really. And every time she tries, she only makes it worse for herself." Slowly, deliberately, she relaxed her hands. "Every interview she gives is free publicity for the film."

"If there's any way she can hurt you, she will. I should've thought of that before I cast you as Rae."

Smiling, Ariel lifted her hands to his arms. "Are you worried about me? I'd like you to be…just a little."

He should have backed off right then. But he needed, badly needed to absorb that contact. Just her hands on his arms. If he were careful, very careful, it might be enough. "Whatever trouble she causes you I'm responsible for."

"That's a remarkably ridiculous statement—arrogant, egotistical." She grinned. "And exactly like you. I've missed you, Booth. I've missed everything about you."

She was drawing him closer, but more, she was drawing him in. Even as her hand reached for his face, he was lowering his mouth to hers. And the first taste was enough to make him forget every promise he'd made during this absence.

Ariel moaned as her lips met his. It seemed she'd been waiting for years to feel that melting thrill again.

More. The greed flashed through her. She pulled him
down so that the hammock swayed under their combined weight.

There was no gentleness in either of them now. Impatience shimmered. Without words they told each other
to hurry—hurry and touch me; it's been too long. And
as clothes were tugged away and flesh met flesh, they
both took hungrily from the other.

The movement of the hammock was like the sea,
and he felt the freedom. There was freedom simply in
being near her again. And from freedom sprang the
madness. He couldn't stop his hands from racing over
her. He couldn't prevent his mouth from trying to devour every inch. He was starving for her and no longer
cared that he had vowed to abstain. Her skin flowed
warm and soft under his hands. Her mouth was hot and
silky. The generosity he could never quite measure simply poured from her.

She'd stopped thinking the moment he'd kissed her
again. Ariel didn't need the intellect now, only the
senses. She could taste the salt on his skin as they clung
together in the moist heat of the afternoon; the dark
male flavor along his throat enticed her back, again
and again. There was a fury of desire in him, more
than she'd ever known in him before. It made her skin
tremble to be wanted with such savagery.

But with the trembling came a mirroring desire in
herself. The top of the hammock scraped against her
back as his body pressed against hers. For one isolated
moment, she thought she could feel the individual
strands, then that sensation faded into another.

His hands were in her hair, holding her head back so
that he could plunder her mouth. She heard his breath

shudder, and saw, as her lashes fluttered up, that he was watching her. Always watching.

His eyes stayed open and on hers when he plunged into her. He wanted to see her, needed to know that her need for him was as great as his for her. And he could see it—in the trembling mouth. His name came from there in a breathy whisper. In the stunned pleasure in her eyes. He could bring her that. He could bring her that, Booth thought as he buried his face in her hair. He wanted to bring her everything.

"Ariel…" In the last sane corner of his mind he knew they were both near the edge. He took her face in his hands and crushed his mouth to hers so that they crested, swallowing each other's cry of pleasure.

The movement of the hammock eased, soothing now, like a cradle. They were wrapped together, facing, with her head in the curve of his shoulder. Their bodies were damp from the heat in the air, and from the heat within. A length of her hair fell over her and onto his chest.

"I thought of you," Booth murmured. His eyes were closed. His heartbeat was slowing, but the arms around her didn't loosen. "I could never stop thinking about you."

Ariel's eyes were open, and she smiled. She'd needed no other words but those. "Sleep with me awhile." Turning her head she kissed his shoulder before settling again. "Just for a little while."

For days and nights she'd thought only of tomorrows. The time had come again to think only of now. Long after he slept, she lay awake, feeling the hammock move gently.

Chapter 11

Ariel sat on a small wooden bench outside the court-room. It was a busy hallway with people coming and going, but no one paid much attention to a solitary woman in a cream-colored suit who stared straight ahead.

The first day of the hearing was over, and she felt a curious mixture of relief and tension. It had begun; there was no going back. A door opened down the hall, and a flood of people poured out. She'd never felt more alone in her life.

Bigby had outlined it for her. There'd been no sur-prises. Despite the legal jargon, the first day had dealt basically with establishing the groundwork. Still, to Ariel's mind the preliminary questions had been ter-ribly cut-and-dried. But the wheels had begun to turn, and now that they had, maybe the pace would pick up.

Just let it be over with quickly, she thought and closed her eyes briefly. *Just let it be done.* The tension came from the thought of tomorrow. The relief came from the absolute certainty that she was doing the right thing.

Bigby came out of the courtroom with his slim briefcase in his hand. With his other, he reached out to her. "Let me buy you a drink."

Ariel smiled, linking her hand with his as she rose. "Deal. But make it coffee."

"You did well in there today."

"I didn't do much of anything."

He started to speak, then changed his mind. Maybe it was best not to point out how much she'd done by simply being. Her freshness, the concern in her eyes, the tone of her voice—all of that had been a vital contrast to the stiff backs and stone faces of the Andersons. A judge in a custody suit, a good one, was influenced by more than facts and figures.

"Just keep doing it," he advised, then gave her hand a squeeze as they walked down the hall. Neither of them noticed the dark-suited man in horn rims who followed. "Tell me how the rest of your life's going," he requested. In his unobtrusive way, Bigby guided her through the doors as he guided her thoughts. "It isn't every day I represent a rising celebrity."

She laughed even as the first wave of heat rose off the sidewalk and struck her. New York in midsummer was hot and humid and sweaty. "Is that what I am?"

"Your picture was in *Tube*—and your name was brought up on the MacAllister show." He grinned as she arched a brow. "I'm impressed."

"Read *Tube*, do you, Charlie?" He was trying to keep her calm, she realized. And he was doing it expertly. She slid a companionable arm through his. "I have to admit, the publicity isn't going to hurt the soap, the film or me."

"In that order?"

Ariel smiled and shrugged. "Depends on my mood." No, she wasn't without ambition. The *Tube* spread had given her a great deal of self-satisfaction. "It's been a long time between shampoo commercials, and I won't be sorry if I don't have to stand, lathered up, for three hours again anytime soon."

They entered a coffee shop where the temperature dropped by twenty-five degrees. Ariel gave a quick shiver and a sigh of relief. "So professionally, everything's rolling along?" Charlie asked.

"No complaints." Ariel slipped into the little vinyl booth and pushed off her shoes. "They're casting for *Chapter Two* next week. I haven't done live theater in too long."

Bigby clucked his tongue as he picked up a menu. The man in the dark suit took the booth behind them, settling with his back to Ariel's. "You don't sit still, do you?"

"Not any longer than I can help it. I have good feelings about the custody suit, maybe because I'm on a professional roll. It's all going to work out, Charlie. I'm going to have Scott with me, and Booth's film's going to be a smash."

He eyed her over his glasses, then grinned. "The power of positive thinking."

"If it works." She leaned her elbows on the table, then rested her chin on her fists. "All my life I've been moving toward certain goals, without really understanding that I was setting them for myself. They're almost within reach."

Bigby glanced up at the waitress before he turned back to Ariel. "How about some pie with the coffee?"

"You twisted my arm. Blueberry." She touched the

tip of her tongue to her lip because she could almost taste it.

"Two of each," Bigby told the waitress. "Speaking of Booth DeWitt…" he went on.

"Were we?"

He caught the gleam of amusement in Ariel's eye. "I think you mentioned him to me a few weeks ago. A man who didn't think much of relationships or actresses?"

"You've quite a memory—and very sharp deductive skills."

"It was easy enough to put two and two together, particularly after Liz Hunter's performance on the Mac-Allister show the other night."

"Performance?" Ariel repeated with a half smile.

"An actor can usually see through another, I'd think. A lawyer's got a lot of actor in him." He paused and folded his hands on the chipped Formica much as he did on his desk. "She put DeWitt through the wringer a couple of years ago."

"They damaged each other. You know, sometimes I think people can be attracted to the specific persons who are the worst for them."

"Is that from personal experience?"

Her eyes became very sober, her mouth very soft. "Booth is right for me. In a lot of ways he'll make my life difficult, but he's right for me."

"What makes you so sure?"

"I'm in love with him." When the pie was brought over, Ariel ignored the coffee and concentrated on it. "Bless you, Charlie," she said after the first bite.

He lifted a brow at the sliver of pie she was in raptures over. "You're easily impressed."

"Cynic. Eat it."

He picked up a fork and polished it absently with a

paper napkin. "At the risk of putting my foot in it, De-Witt isn't the type of man I'd've matched you with."

Ariel swallowed the next mouthful. "Oh?"

"He's very intense, serious-minded. His scripts have certainly indicated that. And you're…"

"Flaky?" she suggested, breaking off the next piece of pie.

"No." Bigby opened one of the little plastic containers of cream that were heaped in a bowl on the table. "You're anything but that. But you're full of life—the joy of it. It's not that you don't face the hard side when it comes up, but you don't look for it. It seems to me DeWitt does."

"Maybe—maybe he expects it. If you expect it and it happens, you aren't as staggered by it. For some people, it's a defensive move." A small frown creased her brow before she smoothed it away. "I think Booth and I can learn a lot from each other."

"And what does Booth think—or am I out of line?"

"You're not out of line, Charlie," she said absently as she remembered how grim Booth had been when he'd come to her door, how intensely he'd made love to her. He'd relaxed, degree by slow degree. Then he'd slept, with his arms tightly around her, as if he'd just needed to hold on. To her, she'd wondered, or to the peace? Perhaps it didn't matter. "It's hard for Booth," she murmured. "He wanted to be left alone, wanted his life to go on a certain way. I've interfered with that. He needs more time, more space."

"And what do you need?"

She looked over and saw her answer hadn't pleased him. *He's thinking of me,* Ariel realized, touched. Reaching over, she laid a hand on his. "I love him, Charlie. That's enough, for now. I do know it's not enough for always, but people can't put a control switch on emotions. I can't," she corrected.

"Does that mean he can?"

"To a certain extent." Ariel opened her mouth again, then shook her head. "No, I don't want to change him, even in that way. Not change. I need the balance he brings me, and I need to be able to lighten some of those shadows he carries around. It's the same with Scott, in a way. I need the stability he brings to my life—the way Scott, maybe children in general, can center it. Basically, I have an outrageous need to be needed."

"Have you told Booth about Scott? About the custody hearing?"

"No." Ariel stirred sugar into her coffee but didn't drink it. "It doesn't seem fair to saddle him with a problem that was already in full swing when we met. Instinct tells me to handle it myself, then when it's resolved, to tell Booth in my own way."

"He might not like it," Bigby pointed out. "The one thing Ford brought up in our last meeting that I have to agree with is that some men can't or won't be responsible for another man's child."

Ariel shook her head. "I don't believe that of Booth. But if it's true, it's something I'll have to deal with."

"If you did have to make a choice?"

She said nothing at first, as she dealt with the ache even the possibility brought her. "When you make a choice between two people you love," Ariel said quietly, "you choose the one who needs you the most." She lifted her eyes again. "Scott's only a child, Charlie."

He leaned across to pat her hand. "I just wanted to hear you say it. To be completely unprofessional again," he said with a grin, "there isn't a man in the world who'd turn down either you or Scott."

"That's why I'm crazy about you." She paused a moment, then touched her fork to her tongue. "Charlie, would you think I was really a hedonist if I ordered another piece of this pie?"

"Yes."

"Good." Ariel lifted a hand and gestured for the waitress. "Once in a while I just have to be decadent."

Amanda's life was a pressure cooker. As she went over the pacing of her lines one last time, Ariel decided she was grateful for the tension. It helped her deal with reality just a little better. She'd spent the morning in court, and the following day she was scheduled to take the stand. That was one part she couldn't rehearse for. But the good feeling she'd experienced the first day of the hearing hadn't faded, nor had her optimism. It was poor Amanda, Ariel mused, who'd continue to have problems that would never completely be resolved. That was life in a soap opera.

The rest of the cast had yet to return from the lunch break. Ariel sat alone in the studio—lounged, that is, on the rumpled bed she would rise from when Amanda was awakened by the sound of breaking glass. Alone and defenseless, she'd face the Trader's Bend Ripper. She'd have only her wits and professional skill to protect her from a psychotic killer.

Already in costume, a plain nightshirt in periwinkle-blue, she continued to murmur her lines out loud while doing a few lazy leg lifts. She'd had some vague twinges of guilt about the second piece of blueberry pie.

"Well, well, so this is the lightning pace of daytime television."

Immersed in the gripping scene between Amanda and a psychopath, Ariel dropped the script and gasped.

The pages fluttered back down to her stomach while her hand flew to her throat. "Good God, Booth. I hope you're up on your CPR, because my heart just stopped."

"I'll get it started again." Placing a hand on either side of her head, he leaned down and kissed her—softly, slowly, thoroughly. As surprised by the texture of the kiss as she'd been by his sudden appearance, Ariel lay still and absorbed. She knew only that something was different; but with her mind spinning and her blood pumping she couldn't grab on to it.

He knew. As he eased down to sit on the bed and prolonged the kiss, Booth understood precisely what was different. He loved her. He'd awakened alone in his own bed that morning, reaching for her. He'd read something foolish in the paper and had automatically thought how she'd have laughed. He'd seen a young girl with a balloon giggling as she'd dragged her mother toward the park. And he'd thought of Ariel.

And thinking of her, he'd seen that the sky was beautiful and blue, that the city was frantic and full of surprises, that life was a joy. How foolish he'd been to resist her, and all she offered.

She was his second chance… No, if he were honest, he'd admit that Ariel was his first chance at real happiness—complete happiness. He was no longer going to allow memories of ugliness to bar him from that, or from her.

"How's your heart rate?" he murmured.

Ariel let out a long breath, let her eyes open slowly. "You can cancel the ambulance."

He glanced at the tumbled bed, then down her very sedate, very appealing costume. "Were you having a nap?"

"I," she countered primly, "was working. The rest

of the cast is at lunch, I wasn't due in till one." She pushed at the hair that fell dark and disordered over his brow. No tension, she thought immediately, and smiled. "What're you doing here? You're usually knee-deep in brilliant phrases this time of day."

"I wanted to see you."

"That's nice." Sitting up, she threw her arms around his neck. "That's very nice."

It would take so little, Booth mused as he held her close. What would her reaction be when he told her that he'd stopped resisting, and that nothing had ever made him happier than having her in his life? Tonight, he thought, nuzzling into her neck. Tonight when they were alone, when there was no one to disturb them, he'd tell her. And he'd ask her.

"Can you stay awhile?" Ariel didn't know why she felt so wonderful, nor did she want to explore the reasons.

"I'll stay until you wrap, then I'm going to steal you and take you home with me."

She laughed, and as she shifted her weight, the script crumpled beneath her.

"Your lines," Booth warned.

"I know them. This—" she flung back her head so that her eyes glittered "—is a climactic scene full of danger and drama."

He looked back at the bed. "And sex?"

"No!" Shoving him away she scrambled onto her knees. "Amanda's tossing and turning in bed, her dreams were disturbed. Fade out—soft focus—she's wandering through a mist, lost, alone. She hears footsteps behind her. Close-up. Fear. And then..." While her voice took on a dramatic pitch, she tossed her hair behind her back. "Up ahead, she sees a figure in the fog." Ariel lifted a hand as if to brush away a curtain of mist. "Should she run toward it—away from it? The footsteps behind her come faster, her breathing quickens. A sliver of moonlight—pale, eerie—cuts through. It's Griff up ahead holding out a hand to her, calling her name in an echoing, disembodied voice. He loves her, she wants to go to him. But the footsteps are closing in. And as she begins to run, there's the sharp, cruel glimmer of a knife."

Ariel grabbed both of his shoulders then did a mock faint into his lap. Booth grinned. A quick tug of her hair had her eyes opening. "And then?"

"The man wants more." Scrambling up again, Ariel pushed the script aside. "The scream's caught in her throat, and before she can free it, there's a crash, a splinter of glass. Amanda jerks up in bed, her face glistening with sweat, her breath heaving." When she demonstrated, Booth wondered if she knew just how clever she was. "Did she dream it, or did she really hear it? Frightened, but impatient with herself, she gets out of bed."

Swinging her feet to the floor, Ariel got out of bed, frowning at the door as Amanda would do, absently pushing back her hair and reaching for the low light beside the bed. "Perhaps it was the wind," she continued. "Perhaps it was the dream, but she knows she'll never get back to sleep unless she takes a look. Music builds—lots of bass—as she opens the bedroom door. Cut to commercial."

"Come on, Ariel." Exasperated, he grabbed her hand and pulled her back toward the bed.

Obligingly she circled his neck with her arms as she stood in front of him. "Now you'll learn the best way to keep that shine on your no-wax floor."

He pinched her, hard. "It's the Ripper."

"Maybe," she said with a flutter of her lashes. "Maybe not."

"It's the Ripper," he said decisively. "And our intrepid Amanda goes downstairs. How does she get out of being victim number five?"

"Six," Ariel corrected. "The saying goes, that's for me to know and you to find out." With a jerk of his wrist, he'd whipped her around so that she tumbled into his lap, laughing. "Go ahead, torture me, do your worst. I'll never talk." Linking her hands around his neck, she looked up at him and smiled. And she was so beautiful, so full of life at its best that she took his breath away.

"I love you, Ariel."

He felt the fingers at his neck go limp, saw the smile fade, her eyes widen. Inside, Ariel felt as though someone had just cut off the flow of blood from her heart. "That's a tough way to find out a plotline," she managed after a moment. She would have sat up if she'd had the strength to resist the gentle pressure of his hand on her shoulder.

"I love you, Ariel," he repeated, forgetting all his plans for telling her with finesse and with intimacy. "I think I always have. I know I always will." He cupped her face in his hand as her eyes filled. "You're everything I've ever wanted and was afraid to hope for. Stay with me." He touched his lips to hers and felt the tremor. "Marry me."

When he would have drawn back, she clutched at his shirt. Burying her face in his shoulder she took a deep breath. "Be sure," she whispered. "Booth, be absolutely sure because I'll never give you a moment's peace. I'll never let you get away. Before you ask me again, remember that. I don't believe in mutual disagreements or irreconcilable differences. With me, it's forever, Booth. It's for always."

He forced her head back. In his eyes she saw the fire and the passion. And the love. "You're damn right." Her breathless laugh was muffled against his mouth. "I want to get married quickly." He punctuated the words with another kiss. "And quietly. Just how soon can they shoot around Amanda so we can have more than a weekend honeymoon?"

Ariel hadn't known anyone could outpace her. Now, her thoughts jumbled as she struggled to keep up. Marriage—he was already talking of marriage and honeymoons. "Well, I, let's see… After Griff saves Amanda from the Ripper, she loses the baby and goes into a coma. The hospital scenes could be—"

"Aha." With a self-satisfied smile, Booth kissed her nose. "So Griff saves her from the Ripper, which removes him from the list of suspects."

Ariel's eyes narrowed. "You rat."

"Just be glad I'm not a spy for another network. You're a pushover."

"I'll show you a pushover," Ariel claimed, and overbalanced him so that he landed on his back. He loved her. The thought brought on such giddiness, she collapsed against him, laughing. Before he could retaliate, they heard someone rushing up the stairs.

"Ariel! Ariel, you'd better take a look at—" Stella skidded to a halt when she saw Ariel and Booth laughing and half lying on the bed. She whipped the paper she held behind her back and swore under her breath. "Whoops!" With the aid of an embarrassed smile she called on all her skill to keep either of them from noticing that she felt slightly ill inside and desperately worried. "Well, I'd've knocked if you'd bothered to close the door." She gestured with her free hand toward the false wall. "Suppose I go out and come in again?" *Right after I burn this paper,* she thought grimly, and grinning, backed up.

"Don't go." Ariel struggled all the way up, but kept one hand tucked into Booth's. "I'm about to bestow a singularly great honor on you." She squeezed Booth's fingers. "My sister, however rotten, should be the first to know."

"By all means."

"Stella…" Ariel stopped because she caught a glimpse of something in her friend's eyes. A glimpse was enough. "What is it?"

"Nothing. I remembered I have to talk to Neal about something, that's all. Look, I'd better catch him before he—"

But Ariel was already rising from the bed. "What was it you wanted me to see, Stella?"

"Oh, nothing." There was a warning, a deliberate one, in her eyes. "It can wait."

Unsmiling, Ariel held out her hand, palm up.

Stella's fingers curled tighter around the paper. "Ariel, it's not a good time. I think you'd better—"

"I think I'd better see it now."

"Damn it." With a glance over Ariel's shoulder at Booth, Stella passed her the paper.

Celebrity Explorer, Ariel noted with a slight flicker of annoyance. As tabloids went it was bottom of the barrel. Half-amused, she glanced over the exploitive headlines. "Really, Stella, if this is the best you can do for lunchtime reading, I'm disillusioned." Absently, she turned it over and scanned under the fold. From behind her Booth saw the tension shoot into her body.

SOAP OPERA QUEEN'S DESPERATE BATTLE
FOR LOVE CHILD

Below the bold print headline was a grainy picture of Ariel sitting on the grass in Central Park with Scott's face caught in her hands. In one part of her mind she remembered that frozen moment from their last Sunday afternoon. As she stared at it, appalled, sickened, she didn't hear Booth rise and come to her.

Something slammed into his stomach—not a hammer but a fist that thrust then ground deep. Even the poor quality of the photo didn't disguise the stunning resemblance between Ariel and the child that laughed into her face. There was no mistaking the tie of blood. As the headline shouted out at him, Booth wanted to murder.

"Just what the hell is this?"

Shaken, Ariel looked up. Scott was not to see it, she thought over and over. This was not to touch him. How? How had it leaked? The Andersons? No, she rejected that thought instantly. They wanted publicity less than she did.

The picture...who'd taken it? Someone had followed her, she decided. Someone had followed her and found out about Scott, the custody hearing. Then they'd twisted it into an ugly headline and an exploitive article. But who...?

Liz Hunter. Ariel's fingers tightened on the newspaper. Of course, it had to be. There were few women who knew better than Ariel what that type of person was capable of. Liz hadn't been able to get to her professionally, so she'd taken the next step.

"Ariel, I asked you what the hell this is."

Ariel focused on Booth abruptly. *Oh, God,* she

thought, *now I have to work my way through the ugliness before I can explain.* Already, she saw the anger, the distrust. "I'd like to talk to you privately," she said calmly enough. "Down in my dressing room."

As Ariel turned to go, Stella reached out, then dropped her hand helplessly back to her side. "Ariel, I'm sorry."

She only shook her head. "No, it's all right. We'll talk later."

As they wound their way through the studio, down the corridors, she tried to think logically. All she could see was that nasty headline and grainy picture. When she walked into the dressing room she went directly to the coffeepot, needing to do something with her hands. She heard the door close and the lock click.

"This isn't the way I wanted to handle this, Booth." She pulled in a deep breath as she fumbled with the coffee. "I didn't expect any publicity... I've been so careful."

"Yes, careful." He jammed his hands into his pockets.

She pressed her lips together as the tone of his voice pricked along her skin. "I know you must have questions. If I..."

"Yes, I have questions." He snatched the paper from her dressing table. He, too, needed to occupy his hands. "Are you involved in a custody suit?"

"Yes."

He felt the grinding in his stomach again. "So much for trust."

"No, Booth." She whirled around, then stopped as a hundred conflicting emotions, a hundred opposing answers hammered at her. Would this be the time of choice? Would she have to choose after all, when she almost had everything she needed? "Please, let me explain. Let me think how to explain."

"You're involved in a custody suit." He remembered those brief flashes of strain he'd seen in her from time to time. He wanted to tear the paper to shreds. "You have this child, and you didn't tell me. What does that say about trust?"

Confused, she dragged a hand through her hair. "Booth, I was already deeply involved in this before we even met. I couldn't drag you into it."

Bitterness seeped into him. Booth hated to taste it… again. "Oh, I see. You were already involved, so it was none of my business. It appears that you have two separate standards for your trust, Ariel. The one for yourself, and the one for everyone else."

"That's not true," she began, then fumbled to a halt. Was it? "I don't mean for it to be." Her voice began to shake, then her hands. "Booth, I've been frightened. Part of the fear was that something would leak out. The most important thing to me was that none of this touch Scott."

He waited, trying to be impassive as she brushed away the first tear. "That's the boy's name?"

"Yes. He's only four years old."

He turned away because the grief on her face was destroying him. "And his father?"

"His father's name was Jeremy. He's dead."

Booth didn't ask if she'd loved him. He didn't have to. She'd loved another man, he thought. Had borne another man's child. Could he deal with that, accept it? Resting his palms on her dressing table he let the emotion run through him. Yes, he thought so. It didn't change her, or him. And yet…and yet she hadn't told him. It was that that brought the change.

"Who has the boy now?" he asked stiffly.

"His grandparents. He's not…he's not happy with them. He needs me, Booth, and I need him. I need both of you. Please…" Her voice lowered to a whisper. "Don't ask me to choose. I love you. I love you so much but he's just a little boy."

"Choose?" Booth flicked on his lighter, then tossed it onto her cluttered dressing table as he took the first drag from his cigarette. "Damn it, Ariel, just how insensitive do you think I am?"

She waited until she could control the throb of her heart at the base of her throat. "Would you take both of us?"

Booth blew out smoke. Fury was just below the surface. "You kept it from me. That's the issue now. I could hardly turn away from a child that's part of you."

She reached for him. "Booth—"

"You kept it from me," he repeated, watching her hand drop away. "Why?"

"Please understand, if I kept it from you it was only because I wanted to protect him. He's had a difficult time already, and I was afraid that if I talked about the hearing to anyone, anyone at all, there was a risk of something like that." She gestured to the paper, then turned away.

"There's nothing you don't know about my life, Ariel. I can't help but resent that there was something so vital to yours that you kept from me. All this time, almost from the first minute, you've asked me to trust you. Now that I've given that to you, I find you haven't trusted me."

"I put Scott first. He needed someone to put him first."

"I might be able to understand that, if you could explain to me why you ever gave him up."

"Gave him up?" Ariel stared, but tears blurred her vision. "I don't know what you mean."

"I thought I knew you!" Booth exploded. "I believed that, and believing it fell in love with you when I'd sworn I'd never get emotionally involved again. How could you give up your child? How could you have a child and say nothing to me?"

"Give up my child?" she repeated dumbly. "But no, no! It's nothing like that."

"Damn it, Ariel, you've let someone else raise your child. And now that you want him back, now that you're involved in something as serious as a custody battle, you do it alone. How could you love me, how could you preach trust at me and say nothing?"

"I was afraid to tell you or anyone. You don't understand how it might affect Scott if he knew—"

"Or how it might affect you?" He swung his arm toward the discarded paper.

Ariel sucked in her breath and barely controlled a raging denial. Perhaps she'd deserved that. "My concern was for Scott," she said evenly. "A custody suit would hardly damage my reputation. Any more than an illegitimate child would—though he's not my child. Jeremy was my brother."

It was Booth's turn to stare. Nothing made sense. Underlying his confusion was the thought that tears didn't belong in Ariel's eyes. Her eyes were for laughter. "The boy's your nephew?"

"Jeremy and his wife died late last winter." She couldn't go to him now; she could see he wasn't ready. And neither was she. "His grandparents, the Andersons, were appointed guardians. He's not happy with them."

Not her child, Booth thought again, but her brother's child. He waited to gauge his own reaction and found he was still hurt, still angry. Whether the boy was her son or not hadn't been the issue. She'd blocked that part of her life from him.

"I think," Booth said slowly, "that you'd better start at the beginning."

Ariel opened her mouth, but before she could speak, someone pounded on her door. "Phone for you, Ariel, in Neal's office. Urgent."

Banking back frustration, she left the room, heading for Neal's office. So much to explain, she thought. To Booth and to herself. She rubbed her temple with two fingers as she picked up the phone. "Hello."

"Ms. Kirkwood."

"Yes, this is Ariel Kirkwood." Her frown deepened. "Mr. Anderson?"

"Scott's missing."

Chapter 12

She said nothing. Only seconds passed, but a hundred thoughts raced through her mind, tumbling over each other one at a time so that none was clear. Every nerve in her stomach froze. Vaguely she felt the ache in her hand where she gripped the receiver.

"Ms. Kirkwood, I said that Scott is missing."

"Missing?" she repeated in a whisper. The word itself brought up too many visions. Terrifying ones. She wanted to panic, but forced herself, by digging her nails into her palm, to talk, and to listen carefully. But even the whisper she forced out shook. "How long?"

"Apparently since around eleven o'clock. My wife thought he was next door, playing with a neighbor's child. When she called him home for lunch, she learned he'd never been there."

Eleven… With a sick kind of dread Ariel looked at her watch. It was nearly two. Three hours. Where could a small boy go in three hours? Anywhere. It was an eternity. "You've called the police?"

"Of course." His voice was brisk but through it ran a thread of fear Ariel was too dazed to hear. "The neighborhood's been searched, people questioned. Everything possible's being done."

Everything possible? What did that mean? She repeated the phrase over in her mind, but it still didn't make sense. "Yes, of course." She heard her own words come hollowly through the rushing noise in her head. "I'll be there right away."

"No, the police suggest that you go home and stay there, in case Scott contacts you."

Home, she thought. They wanted her to go home and do nothing while Scott was missing. "I want to come. I could be there in thirty minutes." The whisper shattered into a desperate plea. "I could help look for him. I could—"

"Ms. Kirkwood," Anderson cut her off, then breathed deeply before he continued. "Scott's an intelligent boy. He knows where you live, he knows your phone number. At a time like this it's best to admit that it's you he wants to be with. If he— If it's possible for him to contact anyone, it would be you. Please, go home. If he's found here, I'll call you immediately."

The single phrase ran through her mind three times. *If it's possible for him to contact anyone...*

"All right. I'll go home. I'll wait there." Dazed, she stared at the phone, not even aware that she'd replaced the receiver herself. Marveling that she could walk at all, she moved to the door.

Of course she could walk, Ariel told herself as she pressed a hand to the wall for support. She could function—she had to function. Scott was going to want her when he was found. He'd be full of stories and adventures—especially if he had the chance to ride in a police car. He'd want to tell her about all of it. The phone would probably be ringing when she opened her front door. He'd probably just been daydreaming and wandered a few blocks away, that was all. They'd be calling, so she should get home quickly. Her legs felt like rubber and would hardly move at all.

Booth was brooding at the picture of Ariel and Scott when he heard the door open. He turned, the paper still in his hand, but the questions that had been pressing at him faded the moment he saw her. Her skin was like parchment. He'd never seen her eyes look vacant, nor had he expected to.

"Ariel…" He was crossing to her before he'd finished speaking her name. "What is it?"

"Booth." She put her hand on his chest. Warm, solid. She could feel the beat of his heart. No, none of it was a dream. Or a nightmare. "Scott's missing. They don't know where he is. He's missing."

He took a firm hold on her shoulders. "How long, Ariel?"

"Three hours." The first wave of fear rammed through the shock. "Oh, God, no one's seen him in three hours. Nobody knows where he is!"

He only tightened his hold on her shoulders when her body began to shake. "The police?"

"Yes, yes, they're looking." Her fingers curled, digging at his shirt. "They don't want me to come, they want me to go home and wait in case he… Booth."

"I'll take you home." He brushed the hair away from her face. His touch, his voice, was meant to soothe. "We'll go home and wait for the call. They're going to find him, Ariel. Little boys wander off all the time."

"Yes." She grabbed on to that, and to his hand. Of course that was true. Didn't she have to watch him like a hawk when they went to the park or the zoo? "Scott daydreams a lot. He could've just walked farther than he should. They're going to call me… I should be home."

"I'm going to take you." Booth kept hold of her as she took a disoriented study of the room. "You change, and I'll let them know you can't tape this afternoon."

"Change?" Puzzled she looked down and saw she still wore Amanda's nightshirt. "All right, I'll hurry. They could call any minute."

She tried to hurry, but her fingers kept fumbling with the most basic task. She needed her jeans, but her mind seemed to fade in and out as she pulled them on. Then her fingers slid over the snap. She tried to think logically but the pounding at the side of her head made it impossible. Holding off the nausea helped. It gave her something tangible to concentrate on while she fought with the laces of her shoes.

Booth was back within moments. When she turned to look at him he could feel her panic. "Ready?"

"Yes." She nodded and walked out with him, one foot in front of the other, while images of Scott, lost, frightened, streamed through her head. Or worse, much worse—Scott getting into a car with a stranger, a stranger whose face was only a shadow. She wanted to scream. She climbed into a cab.

Booth took her icy hand in his. "Ariel, it isn't like you to anticipate the worst. Think." He put his other hand over hers and tried to warm it. "There're a hundred harmless reasons for his being out of touch for a few hours. He might've found a dog, or chased a ball. He might've found some fascinating rock and taken it to a secret place to study it."

"Yes." She tried to picture those things. It would be typical of Scott. The image of the car and the stranger kept intruding. He had no basic fear of people, something she'd always admired in him. Now it filled her with fear. Turning her face in to Booth's shoulder she tried to convince herself that the phone would be ringing when she opened the front door.

When the cab stopped, she jerked upright and scrambled for the handle. She was dashing up the steps before Booth had paid the driver.

Silence. It greeted her like an accusation. Ariel stared at the phone and willed it to ring. When she looked at her watch, she saw it had been less than thirty minutes since Anderson's call. Not enough time, she told herself as she began to pace. *Too much time.* Too much time for a little boy to be alone.

Do something! The words ran through her mind as she struggled to find something solid to grip on to. She'd always been able to do something in any situation. There were answers, and if not answers, choices. But to wait. To have no answer, no choice but to wait… She heard the door close and turned. Her hands lifted, then fell helplessly.

"Booth. Oh, God, I don't know what to do. There must be something—anything."

Without a word he crossed to her, wrapped his arms around her and let her cling to him. Strange that it would have taken this—something so frightening for her—to make him realize she needed him every bit as much as he needed her. Whatever doubts he'd had, and whatever anger had lingered that she'd kept part of her life from him, dropped away. Love was simpler than he'd ever imagined.

"Sit down, Ariel." As he spoke, he eased her toward a chair. "I'm going to fix you a drink."

"No, I—"

"Sit down," he repeated with a firmness he knew she needed. "I'll make coffee, or I'll see about getting you a sedative."

"I don't need a sedative."

He nodded, rewarded by the sharp, quick answer. If she was angry, just a little angry, she wouldn't fall apart. "Then I'll make coffee."

The moment he went into the kitchen she was up again. Sitting was impossible, calm out of the question. She should never have agreed to come back and wait, Ariel told herself. She should have insisted on going out and looking for Scott herself. It was useless here—she was useless here. But if he called and she wasn't there to answer… Oh, God. She pressed her hands to her face and tried not to crumble. What time was it?

This time when she looked at her watch she felt the first hysterical sob build.

"Ariel." Booth carried two cups of coffee, hot and strong. He watched as she shuddered, swallowing sobs, but the tears ran freely.

"Booth, where could he be? He's hardly more than a baby. He doesn't have any fear of strangers. It's my fault because—"

"Stop." He said the word softly, but it had the effect of cutting off the rapidly tumbling words. He held out the cup, waiting for her to take it in both hands. It shook, nearly spilling the coffee over the rim. As it depleted, she sat again. "Tell me about him."

For a moment she stared at the coffee, as if she had no idea what it was or how she'd come to be holding it. "He's four…almost five. He wants a wagon, a yellow one, for his birthday. He likes to pretend." Lifting the cup, she swallowed coffee, and as it scalded her mouth, she calmed a bit. "Scott has a wonderful imagination. You can give him a cardboard box and he'll see a spaceship, a submarine, an Egyptian tomb. Really see it, do you know what I mean?"

"Yes." He laid a hand on hers as he sat beside her.

"When Jeremy and Barbara died, he was so lost. They were beautiful together, the three of them. So happy."

Her eyes were drawn to the boxing gloves that hung behind the door. Jeremy's gloves. They'd be Scott's one day. Something ripped inside her stomach. Ariel began to talk faster. "He's a lot like his father, the same charm and curiosity. The Andersons, Barbara's parents, never approved of Jeremy. They didn't want Barbara to marry him, and rarely saw her after she did. After... after the accident, they were appointed Scott's guardians. I wanted him, but it seemed natural that he go with them. A house, a yard, a family. But..." Breaking off, she cast a desperate look at the phone.

"But?" Booth prompted.

"They just aren't capable of understanding the kind of person Scott is. He'll pretend he's an archeologist and dig a hole in their yard."

"That might annoy anyone," Booth said and drew a wan smile from her.

"But he wouldn't dig up the yard if he had a sand dump and someone told him it could be a desert. Instead, he's punished for his imagination rather than having it redirected."

"So you decided to fight for him."

"Yes." Ariel moistened her lips. Had she waited too long? "Even if that were all, I might not have started proceedings. They don't love him." Her eyes shimmered as she looked up again. "They just feel responsible for him. I can't bear thinking he could grow up without all the love he should have."

Where is he, where is he, where is he?

"He won't." Booth drew her against him to kiss the tears at the corners of her eyes. "After you get custody, we'll see that he doesn't."

Cautiously, she pulled back, though her fingers were still tight on his shoulders. "We?"

Booth lifted a brow. "Is Scott part of your life?"

"Yes, he—"

"Then he's part of mine."

Her mouth trembled open twice before she could speak. "No questions?"

"I've wasted a lot of time with questions. Sometimes there's no need for them." He pressed her fingers to his lips. "I love you."

"Booth, I'm so afraid." Her head dropped against him. The dam burst.

He let her weep, those harsh sobs that were edged with grief and fear. He let her hold on and pull out whatever strength she could find in him. He lived by words, but knew when clever phrases were of no use. So in silence, Booth held her.

Crying would help, he thought, smoothing her hair. It would allow her to give in to fear without putting a name on it. While she was vulnerable to tears, it was he who willed the phone to ring. And he was denied.

The passion exhausted her. Ariel lay against Booth, light-headed, disoriented, only aware of that hollow ache inside that meant something vital was wrong. Her mind groped for the reason. *Scott.* He was missing. The phone hadn't rung. He was still missing.

"Time," she murmured, staring over his shoulder at the phone through eyes that were swollen and abused by tears. "What time is it now?"

"It's nearly four," he answered, hating to tell her, hating the convulsive jerk he felt because her body was pressed so close to his. There were a dozen things he could say to offer comfort. All useless. "I'll make more coffee."

At the knock on the door, she looked around listlessly. She wanted no company now. Ignoring the knock, she turned her back to the door. It was the phone that was important. "I'll get the coffee." Forcing herself to move, she rose. "I don't want to see anyone, please."

"I'll send them away." Booth walked to the door, already prepared to position himself in front of it to shield her. When he opened it, he saw a young woman wearing a bandanna and paint-smeared overalls. Then he saw the boy.

"Excuse me. This little boy was wandering a couple blocks from here. He gave this address. I wonder if—"

"Who are you?" Scott demanded of Booth. "This is Ariel's house."

"I'm Booth. Ariel's been waiting for you, Scott."

Scott grinned, showing small white teeth. Baby teeth, Booth realized. He's hardly more than a baby. "I would've been here sooner, but I got a little lost. Bobbi was painting her porch and said she'd walk me over."

Booth laid a hand on Scott's head and felt the softness of hair—like Ariel's. "We're very grateful to you, Miss…"

"Freeman, Bobbi Freeman." She grinned and jerked her head toward Scott. "No trouble. He might've lost his way a bit, but he sure knows what he wants. It seems to be Ariel and a peanut butter sandwich. Well, hey, I've got to get back to my porch. See you later, Scott."

"Bye, Bobbi." He yawned hugely. "Is Ariel home now?"

"I'll get her." Leaving Scott to climb onto the hammock, Booth walked toward the kitchen. He stopped Ariel in the doorway then took the two cups from her hands. "There's someone here to see you."

She shut her eyes. "Oh, please, Booth. Not now."

"I don't think he'll take no for an answer."

Something in his tone had her opening her eyes again, had her heart drumming against her ribs. Skirting passed him, she hurried into the living room. A small blond boy swung happily in her hammock with two kittens in his lap. "Oh, God, Scott!"

His arms were already reaching for her as she dashed across the room and yanked him against her. Warmth. She could feel the warmth of his small body and moaned from the joy of it. His rumpled hair brushed against her face. She could smell the faintest memory of soap from his morning wash, mixed with the sweat of the day and the gumdrops he was forever secreting in his pockets. Weeping, laughing, she sank to the floor holding him.

"Scott, oh, Scott. You're not hurt?" The quick fear struck at her again and she pulled him away to examine his face, his hands, his arms. "Are you hurt anywhere?"

"Uh-uh." A bit miffed at the question, Scott squirmed. "I didn't see Butch yet. Where's Butch?"

"How did you get here?" Ariel grabbed him again and gave in to the need to kiss his face—the rounded cheeks, the straight little nose, the small mouth. "Scott, where've you been?"

"On the train." His whole face lit. "I rode on the train all by myself. For a surprise."

"You…" Incredulous, Ariel stared at him. "You came from your grandparents', all alone?"

"I saved up my money." With no little pride he reached in his pocket and pulled out what he had left—a few pennies, two quarters and some gumdrops. "I walked to the station, but it took lots longer than a cab does. It isn't as far in a cab," he decided with a small boy's logic. "And I paid for the ticket all by myself—just like you showed me. I'm hungry, Ariel."

"In a minute." Appalled at the idea of his traveling alone and defenseless, she took both his arms. "You walked all the way to the train station, then rode the train here?"

"And I only got a little bit lost once, when Bobbi helped me. And I was hardly scared at all." His lip trembled. Screwing up his face, he buried it against her. "I wasn't."

All the things that might have happened to him flashed hideously through her mind. Ariel tightened her hold and thanked God. "Of course you weren't," she murmured, struggling to hold on to her emotions until she'd both schooled and scolded. "You're so brave, and so smart to remember the way. But, Scott—" she tilted his face to hers "—it was wrong for you to come here all alone."

"But I wanted to see you."

"I know, and I always want to see you." Again she kissed him, just to feel the warmth of his cheek. "But you left without telling your grandparents, and they're so worried. And I've been worried," she added, brushing the hair from his temple. "You have to promise you won't ever do it again."

"I don't want to do it again." With his mouth trembling again, he rubbed his fists against his eyes. "It took a long time and I got hungry, and then I got lost and my legs were so tired. But I wasn't scared."

"It's all right now, baby." Still holding him, she rose. "We'll fix you something to eat, then you can rest in the hammock. Okay?"

Scott sniffled, snuggling closer. "Can I have peanut butter?"

"Absolutely." Booth came back into the room and watched as both heads turned toward him. He might be her own child, he thought, wonderingly. Surprised, he felt a yearning to hold the boy himself. "I just saw a peanut butter sandwich in the kitchen. I think it's yours."

"Okay!" Scott scrambled out of Ariel's arms and bounced away.

Getting unsteadily to her feet, Ariel pressed the heel of her hand to her brow. "I could skin him alive. Oh, Booth," she whispered as she felt his arms go around her. "Isn't he wonderful?"

By dusk, Scott was asleep, with a tattered stuffed dog that had been his father's gripped in one hand. The three-legged Butch kept guard on the pillow beside him. Ariel sat on the sofa next to Booth and faced Scott's grandfather. Coffee grew cold on the table between them. As always, Mr. Anderson sat erect; his clothes were impeccable. But there was a weariness in his eyes Ariel had never seen before.

"Anything might've happened to the boy on a jaunt like that."

"I know." Ariel slipped her hand into Booth's, grateful for the support. "I've made him promise he won't ever do anything like it again. You and your wife must've been sick with worry. I'm sorry, Mr. Anderson. I feel partially to blame because I've let Scott buy the train tickets before."

He shook his head, not speaking for a moment. "An intrepid boy," he managed at length. "Sharp enough to know which train to take, when to get off." His eyes focused on Ariel's again. "He wanted badly to be with you."

Normally the statement would have warmed her. Now, it tightened the already sensitive muscles of her stomach. "Yes. Children often don't understand the consequences of their actions, Mr. Anderson. Scott only thought about coming, not about the hours of panic in between or about the dangers. He was tired and frightened when he got here. I hope you won't punish him too severely."

Anderson took a deep breath and rested a hand on either thigh. "I realized something today, Ms. Kirkwood. I resent that boy."

"Oh, no, Mr. Anderson—"

"Please, let me finish. I resent him, and I don't like knowing that about myself." His voice was clipped, unapologetic and, Ariel realized, old. Not so much in years, she thought, but in attitude. "And more, I've realized that his presence in the house is a constant strain on my wife. He's a reminder of something we lost. I'm not going to justify my feelings to you," he added briskly. "The boy is my grandchild, and therefore, I'm responsible for him. However, I'm an old man, and not inclined to change. I don't want the boy, and you do." He rose while Ariel could only stare at him. "I'll notify my attorney of my feelings on the matter."

"Mr. Anderson." Shaken, Ariel rose. "You know I want Scott, but—"

"I don't, Ms. Kirkwood." With his shoulders straight, Anderson gave her a level look. "It's as basic as that."

And as sad. "I'm sorry" was all she could say.

With a nod only, he left.

"How," Ariel began after a stretch of silence, "could anyone feel that way about a child?"

"About the child?" Booth countered. "Or about themselves?"

She turned to him, puzzled only for a moment. "Yes, that's it, isn't it?"

"I'm an expert on the subject. The difference is—" he drew her down to him again, circling her with his arm so that her head rested against his shoulder "—someone pushed her way into my life and made me see it."

"Is that what I did?" She laughed, riding the next curve on the roller coaster the day had been. Scott was sleeping on her bed, with kittens curled at his feet. He could stay there now. No more tearful goodbyes. "Pushed my way into your life?"

"You can be very tenacious." He gave her hair a sharp tug then captured her mouth as she gasped. "Thank God."

"Should I warn you that once I push my way in, I won't ever get out?"

"No." He shifted so that she could sit across his lap, and he could watch her face. "Let me find out for myself."

"It won't be easy for you, you know."

"What?"

"Dealing with me if you decide to marry me."

His brow rose, and unable to resist, she traced it with a fingertip. "If?"

"I'm giving you your last chance for escape." Half-serious, Ariel pressed her palm to his cheek. "I do most things on impulse—eating, spending, sleeping. I much prefer living in chaos to living in order. The fact is I can't function in order at all. I'll get you involved, one way or the other, in any number of organizations."

"That one remains to be seen," Booth muttered.

Ariel only smiled. "I haven't scared you off yet?"

"No." He kissed her, and as the shadows in the room lengthened, neither of them noticed. "And you won't. I can also be tenacious."

"Remember, you'll be taking on a four-year-old child. An active one."

"You've a poor opinion of my stamina."

"Oh, no." This time when she laughed, it held a husky quality. "I'll drive you crazy with my disorganization."

"As long as you stay out of my office," he countered, "you can turn everything else into a building lot."

She tightened her arms around his neck and clung for a moment. He meant it, she told herself, giddy. He meant it all. She had Booth, and Scott. And with them, her life was taking the next turning point. She could hardly wait to find what waited around the corner.

"I'll spoil Scott," she murmured into Booth's neck. "And the rest of our children."

He drew her back slowly, a half smile on his mouth. "How many is implied by *the rest*?"

Her laughter was free and breezy. "Pick a number."

* * * * *